91100000043073

D1363222

11/6/14

3/7/14

BRENT LIBRARIES

Please return/renew this item
by the last date shown.
Books may also be renewed by
phone or online.
Tel: 0115 929 3388
On-line www.brent.gov.uk/libraryservice

Also available from Delphine Publications!

Kisses Don't Lie by Tamika Newhouse

Who Do I Run To Now? by Anna Black

Her Sweetest Revenge by Saundra

For our full listing of exciting titles,
visit www.delphinepublications.com today!

CRIMSON FOOTPRINTS

Delphine Publications focuses on bringing a reality check to the genre urban literature. All stories are a work of fiction from the authors and are not meant to depict, portray, or represent any particular person Names, characters, places, and incidents are either the product of the author's imagination or are used fictitiously, and any resemblances to an actual person living or dead are entirely coincidental.

Crimson Footprints

ISBN 13 - 978-0984692361
Library of Congress Control Number:

Published by Delphine Publications
www.delphinepublications.com

Printed in the United States of America

Layout: Write On Promotions
Cover Design: Odd Ball Designs
Interior layout: A Reader's Perspective
Editor: Alanna Boutin

Crimson Footprints

PART ONE

Chapter One

With the quiet hiss of an old and burdened bus, the number 62 unfolded its doors and welcomed Deena Hammond to the night. She took the invitation, hand on a sliver of cool metal, gravel grinding under black pumps, and stepped down.

Liberty City. A shitty place in the bowels of Miami. Where she was raised and where her grandmother still lived.

Piss and Hennessey singed her nose, and Deena blinked, giving herself a moment for acclimation. Enveloped in the dark thickness of a Miami evening, an old black man slept, cheek to weathered wood on a bus stop bench. Matted dreadlocks formed a pillow as sheets of *The Herald* covered his middle. Deena stood there, eyes trained on the sleeping man, as her bus disappeared into darkness. Dirt and twigs clung to his hair and valleys creased his face. He was forty, fifty, maybe sixty.

He opened his eyes.

She should've been afraid. Would've been, had she had a different life, been a different woman.

He looked her over, before cracked lips hinted at the beginnings of a smile. But they would get no further. Smiling here was so hard.

She hurried on.

The heat of Miami clung like a sleeve, dampening her neck and smothering her breath, night never alleviating its burden. She was flesh in Liberty City—all flesh. Everyone was.

Used to the stares a near-white woman got when ambling through the hood in a suit, Deena moved, head high, toward her grandmother's house.

Darkness engulfed block after block of dilapidated row houses, public housing that assaulted her architect's eye. Boarded windows. Peeled paint. Sticks that propped up exhausted AC units. Torn fences that imprisoned rather than embellished. Toys, sandwich wrappers, tire irons, lawn chairs, beer bottles, and bicycle parts sat helter-skelter in yard after yard, as if paying homage to the American landfill. Under cover of night, elderly men and women sat in cheap plastic lawn chairs, no doubt reminiscing about the Peppermint Lounge on 79th, back before Liberty City was downright scary. It was a long time ago, longer than Deena could remember.

Black teens in saggy jeans, tall tees, socks, and flip-flops strutted the streets, pockets bulging with the wares of their livelihood. Deena spotted her brother, Anthony, among them.

She stopped to watch him from a distance. He stood on the corner of 14th and 63rd, fists clenched, pretending not to be alert. He was tall, oversized red shirt and golden skin bright against the night. Breath held, Deena waited for what she knew would come. Her brother glanced over his shoulder, paused, and did a sleight of hand with a nasty black man whose head swiveled as he scratched himself.

She looked away, blinking back loathsome tears.

Head lowered, she crossed the street, eager to close the distance between her and her grandmother's front door. A block more and she was there. Another peeling and rotted door, held fast with deadbolts. She'd wanted to replace it, but Housing wouldn't let her. With a sigh, Deena slipped her key in the latch, unlocked it, and stepped inside.

"Listen, girl! How many times I done told you, you better talk to that devil of a brother of yours!"

Greeted by her consistently hostile grandmother, Deena shut the door and gave a half, and what she hoped was a disarming smile.

Grandma Emma placed an authoritative hand on her hip and eyed Deena's Louis Vuitton handbag and chocolate linen suit with stark disapproval.

"Hmph. Why you always got on that high-class stuff?" She waved an immense and dismissive hand in Deena's direction before rolling her eyes in impatience.

Deena frowned. It was more than the massive stature and booming outdoor voice that made Emma Hammond a figure of intimidation. It was the old-school, never-too-old beat mentality her grandmother housed which made her tread in fear of a discipline last doled out better than seven years ago.

Roused by the image of a belt at her backside, Deena dug into her purse and fished out five twenties before hurriedly handing them over. Her grandmother snatched them and continued to stare.

"What?" Deena whispered. She hated that look. The one that said she did nothing right.

Her grandmother shoved the twenties under her barnyard red housecoat and into her bra before turning the scowl back on her once more. Behind her, the furnishings combined for a cluttered, pop art-gone-wrong kind of feel. A corduroy couch, burnt orange and sagging, a tiny TV mounted atop a taller one, and a wood-carved stereo with an eight-track component sat contrary to dozens of old and chipped figurines arranged in a battered china cabinet like a poor man's terra-cotta army. A threadbare peacock blue carpet played host to it all.

Grandma Emma continued to glare. "You heard me the first time, gal. Get out there and talk to that boy before I put him *outta* my house. Now!"

6 *SHEWANDA PUGH*

Deena was turning before she knew it, whirled by two big hands and shoved at the door. She stumbled briefly, righted herself, and resolved to exit with dignity. Apparently, she was talking to her brother whether she liked it or not.

She spotted Anthony outside, not far from the curb where she'd left him. Deena crossed the street and parted the two dark figures that stood near before touching his arm.

"Anthony. I need to talk to you." It came out like a whisper, weaker than she'd hoped.

"Damn, Ant, who's this?"

A dark and burly teen turned a hungry eye on her. His jaw was prominent, his face hard, eyes cruel. Crude tattoos covered his hulking body, one claiming him to be the "enforcer." In addition, the bulge under his ribbed tee was unmistakable. But Anthony turned a cold, corrective, unforgiving glare on "the enforcer," and he looked away.

"What do you want?" her brother snapped.

She met his impatience with a tight smile. "A walk. Take one with me."

Deena turned and headed down 17th. She didn't have to look to know he'd scurry after her. On the opposite side of the street, a black prostitute yanked at her blond wig before giving her leather mini the same treatment. Too-high fuchsia pumps made her stumble.

"Listen," Anthony said, falling in step alongside her, "say whatever you gotta say so I can go. I got business I gotta deal with out here."

Deena stopped. Her brother did the same. They stood under a busted street lamp with a tattered sneaker hanging from a phone line above, the words "Fuck the Police" scrawled in blue below, and an old syringe lying forgotten in the gutter.

"You're so selfish," she whispered, her voice etched with a disbelief she'd been unable to shake after so many years. "And God only knows what else you are. I try not to think about it." She turned, the sight of him sickening her. But he whirled her to face him, his honeyed eyes hard and narrow.

"*I'm* selfish?" he demanded. He shook his head. "Listen. Say what you want, but I make food happen. I make rent happen. I make your fucking safety happen."

Deena recoiled at the curse.

"But at what cost? At what cost, Anthony?" She was somewhere between a sob and shout of enragement.

Anthony inhaled. "Deena—"

"*Please.* You don't have to do this. I can get more money. I can get a second job—"

"You work hard enough as it is."

"I'll work harder if it'll keep you alive!"

They were the wrong words, she knew, even before he turned to leave.

"You're so smart," she said to his back. "You could be anything."

He had the shoulders of their father—broad, sturdy, reassuring, and a mind just as sharp.

"Remember when you were a kid?" Deena whispered. "You wanted to be a—a firefighter." Her eyes moistened. "You still could, you know."

He turned and gave his sister a once-over, eyes sad, smile sadder.

"You could," she insisted.

In the distance, a siren wailed.

"You always could make something out of nothing, Deena."

He placed a hand on her shoulder, leaned in, and kissed her forehead. "Get back in the house, OK? It's not safe." He shot her a single regretful look and jogged back to his corner.

When Deena returned, Grandma Emma resumed her rant about Anthony. As Emma yammered, Deena tried to recall where she left a set of concrete specs for a prep school in Miramar. She needed them ASAP. It was possible she'd left them on the bus. But if they were on the bus, then they were halfway to—

Shouts pierced Deena's thoughts. Grandma Emma, ever the enthused spectator, abandoned her tirade for a glimpse of the outside commotion.

"Grandma!" Deena scolded. "Get away from the door before someone shoots you!"

Emma dismissed her with an impatient wave, wide backside jerking as she tilted forward, cracked the door, and peeked out.

"Goddammit, girl! This your brother out here acting a god-damned fool again!"

Grandma threw the door wide and Deena pushed past, intent on kicking her brother's ass. She'd *just* talked to him. What kind of trouble could he possibly have—

Before she could finish the thought, Deena froze, immobilized by what she saw.

A slender, striking man of Asian descent was on the wrong end of Anthony's .32. Arms raised, his hands were splayed in a show of defenselessness. Despite the growing crowd of onlookers and the pistol in his face, his expression was calm, to his credit. Behind him, an old woman mouthed something and made the sign of the cross.

"Anthony!" Deena cried, rushing forward.

Her brother cast a single sideways glance, but kept the gun level. "Get back in the house," he said, an edge in his voice.

Deena turned her attention to the Asian man once again. She was struck by his eyes, wide and heavy-lidded. His mouth was generous, his square face softened by layers of thick black hair. He had boyish good looks and a long, lean, athletic frame.

Japanese.

She was certain he was Japanese.

It was only when his eyes caught hers and vaulted back toward her brother did she face Anthony once more.

"Will you put that goddamned thing away?" Deena hissed.

The two stared at each other, older sister, young brother, eyes narrowed. When he didn't move, Deena stepped between gun and stranger, eyes level with her brother's. A tense moment passed, and in it Deena thought a thousand thoughts—figures about accidental deaths and the number of people killed each year by family members. Still, she stayed until Anthony lowered his gun. She took the opportunity to snatch it. Only afterward did it occur to her that it could've misfired.

Breathless, Deena turned to the stranger. "I assume that's your car," she said, nodding toward a sleek gray convertible parked haphazardly, a shiny nickel in a murky puddle.

He nodded, glossy black tresses falling into wide almond eyes. "Yeah, um, about that." He cleared his throat. "He, uh, took my keys."

Deena turned to her brother, hand extended in impatience. Anthony dropped the keys into her waiting palm with a sigh, a new Ferrari slipping from his grasp with reluctance.

She passed the keys over and their fingertips brushed. Something warm and foreign turned over and her lips parted in surprise. She thought she saw the makings of a smile in his eyes, but she dismissed it. He took the keys and thanked her. And as she watched him peel off with the top down on his sleek convertible, Deena's pulse skittered then and long after.

Chapter Two

Takumi Tanaka was possessed. Only days had passed since he'd last seen her, but in that time, he'd been consumed. She was everywhere. Pages and pages of his sketchpad were devoted to her, the canvas on his easel, the canvas in his mind. She'd haunted him that first night, that first moment really, so much so that he'd rushed home and put pencil-to-paper like a madman.

There was something about her eyes. He couldn't convey what he saw under those heavy lashes—pain, sadness, defeat? Whatever it was, he'd wanted to smooth it away with his hands, his lips, and his heart.

He stared at the floor of his studio, littered with sheets of ruined canvas, and knew he had to see her again. With a groan, Takumi abandoned his work for the morning paper. He had a love-hate relationship with the Arts Section of *The Herald*, where he could laude their brilliance one minute and curse their convoluted conclusions the next. So, he ventured out into the hall and grabbed the paper from the corner it rested in. He was grumpy and needed coffee, even as he opened the paper, an act that would undoubtedly make him feel worse.

He scanned the front. There, below the fold, was a common South Florida headline: LIBERTY CITY TEEN FOUND SLAIN. And beneath it, a picture of his would-be assailant, the six-foot hooligan who'd put a .32 to his face.

Anthony Hammond's funeral was in three days.

~*~

Anthony's service was held at Emmanuel Rises Baptist Church. It rained the day they buried Deena's brother, and according to Grandma Emma, it meant the devil had come for his soul.

The windows of the limo that housed the Hammond family were tinted, making a steely sky even darker. Deena's gaze fell from the heavens to a puddle in the street and watched it swell with each gray and acidic drop.

"Honestly, I don't know what we expected," Aunt Caroline said. She paused long enough to fuss through an oversized black purse before coming away with a lighter and a pack of Newports.

"We shoulda expected this. Especially after Man-Man got killed."

"But he didn't even do that!" Lizzie cried. "It was just—just a rumor."

She was Deena's last sibling; fifteen, an ancient fifteen.

"Mmm," Caroline said. She balanced her cigarette between fat and rouged lips before lighting up. The drag she took was long and indulgent.

"We shoulda been ready for this," she said with a nod. "I hate that I didn't prepare myself mentally, you know?"

"Will you shut your ass up?" Grandma Emma shouted. "And put that goddamned cigarette away."

She snatched it from her daughter's fingers, never one to wait, put the window down, and heaved it.

"Got a mouth like diarrhea. You keep on and somebody'll stop it up for you."

Silence filled the limousine again. Silence, save for Lizzie's sobs, soft and gut-wrenching. Deena turned back to her puddle and soon a tap on the window interrupted them.

It was time. They were escorted into the sanctuary by twos, an usher flanked on either end by a Hammond. They took their seats on the front left pew, under the watchful gaze of a full house. Standing sprays of white roses, larkspur, and gladiolus surrounded a solid copper casket at the front. But no one would see the beauty of the cream-quilted interior that cradled Anthony's body—four gunshots and Miami heat prevented that. But Deena had seen it, seen him, before the lid of a coffin closed between them forever. And the blood of her brother had painted her nightmares ever since.

Floor arrangements of lilies, statice, and caspia flanked each end of Anthony's coffin, brilliant in sunburst orange, lilac, and ivory. A poster-sized portrait of him in a button-up and tie stood at the back of the casket, facing an audience with standing room only. Walter Haines, an old and weathered black man who'd played at her father's and grandfather's funeral, stroked out gentle gospel from an organ onstage. Deena wondered if he'd play at hers too.

Seven years had passed since the last Hammond burial, when they laid to rest Deena's grandfather. Were he still alive, she knew what he'd say. *Justice.* Anthony's fate was justice, as sin begot sin.

Deena blinked in surprise at the program in her hand. Looking down at the picture of her brother, even now, she couldn't help but smile back. It was a portrait of Anthony in the 10th grade, his grin wide-mouthed and toothy—silly in that contrary way that was his alone. He was love one moment and fire the next, never able to find rest in his mind. She only prayed that finally, he had.

Late mourners poured in, an army of them, as if to make a show of it. Each wore a black tee with white letters that read "RIP Tony Hammond" and beneath it a picture of Deena's brother. In it, his hair was a cascade of toffee coils that fell to his shoulders, so heavy that it parted down the center from its weight. The smile here was ominous as he held a Budweiser in one hand and a .32 in the other.

The picture looked recent. Really recent.

"Deena?" Lizzie whispered.

She turned to face her kid sister. "Yeah?"

"I don't want them here."

Deena nodded. She didn't want them there either.

Takumi slipped into the church and stood at the back of the sanctuary, heart ricocheting with the power of a cannonball. Settling on a place near a cluster of ushers in navy vests, he let his gaze sweep the pews.

He saw her, saw the hair first—coils of honey, cinnamon, and chocolate, cascading like a waterfall. A moment passed, and he remembered to breathe again.

A black woman with short and plastered curls stood from her place on the front pew and approached the microphone. She introduced herself as Rhonda Hammond, aunt of the late Anthony Hammond. Her voice was soft and therapeutic, the way only an aunt's can be. With lips too close to the microphone, she presented an assortment of sympathy gifts, but there weren't very many. A basket of fruit, a vase of Peruvian lilies, a prayer plant from the church. Three dozen red roses from Daichi Tanaka and the Tanaka Firm.

That caught his attention.

Aunt Rhonda found her seat. A short stout man named Mr. Phillips stood and ventured to the piano. His wife, a tall and thick-browed black woman with a hawk nose and long fingers, followed him. Even as a child, Deena thought the couple looked more like brothers than husband and wife. Mrs. Phillips found the microphone, cleared her throat, and closed her eyes. Deena waited, knowing what would follow.

Mr. Phillips came in first, delicate and unobtrusive on the piano with a subtle melody. When his wife slipped in to join him, she pierced Deena with a voice she both loved and hated. It was beautiful and awful, smooth, rich, and melancholy, all with the first damned note. They rose together, piano and woman, never relenting in their melodic sorrow.

"It's time to be with the Lord," she sang, and she for one was ready. "When our time here is through, it's time to be with the Lord."

There were more songs, hopeful, upbeat, rousing numbers sung by a rocking choir in white robes. They served their purpose, Deena supposed, raising the spirits of those around her, until most were on their feet shouting, clapping, jumping in tune to love-filled lyrics. But seven years of Sunday School had taught Deena that Anthony was not in the joy-filled place they promised her. And because of that, she was grateful when all of them shut the hell up.

People shared stories about Anthony next. Aunt Rhonda murmured in a voice too low about his penchant for practical jokes and infectious smile, her eyes rimmed red. A cousin of Deena's, one of Caroline's children, talked about a time Anthony stood up and fought a bully for him. "Never a coward," he said in quiet admiration, "never." Deena wondered if it was bravery that put him in the ground. Others went, including Lizzie, who broke down with the first word and had to be half-carried back to her pew.

When Deena rose, she made her way to the microphone with a wad of tissues in her fist. From her place at the podium, she stared at the coffin. An eternity passed, and finally, her own voice surprised her.

"I didn't want to do this," she said softly. Her eyes found the ceiling, and she struggled to inhale.

"Coming here and talking to you like this is an admission, an acceptance, and I'm not ready to do that just yet." She laughed bitterly and shifted her weight.

"You know, if you knew my brother, you know he was like a train wreck. He had no problem tearing from the tracks and—and running roughshod through the forest." Deena swallowed and shook her head. "And as crazy as this sounds, I admire that. I wish I had that kind of strength."

She lifted her gaze from the coffin.

"I don't want to negate the things he's done or the people he's hurt. No doubt people have stood as heartbroken as I am now, because—" she broke off. "Because of who my brother was."

She surveyed the crowd, meeting them frankly for the first time.

"I need you to know, to believe, that there was good in him. That he was a good brother, that he had value and that people loved him."

Deena opened her mouth to say more, closed it, and retreated to her pew. Once there, she collapsed in sobs.

When the service ended, six pallbearers, all cousins, hoisted the solid copper casket onto their shoulders. They carried Anthony Hammond to the tune of an upbeat gospel about marching up to heaven on an angel's wings. Deena stood, swayed a bit, and found Aunt Rhonda there to steady her. They walked arm in arm, with Deena's gaze on the floor as the Hammonds made their way to the exit. God had given her so few to love, so very few, and saw fit to take even them from her. He hated Deena. And she hated Him.

Deena raised her gaze, though she didn't know why. Searching, searching until she saw him tucked away near the ushers.

Their eyes locked and stayed locked through Deena's slow procession until she was out the door and could see him no more.

~*~

At the front of an empty church, Takumi ran an appreciative hand over the brass cymbals of a drum set. It was a Tama Swingstar, good quality, great price. When he was seven, he fell in love with the sound of a birch Yamaha and had remained true ever since. He didn't get to play much anymore, as the crashing sound was counterconducive to being neighborly. These days, Takumi relied on the guitar or keyboard for a bit of melodic retrospection. But none of that had a thing to do with the price of dairy in Denver. So, why the hell did he linger?

The doors of Emmanuel Rises opened, and he looked up. Just then, his reason for staying stepped in and made her way down the aisle. Automatically, Takumi stood up straighter.

She didn't so much walk as flow, the black silk of her dress like a caress against curves. Ample in that perfect way only a woman could be, the undulations of her body reminded him of the Salween, the last free-flowing river in South Asia.

"It's you," she whispered. She looked up at him with eyes flecked in gold, a shimmering sliver of melted bronze under long, thick lashes. They stole his words momentarily.

"I was thinking the same thing," he said eventually.

She hesitated. "What are you doing here?"

Takumi looked away. He couldn't tell this woman whose name he knew only from a funeral program that he'd not come to pay his respects but because he knew she'd be there.

"I don't know," he said. "I saw what happened in the paper and—and—and I'm sorry."

They fell silent. She gave a rough nod and blinked back obvious tears. When they fell anyway, she dashed them away in impatience. He felt helpless, impotent.

Suddenly, she looked up at him.

"Why were you there? In Liberty City that night?"

He hesitated, not sure why he felt embarrassed. His work had never embarrassed him before. "I was . . . um, looking for inspiration."

She raised a brow. "Inspiration?"

"Yeah." He shifted his weight.

"I'm an artist. I paint."

"Paint what?"

Takumi shrugged. "Oh, I don't know. Hope. Happiness. Regret. Stuff like that."

An almost smile crept to her lips, lips that were fuller than he remembered, like strawberries ripe to bursting. Her eyes widened.

"Fascinating," she whispered.

He couldn't have said it better himself, though their thoughts were far apart, he would bet.

"So . . . Did you find it? Did you find your inspiration?"

And there it was—a twinkle, a twinkle behind weary hazel eyes. She was teasing him. And he liked it.

Takumi grinned. "Like you wouldn't believe."

He caught a glimpse of a cross behind her, and his smile faltered with the memory of why a Buddhist stood in the middle of a Baptist church. He shot a look at the double doors.

"Sweetheart, if you—if you stay any longer you'll miss the burial."

He wanted the words back instantly; the words that stole the twinkle and almost-smile she'd given him so willingly.

But they were gone.

With a heavy sigh, she took a seat on the front pew. "I'm not going," she admitted heavily. "I—I can't watch."

Deena dropped her head, as if ashamed, and stared at the slender, manicured hands that rested in her lap.

Takumi sat down next to her.

When his *ojiichan*, or grandfather, had died, he'd taken it hard. Had, in fact, sobbed like a brokenhearted baby, despite the full year a diagnosis of colon cancer gave him to prepare for it. It was only his father who—

He looked up, roused with the memory of an earlier point in the service.

"You, uh, know Daichi Tanaka?"

She looked up in surprise.

"Know him? The asshole's my boss."

Takumi grinned.

"Well, I'm Takumi Tanaka. The asshole's my father."

Deena's eyes widened with the sort of white-hot horror you only got from imminent danger. She searched and searched, registering with pain each of the physical similarities this stranger shared with her boss. And there were many.

He extended a hand.

"You can call me Tak."

"Oh my God." Deena breathed. Her hand found her mouth. "I'm so sorry. I—I just—I'm stressed and—oh my God."

He held up a hand.

"Really. It's alright. I've called him a lot worse."

She smiled weakly, lowering her hand just a tad.

"Yeah? Like what?"

He shrugged, nonchalant, the way only rich kids can.

"Oh, I don't know. Nosferatu, Pinhead, Skeletor—"

"Skeletor!"

"Yeah." He raised a brow. "Come on. You know the cartoon. He-man? She-ra?"

"You're insane!" Deena hooted.

"Yeah. By the power of Grayskull."

She clamped a hand over her mouth to stifle a laugh, the first in a long time. But when he proceeded to prattle off a never-ending list of cartoonish villains he likened to his father, Deena found she could hold back the laughter no more. Not even there, with the foliage of her brother's demise all around her, could she hold back that unaccustomed sound.

Chapter Three

Deena hated the awkwardness of grief. As a girl, she'd experienced it with the death of her father. The staring, the avoidance, the uncomfortable ramblings of people who felt obligated to speak, yet wanted nothing more than to put distance between them and you.

Though a decade had lapsed between the death of her father and that of her brother, she found that people hadn't changed all that much. So when Deena entered her office on the third floor of the Tanaka Firm Monday morning, she was relieved to put a slab of wood between them and her. She didn't want their damned condolences or sickening sympathy—constant reminders that her brother was dead. What she wanted to be reminded of was that she wasn't.

She couldn't say for sure how long she stood there, eyes shut, back pressed to mahogany. But when she opened them, a bouquet on her desk took her by surprise. Peek-a-boo pink plumerias, golden stargazers, jutting purple larkspur, and mango calla lilies seemed to dance on her desk, overshadowing her little bonsai with their beauty. And could she really smell their sweetness from the door? Certainly not.

Briefcase aside, she took a seat in her leather swivel and brought the flowers in for a sniff. Deena froze mid-smile at the sound of the office intercom.

"Ms. Hammond, Mr. Tanaka's here to see you."

Deena frowned. So much for indulgences. Her boss Daichi was many things, but indulgent was definitely not one of them. So, it was back to business as usual. Could she really expect something else?

Deena met Daichi Tanaka while in her final year at MIT. She could still recall the thick and cramped feel in Kresge Auditorium as faculty, students, and the community piled in, in mouth-foaming anticipation of the avant-garde of architecture. She arrived early, though not early enough, as she had to step and stumble her way to a seat. Despite the darkness of the auditorium, she noted that scores of people clutched a recent copy of *Time* magazine. Daichi Tanaka was on the cover.

"May I?" Deena whispered, nudging the old hawk-eyed woman she'd settled in next to. With a nod, she handed it over, dark eyes wary and watchful.

Deena turned her attention to the magazine.

Behind a Hitchcock-style silhouette of Daichi was a collage of a dozen major city skylines—New York, Mumbai, Moscow, Miami, Hong Kong, Karachi, Cairo, L.A., and more. Underneath was probably the boldest declaration ever attributed to a single architect: DAICHI TANAKA: ARCHITECTURAL GOD.

Though bold, the phrase was apropos. His was the biggest firm in the world, the most influential, and by far the most daring and cutting edge. Tanaka tempted fate with his designs, implored homemade theories, and thumbed his nose at the very laws of science and society.

As a junior, Deena read about the power of a single architect to reinvent a nation. Daichi Tanaka and his project Cityscape was the example, a miniature world unto itself made of glittering, twisting, turning buildings that seemed to cut into thin air and defeat the laws of gravity. Part beauty, part resort, part fantasy, the lush acreage of Cityscape was suddenly a status symbol throughout the world, a tour de force for an impoverished Guatemala. As the privileged world rushed in for the opportunity to eat four-hundred-dollar plates of carne adobada while hovering over the Pacific, Hollywood elite built mansions along the coastal mountainside. But Daichi's greatest triumph came not from single-handedly creating a tourism vacuum in a once unappealing place, but from doing what no one else dared dream. In a country little more than a decade removed from civil war, Daichi shifted power to the masses—to the rural Mayan farmers who'd been victims of state-sponsored terrorism. He paid them fair prices for the land he used and negotiated so that the influx of hotels and restaurants used locally farmed foods. And suddenly, with the rising of the sun, the Guatemalan people had a voice.

Daichi, with his vision, blurred the line between architect and statesman, statesman and ideologue, demonstrating to the world the limitless power of an architect. So it came as no surprise that the people of Kresge Auditorium looked around as though a god would soon be among them. An architectural god.

After wilting under the professor's prolonged glare, Deena slipped the magazine back to its owner. A thunderous applause startled her as the room rocked with the approval of a clamoring crowd, a crowd enamored by the pop icon of architecture now before them gracing them with his presence.

Daichi took to the podium with a scowl. He bypassed preamble and dove directly into the lecture, accusing and verbally accosting them.

He ridiculed his colleagues for their ignorance, for traveling to far-flung locales without studying the correlating history and culture—without respecting it. He called them presumptuous, privileged, narrow-minded.

"You all look the same and think the same and pick people of the same vein to attend your illustrious universities. Why? Because you need validation. Because you serve yourself. But an architect is a selfless being, reflecting the client and society that seeks his services. And in this regard, you've failed."

He should've been shouted down, run off, or at the very least challenged. It was a rant more than a speech, hurled at them by the most privileged architect of them all. But he was met with a boom of approval, a roar of allegiance from an otherwise sane and brilliant bunch. They were the choir to his sermon, amen-ing his every utterance. And Deena understood. It was hard not to feel dazzled by his presence. After all, when was the last time an architect had changed the world with his vision? Ancient Rome? They had every right to be at least a little starstruck. And they were. Even Deena.

Daichi took questions for half an hour.

Deena stood in line among the hopeful, waiting for an opportunity to ask something, though what she had no idea. The questions from fellow students were predictable: What drew him to architecture? What were his inspirations? How did he handle criticism? When a professor Deena recognized as an architectural one-man think tank rose, she knew a challenge was coming. Not everyone wanted to admire Daichi Tanaka. A few wanted to unseat him.

"In *Time* magazine, you credited your success in Guatemala to Architectural Determinism, a theory that has largely been disproven. Given that, isn't it fair to say that you have no idea why you've been so successful?"

Dr. Cook was met with a forbidden sort of silence. In it, Deena could practically hear his celebratory smile. When Daichi looked up at him, it was with a look of expectancy.

"Michael, if you can recall from our days at Harvard, Architectural Determinism simply espouses that the built environment is the chief determinant for social behavior."

"I know what Architectural Determinism means!" Dr. Cook sputtered.

"Good," Daichi said brightly. "Then perhaps I can influence the learned with a bit of common sense. Consider this, if you will. If you build beautiful things and charge high prices, then beautiful people with deep pockets will pay for them. No need to consult a thick text on that trinket. There's a charming little boy in Nassau that carves wooden figurines on request, just about anything you can imagine, and charges a pretty penny for them, too. No doubt he could counsel you more on this matter."

The room erupted with laughter and the professor's face turned red. Deena was glad to see the professor get his comeuppance. After all, he was the sort of teacher that couldn't be bothered with learning students' names, or helping them, for that matter, the kind who sneered down at his own breakfast as though not even it were worthy.

The questions continued and no one else dared challenge Daichi. And when it became clear that he would never get to her, Deena slipped out of the winding line and tiptoed around to the side of the building, where she knew he would exit.

She didn't have to wait long. The moment Daichi stepped out of the auditorium and into the snow-covered parking lot, Deena scurried toward him.

"Mr. Tanaka! Mr. Tanaka, if you could just give me a second—"

"The time for asking questions was back there, in line." He never slowed.

"Yes, sir, I know."

Deena quickened her pace and fell in step alongside him, his stride long despite his average height.

"But we ran out of time, sir. And I really wanted to talk to you."

"Yes, yes. Everyone really wants to talk to me."

They moved faster. She scurried to keep pace. "I—I understand that, sir. It's just that I'll probably never see you again and my question isn't the sort I'd want to ask in front of all those people—"

Daichi stopped. Deena halted; startled he'd heard anything she said.

"What's your name?"

She opened her mouth and found that it worked only with effort. "Deena Hammond, sir."

"Deena Hammond."

He frowned as if trying to determine whether he liked the name. "And what is your question, Deena Hammond?"

She swallowed. There was something about a person calling you by your full name that did a job on the nerves.

"As a—a person of color, sir, I w—wondered—"

"Shall I give you a minute, Deena Hammond? To gather your thoughts and formulate an articulate statement?"

Her eyes widened. "No, sir. Certainly not. I—"

He appraised her frankly. "What is your ethnicity, Ms. Hammond?"

She froze. "I'm black—black and white, sir."

"I see." Daichi frowned. He looked past her to the auditorium at her back, a thin shell of a dome with glass on two sides.

"Ms. Hammond. How is it that you pay to attend this illustrious institution?"

She lowered her gaze. "Sch—scholarships, sir. That, and I work in the cafeteria."

"And where did you say you were from again?"

"Miami."

A brow shot up. "Where in Miami?"

"Liberty City, sir."

Suddenly, he eyed her with interest. "My firm is headquartered in Miami."

"Yes, sir, I know." Her eyes were still on the snow-covered ground.

"You know that and yet you ask about diversity?"

The sharpness in his voice caused her to look up.

"Am I to believe that you're not here to clamor for an internship?"

"I'm not," Deena whispered.

"Then you're a fool."

He turned from her and dug in his pocket, coming away with keys. Daichi deactivated the alarm to a sleek black Town Car mere steps away. She was losing him.

"Sir, please listen to me. I wouldn't dare presume to—"

He shot her a look of impatience. "Did you get that from them? In there?" Daichi nodded toward the auditorium. "Unless you've plans to return to that hell you call home I would suggest that you beg, barter, and presume, Ms. Hammond."

He opened the trunk and tossed in his briefcase. "You're a smart woman, no doubt, since you've made it this far, but the floodgates won't open with your degree. Opportunities are few, especially in these times, and fewer still for those that don't look the part."

Deena blinked. It was what she hated most about being from the slums. Dress it up or dress it down, it didn't take much for someone to peel it back and see who you really were. A "where are you from?" was rarely satisfied with a single word. A city became a neighborhood, and a neighborhood the truth. The truth, in her case, revealing far more than she ever intended.

Trunk closed, he turned to her again. "Tell me this, Ms. Hammond. What are your thoughts on deconstructivism?"

She hesitated, remembering the folly of Dr. Cook and knew that he saw her thoughts.

"Do you not even know what deconstructivism is?" he demanded.

Of course she did. Considered a brain even by MIT standards, she was a self-made outcast, never socializing and instead, finding solace and affirmation in the only thing she fully immersed herself in—academics. There could hardly be a topic in the field that she knew little about.

Deconstructivism was a postmodern notion that thrived on fragmentation—in other words, it sought to distort and dislocate the various elements of architecture. And she loved it.

Suddenly, she remembered an article in *Architectural Digest* where Daichi had slammed deconstructivism as an affront to the eye.

He was testing her. Problem was, she didn't know on what.

"I like deconstructivism," Deena said and immediately winced at the volume of her voice and the childishness of the declaration.

Daichi strode to the driver's-side door.

"I—I know that you think, it's an affront to the senses," she rushed up to him, blocking his way with her body. "But if you ask me, all architecture is an affront to the senses."

Daichi paused, lowered his gaze to the car, and returned it to her. "I'm listening," he said quietly.

Deena swallowed. She'd half-expected his next words to be a shout for security.

"Architecture isn't nature, and it can't replace it. Nature stimulates the senses, whereas architecture assaults them."

Deena paused.

"Take Miami, for example. A place that seduces the senses. It's where blistering heat drenches you in sweat, where sweltering, breezeless nights leave you panting, and where ocean waves pound against the sights, sounds, and flesh of the city."

Deena fell silent; her cheeks flushed red. Had she *really* just said that? To Daichi Tanaka?

He turned on her, nearly smiling. "And architecture? What does architecture do?"

She lowered her gaze again. "Not that."

"Then why are you here? Why aren't you—an environmentalist?" he spat.

But she raised her head anyway. "Because I'm going to make it do that."

She met his gaze and found that his dark eyes danced. "Make it do what?" he said quietly.

Somehow, she was no longer afraid. She'd been laughed at most of her life. What difference did it make who was doing the laughing?

"I'm going to make architecture like nature. I'm going to make it stimulate the senses."

Daichi's gaze traveled the length of her body. Were he another man, she might've thought it suggestive. Finally, he cleared his throat. "Much as I'd love to finish this conversation with you, Ms. Hammond, I've a flight to Nepal, and as it is, I'm already late."

He nudged her aside and climbed into the Lincoln. Door closed, Daichi lowered the window. In his hand was a thick ecru business card with a gilded logo in gold flourish. "Call me when you graduate."

Daichi peeled off, leaving Deena to clench the crisp card in her fist as she stood in that snow-covered parking lot wondering just what happened.

~*~

When Deena worked up the nerve to contact Daichi, she was two weeks past graduation and back at her grandmother's house in Liberty City.

"I take it you're in Miami now," he said dully.

"Yes, sir."

"Good. Meet me at my firm in two hours. Bring some drafts with you."

"Sir?"

"One more time since I'm feeling particularly patient today. Firm. Two hours. Portfolio." He hung up.

Deena borrowed the cab fare from her cousin Keisha and rushed to meet the architectural icon at his office in Brickell.

The Tanaka Firm had twenty-five locations, in cities that included London, Rio, Mumbai, and Tokyo. The U.S. headquarters, in Miami's posh Brickell district, reflected Daichi's affinity for forward thinking. A reenvisioned variation of modernism, the thirteen-story Tanaka Firm formed a right-angled triangle, with a glistening waterfall running the length of its straight side. Sheathed in mirror-surfaced steel and brushed aluminum, the building gleamed with the rise of the sun each morning. Among the perks of the office was the dock at the rear, with its access to Biscayne Bay, and ultimately, the Atlantic Ocean. Some days, Deena eventually discovered, Daichi took his yacht to work.

When Deena stepped into the firm's brilliant gold lobby for her initial meeting with her future boss, she had fifteen minutes to spare.

"Can I help you?" asked the security guard behind the desk.

Just past the sensory-automated glass doors with the gold inlaid Tanaka logo, an automated message welcomed her in English, Spanish, French, and a few other languages she was too uncertain to name. Deena wiped the sweat from her brow and took a deep breath, muttering a silent mantra of encouragement before stopping to survey her surroundings.

Turkish marble onyx covered the floor—the first time she'd seen any in person. She was surprised by how much she liked it. It should've been presumptuous, over-the-top, obnoxious. But when paired against the gleaming, unassuming maple walls, and an ultrahigh vaulted ceiling, the gold and chocolate marble suddenly seemed bold and elegant.

To her right was a broad and high brass desk, so polished it bore her reflection. Behind it was a security guard, short and thick-chested with dull black hair and a big, bulbous nose.

"Can I help you?" he said too loudly, and she dropped her tubes.

Deena bent to retrieve them, shuffled to the desk, and nearly lost a single navy pump on the way. Tubes back in hand, she brushed a tuft of hair out of her eyes and smiled. "I'm—I'm here to see Daichi Tanaka," she breathed.

The thickset Cuban man had a porn moustache that quivered with a smile. Deena had never actually seen an adult movie but assumed that thick moustaches were standard in them, as that was what her old roommate used to call them. That and lip afros.

The Cuban guy raised a brow. "Here to see Daichi Tanaka? Is that so?"

Her tubes clattered to the floor for an encore and she cursed. "Yes. It—" Deena disappeared from view and reemerged with the plastic cylinders.

"Yes, it is."

"Listen, sweetheart, you can't just walk in here and expect to—"

"It's alright, Carlos. I'm expecting her."

Deena turned, sweaty-faced and surprised, at the sound of Daichi Tanaka's voice.

He'd stepped in from the street, as urbane and intimidating as ever in his tailored Armani. Daichi stood motionless as Deena's work clattered to the floor for a third time. She retrieved them and brushed the sweat-heavy hair from her face yet again.

"About done?" Daichi said.

She him gave a weak nod.

"Good."

He took off across the spacious lobby, his Versace-loafered stride confident. Deena glanced at Carlos, though she wasn't sure why. When he nodded for her to follow, she scurried for the elevator. Daichi punched the brass UP button and turned to face her.

"Why don't you have a portfolio case?"

Deena lowered her gaze. She couldn't even afford cab fare, let alone the $200 to $300 those things cost.

When she opened her mouth to make up an answer, he held up a hand to stop her. "Let me see something," he said, nodding at her tubes.

"Anything?"

"Well, I certainly can't request anything specific, now, can I?"

Mumbling a calming mantra in her mind, Deena reached first for one tube, then another, before deciding to show him drafts for a small-scale subdivision she'd created in a senior level drafting class. Just as Daichi unrolled the sketch, the elevator doors opened at the top floor, and he stepped off without looking. A healthy brunette with a stack of manila folders toppled in an effort to avoid him.

"What am I looking at?" He stared at her drafts as though they were the blueprints for madness.

Deena rushed to his side, stepping over the folder-laden lady on her hands and knees. "It's a—a mimic of nature."

He handed the draft back to her. "You have thirty seconds to tell me what this is." He fished out his cell phone and began to punch keys.

"It's—it's a luxury community," she blurted. "I—I planned it with Miami in mind. There'd be lush tropical foliage, bird life and cul-de-sacs. The plan is for an eco-friendly construction and green building practices."

Her words were frightened fragments, but she hoped they made sense. The phone was at his ear and she presumed another one, somewhere else, was ringing. She needed to do better.

"The exterior of each town house would resemble a thatched roof bungalow and the interior would have an open-air approach. Cathedral ceilings. French doors. Huge Palladian windows. Also, there'd be views of a manmade semitropical jungle. The foliage would . . . keep heating and cooling costs down," she trailed off lamely.

He wasn't even looking at her.

"I also plan to use hammocks, wildlife, true to the habitat and safe, of course, and a waterfront setting to give the homes a sense of privacy and seclusion in the community setting," she mumbled automatically, certain she was jabbering to herself.

Daichi glanced at her distractedly. "Is that your best design?"

She blinked back the sting of tears. "Yes, sir."

"Fine. Start a preliminary proposal. Angela'll show you to your desk."

Deena followed Daichi's gaze to the brunette still on her hands and knees. When she turned back, it was just in time to see his office door slam.

And that, in a gist, was Daichi Tanaka.

A few short years later, with the first test behind her, she sat at her desk just as anxious as ever.

"Shall I send in Mr. Tanaka?" The intercom jarred her back to reality. The notion of Daichi Tanaka having to ask twice to enter her office had a sobering effect whose only equivalent was a pink slip.

"Jesus, of course!" Deena cried. "Tell Mr. Tanaka that there's no need to ask. Please, send him in."

Breathless, she stood and rushed to the door, opening it with a potent sort of dread. A short pause later, she was met not with the senior Tanaka, but the decidedly more favorable junior.

"If only I were welcomed so warmly everywhere I went," Tak sighed as he stepped into her office.

Deena stared after him. "I thought you were your father. I thought—"

He held up a hand. "Don't. You'll spoil the warm feeling your gushing invitation gave me." He turned to the flowers. "Did you like them?"

Her eyes widened. "They're from you?"

Tak shrugged. "Thought you could use a little sunshine. Was I right?"

The corners of her mouth turned up just a tad. "Yeah."

She turned from him, eyes suddenly wet. Counting backward, Deena waited until the tears abated, pretending to fuss over the larkspur. Once safely dry-eyed, she turned back to him. "So, Mr. Tanaka, what brings you here?"

"Stopped in to see my dad—the asshole, as you like to call him."

He smiled at her sudden blush and ventured over to the flowers. Tak fingered them halfheartedly.

"And to see you," he said quietly.

"Oh?"

She heard the breathlessness in her voice and frowned. What the hell was that?

"You know—"

He slipped a calla lily from the bouquet and held it up for inspection. The stem was long and olive, the bulb mango and vaulted. It made her think of a ballerina in repose.

"I saw this thing," he said. "And it made me think of you."

"Thing?" she echoed.

He looked up.

"An article. About curry addiction. Have you heard of it?"

Deena shook her head, more confused now than before he'd begun to elaborate.

He stuck the lily back in its vase. "Well, it's a just a theory, really. Some people think that when you eat really hot food, that the pain from it makes the body release endorphins." He leaned against her desk. "Supposedly, you get this natural high from eating hot foods, and it leads you to want more and hotter curries, the same way any other addiction makes you want more."

"And that made you think of me?"

"Sort of. When I read it, I thought to myself, hell, if anyone needs to get high, it's Deena."

She paused, unsure of how she should respond, certain she was supposed to be offended. But she laughed. The boy had no idea how spot-on he was.

Tak smiled, clearly pleased with himself. "No rush to go curry hunting, mind you." He nodded toward the flowers. "Maybe when the sunshine wilts and you could use some of a different kind."

Deena lowered her gaze, suddenly shy, exposed.

"Unless . . ."

"Unless what?" She bit down on her lip, taken back by the automatic need to answer.

Tak shrugged. "I don't know. I just hate to think that you're going to spend your evening alone in some apartment you've got decked out like this sad-looking place."

Deena looked around. "You don't like my office?"

He stared. "You do?"

She laughed, despite herself. That made three—three times she'd done so since her brother's death—all three because of him.

"I think this place is cozy. Streamlined. And conducive to work."

"It's barren."

Deena balked. "What are you talking about? I have Hope and your bouquet. It's positively radiant in here."

He looked around. "Hope?"

Deena blushed. "She's my bonsai."

Now he would laugh. But he didn't.

"Maybe one day you'll tell me how she got that name," he said softly.

She lowered her gaze once more. "Maybe."

They fell silent.

"So," Tak said suddenly, loudly. "Dinner? Six? Meet you in the lobby."

Deena sputtered. "Oh, I don't know, I—"

He held up a hand. "Listen, you don't even have to talk to me. Just a little company and good conversation if you want." He shrugged. "At least, I hope it's good."

Briefly, she thought of the box of tissues that had been her constant companion for the last few nights.

"And you don't mind if I'm not good company?" she squeaked.

He was already heading for the door. "Not at all."

She smiled at his back. "Okay, then."

He paused, a hand on the doorknob. "Excellent. There's a new place on Ocean Drive called Spiced. Everything's lava hot. We can burn a hole in our mouths, then try to cool it with ocean water. You'll love it."

Deena grinned, watching the door slam behind him. Something told her she just might.

Their first night together was filled with incendiary curries from India and crashing waves from the Atlantic. Dinner ran long and the coffee cold before Tak and Deena were ushered out at closing. They returned again the next night and opted for decidedly more adventurous fare—a black bean and squid ink soup for her, Moroccan sea bream and braised rabbit for him—all made searing with a bevy of chilies, pastes, powders, and spices. And after closing this time, they walked along the shore with a sliver of moon illuminating the sky and plans for a third night on their lips.

Chapter Four

Deena slipped into the silent sanctuary of Emmanuel Rises, pumps muffled against the ruby carpet. Her gaze skittered past scores of bowed heads before spotting her family in the front, in their pew for the last thirty years. Despite the diligent tiptoe, Grandma Emma snapped to attention midprayer, as if connected to her granddaughter in some basic biological need for admonishment. So when that old finger jerked in impatience at the pew, Deena hustled down the aisle and squeezed in between Caroline and Rhonda, just in time for the amen.

"Mmm," Emma murmured, running a critical gaze over Deena's smoke gray pants suit. It featured an angled collar and V-neckline alongside boot-cut slacks that lay just right. Retail price for the Gucci ensemble—jacket, black silk shirt, slacks, and high-heeled shoes should've been in the neighborhood of thirty-five hundred, but a secondhand consignment shop in Bal Harbor brought it home for less than two.

"It was all I had to wear," Deena mumbled.

Aunt Caroline gave her a once-over. "Well, you wore pants two Sundays ago, too." Newport breath singed Deena's nose and she sighed.

Emmanuel Rises was a conservative church, baptized in the holy fire and washed in the blood of the lamb. Still, there had to be room for reason. Could they really argue that Deena's understated pants suit was less appropriate than Aunt Caroline's dimpled cleavage and leopard print dress?

Caroline shot Deena a sideways look of disdain before pulling out a mirror and primping fat blond curls. Her platinum hair was sharp against dark skin, sharp against crimson talons, and sharp against gold teeth.

Fuchsia lipstick, a leopard print dress, and scuffed white pumps was the whole of Caroline's sordid church attire. The oldest of Eddie and Emma Hammond's four children, she was a mother at sixteen, a grandmother at thirty-three, and at fifty-two, Caroline Hammond was a great-grandmother. Even so, she'd never been an outcast in their family. On the contrary, she set precedent for what was to come.

Three women of childbearing age in the Hammond family were actually without children. Aunt Rhonda, who constantly fielded unfounded accusations that she was a lesbian, Deena's teen sister Lizzie, who would surprise no one if she stood up and declared she were pregnant that moment, and Deena, who avoided men like the malice they were.

"Where's Lizzie?" Deena asked suddenly, scanning the pews for her sister.

Emma shook her head. "Didn't come home last night."

Deena sighed. How many nights would a teenage girl have to disappear for it not to give her grandmother cause for alarm anymore? Whatever the number, she didn't want to know.

Lizzie's descent into anarchy began with adolescence. To Deena, it seemed that budding breasts and a menstrual flow brought with it an exponential madness that worsened each year. At eleven, her sister was suspended for wearing a transparent tee with the phrase *Pay for Play* on it to school, at thirteen it was for offering sexual favors to her math teacher in exchange for a passing grade, and at fifteen, it was for giving fellatio to a waiting line in the boys' restroom. How had two sisters, so similar in appearance and upbringing, made such drastic departures? One regarded her virginity as indisputable proof against their grandfather's claims of inherent whoredom, while the other sought to authenticate his accusations with a come-one-come-all attitude. Still, Deena held out hope that her sister could be rehabilitated.

"You wasting your time," Caroline murmured, shifting in her dress to reveal the puckered thigh that matched her cleavage. "Lizzie is who she is. Anthony was who he was, and you are who you are. End of story. No damned sequel."

Deena frowned. Indeed, she could only be who she was. But the statement only begged a question. *Who the hell was she?*

She turned her attention to the pulpit.

Lenora Howard, the pastor's wife, was a dark and thick woman with ample curves. She sauntered to the podium in a golden knee-length dress and broad-brimmed hat of satin and organza. With a gracious smile and a voice of theatrical formality, First Lady Howard welcomed the church's visitors before diving into announcements.

The youth group was selling raffle tickets, Thursday night's choir practice was cancelled, and Sister Laura Marshall's niece was being added to the sick and shut-in list.

"Also, as you all are aware, the Fellowship Hall is in need of renovations. The church is requesting a volunteer to spearhead the organization and to plan these much-needed improvements."

Grandma Emma struggled to her feet. "I would like to volunteer my grandbaby, Deena Hammond, for the job."

"What!"

Emma gave Deena a look of warning before turning her attention to First Lady Howard. "As I'm sure the church knows, my grandbaby be in charge a-building them big ole buildings, what you find down there on the rich folks' part a town. So I 'spect this would be nothing to her."

Nothing?

"Well, praise the Lord," Lenora Howard crooned.

"Praise the Lord!" the congregation echoed.

Deena balked.

She wanted them to stop praising the Lord, but the words wouldn't come.

"Amen! Amen! Deena Hammond, Emmanuel Rises's own certified architect, is going to bless us with a new Fellowship Hall," Lenora continued.

"I can't—I don't have the time—" she mumbled. Deena sunk into her seat, horrified as her pleas were muffled by applause.

When the family arrived at Grandma Emma's place after the eleven o'clock service, Deena washed her hands and went to work prepping Sunday dinner. Her grandmother labored next to her in silence, coating catfish with cornmeal and chicken with flour so both could be fried. Afterward, she would dice the boiled chitterlings.

Chitterlings.

Deena could remember the first time she laid eyes on the pig entrails—in fact, most of her family could. She'd sampled the offal without knowledge of what it was before spewing it into Grandpa Eddie's face. He'd wanted to beat her; he always wanted to beat her, but the family laughed until it would've seemed as though he were a poor sport for hitting her.

Eventually, Deena grew to like chitterlings, or chitlins as they were called, boiled in a broth and served up with a dash of hot sauce. In fact, she grew to love many of the foods that had been so foreign to her when she first joined the family—fried chicken gizzards and chicken livers, okra and black-eyed peas, pigs' feet and neck bones. As a child, she'd been curious about the hodge-podge assortment of food on their table; while delicious, she knew scraps when she saw them. Grandma Emma explained to her that the African American food tradition was born of a necessity for survival. Slaves would make do with what they had—things they could grow and meat discarded from the master's kitchen. As a young girl, it fascinated her that black people had such a rich food tradition, an actual meaning attached to the food they favored. Her mother's spaghetti Wednesdays and meatloaf Sundays could hardly boast the same.

It wasn't long before Grandma Emma took Deena under her wing and showed her how to clean chitterlings, pick the freshest collards, and deep-fry a catfish. Each Sunday, Deena studied hard in an effort to cook like her grandmother, like a black person.

She studied other things in her effort to seem blacker. She watched her cousins for the appropriate fashions, the proper use of vernacular, and suitable music and television programs for a young black youth. As a teenager, she pretended to love hip hop in public though she listened to pop and classic rock in secret.

It was all an attempt to fade into the fabric of the Hammond family—and by fade, she meant disappear. Oh, there were times when she was the center of attention, when her contrary ethnicity came up, but many more when she simply went unnoticed. And while unnoticed wasn't synonymous with acceptance, it was a step in the right direction.

Two hours past the end of church service, the Hammond family gathered around the supper table. There were two of her three aunts, a smidgeon of cousins. For a painful moment, Deena's thoughts turned to Anthony, who would never be around to lie about why he'd skipped dinner again.

"So, I was thinking that you could put one of those pretty roofs up in the fellowship hall. You know, like them ones that ain't nothing but windows. That should be good," Grandma Emma said.

"Naw, what you should do is a regular roof but paint like angels and demons and stuff like the one they got overseas," Aunt Caroline said.

Did she mean the Sistine Chapel?

Deena looked past her aunt in a plea to her grandmother.

"Grandma, please. I can't do this. I don't have the time to work on a new fellowship hall." She stabbed at her collard greens in despair. "You just don't know my boss. He keeps us on a short leash. In-kind donations have to be vetted through the proper channels. And anyway, I'm swamped at work."

Emma glanced from Deena to Caroline tapping ash on the side of her dinner plate.

"If you don't put that goddamned cigarette out at your father's table," Grandma Emma said through gritted teeth.

"Alright, alright." With an exasperated sigh, Caroline stumped her Newport on the plate, ashes cascading into three fat pieces of catfish. She shifted in her seat and with two fingers, plucked the fabric of her dress from the wet folds beneath her breasts.

"Listen," Grandma Emma turned back to Deena, "I gave them people my word that you gone do that hall, now you ain't gone make no lie out of me," Emma said with the point of her fork. "You understand?"

Deena lowered her gaze. "Yes, ma'am."

Emma turned to her granddaughter, Keisha, Caroline's fourth child. She was the same age as Deena.

"Now where's that eldest child of yours at?"

"With his daddy," Keisha said as she poked at butter beans with a fork. "He's the only one that really comes to see about his kid, you know? Snow's a good dude."

Caroline nodded. "He's got some ways about him, but he does handle his business."

Aunt Rhonda looked up. "So he still deals drugs?"

Deena grinned. She loved Aunt Rhonda. The woman was an oasis of sanity in the Hammond desert of madness. The youngest of Emma and Eddie Hammond's children, she fled the Hammond household three months shy of her eighteenth birthday to pursue a nursing degree at the University of Florida. Now she worked in the maternity ward at Jackson Memorial.

"Not everybody can go to college, Rhonda," Caroline said with a roll of her eyes. "Like I said, he's got his ways. But my grandson Curtis don't never go hungry."

"Mmm," Rhonda said, lifting Coca-Cola to her lips. "But shouldn't you thank the taxpayers for that?"

Deena giggled.

"And what the hell are you laughing at?" Keisha snapped.

"Nothing." Deena lowered her gaze. "Nothing at all."

"Right answer," Keisha snapped.

The smell of weed met Deena from across the table. When she looked up, her eyes met Keisha's, darker and flitting with scorn. Never had she been able to figure out what she'd done to earn Keisha's wrath, but she'd owned it from the start. Memories of an eleven-year-old Keisha flaunting Deena's wardrobe at school each day still ate away at her. The last gift of a once doting father, Keisha had taken Deena's clothes with glee, relishing both them and the shock on her classmates' faces each time she recanted the story of how Deena's father had died.

"Bet if the church was payin' ya, you'd have time for the hall," Keisha smiled. She plopped a sliver of corn bread into her waiting mouth and grinned.

"Mmm," her mother Caroline agreed.

Emma grabbed a few thick pieces of fried chicken from the tray and dropped them on her plate before turning a critical eye on Deena's food. Collard greens, stewed okra with tomatoes and onions, butter beans and corn bread. No meat. Not a single piece.

"Chile, what in the world wrong with your plate?" Emma demanded.

Keisha and Caroline snickered.

Deena glanced down. "Nothing. I thought I'd try to eat a little healthier." That, and she was saving room for dinner with Tak.

"Child, gimme that plate."

Emma produced a large, demanding hand. "You gone starve yourself listening to these white folks 'bout what you gots to eat. You gots black blood in ya. You needs to eat black folks' food. Simple as that."

Deena handed the plate over and watched in dismay as her grandmother dumped an assortment of chicken and catfish on it. Her gym's treadmill didn't have a setting high enough to run off all that fat.

Emma dropped the plate in front of Deena with a scowl. After succumbing to her stare, Deena reluctantly poked at a crispy piece of chicken thigh.

"Eat!" Emma snapped.

And with a sigh, she dug in.

"So," Aunt Rhonda said brightly, "what are you working on these days, princess?"

Deena was the only one she called princess, and the only one whose job necessitated variation.

"Renovations for a parochial school. I'm making it handicap accessible." She tasted the collard greens. They were salty.

"So, basically, you putting a wheelchair ramp in," Keisha said.

"Well, not exactly. There's a complete reenvisioning taking place. We're turning over every stone to make the place not just handicap accessible but handicap friendly, as well. Hallways are being widened, walls knocked down. We're even putting Braille—"

"It's a lot of crackers that work with you, huh?" Keisha said.

Deena froze. "What?"

"Crackers. White folks." Keisha rolled her eyes in exasperation. "Never mind."

Her mother laughed. "She ain't notice them, girl. She one of them."

Keisha's laughed reminded her of a siren.

"I'm black," Deena snapped. "Just as much black as I'm white." But her aunt laughed. "Well, I can't tell."

"She right, Deena, whether you like it or not. You ain't got nothing from your daddy. It's like that white woman just spit you out," Grandma Emma said. "White as snow, don't 'cha know. White as snow."

Deena lowered her gaze. It was always the same. She was Gloria Hammond's daughter. *White as snow, don't 'cha know.*

Chapter Five

Tak's condo was a high-rise on Ocean Drive, center stage on South Beach. "The Jewel on the Beach" was what they called the property, and from what he could gather, they took the claim literally. His loft, a three bedroom on the twentieth floor, had been purchased by his father at the vision-blurring price of 2.5 million. With it came private ocean access, a spa and fitness center, and 24-hour white-glove service. He was still trying to figure out what that one meant. Still, his place was a tattered old tent compared to the Mediterranean masterpiece his parents called home.

The Jewel was a thirty-story, sleek and lofty postmodern design envisioned by an MIT professor who was once his father's classmate. Tak remembered visiting the property as a potential buyer with his father and watching him scrutinize fixtures, pull out a measuring tape, and harass the real estate agent for blueprints. When Tak asked him just what he was doing, his father frowned with that all-too-common sneer of impatience and said, "Michael Cook was a B student. Any work by him needs to be double-checked."

When Tak graduated from UCLA, there'd been no discussion about him remaining in Cali. His father simply told him that he was to pick a condo somewhere in South Florida and that would serve as his graduation gift. Had he been a different sort of father, Tak would've taken the gesture as an indication that his father wanted him near. But since he was Daichi Tanaka, he figured it simply never occurred to him to ask his son's opinion about where he might want to live.

Still, the condo was beyond generous, and Tak couldn't help but be excited about it. And though it was expensive, he could afford the property tax on it. Thanks to his father, he'd never had to prescribe to the struggling artist routine. A trust fund of upward of twenty million released to him the day he graduated from college had ensured that Tak would never have to lift brush to canvas should he not desire to. But he enjoyed work and enjoyed earning his own income.

No one, it seemed, knew how much his father was worth. He kept his wife, children, everyone save the IRS and a lone accountant swathed in ignorance. For years, Tak ran a guesstimate, tallying projects and expected payouts in the hopes of figuring out his father's elusive worth. But when he gained access to his trust fund and found that it alone was more than what he'd figured his father was worth, he knew that math wasn't his field.

After graduation, Tak educated himself on market trends, invested his money aggressively, and kept up the frugal spending habits he'd developed in college. The result was a net worth that swelled from twenty to twenty-five million, and more importantly, the sense that he shared responsibility for his fate and success.

His first artistic triumph came as an undergraduate at UCLA after winning a citywide collegiate competition. The grand prize was an art gallery showing with major press. From it, he was able to segue a short-lived fame into a full-fledged gallery deal, first in Miami, and then eventually in Manhattan.

He should've considered himself successful. Last year, he'd been commissioned to do an oil painting for the Miami Museum of Art and the earnings for it alone were stellar. Better still, his gallery showings were always well attended and always profitable. But his scale for weighing success was tilted and broken—after all, he was the son of Daichi Tanaka. Short of morphing into Picasso, Van Gogh, or his father, his version of success was all but unattainable.

Chapter Six

Deena arrived at her grandmother's house in time for breakfast. There were grits on the stove alongside sausage links, eggs, bacon, and flapjacks. Coffee brewed in the percolator while orange juice waited on the table. But Deena could stomach no food. Not before what she had to do.

She stared at the flimsy slab of door that stood between her and Anthony's room. White and peeling, he'd slammed it in her face in a thousand variations of exasperation, anger, annoyance.

What she wouldn't give for him to slam that door once more.

Deena brought a hand to the brass knob and hesitated. Never had she walked into Anthony's room unannounced. There was something so final about presuming to do so, so irreversible, that her body seemed unwilling to do it. She turned the brass knob and the door slipped open.

There.

It's done.

The room was stale; the white curtains drawn and already gathering dust. Air Jordans were strewn about—an orange and red one near the entrance, its match near the window, a purple one at her feet, the other absent. Deena stared at those shoes, her brother's pride, and a bitter sort of amusement washed over her. How many times had Anthony declared that his shoes were off limits, that they would be touched only over his dead body? How right had he been.

Deena moved to open the lone window. The heat and smell of old sneakers threatened to smother her. His window caught, refusing to open; she abandoned it. Looking around, Deena realized she'd neglected to bring a box or bag for mementos. She headed for the kitchen and returned with a fistful of Glad bags.

Deena worked slowly, gathering and folding his shirts and pants, paying them the attention that he never did. Her mind was on auto-pilot, processing data and giving orders through the ripest pain she'd ever known. She bagged shirts, shoes, and sneakers for Goodwill before digging out a pair of Jordans for herself. They were his first pair, as gleaming as the day he'd bought them. Varsity red and white, the sneakers were a vintage tribute to originals released two decades earlier. Deena set them aside. They would join a fitted Miami Heat cap and a bracelet he used to wear, now in her closet at home.

She moved on to his dresser, an old oak hand-me-down with five drawers and froze at the sight of his keys.

Air eluded her.

Silver and unassuming, the keys sat, forgotten.

Deena lifted them with trembling fingers and closed the keys in her fist.

He'd forgotten them that night, left there on the dresser as he went to his death. Would he have returned had he remembered? Would he have lived had he remembered?

She brought the keys to her heart. Choked on a sob. Never would they be used again. Not at her house or her grandmother's or anywhere.

Ever.

In the end, it was the keys and that single, unforgiving word that brought her to her knees. Never would she see her brother again.

Ever.

Chapter Seven

Deena reached underneath the leather bucket seat and felt for a lever. When she found it, she adjusted her chair so that the back was bone straight and knees brushed the steering wheel. With a deep breath, she turned and looked at Tak.

"You can't drive like that," he said.

Deena frowned. "But, I want to be sure I can reach—"

He leaned over and yanked the handle. Her seat shot back.

"I said you can't drive like that. It's too close. Plus, you look ridiculous."

She pursed her lips. "Fine. But can I at least get close enough to reach the steering wheel?"

"Steering wheel, yes; headlights, no."

She rolled her eyes. "You exaggerate, as always."

"Probably. Now come on. Hands at ten and two."

Deena swallowed. For a much-welcomed twenty-fifth birthday present, these driving lessons were causing her a fair amount of stress.

"Can you give me a sec? I mean, I'm wrestling with nerves here. You're teaching me to drive in a Ferrari." She stared at the instrument panel. The car had six speedometers.

"We'll go slow. I promise. But we've got to start to go at all."

She nodded.

"OK. What first? I'm all yours."

Tak grinned as if tempted beyond reason. "Don't, Deena Hammond. I'm but a man." He smiled at her blush.

"Tell you what. Let's practice changing gears. Foot on the clutch. As you push in shift from first to second."

Deena nodded; her left foot sliding to the clutch as her right hand found the gearshift.

"Do that up to six, then back down to one a couple of times."

"But this feels silly."

"Good. Let me know when it feels natural."

Deena sighed.

After absentmindedly whistling *Sakura, Sakura* for a few moments, a song he'd told her was from his childhood, he turned to her once more.

"Put the car in neutral."

"Am I going to drive now?"

"That's the plan."

He sat up straighter. "Now, push the clutch in, start the car, then slowly take your foot off the clutch."

She smiled weakly but stayed planted. There'd been no driver's ed, no uncle with an old jalopy, and certainly no dad to teach her to drive. In fact, at twenty-five, this was her first time behind the wheel of a car. She just wished it wasn't a Ferrari.

"It's okay. I promise, I've paid the insurance," he said.

She knew it wasn't okay if she wrecked it, and that he was just making her feel better. She appreciated the effort.

"Okay," she whispered.

He placed a hand over hers, warm and strong. "Foot on the clutch?"

"That's the one on the left, right?"

"That would be it."

"Then, yes."

Palm over hers, he turned the key in the ignition. She glanced at the hand, larger and lighter, and exhaled at the slight pressure he applied. They were the hands of a painter—nimble, skilled, practiced. His livelihood depended on the preciseness of his touch, the softness or hardness of the pressure he applied, the stroke that he used.

Deena exhaled noisily. There. That was enough of that kind of thinking.

"Okay now, shift to first, then off the clutch. Easy does it."

She inhaled and her foot inched until it pained with the careful, creaking way she moved it.

"It's moving! What do I do?"

There was wide-open parking lot before her and beyond that, a fence.

"Give me a little to the left."

He covered her hand on the steering wheel and used it to turn.

She gripped the ten and two o'clock positions and attempted to turn the wheel. The result was an awkward twist of the body that made Tak laugh.

"What?" Deena said. But she was smiling. He didn't laugh at her the way Aunt Caroline or Keisha did; when he laughed at her, it made her smile instinctively.

"You can't keep your hands there, Dee. It's just a starting place."

Dee. He'd begun to call her that lately, and she liked it. She'd never had a nickname before. She glanced at him.

"I knew that."

"Liar."

He turned his attention to the parking lot. "Start turning left. We're just going to circle this thing until you get the hang of it."

"And until I can go straight?"

He grinned. "Yeah. That too."

There was driver's ed at her high school, but with one teacher and 3,600 students, enrollment was near impossible. Likewise, when she was a teenager, there'd been no one in her family with money enough for a car, let alone private instruction. Hence, her first lesson so late.

After stalling the car three times in a hasty abandonment of the clutch, Deena now inched around the near-empty parking lot of a Miami Beach retirement home to the backdrop of a setting sun. A slung-low chain fence circled the property, accented by a series of low and manicured hedges. Three cars were parked at the front—an old white Chevrolet, a green Ford pickup, and a red Toyota Camry. Behind them were six rows of empty spaces, spaces that Deena weaved through pitifully.

"You're doing great," Tak said.

She grinned. It wasn't true, of course, but she couldn't remember the last time someone had lied to spare her feelings.

"Thank you for that," she said. "And by 'that,' I mean the lie."

"Well, progress is great in my book. And moving is progress." He patted her knee. "Besides, you're way too hard on yourself."

She concentrated on the asphalt between the front row and the empty spaces. He was right, of course, but his intuition with her was unnerving.

"You can't possibly know that. You don't even know me."

He glanced at her. "You don't believe that. At least not the way you're saying it." He was right again, of course, but he needn't be so damned confident about it.

"You want to say something."

He grabbed the wheel and sharpened her turn to avoid a slow collision with the fence. She snatched her foot from the clutch and again, the Ferrari shut down.

"Sorry," she said.

"Relax. No harm done. And anyway, it's just a possession."

She grew up in a carless family. She knew what it was to need a ride, miss a bus, find a place inaccessible because of the public transportation route. A car was *not* just a possession.

"Spoken like a rich kid," she said and started the car again, foot on the clutch.

"I wasn't always rich," he said. "But you're right, I've never been poor. Not even close. Unless you count the time I called my *otosan* an asshole and he emptied my bank account."

"*Otosan?*" Deena echoed.

"Dad."

"You called Daichi an asshole?" She'd seen his father fire someone for accidentally calling him Mr. Tanala. She couldn't imagine he'd have much threshold for profanity.

"Yeah, he took it about as well as you'd expect. Told me he'd show me what an asshole was, and yeah, he did," Tak grinned.

"I can't believe you have your teeth. Boy, my grandma doesn't even allow back talk, let alone cursing at her."

He glanced at her. She was circling the parking lot again.

"What?"

He shook his head. "I thought you told me your family was kind of rough. Jail, teen pregnancies, that kind of thing."

Deena nodded. "Yeah? So?"

"So, I'm thinking, maybe back talk is the least of her worries."

Deena burst out laughing. Her sentiments exactly.

PART THREE

Chapter Eight

Grandpa Eddie used to say that everything had a beginning, middle, and end. Lizzie's beginning was in the sixth grade when her math teacher offered to pass her if she showed him her tits.

Mr. Carson was his name, and he was a pudgy and pale-faced guy who sweat all the time. He locked the door to his classroom that day and pulled down the shades before turning to an eleven-year-old Lizzie.

"You just—want to see them?"

Carson nodded, and his eyes darted briefly, always on the alert. "If you don't want to, you don't have to, you know."

Lizzie shook her head. She knew a good deal when she heard one. "So, let me get this straight. I take off my shirt, and you fix my grade?"

Carson swallowed. "Not for the whole year. Just . . . a couple of test grades."

Lizzie's hands faltered at the hem of her pink T-shirt. "But I could still fail."

He shook his head. "I won't let you. Your grades won't be the best, but I'll still pass you."

Lizzie nodded, satisfied with the answer. She pulled her pink tee up and over her head to reveal two budding, rounded breasts, clad in a tan bra.

"That too," Carson said. He glanced at the door, then led her away from it, despite it being locked and the shade pulled. "I want to see everything."

Lizzie shrugged and reached around to unsnap her bra.

"S—slower."

With a sigh, Lizzie peeled away the bra.

"Give it to me."

Carson held out a hand, and Lizzie gave him the bra. He inspected the seams, ran a finger along the clasp, raised it to his face, and sniffed. His pants bulged.

"That all?" Lizzie demanded when he handed her back her bra.

Carson nodded. "That's all."

With a shrug she put it back on, surprised by how easy it had been.

Mr. Carson had been her beginning, all those years ago. He'd taught her that men lived for their cocks, and that if you knew that, you knew everything. So, she returned to him again and again, for more than just grades. And Mr. Carson obliged, at first for a peek, and then for a grope, and finally, for no less than a blowjob each time.

For Lizzie, it was a short leap from swallowing cock for a good grade to swallowing cock for most anything. No man, it turned out, was immune to a young and willing girl with a wet and eager mouth.

Chapter Nine

Architecture. **It was order** in a world of chaos, sense in a world of madness. It relied on math and science instead of grievances and emotions and rewarded hard work, dedication, and achievement. For Deena, it was the only thing that made sense.

Some days she felt like her grandmother loved her. Those were the times when she would welcome Deena, fix her breakfast, and fawn over her. They'd talk about whatever projects Deena had planned and the day she would open her own firm. Her grandmother would be so proud of her, tell her how smart she was—as smart as her father.

Then, there were the other days. The days when she looked at her with disgust, spitting venomous words about the similarities between Deena and her mother.

She hated those days.

Standing in her grandmother's kitchen with the sleeves rolled up on her crisp white blouse, Deena grated cheddar for the mac and cheese. She and Lizzie were alone this Sunday, chatting as they waited for their aunts and grandmother to return from a run to the store. She was careful to keep the conversation light—no school, no family, no expectations for the future. So, they stuck to music and movies and other things that didn't matter. And as they talked, their cousin Keisha arrived with two of her four children in tow, and the father of the eldest, Steven "Snowman" Evans.

Deena's back was to the entrance of the kitchen—a gaping squared-out hole in the middle of puke green walls. So she didn't see Snowman until it was too late.

"Deena, my favorite girl," he said, his voice throaty and intimate at her back.

Snowman was a tall and brawny creep with a pool ball head and deep toffee skin. His moustache and beard looked penciled in, while his fronts glittered with diamonds. Most days he wore an oversized white T-shirt with the hem near his knees and jeans he was forced to hike up. He was the sort of guy that a girl kept an eye on, unsure as to why, but certain it was needed.

"Steven," Deena said.

She could feel the eyes of Keisha on her back. Whenever Snowman was around, she clung to him like asphalt to earth.

Snowman inhaled. "Damn. You always smell so good."

Deena swallowed. Her skin begged to flee. And she could smell his breath, too, beer and tobacco early on a Sunday afternoon. Either it—or he—made her stomach turn.

"Please, move."

She closed her eyes, desperate to control the tremble in her voice. "Please," she repeated.

These were the times when she hated herself. When her body shook and fear kept her from doing what was right. Then, more than ever, she hated herself.

"You want me to beg for it. I know you do." He released a tremulous exhale, his voice a tease, and God help her, he touched her—fingertips at her arm.

"And you still a virgin, ain't you? Yeah."

He trailed icy fingers along her elbow as though they were the only two in the room. "Tight like a virgin."

She had nothing but a flimsy aluminum grater in one hand, knuckles blanched from clenching, and a nub of cheese she'd shredded to nothing.

Finally, Keisha spoke. "Snow?"

Nothing.

"Snow!"

"What?" he barked.

Deena kept her eyes on the sink. But before Keisha could answer, they were interrupted by the clamor of Hammond women returning from the store. Deena finally turned to face them—and Snow.

It was no surprise to her that Emma, Caroline, and Rhonda were met by a wholly reimagined Snowman, who greeted them with hugs while taking their bags. He called Caroline "Mom" and Deena's grandmother, "Grandma." The exchange with Rhonda was stiff but civil.

"'Lizabeth, there's a girl outside asking after you," Grandma said, still glowing from Snowman's affections.

Lizzie stood. "Did you catch her name?"

Emma shook her head, and Lizzie dashed out. Then Emma turned to Deena. "Put these here groceries away. I need to get off my feet."

No sooner did Deena turn than did Keisha grab her wrist. "You better learn your damned place when it comes to Snowman."

Deena stared back, wide-eyed, Keisha's grip tight on her arm. "I don't want him," she hissed. "And you shouldn't either."

Keisha's gaze narrowed. "Stay away from him, Deena. Last warning."

"I will. You don't have to worry."

Keisha heaved Deena's arm aside, leaving her to rub it absentmindedly.

"Worry? You're the only one who should be worrying. The last time a 'girl' was here to see that slutted sister of yours, it turned out to be a fifty-year-old man."

Deena stared, blinking her way to comprehension. When it came, she dashed out after Lizzie.

A cherry red Escalade with custom spinning wheels, a scantily clad teen in a scoop neck tee, and as Keisha had predicted, a paunch-bearing, middle-aged man with a receding hairline were there to greet Deena before Grandma Emma's house.

Lizzie leaned against the door of the Escalade and giggled as the black with a severe widow's peak ran a finger down the crease between her breasts. Deena stormed them, outraged without surprise, disgust without disbelief, fueling her every step. Down the walkway she tore, shouting her sister's name, and when she reached them, Deena snatched for Lizzie mightily.

"What the hell is going on? There was a girl out here! Grandma said there was a girl—"

"This is my friend," Lizzie said.

"Your friend?"

Deena wondered where in the hell a fifteen-year-old girl met a dark and thickset old man with fish eyes, kinky facial hair, and a pop-up belly. And better yet, what would make her call him "friend"?

The man offered a corn-yellow grin. "Normally I don't respond to shouting, but since you're so pretty, I'll do you a favor."

He extended a calloused hand. "The name's Larry Wilshire."

Deena's gaze narrowed. "Are you aware that fucking a fifteen-year-old is illegal, Larry Wilshire?"

"Baby girl, they ain't got a cell big enough to hold all the guys they'd round up behind this fifteen-year-old girl." He laughed. And when he did, Lizzie joined him.

"I—I'll tell you what," Deena said. "How about I have the authorities give you a call? They can shove you in the cell first and see about fitting the rest later as far as I'm concerned."

"Woo-woo, Deena's getting some nerves," Lizzie jeered, wrestling free of her grip.

Deena rounded the fat Escalade, dug out her phone, and punched in the tag number.

Larry joined her around back. "Listen, why don't you take that phone, punch in my number, and make plans to go out with me?"

His indifference was staggering. Unable to speak, Deena snatched her sister a second time and dragged her indoors.

"What the hell was that, Lizzie? What is he? Forty? Fifty?" Deena shoved Lizzie into her bedroom.

"Girl, stop trippin'. I ain't tryin' to marry the dude. Just having a little fun."

The teen turned on her sister, arms folded. Once again that day, Deena gawked at the hot pink baby tee with its spill-over cleavage and the tiny shorts she'd coupled with it. Pink Converse and hoop earrings rounded out the ensemble.

"Where in the hell do you get these clothes anyway?"

"My *friend* bought them for me." Lizzie collapsed on her bed.

"Your friend, huh? And what does he tell you? That he loves you? That you're the only one for him?"

Peels of laughter erupted as Lizzie rolled onto her belly. "Don't be such an idiot, Deena." She dug into the miniature pocket of her shorts and retrieved a pack of Juicy Fruit. She unwrapped a piece and stuck it in her mouth before tossing aside the packet. Deena plopped down on her bed.

"He told me that he's got money. And that's exactly what I want to hear."

Lizzie fluffed her pink pillow and stretched out on her back. Hands folded over her abdomen, she crossed her legs and bounced a foot midair.

"Money? Money for what?"

Lizzie shot her a look of impatience. "Same thing you need it for. *Stuff.* I see you got Gucci and Prada. I'ma get mine, too."

"Gucci and Prada are my reward for hard work," Deena said. "Damned hard work."

"Well, I work hard for mine, too," Lizzie said. "Damned hard." She took a glimpse at Deena's face and laughed as if delighted.

"And how do you do that? Cause I don't see any job uniforms around here."

The teen grinned. "Girl, I'm wearing it."

Deena's stomach pitched. The room was suddenly too tight and bright, with all of its hot pink and fuchsia, coral and salmon. How could a girl, a child with a Hello Kitty throw on her bed and a mammoth collection of teenybopper posters, talk like this?

"I can't do this," Deena said. She threw up a hand. "I can't listen to this."

Lizzie stared at her. "Look, it's not that big a deal. The way I figure it, you're gonna have sex anyway. So, you might as well get something for it."

Deena blinked back fresh tears. "Yeah. You do. It's called love. And it's supposed to be reciprocal."

Lizzie shrugged. "Well, what you call 'love,' I call clothes, purses, and shoes. I want what I want, and I do what I gotta do to get it. So, deal with it."

Chapter Ten

Weather in Miami rarely took dictation from a calendar, and this winter's day was no exception. The air was thick, and the heat smothering as ocean waves crashed and receded in a natural spring sonata. Sun and moon worked to trade places in the sky as Tak and Deena walked, footprints trailing along wet sand, faint glimmers of day receding in a rush.

"God, you know what? I tell you everything," Deena said. "And I have no idea why."

Tak shrugged. "Just one of those things. Like figuring out where we all came from, and what we're doing here."

Deena's eyes widened. "You kidding me? My family's got it all figured out."

"And you? Have you got it all figured out?"

She frowned. "No. It just seems to me that if you've already made up your mind then you can find evidence corroborating whatever it is you believe."

"So what are you telling me? That you're an atheist?"

Her eyes widened. "It's not God that I doubt, it's people."

They continued in silence.

"And what about you?" she said.

Tak sighed. "I'm sure you've heard of cafeteria Catholics," he said.

"Yeah?"

"Well, I'm an ambivalent Buddhist. You know, it's more about family ties than any clear and all-encompassing notion."

"Hmm," she said in quiet understanding.

On they went.

"You know what I wish?" Deena said suddenly.

He shook his head.

"I wish that I didn't want my family's love so bad. I wish I could be one of those people who wore leather jackets and just didn't give a damn."

He shot her a look. "You'd be musty if you wore a leather jacket in this heat."

She grinned. "You know what I mean."

He shrugged. "Who doesn't want a decent family, Dee? It's not much to ask for."

He paused to pluck a seashell from the sand. Chipped and polished by time, it shone under the glint of a fast-setting sun.

"I don't know the answers," he said. "But they seem to be in things like this." He held up the shell.

She frowned. "I don't follow."

Tak simply shrugged. "Well, think about it. What's a shell? It's just a—a hard, protective outer layer. The same is true with family. They're an outer layer, a protection from the world. At least that's what they're supposed to be." He paused. "Think about what happens when you screw with an animal that has one of those hard shells. What does he do?"

"He goes into it."

"Right. He retreats." He thumbed the shell thoughtfully. "Now imagine if you were to rip the shell off a turtle and expose him. What do you think you'd find?"

Deena cringed. "Something soft and hurting."

"And dead, if not close to it. So, our hypothetical turtle, who's able to stand our shell transplant for the sake of comparison, needs another shell, another form of protection. And so do you." Tak handed the grooved and sand-polished subject to Deena. She looked down at it.

"So, how've I been surviving all this time then? What's my shell?"

Tak grinned. "Tell you what. I'll let you know when I crack it." He plucked the shell from her hands and tossed it in the water. The two stopped, ocean rushing their feet, saturating then receding.

"Who the hell told you to take my shell?" Deena demanded. She would've sounded more incredulous if she could've kept from smiling.

"*Your* shell? I'm the one who bent down and plucked it. All you did was stand there with your hand out."

Deena giggled. And before she knew it, she'd shoved him. Never had she pushed someone before. But the feeling it gave her, watching him stumble just a tad, was enough to make her squeal in mischief. She darted off, hoping he would follow.

He did.

Through the sand they dashed, laughing as their footprints grew closer and closer before merging with her capture.

Chapter Eleven

When **Deena went to** work for Daichi Tanaka as an intern four years ago, she was shoved into a cubicle with the breadth and gloss of a sterilized broom closet. Her desk back then was a flimsy white contraption, held steady by the half dozen texts she memorized as per Daichi Tanaka's request.

Of the twenty interns Daichi took on each year, Deena had been the first he'd ever offered employment. With that vote of confidence, Deena's workspace moved from a broom-closet cubicle to an office on the third floor. It had a single window, bare white walls, and a drab gray carpet. But it was hers.

Her desk as an intern and the one she had now had both been adorned with a single potted plant—a bonsai named Hope.

Hope was a forgiving bloom, hacked in inexperience, frustration, and anger. Ever lending a patient ear, she listened as Deena prattled about her apprehensions and fears, and forgave her for skipped feedings and sunlight. Hope flourished no matter her treatment, almost as if aware of how much Deena needed her to.

Deena's reliance on Hope was beginning to wane. These days, she found it much more rewarding to seek out a certain guy with an easy smile and a tender touch when she wanted to talk. She hoped the bonsai didn't mind.

Despite the shimmering sunlight of an early spring day, Deena was behind her desk. Her workspace was a streamlined one because a cluttered mind led to cluttered work. She had only her MIT degree on the wall, hung with a single nail. A drafting table, L-shaped desk, and charcoal gray swivel chair sat in the center of the room. On one side was a bookshelf crammed with must-have references, on another, a high-backed guest chair, and in the center of it all, was Hope.

It was the sort of day when the sky was a silky seamless blue, when the ocean shimmered as if buffed to a high gloss and sunshine glistened like melting honey. It was the kind of day that emptied out the Tanaka Firm like a fire drill. Daichi's employees found countless ways to get out of the office—lunch with a client, site evaluations, scouting potential construction locations—anything, really. But not Deena. Deena was business without fail.

She spent the morning working on the plans to remodel a preparatory school, all the while loathing the subsequent phone call with the school's chancellor. She was a nasty old woman with a penchant for drama who preferred to choke rather than hold the school's purse strings. The woman salivated over haggling, and when the time came, Deena knew she wouldn't disappoint.

"Is it really necessary to raise the toilets?" croaked the disciplinarian. "It seems to me that if we left the toilets as they were we could save thousands of dollars."

Deena stared at her fingernails, already annoyed. "It's a matter of safety, Miss Gleason. It's the same way with the grab rails. These are small alterations with big benefits."

"Big benefits? Benefits to your firm, perhaps. I've heard that you guys mark up the price on everything anyway."

She hated this part. The haggling, the selling of a vision, the educating of the ignorant.

"Miss Gleason, I can assure you that you're being charged the customary 8 percent of construction costs and not a penny more. I've slashed every possible expenditure to make this affordable—there's nothing left to cut."

"That's what you say. But why is it that when St. Charles was renovated, it cost half of what you're quoting me?"

Deena sighed. "I don't know, Miss Gleason. It could be anything. Your building might be older, or larger, or, or—"

"Or it could be *you*. You ripping me off."

"If I wanted to rip you off, I wouldn't suggest cost-saving measures, now, would I?"

"I don't know what you'd do. But I'll tell you this. I don't like your tone. And quite frankly, I never have. I think you're a snob."

Deena froze. "I beg your pardon?"

"I said you're a snob. Right from the beginning you've been rude and impatient and—and—"

"Miss Gleason, hold on a moment. I don't think—"

"Don't tell me to hold on. *I'm* paying *you*. Now all you've tried to do, right from the beginning, is rip me off. 'We need this and we need that'—way more than what we asked for!"

"Your building wasn't up to code!"

"Says you. Look, I don't have to tolerate this," Miss Gleason said. "I refuse to work with you one more moment. Not one more!"

"Miss Gleason, please. Let's gather our bearings and—"

Dial tone.

With a sob of frustration, Deena heaved the phone across the room and buried her face in her hands. All that work, all that fighting, only to be fired.

The woman was impossible. Life was impossible. She wished herself away from this plain-faced office and on a beach. With Tak and his guitar.

The first time she heard him play was the evening she cleaned out Anthony's room. The hour grew late as they sat on the beach, nothing but the gentle strumming of his guitar between them, and on occasion, a few melodic verses he'd conjure on the spot.

She'd been stunned by his voice and the feelings it stirred in her. Smooth and sultry, his tenor was lulling and seductive, and on that night, made exquisite by grief. She'd closed her eyes and let his sound wash over her, pain alleviating with the notion that he somehow shared it.

Deena closed her eyes with the memory, attempting to recall something of the notes which soothed her.

"That bad, huh?"

Startled, she lifted her head to find Tak. Deena smiled.

"How long have you been standing there?"

He shrugged. "Long enough to know you need a raise."

Deena grinned. "Try getting that one by your dad."

He stepped inside and closed the door. "Schoolmarm?" he said with a sympathetic smile.

Deena sighed. "Schoolmarm. Not to worry though. She fired me this time."

Tak waved a dismissive hand. "Screw her. She was beneath you anyway."

"No one's beneath you when you're as poor as me."

He shook his head. "Deena, listen. Sometimes the slammed door is just a distraction. You know, to the opportunity in the other direction. Every week that woman took a hacksaw to your work, stifling your talents. She had no vision, no appreciation. Trust me. Better things are in store. Soon." He pinched her cheek. "Alright?"

"Alright."

Again, she smiled.

"How long has that woman been badgering you, anyway?"

"Too long. And I rushed through two other projects, small ones true, but still, rushes—because she said that I wasn't giving her enough attention."

"And this is how she thanks you." Tak frowned, leaned against her desk. "And the fellowship hall? Are they still beggars being choosy?"

Deena sighed. "Yeah. Draft number five was finally approved. And all it cost was my sanity."

"You need a vacation, Dee."

Dee. She still churned at the nickname. Never had she known how sweet endearments could be on the right lips.

Was that what she thought of him? Of his lips? That they were somehow right for her? Deena blushed.

"Let's do it," Tak said as he slammed a hand on her desk and Deena blinked.

"Do what?"

"Take a vacation."

He rounded her desk, warming to the idea. "Let's hit the road. You, me, and the top down on the Ferrari." His hand sliced through the air. "Just open air and speed."

Deena frowned. "But when? Where?"

"Who cares where. Anywhere. Everywhere. The going is what's important." He leaned against her desk again.

"Now the way I figure it, my dad gives two weeks of vacation for every year of employment. Considering what I know about you, that you've been here three years and you've probably never used a day; that gives us eight weeks of vacation time to play with. Who knows where we could go with that."

Deena lowered her gaze. She was considering it. She could hardly believe it, but she was considering it. The woman whose life was charted out on an Excel spreadsheet titled "Expectations," the woman whose Monday, Tuesday, and Wednesday of each week had been nearly identical for the last three years, was considering it.

How had he done that to her? How had he penetrated her life so thoroughly, that she would consider throwing her hands in the air and following him blindly round the country?

But the thought of it made her shiver. She wanted to. God knows she wanted to.

"But—I have a new project. What about Skylife?" Deena said. "I can't skip out on that. I mean, we haven't started or anything yet . . ."

His father had given her an opportunity, singling her out among the hundred or so architects that worked for him, pegging her to collaborate on a project with him. She was the youngest at the firm, and after that day, the most loathed.

Tak waved a hand. "Dad's in Prague. He left yesterday. From there, it's Tokyo for two weeks, then London for another two. Gives you at least a month until he comes looking for you, probably more." He paused. "I could get an estimated start date if it'll make you feel better."

"But I've got other stuff . . ." Deena said lamely, glancing at her desk.

Tak sighed. "You've got a wheelchair ramp for K-Mart. I know you, Deena. You can have the concrete specs out for that in fifteen minutes."

Deena smiled. It was her misfortune to find a man whose mind didn't wander when she yammered about her work. "Well, there are channels. It takes forever to get approved for time off here. If I put in now I might get cleared in six months."

"Let me worry about that. Being the boss's son must come with some perks. You just make plans to leave tomorrow."

"Tomorrow?"

He smiled slyly. "Tomorrow, Deena Hammond. Handle the concrete specs today. And tomorrow," he winked, "belongs to me."

He left with a bounce in his step, oblivious to her sharp intake of breath.

Tak bounded the stairs two at a time, always keen for exercise, as he ascended to the top floor, his father's. Broad and winding, the staircase gleamed with white marble and wrought iron banisters. At each landing was the Tanaka logo, his father's pompously grand signature etched in gold, with a transparent globe of the same color in the background. The earth signified his global approach to architecture and the signature, which omitted his first name, stemmed from his conviction that a Tanaka would always be at the helm of his firm.

The thirteenth floor belonged to Daichi and his secretary of fifteen years, Angela. Heavy glass doors etched with the company logo glided open to meet Tak when he reached the floor. He conjured up his most charming grin and crossed the bright white lobby to Angela's desk.

She looked up and smiled at the sight of the boy she'd watched become a man over the years.

"You must want something, Takumi. That smile is far too big."

Tak leaned on her desk, a hand on several of his father's files. "You've done something new with your hair, Angela. Looks great. Glamorous, even."

She grinned. "Now I *know* you want something. Out with it, *por favor.*" Though she'd worked for Daichi Tanaka for fifteen years and knew that he and his sons were fluent in Spanish, she wouldn't have dared used it with her boss.

Tak shook his head. "I'm so disappointed. I came to see you. I just . . . needed a little sunshine in my day."

Casually, he picked up a manila folder, only to have it snatched away.

"*¿Que?* You want me on the unemployment line?"

Tak rolled his eyes.

"Right. My dad would sooner get rid of me than you." He watched her organize the files he'd skewed.

"Listen," he said finally, "I need a favor."

She didn't look up. "A favor?"

"Yeah."

He glanced behind him, as if worried his father would show up.

"*Su padres en Prague,*" she reminded him.

"Yeah, I know." He leaned forward. "There's a girl who works here. I need you to clear her for vacation."

Angela's mouth dropped. "I knew it!"

Tak tried not to smile. "You knew what?"

"You and your 'oh, I just had to see you. You just brighten my day.'"

She came around the desk and folded bronzed arms, a lock of auburn hair slipping into her eyes. "Who is it?"

Tak grinned. "Deena Hammond."

"*Deena Hammond.* You say her name like that in front of your father?"

"You kidding me? He doesn't even know I know her."

Her face went serious. Angela returned to her desk, hands trembling as she sorted paperwork for filing.

Tak watched her.

"What? What did I do?"

"Go away, Takumi."

"Go away? Why?"

She shook her head. "Because I said so."

Angela went to work filing her stacks. When she looked up, she found him still standing there.

"I can't get between you and your father. The job market isn't good, and anyway, I'm too old to start over."

"I'm just asking for a few days off, days that she's already earned. Paid."

"Paid?"

"Come on! You can do it. You can do anything. Dad says so all the time."

"You went too far, Takumi."

"Sorry."

Angela dashed the hair from her eyes and sighed at the hopeful expression on his young face. As a boy, he'd worn that same expression sitting outside his father's office as he begged for pizza instead of sushi for lunch. And as a teen, he wore it when he needed help getting a dent out of his new Mustang before his father was any the wiser. And now, as he needed her to bend company rules for a girl, he wore it one more time.

Angela sighed. "How many days?"

Tak lowered his gaze. "A month."

"A month!"

"Angela, come on. She has two. Go ahead and put it through."

"No one's ever been approved for a month at a time. No one."

"Please," he clasped hands in desperation.

With a groan, Angela turned to her PC, usurping the human

resources department as she went to Deena's file.

"Well, she's never taken a sick day. Just bereavement."

Tak came around her desk for a closer look, and Angela jabbed the monitor's OFF button. "Jesus! *¿Estás loco?*"

"Well, you're sitting here reading it to me! What's the difference?"

"I'm not reading it to you, Takumi, I'm thinking out loud." She scowled at him until he retreated, then turned the monitor back on.

"I'll give you two days."

"Two days? I need a month."

This was why he didn't belong in corporate America. He needed to be free to roam, at will.

"Well, you're in here at the last minute. There are people who have been waiting for months—"

"Come on. We don't care about them. It's me. Why're you going on about a bunch of strangers, anyway?" He gave her his most doleful expression.

"I'll owe you," he promised.

"You have nothing I want!"

"Well, when I get something it's yours." Tak leaned against her desk. "Please, Angela? I'm crazy about her."

That was the other thing. She was a sucker for love. Married for thirty-two years, the mother of four children, the daughter of a couple together for sixty. She devoured romance novels and soap operas and thrived on the love affairs of celebrities. She was always, always disappointed when love didn't work out.

Tak smiled, knowing he'd baited his fish.

"The first time I touched her, there was this, this awareness I've never felt." He exhaled nosily.

Her eyes widened. "And you met her here? At the office?"

Tak shook his head. He knew this next part would send her over the top. He had to be careful though, as the truth was sensational enough. Any embellishment would make it implausible.

"She saved my life. We were strangers, and she saved my life."

Angela gasped. "Someone tried to kill you?"

He nodded.

"Father in heaven!" She made the sign of the cross. "Pull up a chair and tell me *everything*. I'll put in for her vacation time."

"Well, I think you should go, Deena."

Rhonda shifted to adjust the slim black phone wedged between her shoulder and ear and waited for her niece's protests.

"You can't be serious. I'd be gone a month. I don't even know where I'm going. What if Grandma needs me? What if Lizzie needs me?"

Rhonda thought about her niece Lizzie, the lost and promiscuous soul who would be unwilling to accept help from her sister even if she did need it.

"They'll just have to manage."

"Grandma doesn't want me to go. She says she might need me for something."

Rhonda sighed. "And what about what *you* need?"

Deena laughed. "I don't even know what I need."

"No? Well, I'd start with this vacation." Rhonda gave a tired sigh. "Sweetheart, listen. You're twenty-five, and you live like a nun. You work, come home, and spend all your free time trying to please everyone else. There's got to be more to your life."

Rhonda stood, folded her arms, and crossed the length of her spacious master bedroom. With a lean on the windowsill, she gave her lover, stretched out on the broad and accommodating platform bed, a wink. Black lace on soft curves made her irresistible.

She turned her attention back to Deena.

"You need a life of your own, sweetheart. An adventure. Wind in your hair and laughter in your heart. You need to feel alive, to do more than just be. And you have the right to happiness. But you have to take it and own it."

"And what? You think I'll find it? On this trip with him?"

Rhonda shook her head. "It doesn't matter if I think you'll find it with him. The question is, do you?"

Chapter Twelve

Deena stared at the pile of clothes on her bed. She had no idea what to pack. She had a few sweaters, relics from her days at MIT, but wasn't sure if they'd be traveling far enough north to need them. It was March, and already the unrelenting Florida heat was upon them like summer in a desert wasteland. He'd warned her not to pack much, that they would go where the wind took them, but she found the idea of being unprepared frightening. So she threw in the sweaters, jammed in the jeans, and frowned at the stack of short and long sleeve shirts on her bed. Not everything would fit, and for the first time in her life, planning alone couldn't give her comfort. For the first time in her life, she would have to trust someone else.

For years, Deena, as the older sister, practiced a life of piety, determined to be the shining example her siblings so desperately needed. Every decision was a conscious choice, painstakingly determined after weighing all options and ascertaining every possible outcome. From obsessing over course material to ensure that her grades remained stellar to skipping parties and dating because they were unproductive distractions, all of it had been for Anthony and Lizzie. Anthony, who lived and died by the sword, and Lizzie, who lived and might die like a whore. For once, there was no great and noble purpose behind Deena's actions. She was responding to a voice thought long dead, bullied and smothered by her grandparents and a file on her hard drive boldly named "Expectations." It was a file whose dense itinerary contained no mention of a monthlong vacation or a schoolgirl infatuation. But the junior Tanaka had done the impossible. He'd resurrected that voice, weak though it was, and gave it reason to shout.

It was a drab and damp Friday morning when they left for destinations unknown. Deena ventured out with a stone gray duffle bag in hand—large, but singular. On her face was the uncertainty that plagued her. But it was coupled with something else, something wholly unfamiliar—excitement. Tak spotted her and smiled. He saw the apprehension, but he saw past it to the single bag and the simmering anticipation in her smile. He needn't be told that she'd spent half the night packing and unpacking in an effort to meet every anticipated need, only to realize it was impossible. And he needn't be told what this large, lone bag meant to her, or meant to them. In her own way, she was giving herself to him. She trusted him.

There was something about the patter of rain on a windshield, the mundane nothingness of an overcast sky, and the gentle hum of a car on the interstate that could lull even those with the heartiest resolve to sleep. Tak glanced at Deena, with her knees drawn to her chest, head against the door, and a few unruly wisps of hair in her face as she slept, and he smiled.

He could recall a conversation they'd had last year, shared over two lattes in Brickell. In particular, it was the wide-eyed wonderment with which she looked at him as he confessed that he'd seen most of the country.

"But how is that possible?"

He'd shrugged. "A combination of things. Road trips, family vacations, just visiting people mostly."

She'd been to two places in her life, Cambridge and Miami, and neither had been vacations.

It'd been his turn for disbelief. Never had she crowded into a jazz joint in New Orleans because a melody had intoxicated her. Never had she tasted Memphis barbecue, Chicago deep dish, or Philly cheese steak. Never had she shopped on Rodeo, blew money in Vegas, or watched the ball drop in Times Square. Her words burned him, and in that moment, he'd wanted nothing more than to change that. He wanted those things for her, and wanted to be there with her when she experienced them for the first time.

Tak thought about his own life, and the endless opportunities he'd had. Sure, it hadn't begun in wealth, but by the time he was in the fifth grade, even he could see where the family fortunes were heading.

His father was catapulted to fame quite suddenly when, at thirty-two, he won an open competition to design JP Morgan's new headquarters in Manhattan. His design had beaten a whopping seven hundred entries, including several legendary architects, and in doing so had jammed his name into the mouths and magazines of everyone who mattered.

Tak remembered when the call came to their home in Miami Shores. Just the night before his father had been pouring over the records for his fledgling firm, fretting over whether it could get through the month. His father was at the kitchen table frowning over drafts when the phone rang. It was a then ten-year-old Tak who dashed to answer. The man on the phone had an odd accent, so peculiar that Tak felt compelled to hang up on him.

"There's no Morgan here," Tak said, gleaning a lone word from the garble on the other end.

His father looked up.

"No JP either," Tak insisted. As he moved to slam the phone back in its cradle, Daichi snatched it, rescuing his career in the process.

A $750 million contract. He would never forget the look on his father's face in the moment when he transformed from a man of meager means to one that good fortune had suddenly found. In the days following that phone call, their family was at its happiest.

His mother was not yet an alcoholic, and his father still had time to toss a football.

Then the phone calls came. First, industry insiders like the *Architectural Digest* and *Architectural Record*. Then the rest. They called it a coup d'état, an ousting of architectural aristocracy and a supplanting of a brazen new face. It was the beginning of the end, they'd all proclaimed.

They were right in more ways than they knew. Within months, the Tanakas moved from the quaint house in Miami Shores to a posh condominium in Coral Cables. With the move came a new school and new friends, a new life where Tak could have whatever he wanted, so long as it didn't include his parents. And as the work poured in and the Tanaka Firm grew from a single desk in the back of a house to a monolith with twenty-seven locations on five continents, the rift between his mother and father, between him and his parents, slowly but surely, became an abyss.

His younger brother Kenji had been a surprise. Wedged between the JP Morgan account and the revamping of Bayfront Park, no one seemed more agitated with the news than his father. His firm was doing well, he'd hired two architects, the first of hundreds to come, and he hadn't the time for fatherhood. The wince on his face told his son that he regretted those words, but for Tak they were little more than a Freudian slip.

He wasn't sure about the exact time his mother began drowning herself in alcohol. Like Kenji, it was wedged firmly between JP Morgan and Bayfront. Whenever Tak was in a particularly forgiving mood, he told himself that she hadn't drunk a drop of alcohol during her nine months of pregnancy, but when he was especially incensed with his mother, he would say that she'd probably all but succumbed to alcohol poisoning. The truth, he suspected, was somewhere in between.

Tak glanced at Deena as she stirred in her seat. He couldn't look at her and feel sorry for himself though. Sure, he had a callous father and a drunk for a mother, but hell, he had parents. What's more, neither of them, at their worst, had ever struck him in anger. He'd never known what it felt like to be unloved, unwanted, rejected. Even his father, in all his iciness, had never caused him to feel rejected. Forgotten, most certainly, but never rejected.

Deena had lost both her father and brother to murder. His closest comparison was his grandfather, George Tanaka, dead from cancer at seventy-seven. And while they'd both experienced grief, hers, of course, was incomparable.

Deena was good for him in an unexpected sort of way. She forced him to reevaluate, to cherish things he'd taken for granted. Things like life and love, money and security. And she ignited him in a way that was as thrilling as it was unfamiliar. Deena, with her toffee-colored curls and fawn-brown eyes, seemed to fit into his life like the perfect puzzle piece, albeit doused with kerosene. He couldn't wait to ignite it.

When Deena woke, she found herself on a bare stretch of interstate skating at close to a hundred miles an hour. She glanced at Tak, who tapped out accosting notes to an '80s rock song with one hand as he drove.

"Did I wake you?" He turned down the volume.

Deena frowned. "Maybe you should slow down."

He eased off the gas. "Sorry. Lead foot."

Deena's neck creaked as she turned to the window. "Where are we?"

"Half an hour outside of Gainesville."

"Gainesville! How long have I been asleep?"

Tak shrugged. "Awhile. About four and a half hours. Figured you were pretty tired."

She couldn't remember the last time sleep had come so easy. She brought a hand to her face and felt the creases left there from the door.

"You should've woke me. Why'd you let me sleep so long? You don't have to be a chauffeur, you know."

She had her license, a crisp new piece of plastic in her wallet that she was dying to put to use. But he waved her off.

"You were tired so I let you rest. And anyway, I don't mind being your chauffeur, sweetie."

She turned away, ignoring the customary flutters she felt at his casual endearments. He was always dropping sweet nothings like that—a "baby" here, a "sweetie" there, and she dared not take them for more than face value. Her experiences with men were painfully lacking, never a lover, never even a kiss, so she felt insecure about what constituted harmless flirting versus a sign of sincere interest.

Deena sighed. It wasn't that there'd been no opportunities for her, but rather that she'd shied away from men; first because she feared her grandfather's wrath and later because she feared the men themselves—their expectations, their experience, and their laughter when they discovered she was still a virgin. In the back of her mind, she buried Snow's derisive laugh when he'd stated with all certainty that she was, in fact, still tight like a virgin.

As always, Deena buried her fears with reason. She was a busy woman and had no time for men. Driven by the need for success, she needn't be bothered with cumbersome relationships anyway. So she shied away from the obvious advances, the inherent confidence of her pursuers only serving to intimidate her more. And she shied away from the awkward innuendo of geeks who figured she wanted an intellectual match instead of the bare bones brawn and good looks of other pursuers. And on the occasion when a man crossed her path with that rare combination of looks and smarts, she, of course, was far too shy to do anything about it. And so, she would stay seated, daring not to approach such a man, and in doing so, would lose him to far more forthright women. Still, she always found it comforting that these lost opportunities affected her so little. Her feelings toward men had always approached indifference. For Deena, men were like museum paintings—ideal to admire, forbidden to touch, and always, always, too costly to bring home.

They stopped for gas in Gainesville, and while filling up, Tak pulled a map from his glove compartment and spread it over the hood of his Ferrari. Despite the GPS of his car, he insisted he liked the feel of a map in his hands.

"How's Atlanta sound to you?"

Atlanta. Home of the Bank of America Plaza, the tallest building in the country outside of New York and Chicago. Also home of the Flatiron, a wedge-shaped, window-wide building that was the second-oldest skyscraper in the nation. In fact, some of the greatest architects in the world had shaped Atlanta's skyline— Richard Meier, Michael Graves, Daichi—

"You know your father—"

"Yes, yes, I know. My dad designed Peachtree Emporium."

Tak crumpled the map and jammed it in his pocket. "Listen, I'm sure Atlanta has some great architecture, and I'll make sure you see as much as you want. But keep in mind we're going a lot further than here, and time is finite."

He took a breath, paused, and offered her a smile, first forced, then broadening with each second that passed.

"So," Tak continued, natural this time, "I'm thinking a show at the Fox Theatre, the night scene in Underground Atlanta, and maybe a stroll in Olympic Park. We could tour CNN or Coca-Cola if you want." He withdrew the nozzle from the car and placed it back on the gas pump.

"How's that sounding, love?"

He glanced back at the Ferrari, scrutinizing the exterior, before declining a car wash.

Deena lowered her gaze. It was there again, sweet words warming her. And even as she uttered the phrase "It sounds wonderful," she couldn't help but wonder if she was talking about the itinerary or the sound of love on his lips.

They arrived in Atlanta at four thirty and at Deena's insistence, checked into The Mansion on Peachtree, a luxury hotel designed by renowned architect Robert A. M. Stern. As Tak retrieved the bags from his car, she lectured him endlessly.

"Stern's generally classified as a postmodernist, but he prefers the label 'modern traditionalist.' You can see why though when you actually look at his work. He's really big on tradition. He—"

"Hey, are you bringing this stuff inside?" Tak held up a pair of fuzzy pink slippers, wretched free from Deena's partially closed duffle bag.

"Damn it, the zipper gets stuck and everything falls out." Deena jammed the shoes underneath her arm, and Tak slammed the trunk and followed her toward the hotel. He nearly collided with her when she stopped.

"What? What is it?" he said.

"Look at it. It's wonderful. The limestone and cast stone create such a dramatic effect." She glanced back at him. "I'm sorry. You're bored."

She did that sometimes—use architecture as her fail-safe. She could spout arbitrary facts at awkward moments and prattle on about nuances till her nerves calmed or a blush subsided. Though she did enjoy the work before her it wasn't to the exclusion of all else.

But Tak shook his head. "No, it's okay. I'm Daichi's son, remember? I'm used to marveling at concrete structures for hours on end."

"Limestone."

"What?"

"It's limestone and—" Deena shook her head. "Never mind. For once, I want to forget about the structure of a building and enjoy whatever's inside. Maybe there's a hot tub. I'd love to soak in one."

He glanced at her as if he'd love for her to soak in one, too.

They settled on a deluxe room, a marble and velvet delight with an enormous tub, a 37-inch flat screen and two queen-size beds. The two showered and dressed before deciding on dinner.

"How do waffles sound?"

Deena glanced at her watch. "It sounds like breakfast at 7 in the evening."

Tak threw an arm around her, grinning. "Come on, Dee. Waffles it is. Allow me to rock your world."

"Two pecan checkerboards, four eggs wrecked, and two heart attacks on a rack. Sweep the kitchen and give it to me scattered, smothered, covered, chunked, topped & diced!" Deena's waitress cupped her hands over crimson-painted lips, gave her chewing gum a few more pops, and sauntered off in her crisp white blouse and black slacks.

Deena scrutinized the diner. They were at the Waffle House, a place she'd never heard of until half an hour ago, despite Tak's insistence that such a thing was impossible. The place was a diner in every sense of the word, from its broad counter and weathered stools where patrons speculated about Georgia prospects for the upcoming football season, to the single row of tables and chairs waited on by sassy waitresses who insisted on calling you "hon" even when you asked them not to.

"So, what does my little architectural scholar think of the Atlanta skyline?" Tak took a sip of his sweet tea.

Deena lowered her gaze. It was the right question, a deterrent from the jitters she felt from being hundreds of miles away from home with a man who made her wake up in a peculiar, mysterious, and acute sense of desperation.

She attempted to shrug nonchalantly.

"Oh, I don't know. There's a lot of modern and postmodern stuff here, but that's not surprising. Atlanta's a southern city, but it's a hybrid one. In a time when much of the South rejected what they saw as an encroachment on an old way of life, Atlanta was going through a transformation. They wanted to be seen as a progressive city, a beacon of the 'New South.' You know how some of the best architecture reflects the values of the people around it? Well, Atlanta's no exception. You can see the rejection of antebellum roots and—"

Deena paused, her cheeks coloring. She's was being nervous and stupid again.

"I'm sorry. Before this is over you'll wish you asked some other girl to come with you."

Silence followed. Her words implied more than she'd intended about their reasons for being there. They implied more than the careful friendship they'd maintained to that point.

A slight smile played across Tak's lips. "Don't be silly, Dee." He watched her as she shifted, before deciding she'd squirmed enough. "You're a genius. My *otosan* must love talking to you."

Deena shrugged. "It's a big firm. I don't really spend time with your father."

Tak laughed. "You do. You just think you don't."

She frowned. "What in the world does that mean?"

"My dad's brilliant, and his whole life is wrapped up in that firm. He hired you because he saw something. While you were his intern, he studied you, figured out what you were made of, and decided that he liked it. In other words, he was spending time with you, even if you weren't spending time with him."

Before Deena could respond, the waitress returned with their food. Pecan waffles and scrambled eggs, biscuits and country gravy and two unidentifiable piles on saucer plates were placed before them.

"What in the hell is this?" Deena said, lifting the edge of a saucer for inspection. Her nose crinkled at the mass.

"It's hash browns. Try it."

Tak grabbed a bottle of syrup and went to work on his waffles.

"Hash browns *where?*"

Tak grinned. "Hash browns *there.*" He jabbed at the mass with his syrup-covered fork. "There's also onions, ham, cheese, chili, and tomatoes." He pointed at each item with the utensil before returning to the slicing of his waffles. "And it's all quite good."

She looked at the red and yellow goo that covered the potatoes in distrust. She didn't want to think of how many calories might be in that little saucered dish, with its fried potatoes and ooze of cheese. She didn't want to think of what her ass would look like in a swimsuit after a bite of that mess.

"Come on, Dee. Open up already."

Tak dipped his fork into his mouth to clean it before taking a stab at her hash browns. He came away with a thick wad and trained it toward her mouth.

"Just a little now."

With a hand beneath her chin, he guided the gooey hash into her mouth.

An explosion of flavor slipped between her waiting lips, and with it, the fork that had once been in his mouth. She blushed.

"Uh-oh," Tak said as he caught chili with his thumb. Quickly, he returned the finger to her mouth; her lips parted to accept it. His breath caught. Their eyes locked and a sudden, painful throb ailed him. It took too long for either to look away, neither speaking, even as he drew thumb from mouth. Wide-eyed, Deena cleared her throat and looked away, red-faced and stiff. Tak stared, a sober and dry-mouthed astonishment on his face. Just what the hell was it with him and this girl that made him act as if he'd never known another? He exhaled, and once again, resumed his natural course of his breathing.

Three days in Atlanta. In it, they strolled the lush greens of Centennial Olympic Park, admired the architectural wonders of Peachtree, and danced till exhaustion in Underground Atlanta—Deena's first foray with a nightclub.

Underground Atlanta wasn't so much "underground" as it was downstairs. Furthermore, the entrance to it looked seedy and suspect, but she took Tak's hand and allowed him to lead her in. There were nightclubs down there, at least half a dozen, and that night, he promised, they would dance.

Deena produced a shiny, laminated new driver's license for entrance to the club. The bouncer who took it was tall enough so that the back of his head pressed against the bit of wall above the door. He scrutinized the picture and handed it back as if unimpressed. The bouncer repeated the ritual with Tak before they were finally admitted.

They stepped inside and darkness swallowed them. People were pressed on a vast floor, swaying to a trance-inducing beat. Deena blinked. It was damp and humid as the fumes of sweat and liquor coalesced midair. The music throbbed, a light, poplike tune that was almost disco, paired with an airy voice.

Tak squeezed her hand. "Want a drink?" he had to shout over insistent bass.

Deena nodded gratefully.

They weaved through the club, hands clasped out of what Deena told herself was necessity, till they reached the bar at the back. He ordered a Heineken draft and a Strawberry Daiquiri before looking down at her hand.

"You okay?"

She blushed, grateful that it was too dark for him to see. Her grip was clammy and tight, her resolve to keep him in reach unshakeable.

"A little nervous." She peered around. "You're probably eager to dance."

At UCLA, he'd been a beer-chugging frat boy of a stereotype who partied four times a week. So tonight, he was in his element.

Tak shrugged. "Whatever you want to do."

She lowered her gaze. "Just—enjoy my drink, maybe?"

He nodded. "Sounds good to me."

He released her when his beer arrived and tossed back a big swallow. She brought the daiquiri in a big pilsner to her lips for a sip.

"Good?" Tak asked.

Deena nodded. "Very."

She drank the first one and had a second. The music was southern rap now, so it had a slower tempo, claps on the backbeat, and constant references to sex, strippers, and alcohol.

The liquor had a warming effect. She peered in her glass. What was in a daiquiri? She had no idea, but it was marvelous.

"You, uh . . . want another?" Tak smiled.

Deena nodded. "One more. Not too much."

Her words didn't sound right. Running together and enunciating all at once. She frowned.

Another daiquiri was placed before her and again she peered in the glass. "These are very good. You should try one."

Tak grinned. "I generally steer away from drinks with umbrellas and sliced fruit adorning it. Not good for the image."

"Fine," Deena said. "Suit yourself." She tossed some back in a big gulp and got brain freeze. "Ow!" She gripped her skull with both hands.

"Just let it pass," Tak advised. "And drink slower."

She looked up at him suddenly. "Wanna dance?"

He looked surprised. "Uh—sure. If you're okay with that. I'd love to."

She took another gulp of her drink and abandoned it, near full. Then she started for the floor. Tak dropped a few bills on the counter and followed.

"I've never danced," Deena gushed. "Tell me what to do."

"Not much to tell. Just feel it. Feel it and have fun."

"Feel it. Fun. Got it," she said.

Tak smiled. "Follow me."

The music was club rap with intoxicating beats, a breathy male voice, and a few sexy and well-placed hooks. He pulled her into his arms and began to sway. She followed with ease.

"Like this?"

Tak grinned. "Just like that."

It was easier than she thought. When she told him that she'd never danced, what she meant was that she'd never danced in public. In her room, with a radio and a broomstick, she'd held jaw-dropping concerts for an audience of none. She'd danced in those days, as a girl all alone. But in his arms it seemed her selfless abandon had found her again.

"Someone told a lie," he teased.

He pulled her closer, till their bodies molded—his arms around her waist, hers at his neck. He was hard and hot and moved like liquid. She imagined him a skilled lover for the motions came so easy. It wasn't the first time they'd been so close; after all, they hugged each time they saw each other, but this was different. This was lingering and indulgent and . . . stimulating.

She knew what was happening, happening to her, to them— between them. She wanted to stop it, felt like she had to, to avoid pain down the road. But her heart took no heed from the tyrannical rule of her mind. It wanted him near and was willing to do anything to make that happen.

Chapter Thirteen

From Atlanta, it was on to the Big Easy for jazz and jambalaya in The Quarter and riverboat gambling on the Mississippi. For two days they combed the streets of that old historic district, marveling at the Creole town houses by day and downing hot Cajun food and big-ass beers by night.

With New Orleans behind them, they headed for Memphis in a six-hour tear up I-55. There, Tak insisted, they would find the best barbecue on the planet. But they did more than gouge on butter-soft baby back ribs and pounds of pulled pork; they lost themselves in the melancholy sound of blues on Beale Street, danced rooftop at The Peabody Hotel, and strolled the banks of the Mississippi by moonlight.

"My mom never said why she killed my dad," Deena said, the Mississippi River to her right as they strolled. The moon was high and shone on the water, shimmering with an imminent fullness as if promising to pop. The air pressed with the heat of the South and summer.

"Not even after conviction?" Tak said.

Deena shook her head.

A white couple passed, staring. Tak either didn't notice or didn't care. Deena figured it was the second one.

"You said you didn't remember much. Is it possible you suppressed her explanation?"

Deena shrugged. "I suppose. But I doubt it. When I say I don't remember much, I mean about the murder. Like, it comes in snippets for me. The blood, my mom with the gun, things like that. Never in sequential sense."

"And when you dream, is it the same way?"

She hesitated. "I don't dream about that much anymore."

Instead, images of her parents were being ousted in dramatic fashion by lurid snatches of sex, courtesy of a sweating and shirtless Takumi Tanaka.

He glanced at her. "You don't dream about them much? Really?" He sounded thoroughly surprised.

Deena shook her head.

"Well, that's odd, considering it went on for so long. When did it stop?"

Instantly, she wanted to say, right about the time I started wanting you inside me. After all, they were the same moment.

But she cleared her throat instead. "Um, I'm not sure."

When he glanced at her, she looked away. Deena didn't dare look up, so afraid was she that he knew her secret, so certain was she that everyone did.

Chapter Fourteen

Four hours separated Memphis from St. Louis, next on their list of "must-sees." The I-55 corridor linking the two cities weaved them through highlands and plains before dumping them in St. Louis, the self-proclaimed "Gateway of the West."

They were hurdling toward exhaustion, crisscrossing first the South and now the Midwest at breakneck speed. By the time they arrived in St. Louis, they'd clocked better than 1,800 miles over two weeks in Tak's Ferrari. More telling, however, was the way they traveled—top down, wind in their hair, his arm around the back of her chair.

Deena identified with the conundrum that was St. Louis, Missouri. An independent city, it seceded from its county better than a hundred years ago. It was a speculative place, being equal parts North and South, East and West, and therefore, a different thing altogether. It endured extremes with sweltering summers and frigid winters; and whole sections of it had been abandoned. Deena could definitely relate to St. Louis.

They were touring the city, architecture, and art museums, sights and tourist traps, when they decided to stop at the Gateway

Arch for pictures. A massive and gleaming structure of stainless steel, it was the tallest monument in the country.

Deena brought a hand to that iconic image, the identity of St. Louis, made not by others, but by what it envisioned itself to be. It was then that her phone rang.

A sort of resigned indifference passed over her at the sight of her grandmother's name on the caller ID. Deena answered with a sigh.

She was calling to complain, to do nothing but bitch. Lizzie had been suspended again, this time for fighting. When Deena breathed a sigh of relief, she nearly laughed. How desperate did she have to be to be relieved that her sister had only been fighting? But as far as Deena was concerned, fighting was a damned sight better than nickel-and-dime blowjobs on the bathroom floor.

"They talking about putting her out of school, for good, 'cause she so much trouble," Grandma Emma said. "And when they do, you gonna be the one to pay for private schooling."

Deena chuckled. She loved the way her grandmother thought that a college degree came standard with an inflated bank account. If she only knew, her granddaughter could barely afford the vacation she was on.

In the end, she promised to speak to Lizzie when she returned to town and hung up before the old woman could protest.

"Everything okay?" Tak said, eyes on her expectantly.

Deena nodded. "Everything's fine. Lizzie's suspended. Same as usual."

She offered him a bright and false smile. "Now what were we doing? Pictures, right?"

"Right," Tak said.

Deena pulled the zipper up on the white parka she wore and gave him a grin. "Well, what's the hold up, buddy?"

Tak responded with a smile.

They ventured a good distance from the Arch, then they waved down a passerby for pictures. It was a sweet-faced old lady that stopped, took Tak's digital camera, and waited for the pose.

They stood arm in arm, lucky enough to have a pond and good deal of the Arch in the shot. In the instant when the old lady went to snap their picture, Tak stole a kiss, a single kiss, on Deena's freckled cheek. She squealed and blushed scarlet as the old lady gushed, insisting they were as sweet as Tupelo honey. When she returned the digital camera with the image of Tak's stolen kiss still emblazoned on it, Deena stood there, her cheeks still flushed. She stared at that frozen screen in silence, the image of Tak's kiss burning into her mind. Behind her, he peered over her shoulder with his four-inch advantage and smiled down at the camera.

"Perfect," he said. "Absolutely perfect."

Chapter Fifteen

Lizzie was glad her sister was gone. Unlike her grandmother, who acted like she needed Deena to come and flip the oxygen on each morning, Lizzie could do without the old maid. Deena spent her days at a desk and her nights in a book, barely existing, if at all. She lived on the beach yet never went there, was pretty and never took advantage of it, and at nearly twenty-five, was a jaw-dropping virgin. Had she not known Deena, she wouldn't have believed such a person existed.

Lizzie lost her virginity three days before her twelfth birthday and never once did she look back. A whole world opened up to her that day, a world where clothes and jewelry, money and drugs could come with a few quick thrusts and a moan here and there. It was easy really, once you got past those first painful moments, easy and sometimes enjoyable. She had a pretty face and an impressive body, an inheritance from a mother she never knew, and a curse according to the family she hated.

Everyone thought that the first time she'd had sex was in school or a crack house, or somewhere equally unforgiving. But it wasn't. The first time Lizzie had sex was at home, with a guy they all knew.

Lizzie and Keisha were arguing that afternoon, arguing over Lizzie's tight red dress and jiggling tits and whether it was all for Snowman's attention. For that purpose or not, Snowman took one look at Lizzie, bit his lower lip, and Keisha detonated.

But the girl was mistaken. Lizzie was no Deena. She was no martyr and took no shit. She screamed when someone screamed at her, hit back when someone hit her, and played tit for tat every goddamned chance she got. So when Keisha called her a slut, and Aunt Caroline laughed until her makeup ran, Lizzie decided to show them just how right they were.

She waited an hour. Long enough for Keisha to begin arguing with her mother about restrictions on food stamps, long enough for Grandma Emma to fall asleep in the middle of *Matlock*, and long enough for Lizzie to grab Snowman's wrist and lead him to her room.

She was eleven at the time, but a mature eleven. Already she was known for toe-curling talents with her tongue. Just that past year her mouth had served her well, and had meant the difference between passing and failing, Payless and Prada.

He was rough from the start, gripping her head, holding it steady. Suffocating and brutal, she'd wanted him to stop, tried to pull away—but found his grip firm and determined. She remembered his words when he finally turned her loose, words that had chilled her, scared her.

"Come on," he said, "time to feel that pussy."

She'd told him no, that she was a virgin, but he laughed. *"Not giving head like that, you ain't."*

The look in his eyes was hard and unforgiving, and the look of his cock was the same. So, she asked him to be gentle, but he wasn't. She asked him to go slower, but he wouldn't. And when her bedroom door opened and there Keisha stood, Lizzie's adult cousin didn't scream or call the police. She simply backed from the door, leaving Snow to finish.

Lizzie thought it was their secret—hers and Snow's and Keisha's. But three days later, Snow's car was riddled in a hail of bullets, leaving him shot in the thigh, shoulder, and chest. Anthony, it seemed, had found out.

Snow came to her, hours after being released from the hospital, begging, crying, convinced there was a bounty on his head. "Talk to him," Snow begged, "tell him nothing happened."

So, Lizzie went to Anthony and persuaded him, surprised by the conviction with which he spoke. He could deal drugs, he said, and he could rob or kill, but what he couldn't stomach, what he wouldn't, was a grown man with a little girl. That kind of man, Anthony reasoned, needed to die.

After that, boys were afraid of Lizzie. They would fuck her, but in a brief and nervous sort of way, as if half-expecting to be murdered midstroke. It didn't matter how many times she explained to them her brother's only beef had been Snow's age; still, they were afraid.

But when Anthony died, so did their fear.

Chapter Sixteen

Tak held out his ice-cream cone, and Deena took a lick. Three kids nearly collided with them as they tore for a monstrous red roller coaster.

"Wow, Tak. That's good. What is it again?"

"Double chunk chocolate chip. Told you to get it."

He took a bite of the frosty treat, and Deena frowned. She turned to her suddenly plain vanilla cone as they walked.

"Trade you."

Tak raised a brow. "Hmm, let's see. You've got plain Jane vanilla while I have mouthwatering double chunk chocolate chip. I mean, would you look at the chunks in this thing? We've got nuggets of fudge here, bits of chocolate chips there, and this enticing swirl of white chocolate comfort."

He shrugged. "Mmm. Sorry. Just don't see the benefit."

Deena turned back to her cone, bottom lip out. "But I want yours."

Tak rolled his eyes in exaggerated fashion, fully aware that he intended to give her his cone. Still, he loved the pouting.

"Deena, I've got to tell you, you're not much of a negotiator."

He handed his two scoops over and took her single vanilla. "Now, let's hurry. We've got a date with the Screamin' Eagle."

Deena froze. The Screamin' Eagle was a wooden roller coaster a hundred and ten feet high and one she seriously doubted she had the gall to ride. Till then, she'd been charmed by the costumed characters of her childhood, waving and posing for pictures with glee, delighted by the sticky and sweet treats they'd devoured with abandon, and giddy with the sophomoric way they tore through the park. And when the Screamin' Eagle's cherry train barreled past with its cartload of screaming passengers, all that changed. Deena's jaw went slack, her cone plummeted, and she gripped Tak's arm in terror.

"I can't, Tak. I can't get on that."

Tak glanced down calmly at the manicured fingernails that blanched his flesh before returning to her face.

"Of course you can do it. You wanted to do this, remember?"

As if to contradict him, the train tore through the sky again before plunging toward the earth.

Deena's eyes widened. "People pay money for this? To be terrorized like this?"

Tak laughed. "Definitely. Now what do you say? One try?"

She lowered her eyes. Before their visit to Six Flags, she'd never been to an amusement park. Her mother Gloria, amazingly enough, used to be something of a worrywart and would never allow her child to attend the fair when it came to town. The fairgrounds were unkempt, the rides unsafe, and the food unhealthy. And later, when her mother was in prison and her father dead, it was pretty clear that asking Grandpa Eddie was not an option.

But of course, Tak knew all that.

"I'll be with you, Dee. I promise. And you can hold on to me as tight as you like."

Cone tossed, he tilted her chin so that she met his gaze. He had to redirect it when a fresh cartload of passengers careened by. "Tell you what. Afterward, I'll have a surprise for you."

Deena's eyes widened. Surprises were that other Tak novelty.

"Really? What?"

Tak shook his head. "Uh-uh. Screamin' Eagle first. Surprise second."

Deena looked at the ride. It made her heart thud, her palms were sweaty, and her mouth dry. But as she stood there with Tak's undivided attention, she knew that her reaction was only partly because of the ride. And in the end, she agreed to the Screamin' Eagle.

Two to a row, twelve rows of carts, each connected by ball and socket joints. 3,872 feet of track rose a hundred and ten feet into the air. Laminated steel set against wood gave each passenger the roughest, wildest ride possible, as they tore through the air at better than sixty miles an hour. The ride would last for two minutes and thirty seconds and the highest drop would be from ninety-two feet. Deena knew all of this because she insisted on being briefed by the ride's attendants before boarding.

Deena adjusted her harness from what she ascertained to be the safest locale within a relatively unsafe place—the middle seat. She looked at Tak; her eyes unusually large with terror, and was grateful when he extended a hand to her.

"It's gonna be great. You'll see."

Tak adjusted his long legs, tight against the safety bar of the cart, and smiled.

Deena turned her attention back to the track. She would use reason and science to battle fear, as always. The ride was heinously tall and climbing; it would employ positive gravitational forces, which were the easiest for the human body to endure. The name of the game was fear, and the expectation of climbing to towering heights combined with the average body's ability to endure about five times the pull of gravity meant that a designer would seek to push the limits in that regard. There was also whiplash to think about. The human body needed time to sense changes in speed and—

"Deena, stop," Tak said.

She blinked, startled. "What?"

"I know what you're doing, and I want you to stop it."

"What? I'm just—getting ready."

With a sigh, Tak leaned in until his mouth brushed her ear. The feel of wet lips coursed heat to her core.

"Trust me. Not logic or science, but me."

He brought a hand to her cheek and traced the line of her jaw, eyes on her mouth. Her breathing came fast and shallow. Instinctively, her lips parted. Tak leaned in, and Deena's eyes closed, chin tilting.

The pair jolted, the ride began, jarring them sheepishly to the far ends of the cart. They glanced at each other and quickly looked away.

With a pull of the chain, Tak and Deena were dragged up a steep incline. Above the trees, above the park, they continued to climb at a steady rate. The creaking of tracks, the rattle of chains, and the steepness of incline combined to topple Deena into near hysterics. In desperation, she gripped Tak's arm when she could stand it no more and buried her face into the crook of his shoulder.

They fell out of the sky. Eyes watering, Deena shrieking, feet digging for footing in vain. Next to her, Tak hooted in glee. They rose and fell, the third of the drops by far the harshest. And just when Deena felt certain her nerves could take no more, they were hurled into a 180-degree turn and heaved toward the exit.

He wouldn't do that to her again. She'd been terrified, far more than he thought one person could ever be. She'd shrieked and clawed like a cat in a hot bath, and halfway through, he felt ashamed for making her ride.

As they weaved down the walkway Tak hurried to keep up; Deena, it seemed, was hell-bent on escape.

"Dee, wait!" Tak called as they dashed toward what he figured was the park's exit. "I'm sorry! I shouldn't have pressured you. Forgive me."

He'd asked her to trust him, and just when she did, he'd heaved her into horror.

Deena turned on him.

"Forgive you? What are you talking about? I'm getting back in line. That-was-incredible!"

She snatched him by the arm and dashed toward the waiting queue, dragging a baffled Tak behind her.

As it turned out, Deena was a thrill junkie. Slicing through the heavens on Mr. Freeze, toppling twenty-three stories on Superman: The Tower of Power, and catapulting through head over heel loops on Batman: The Ride. She wanted it all. White knuckles, corkscrewing, free falling gushes of adrenaline—she wanted it all, it turned out, while clinging to Tak.

Tak squinted under the Midwestern sun, his favorite UCLA cap pulled low on Deena's brow.

"Ready for your surprise?" he asked as he draped an arm about her shoulder midstep.

She glanced at him. "That depends. What is it?"

He stopped before a slew of games. "A stuffed animal. Pick one and I'll win it for you."

Deena looked at him doubtfully. "Tak, these games are difficult. In fact, I wouldn't be surprised if they were rigged."

"Just come on, already." He led her to the long-range basketball booth. "Last I checked I had a pretty decent jump shot."

Despite her objections, Tak nodded toward the crater-faced attendant and dug out his wallet. He slipped the kid a five and turned back to Deena.

"No worries, you'll see. Besides, every girl should have a guy to win her something."

An hour later and $45 lighter, Tak and Deena left with an over-sized panda she could've bought for twenty. Still, she was surprised at the tenderness she felt when he handed her that prize. It was a sweet feeling, having that panda to cradle as they exited the park, his UCLA cap pulled low on her brow. And as they walked, Deena felt something extraordinary and exotic—something she'd all but forgotten. Deena felt . . . normal.

They did all the things they were supposed to in St. Louis—pose for pictures at the Arch, gulp beer at Anheuser Busch, and nearly hurl at Six Flags. They toured the wineries on the outskirts of the city, caught an indie film at Tivoli, and took a horse drawn carriage through Tower Grove Park. And when it was time to split the state of Illinois in two with an I-55 trek north, neither Tak nor Deena had any regrets.

As Tak drove, Deena made plans for their next stop. The Chicago skyline was an architecture lover's dream. When the Great Chicago Fire destroyed so much of the city, its visionaries began experimenting with steel frame construction and large plate glass, and in doing so, created the first modern skyscraper. Their work would give birth to the most awe-inspiring structures the American landscape had ever seen.

While in Chicago, Deena would be able to appreciate the wonders of the greatest American architects: Louis Sullivan, Frank Lloyd Wright, and Mies van der Rohe—their work all dotted the landscape.

And she looked forward to the art, too. The Art Institute of Chicago housed an impressive collection of Impressionist and post-Impressionist work by people even Deena had heard of, Gogh and Monet, among them. And while she'd never been one to linger in the halls of a museum per se, she found Tak's excitement about their work contagious.

Tak's phone rang as Deena flipped through the Chicago guidebook and deftly, he slipped it from his pocket without so much as a swerve.

Impressive.

Every city was a battle, Deena thought, a constant crunching of time, always pressed with the question of must-see versus must-wait. Sure, they could linger in Chicago. But six days in Chicago meant no days somewhere else, and Deena was becoming far too greedy to let that happen.

They would have to compromise. His art and her architecture were tops on the list, as were a few restaurants and a night on Lake

Michigan. But after that, both time and activities got complicated. He wanted a Bulls game, and she wanted a chocolate tour. There would be time for one or the other, but definitely not both.

Deena frowned at the glossy photo of gooey milk chocolate dripping from a spoon and felt her mouth go wet. There was a time in the not-too-distant past when discipline had been the lifeblood of her existence. But as their trip lingered and Tak continued to pander to her every whim, discipline gave way to indulgence, and restraint to satisfaction. But Tak wasn't the only one who could be indulgent.

"Tak, I was thinking—"

Deena froze with the realization that he was still holding the phone.

"Listen, I told you I don't know how long I'll be gone. I'm with a friend." Tak drummed the steering wheel in impatience. "Of course, that's important to me. You're important to me. All I'm saying is—"

Tak paused, glanced at Deena who continued to stare, and returned to the call with a sigh. "Listen, I can't talk right now. It's just not a good time. Later."

He powered off the phone and turned to Deena's wide-eyed stare. The scowl he wore morphed into a smile. "Admiring the view?" he said.

Deena blushed, her curiosity promptly forgotten.

Chapter Seventeen

A **hotel room high** enough for views of the skyline at the junction where the river met Lake Michigan. A top-level suite with hardwood floors, two broad platform beds, and an ebony-paneled Jacuzzi. Soft ecru wallpapering covered three sides of the room, and on the forth, a floor-to-ceiling glass door led to the balcony. These features, combined with a fully stocked wet bar and 47-inch flat screen, promised that they could enjoy Chicago quite well, all without leaving their hotel room.

It was late when they arrived, so the two ordered in. A loaded stuffed pizza with three kinds of sausage, made right with a garden salad for Deena's wary conscience. They mixed Long Island Iced Teas and chatted while they drank, and afterward collapsed into bed for the night.

When Deena woke, it was with a start. Breathless and confused, she blinked at the darkness in an effort to orient herself. She felt ladled in sweat. Entangled in the bedsheets, her womanhood throbbed with the flickers of a memory. A swipe of the tongue. An arch of the back. A moan. Another.

She brought a hand to her throat, and it came away wet. She glanced at Tak, snoring in the bed, razored edges of his hair sweeping his face. In her dreams, those locks had swept her body as he hovered over her, had his way with her, kissing, teasing, pleasing.

She wanted so badly to touch him. Always had. But the voice of her grandfather, strong even in death, maimed her desire.

"The Lord God created the races and separated us water, appearance, and language."

It was a cautionary tale about life, and the reason Deena should've never existed. Her parents had been a brazen affront to God, and she, the by-product of disobedience. And in the past, his voice had been enough. When no other reason seemed compelling enough, the voice always was. It stopped her from clasping Tak's hand a moment too long or holding his embrace a second more. But the voice was losing its luster. No longer was it the loudest or the most insistent. No longer so persuasive.

Chapter Eighteen

A **morning at the** museum, an afternoon on Michigan, an evening of Chicago blues. Day one was done, and for another day, another round of delights. Sunrise on the balcony with mimosas in tow, sunset on the Sears Tower with a view of four states, and jammed between it all was a sublime array of artwork and architecture, exquisite food and music.

Chicago was a complicated city. Ten million people comprised the metro area, three million in the city proper. It was a place where towering high-rises met natural beauty, and where a segregated past battled an inclusive future. It was where a Jewish synagogue could stand three blocks from an Islamic mosque, yet ethnicities could cling to neighborhoods as if gentrified by law.

Nowhere did Deena's increasingly contrary life seem more illuminated than in Chicago. Raised by a family that subscribed to voluntary segregation, she found herself in perpetual violation of this tenet. She spent her days in Tak's company and her dreams in his arms, all the while leading her family to believe she was with a girlfriend from college. A black girlfriend at that.

Deena and the Windy City were of a common variety, clinging to the past out of habit, aware that it hindered, not helped. Deena stood on the patio of her room, gaze sweeping the steel mountains of Chicago, as color and creed, race and religion pressed one upon another in the landscape below. She knew that practicality would eventually force change, in Chicago, in her. But as she stood next to Tak with all the hues of ethnicity beneath her, she wondered. Wondered if she and the city could change together or if fear would force it to go alone.

On their final night in the city, they visited an old friend of Tak's. His college roommate, Eddie Spruce, was a fledgling artist with a grungelike appearance who lived in Wicker Park. An enthusiastic sculptor and aficionado of graffiti, Eddie Spruce boasted that he could down six shots of Tequila, all without flinching.

"Eddie's an enthusiastic guy," Tak explained, as he slowed at a red light midjourney to Wicker Park. "He means well, but his personality can be kinda strong."

"I hope he likes me," Deena said. "Do you think he'll like me?"

He glanced at her, surprised. "Yeah. I'm sure of it." He gave the steering wheel a nervous tap.

"And you're okay with spending the night here? Instead of a hotel?" He was speaking rather loud.

Deena shrugged. "I guess so. I mean, it's a practical idea. And people do that all the time, don't they? Stay with their friends when they visit?" She paused. "Anyway, I'm looking forward to meeting him."

Secretly, she felt thrilled that he would reach into the farthest corners of his life and seek to include her.

When Eddie opened the door that evening, he was clad in a pair of ripped jeans and a T-shirt that proclaimed art dead. His greasy red curls were shorn short and tucked behind his ears; his green eyes glassy—no doubt from the alcohol Deena smelled.

"Tak-man!"

Eddie clapped his old roommate on the back before sweeping him into his arms. Behind Eddie, a slender, wide-mouthed blonde sat on the couch.

"What's happening, Spruce?" Tak said.

Eddie grinned. "That's what I'm trying to find out."

He turned to Deena with interest. "This her?"

Tak nodded. "Yeah. This is Deena."

"Sweet!"

Eddie snatched her into a hug. When he released her, Deena was breathless.

"Man! I feel like I already know you! Tak-man here talks about you all the time."

"He does?" Deena whispered, wide-eyed.

Eddie grinned. "Wouldn't you like to know?"

Tak gave Eddie's chest a shove. "Let us in, already."

"Yeah, sure thing. Anyway, I want you guys to meet my girl." He shot two trigger fingers at the blonde on the couch. "Nan, this is the old roommate I'm always talking about. The Tak-man. And this hot tamale is Deena. Deena, Tak, this is my girl, Nancy."

To Deena, Nancy looked like the sort of girl who dated a Phi Beta Kappa jock from Princeton, whose family owned property on the lake, and whose father had a flourishing law firm handed down from father to son, all of whom sipped martinis before dinner each night.

As Nancy smiled, soft, blond curls framed her doll face, offset by sea green eyes. She wore a navy button-up and smart gray slacks with a charm bracelet from Tiffany's.

She extended a hand to Tak. "I'm assuming no one else calls you Tak-man but Eddie."

"You'd assume right."

Eddie inserted a head between the two, a hand at each of their backs.

"Nan went to Northwestern, Tak-man. Majored in psych so don't talk too long, or she'll weave you into her web of psychobabble."

Tak laughed.

Forty-five minutes later, the four sat around a deep-dish veggie pizza, each with a glass of rum and Coke in hand. They learned that Nancy enjoyed horseback riding and golf, was getting her master's in clinical psychology from the University of Chicago, and that her family preferred to summer in the Hamptons or Martha's Vineyard.

Eddie, on the other hand, was in his fourth year of a two-year master's degree in art therapy. In his free time, he preferred to veg out in front of whatever happened to be on MTV, protest the establishment, or play his guitar to drum up a little cash.

The four downed a bottle of dark rum as Tak and Eddie reminisced about college with good-natured banter, updates on old friends, and UCLA football prospects for the upcoming year.

"So, Deena," Eddie said, as he topped off her glass despite her protests, "Tak-man tells me you're an architect."

Deena nodded.

"I, uh, work for his father." She took a polite sip, her thoughts staggered by liquor. She looked at the others and noticed they were all faring better.

"Yeah, well, I met the old man once. Definitely hard-core." Eddie refilled his glass before turning to Tak with a grin. "What was it he called me?"

Tak smirked. "I believe it was 'a feebleminded burden to society.'"

"That's it!" Eddie hooted and slapped his knee. "Your old man is fucking hard-core." He shook his head. "I tell ya, they don't make 'em like that anymore." And he actually sounded regretful.

Deena shrugged. "Daichi's a serious man. With a low threshold for—for—"

She fell short of saying foolishness, opting instead to fade into silence.

Tak jerked a thumb at her. "You're talking to the wrong one. Remember, she's an architect. She drank the Kool-Aid a long time ago."

Deena turned to him and stuck out her tongue. Tak grinned.

When Tak and Deena lay side by side on the couch's foldout bed, darkness, silence, and half a foot of mattress separated them.

"So," Tak began, "what'd you think of Eddie?"

Deena cleared her throat. "He was . . . lively."

"You don't like him."

Deena turned to face him. "I didn't say that. Of course, I like him. He's your friend. He's important to you. Anyone who's important to you is . . ." She trailed off in horror.

"Is what?" he said softly.

"An . . . important person," she said lamely.

Tak sighed. An awkward silence floated between them, penetrated finally when he wished her good night.

Quiet lasted for five minutes. Then, a violent slam of wood against wall pierced the night. Faint at first, and then with insistence, a nearby headboard banged out a rhythmic tune. Nancy's cries and Eddie's moans meshed and lingered. With brutal clarity, she demanded he fuck her, and apparently, he did.

Tak groaned.

He tossed covers over his head as next to him, beads of sweat pricked Deena's face, aware of how close they lay in that single, flimsy bed.

Nancy screamed.

"Jesus," Tak breathed. "Am I supposed to—?"

"You want to go for a walk?" Deena blurted.

"What?"

"I could use a walk. Do you want to come?"

Tak sat up and flipped on a lamp. Red blotches patched her face.

"Yeah," Tak said. "Definitely. Let's go."

With the Chicago River to the east and Bloomingdale Avenue to the north, Tak and Deena strolled the streets of wind-whipped Wicker Park. One of the oldest communities in Chicago, Wicker Park was home to a horde of artists and musicians. As Deena passed the two- and three-story brick lofts, she could see how the neighborhood had earned its trendy and bohemian name.

"They were an odd couple," she said softly, suddenly.

Conversations began that way with them; an internal dialogue hurdled in the recesses of one mind and tossed out midthought to the other.

"Yeah," Tak said, "but they make it work."

He slipped hands into the pockets of his ripped jeans. "A relationship worth anything takes work."

"People must stare."

Tak shrugged. "Anytime something isn't what people expect, they stare. Doesn't mean anything."

Deena frowned at her feet, clad in a pair of white Reeboks. "I wonder what her family thinks."

The two approached a broad white fountain, an oasis in a concrete desert. There was no need to ask if she could stop; instinctively he headed in its direction, knowing she would want to.

"I don't know what her family thinks, and I'm not sure it matters. He loves her, so if she loves him, then that should be enough."

"She loves him, it's just—"

"Just?"

"Well, he's asking a lot of her. How is she supposed to know whether it's worth it?"

Tak paused. "She couldn't. Not without taking a chance."

They continued in silence.

"Eddie tells me she's a private girl," he said finally. "That her family is kind of on a need-to-know basis." He took a seat on the fountain's broad white edge, slipped a hand into the water, and watched it submerge. "So, she'll tell them when she's ready."

Deena stared, wide-eyed. "And—and how does he feel about that? Is he okay with it?"

Tak frowned at the water and withdrew his hand. "I don't know. Maybe. Point is, he's willing to try."

Chapter Nineteen

The next afternoon, Tak and Deena began the thirteen-hour trek to New York. They spent the evening in Cleveland with a late-night meal of pierogies, or boiled dumplings stuffed with jalapenos and chicken, before passing out for the night. They woke before checkout, grabbed dim sum in Asia Town, and continued on their journey. Tak ripped through Pennsylvania and Jersey before arriving in New York at close to nine P.M., some six hours after their Cleveland departure.

The Statue of Liberty. The Empire State Building. Times Square. Deena had all the giddiness of a girl stepping into the hub of the cosmopolitan world for the first time. Her heart was palpitating and her palms sweaty, and she battled a constant need to grab Tak's sleeve to point out one landmark after another. She wanted a show on Broadway. Pizza in Brooklyn. A glimpse of the Apollo Theater. And she refused to wait another minute. At twenty-five, she'd waited long enough.

Tak's silver Ferrari crawled along the theatre district, stopping and starting on Deena's whim, as he attempted to find a hotel. Up and down the streets of Manhattan they staggered, until finally, he made a turn on 8th and another on 42nd. Deena screeched for him to stop.

"That one. That one there!" Deena jabbed a finger at a single soaring hotel.

It was the Westin. A towering prism split by a curved beam of light and sheathed in multicolored glass. The hotel's mirrored surface shimmered with the reflection of Yellow Cabs and dashing pedestrians. She turned to Tak. "Please."

He turned in, killed the engine, rolled down his window, and handed the curbside valet his keys. Deena squealed at his automated indulgence.

They were forced to take a suite on one of the lower floors, as the closing of some Broadway show had the hotel inching toward capacity. One look at her face as they entered the room, however, told Tak that Deena was far from disappointed.

The room ran a gamut of earthy tones offset with a splash of red. Thick chocolate carpeting and textured ecru walls complemented two broad platform beds with plush white bedding. A dash of red from an armchair, decorative pillows, and a seascape painting all lent to the room's sense of serenity. But they would have to save their appreciation for another day. Exhaustion from the nonstop trek from Cleveland left Tak and Deena skipping dinner to bid each other good night, almost at once.

When Deena woke in the morning, she was alone. The bedside clock told her it was ten A.M., and briefly, she wondered why Tak would let her sleep in so late. Deena showered and dressed, figured he was at the gym, and decided to wait for his return.

The Weather Channel reported a pleasant sixty, considerably warmer than a traditional March in New York. Excited by the news, she dug out a flirty blue blouse with a low-scooped neckline and paired it with a linen skirt. They were the latest additions to her newly emerging casual wardrobe, complements, of course, of Chicago and Michigan Avenue.

Deena waited for an hour. Yesterday's decision to skip dinner haunted her. She glanced at the clock and decided to put in a little more time.

At a quarter to noon, she dialed Tak's cell. Met with his voice mail, she made up her mind that hunger couldn't wait. Deena rose, slipped her room key and a few dollars into her skirt's hidden pocket, and made for the door. New York waited.

Deena headed east on 42nd toward Broadway and the Times Square Building, keeping her eyes peeled for restaurants all the while. She was wary of the overcast sky but certain she'd find something soon before eruption threatened to saturate her.

Wedged between the Bank of America Tower and Condé Nast was the Garden of Eden, an eclectic restaurant that bordered on blasphemous with its claim to be the favorite dining locale of Adam and Eve. She stopped to view the posted menu. An apple pie à la mode that promised to be sinfully sweet. A chocolate cake stacked like the Tower of Babel. Adam's ribs, slow cooked and braised to buttery perfection. She liked the presumptuousness of such a place. She would save it for later. Save it for Tak. It was just his style.

As Deena turned to leave, she froze at the sight of him. Third table from the back, head lowered, reading a menu. The man who'd made her smile in her grief, who made love to her in her dreams. There. With another woman.

She'd been a fool.

He looked up. Their eyes met.

Slowly, Deena backed away from the window, turned, and fled.

The tears came hot and fast, faster than she'd ever thought possible. Her breathing staggered and painful, her heart was broken.

Deena barreled down the street and through the crowds, intent on losing him in the press of Times Square.

He was calling her.

He'd given her no reason for this. No reason for jealousy. To have laid claim to him. Never in her waking hours had he kissed her or whispered words of love in her ear, and yet, it hurt no less.

She was a fool—infusing his every word with innuendo, every touch with fire, all the while believing that it alone could satisfy her.

Raindrops began to fall. Fat and mocking, they pelted her, plastering toffee coils to her face and blouse to her body. In an instant, she was drenched.

When Deena reached the Westin, she tore across the lobby in slippery sandals, nearly plummeting in her distress. At the elevator, she jabbed the UP button, caught sight of Tak, and dashed for the stairs.

"Deena! Deena, please! Would you wait?"

The sound of his voice only fueled her hysteria. She burst into the stairwell, gut-wrenching sobs seizing her like violent gusts of wind. Up three flights they went, as her hair, her nose, her lips dripped with rain mingled with tears. Her vision blurred, as behind her, Tak's footsteps thundered. She reached their floor, their door, and fumbled to unlock it.

"Deena, please. *Listen* to me."

He was there, beside her, as she trembled with emotion. He reached for her, and she recoiled.

"Don't. Just—don't make it worse." She turned to the door, fumbling.

"God, would you listen?"

She began to mutter to herself, enraged with the lock that wouldn't open.

"I'm so stupid," she whispered. "I had no reason to think you loved me. No reason to hope. I just—" She dashed away tears.

"She's my agent, Deena. That's all."

He reached for her, turned her, and she went stark still.

"Now, are we done playing games?" Tak whispered.

Deena closed her eyes. Attempted to swallow fear. "I don't know what you mean," she mustered weakly. Something in her burned with the lie.

"No?"

He snatched her to him, brought his mouth down hard on hers. She opened to meet him, willing, and a moan escaped. Resolve, resistance, rationale—all gone. When he finally withdrew, he was smiling.

"That's what I mean."

He returned to her mouth, his kisses demanding, impatient. His hands found her back, her waist, her ass in greed. Deena was breathless with fear, anticipation, and arousal as her body told her what her mind had feared—that it was his. That it always had been his.

Blindly, he fumbled with the lock and opened the door before backing her into the suite. She clung to him, whimpering, as his tongue ravished her mouth.

He pulled away her blouse, exposing two bronze breasts, clad in frilly white.

"Jesus," he whispered.

His mouth came down on hers again, swallowing, consuming her whole. He found her skirt and tossed it to the floor, before pulling at his own clothes with impatience. She helped him, trembling fingers at the buttons of his shirt, near desperate to feel him.

Tak lifted her and instinctively, Deena's legs wrapped his waist. Their mouths met with abandon as he lowered her to the bed.

"You want this?" he whispered.

Deena blinked back tears. She felt so many things in that instant—alarm and passion, nervousness and desire—and yes— she wanted him that bad.

She brought a hand to his cheek and nodded, hoping he couldn't feel the tremble. Tak kissed her, a soft kiss, before lowering his mouth to her body. He trailed lips to her thighs, parted them, and licked. Deena yelped, back arched as she gripped the sheets and thrashed beneath him. Hot waves swept her, drowning her, drowning her completely. With a flick of the tongue, he'd humbled even her most impassioned dreams, relegating them to mere mediocrity.

He climbed atop her. Her breasts crushed beneath him, soft and round, supple and yielding under hardness. His lips found her mouth again for a soft, sweet, and lingering kiss. Deena closed her eyes, relishing it, and was met with a thrust. White hot and searing, she let out a sob, as a gush of crimson met him.

Tak gasped. He was poised above her, inserted, overwhelmed. Overwhelmed by the tightness of her opening and the knowledge of what she'd given him. Never more had he felt the limitations of manhood. He was weakened by her—by the sight of her body, by his name on her lips, by the perfectness of it all.

She whimpered, and God, the sound drove him mad. He moved against her in slow and staggered strokes, working to forge an opening where none existed. He throbbed in her, pulsing and stirring with the compact fit. Slowly, carefully, together, they found harmony, fed hunger, fueled greed. He struggled to temper his thrusts with tenderness, but he was on fire. He dug fingers into the flesh of her hips, sinking and gripping, losing his battle. Steadily, her words came frenzied and incoherent, as frenzied as his strokes desperately wanted to be. She was meeting them now, each one, with an ardor that sent blazes through his body. She said his name, not once, but until he begged her to stop, certain she'd kill him. And when her body began to quiver and he could hold on no longer, he forged ahead, an apology on his lips. Together, they found harmony, fed passion, and fueled lust. Together, they found a perfect, yet powerful finish.

Chapter Twenty

Deena's body was damp and her pulse still staggered. Having left Tak in the bed behind her, she brought a hand to the room's wide window. It felt cool to the touch. Her view from the third floor was unimpressive—a pharmacy, a few pedestrians, a billboard for *Lion King the Musical*. Both the sky was and ground registered the same dull slate. Rain fell in an indifferent sprinkle, leaving droplets on her windowpane and the ground below.

Midintersection an umbrella unfolded, a burst of red in an otherwise gray day. She thought of Tak. He'd slipped into her life like that red umbrella, bursting open in her private storm of gray.

Behind her, Tak's arms slid around her midsection and kissed it. Silently, they stood there, watching the rain fall. And when Deena brought a hand to the window this time, Tak reached for it, covering it with his own.

Sitting across from each other on the bed, Tak and Deena dug into cartons of Moo Shu Pork with chopsticks. Deena, donned in Tak's gray UCLA tee, frowned at the food as she picked through it.

"There aren't any peanuts, Dee," Tak scooped out a thick wad of pork and noodles before dropping it into his mouth.

"Are you sure? I thought I saw one."

"You didn't. Now eat. You must be starving."

A shadow passed over Deena's face and Tak sighed.

"You can meet her, you know."

Deena's gaze found her lap. "I don't know what you mean."

Tak smiled. "The last time you said that, it turned out you did." He grinned at the rush of color to her cheeks.

"Come on," he placed a hand over her knee. "I'll call Bridget, my agent, and you can meet her."

Deena withdrew her hand. "I don't want you to think I don't trust you."

He returned to his food. "How about we don't even go down that road? How about you meet her, find out for yourself that she has absolutely no interest in me, nor any other man, and then we get on with our lives?"

Deena's eyes widened. "What do you mean 'no interest'? Did something happen to her?"

Tak grinned. He loved the irony of Deena's innocence. Tough, underprivileged, a fighter if he'd ever seen one, and still naïve as hell half the time.

"She's a lesbian, Dee. So she might like you." He winked.

"I don't need to meet her," Deena said quietly.

Tak shrugged.

"The more I think about it, the more I like it. In fact, I insist the two of you meet."

This time his grin was met with a pillow to the face.

"You're such a pig!"

"Your pig now."

She met his gaze with a shy smile.

When the heat of it proved too much, Deena stood and went to the cherry wood desk at the rear of the suite. She returned with a *Fodor's* guide. "I don't know what we'll do about our itinerary. We've wasted a whole day."

Tak shook his head. "And here I was ready to declare New York the best city ever."

Deena blushed. "But we haven't seen anything."

"You kidding me? I've seen *plenty*."

She hurled the book at him and Tak ducked. "You're getting violent, Dee. Can't say I approve." He returned to his Moo Shu Pork.

"Tak! We've only got two days here. We need to make plans."

He turned his carton upside down and shoveled the last of the food into his mouth. "How's this?" He stood, tossed the white box into a wastebasket, and headed for the bathroom to wash his hands. "How about we stay here a few more days. Two, three, five, I don't care. Then afterward, if we can, we squeeze in one or two more places on the way home."

Deena frowned. "If that's what you want."

"No," Tak said, returning to the bed. "We'll stay longer if that's what *you* want. Whatever makes you happy."

It was the first time she'd ever heard the words, directed at her at least. She found they fell oddly on her ears, like the sound of her name being pronounced incorrectly. While she understood the meaning, it still rang as bizarre.

"Let's see how it goes," Deena murmured.

Tak nodded, stood again. "Great. Anyway, tomorrow night my cousin's dropping by."

Deena sat up straighter. "Cousin? What cousin?"

Tak laughed. "Why? Is there one you know?"

"No. It's just—" Deena fell silent.

"My cousin John. The one I'm always telling you about. He's at Columbia."

Deena stared at the bedspread. His cousin. His family. She raised her gaze. "What about Daichi?"

"What about him?"

"Won't he find out that we were here? Together?"

Tak shook his head. "No. He and John aren't exactly text message buddies."

Still unconvinced, Deena watched him as he pulled on a close-fitting chocolate tee and a pair of relaxed jeans. "Still, Tak, you told me a long time ago that your father was like my family in some ways. That he wouldn't approve of you dating a girl who wasn't Japanese."

"So?"

"So I'm not Japanese."

Tak sighed. "It'll be fine. Trust me. When you meet John, you'll understand."

"What in the world does that mean?"

"Well," Tak said, "he'd be a fine one to talk. Considering he's only half Japanese himself."

Chapter Twenty-one

Deena didn't need to be told that the tall and sinewy man with silky black hair was John Tanaka. The square face, heavy-lidded eyes, and broad mouth all gave him away. They were mirrored images, Tak and John, albeit with subtle differences. John's eyes were a honey brown, whereas Tak's were near black. John's skin was like porcelain, Tak's soft wheat. And where John wore his hair in a short and conservative comb-back, Tak's was blunted with a razor and constantly in his eyes.

Tak swept John into a hearty embrace before holding him out at arm's length. "You're looking more and more like your father," Tak said.

John grinned. "Those late-night pan pizzas must be showing." He patted his washboard stomach.

"I'm thinking it's the receding hairline."

"What!" John cried. He pounced, but Tak was ready and swept him into a headlock. The two laughed as they tumbled about the suite as John tried his damnedest to get free.

Deena rolled her eyes and turned to the blonde near the door. She was a saucer-faced girl with gooseberry eyes, short with slight curves. Once it became clear that no introductions were forth-coming, Deena strode over to her.

"I'm guessing you're Allison." She extended a hand. "John's girlfriend?"

The girl nodded.

"And you're Deena? Tak's girlfriend?"

It was news to her. But she liked the sound of it. She smiled shyly, gave a short nod.

"Are they always like this?" Deena asked, peering at the two men, their wrestling match now down to the carpet.

Allison sighed. "John's rowdy, but—Tak brings out the worst in him."

"I should expect more of this?" Deena asked.

"Basically," Allison deadpanned.

Finally, the pair stood and dusted themselves off. Tak clapped his younger cousin on the back.

"John, I swear, you never get tired of an ass kicking."

"What? I'm guessing you need medical attention right now. Don't be too proud to seek it out."

John turned to Deena and smoothed out the white Polo he wore. "John Tanaka," he said and extended a hand.

Deena took it. "Deena Hammond. Pleased to meet you."

John shook his head. "Pleasure's all mines. Finally, I get to meet the great warrior that conquered Takumi Tanaka," he lowered his head. "Honored."

Deena giggled. "I don't know if 'conquered' is the right word."

John raised his head and smirked. "Trust me. It is."

Tak sighed. "And if ever you wondered whether John could keep a secret," he nodded toward Allison. "Here's your answer."

"What! With all the secrets I've kept for you? You ungrateful louse."

John grabbed him and the two tumbled to the floor again.

Allison, Deena eventually learned, had a father who taught international law at Columbia and a mother who taught economics at NYU. John's girlfriend was a pert and saucy blonde with Jersey panache, while he had Tak's predisposition toward silliness, and seemingly, Daichi's hunger for success. It took Deena but a moment to decide she liked them both. A lot. And quickly, the evening out they spent with the couple ranked up there as one of her favorites on the trip. Though behind, of course, one that was *especially* memorable.

It was past noon, and Tak and Deena should've been seizing the day. Instead, they were in bed, having risen only to accept room service, with no more than a passing desire to leave. They were like two colts at play, him nuzzling her, teasing her with exaggerated kisses, and her squealing, pretending not to enjoy it. She could've spent a lifetime in that city, in that bed, in his arms. When the silliness stopped, it was only because her phone insisted on ringing.

"My grandmother," she said.

Tak collapsed on the bed with a groan. "Don't answer," he said even as she said hello. "Emma Hammond never had good news," he muttered. "Never."

"Chile, where you been?" Emma cried. "I've been calling you since yesterday!"

Deena sighed. "I'm in New York. Is everything OK?"

"No! Everything ain't okay! That sister of yours was round here tussling with Keisha behind something, and that's on top the fact that it ain't no food in the house."

No food? Her grandmother received welfare, food stamps, income from the VA, and $400 a month from Deena. All that was to support her and a girl who was never there.

Deena glanced at her watch, noting the date. "Didn't your check from the VA come? Grandpa's pension?"

"Girl, who think you are asking me about that? And anyway, if it did come, it ain't for me to be spending on that fast-ass sister of yours."

No, that's what the welfare, food stamps, and everything else is for, Deena thought. She sighed again.

"You should have something, Grandma. Did you use up all the emergency money, too?"

Emma sucked her teeth. "Chile, that money been gone. Two Sunday dinners ate through dat."

"Sunday dinners! You weren't supposed to treat the whole family with it! It was supposed to be for necessities for you and Lizzie."

"Chile, you act like you left some big-time money."

"I left $400 extra. That's eight hundred this month. It's not a lot, but it was all I could afford."

"Yet you got money for New York."

Deena sat up with a sigh. "So, basically you're calling for more money, right?"

"That's it. I need you to bring more money over."

Deena paused. "Grandma, please. I can't bring it. I'm in New York City."

"Well, how the hell I'm supposed to get it?"

She shook her head. "See, this is why I tell you to get a bank account! You listen to Caroline, who's always going to these predatory lenders. How do you function like this?"

"I don't need no bank account! Mr. Evans up at the liquor store cash whatever kinda check you got. Been cashing my checks for thirty-something years. So don't tell me about no bank."

"I bet Mr. Evans has a bank account."

"How I'm supposed know what Mr. Evans got?"

"Well, anyway, I can't wire money to Mr. Evans at the liquor store."

"Then you just gonna have to come back. Cause we out of money."

Deena thought about the cities that lay ahead and the possibilities—Philadelphia, Baltimore, D.C. She thought about all the moments they'd shared—the Waffle House in Atlanta, the Screamin' Eagle in St. Louis, Lake Michigan in Chicago, him making love to her in New York. And as her grandmother shouted, her eyes began to water.

"Grandma, I'm nowhere near Miami. I could wire you some money, but, but—" Deena brought a hand to her face.

"Listen. I don't deal with nobody but Mr. Evans. Now, unless you gone get this money to him, you need to find yourself another idea."

Deena wiped her face. She should've known she could never get away with such freedom; that she could never get away with happiness. She was forever tethered to this family, forever a Hammond.

Tak touched her shoulder. "Call her back, Dee."

She looked at him and turned away. He repeated himself, sterner. "Call her back."

"You want to ask me about this little bit of money I got. You wouldn't even have nothing if it wasn't for me! You want to be selfish and talk about what you is and ain't gone do?" Grandma Emma spat.

Tak took the phone and hung up. Deena stared at him, eyes shimmering.

"I—I have to call back. She wants me to come home now." Deena swallowed. "She needs more money, but she won't let me wire it because she doesn't trusts banks and—and—"

"Do you want to go home?"

She drew back, horrified. How could he even ask her that? After all this? All that's happened?

"Of course not."

"Then stay." He tossed the phone onto the bed.

"But she needs money. She needs me."

"She doesn't need you. What she needs is a lesson."

He swung his legs out from the bed and stood. "Show her how valuable you are. That you're not at her beck and call."

Deena lowered her gaze. Lowered it because she knew that she was.

"Alright, have it your way. If she really needs money, then we'll wire her some."

"But my grandmother doesn't have a bank account! And—and she'd never go to Western Union. She only deals with Mr. Evans at the liquor store."

Tak's gaze narrowed. "No one who needs money would put so many stipulations on how they get it."

Deena sighed. "Well, it's not like I want to go. I want to stay here. With you," she added miserably.

His face hardened. "Then do that. Call her back and tell her we're wiring money to a Western Union. She can pick it up if she wants to or not."

Deena looked at him doubtfully. Sure, it made sense, but, well . . . she just didn't know.

"Tak, please. I'm not strong like you. It's hard for me to stand up to people."

He sighed. "What're you talking about, Dee? You're as strong as they come. Just look at all that you've done with the little you've had."

She shook her head, slowly. He just didn't get it. This was Grandma Emma. Telling her no meant . . . well, she didn't know what it meant.

Tak stood. "Listen to me. Life's not fair; believe me, I get that. And I know a lot of things have been beyond your control."

He rounded the bed to her. "But not this. You decide how this turns out. For better or worse."

Chapter Twenty-two

With the sun perched hot and obnoxious in the sky, the Hudson River meandered at the side of Tak and Deena, Allison and John. It was a pleasant day, especially warm for New York, warm enough even to shirk sleeves. The Tanaka cousins walked side-by-side, steps ahead of the girls, careful to speak low.

"You seem to be taking life a little more seriously these days," John said.

Tak shrugged. "I guess. I don't know if 'more seriously' is the term I'd use."

John raised a brow. "I would. The last time I saw you, your biggest gripe was that Ferrari had discontinued the 360. We've been out here for half an hour now and you haven't mentioned your car, your art, or a piece of ass once."

Tak grinned. "Speaking of ass, how's that weird-ass brother of yours?"

John snorted. His older brother, Mike, an MIT grad with a major in computer science, was the painful sort of geek usually reserved for cinema and stalking-type cases.

"Good, I suppose. Still in Seattle. Ma's wants him to settle down."

"Yeah," Tak said. "Good luck with that."

"I know, I know," John rolled his eyes.

While Mike was similar enough to John and Tak, he still managed to diverge from them radically in appearance. The bulky black frames, the pointed and protruding ears, the inexhaustible supply of tucked in screen tees—

Ghostbusters, Marvel Comics, Star Trek—good Lord, he had enough Star Trek to leave with excess after a geek convention.

"Mike's of the opinion that he'll meet a beautiful woman with a brain to match his," John said.

Tak frowned. "I'm not sure there is a brain to match his," he said, considering his cousin's near-perfect SAT score.

John shrugged. "Well, if she does exist, I'm not sure she'd want to spend her days watching B-rated horror."

Tak paused at the inverted railing for a view of the Hudson at the promenade in Battery Park City. The World Financial Center was in their sights; a megacomplex of power corporations like Merrill Lynch, Dow Jones, and American Express, all clustered in this concrete-laden, carefully constructed prism of nature.

He caught a glimpse of Deena and Allison a few yards back, their arms entwined like two old ladies as they talked. He thought of Deena standing up to her grandmother and wiring the money with a declaration of "it'll be there if you need it," and smiled.

John followed his gaze.

"I think they've given up on us. My guess is that they're seeking solace in each other's arms."

"Yeah. I could see why Allison would give up on you. She's had enough time to see you're not worth it. But me, what have I had? Three days?"

John smiled. "Well, your shortcomings are painfully obvious."

Allison stared at her boyfriend of three years and scowled before turning back to Deena. "So I told him, Deena, I said, 'John, I'm no bimbo. You either commit to me or I'm out of here.'"

"And that worked?"

Allison smiled. "I'm still here, aren't I?"

Deena lowered her gaze.

"Still, Tak's such a free spirit. He's always talking about how he needs to live untethered."

"And what about what you need?"

"I'm not sure I know what I need."

"Okay, fine. Let's clarify." Allison turned to Deena, placing a hand on each of her shoulders. "What would you do if this absolutely stunning woman, and I mean *stunning*—big breasts, narrow waist, long, beautiful hair—if she just walked up to Tak and kissed him?"

Deena recoiled. "Cry."

Allison sighed. "Cry?"

"Go home?" Deena tried again.

Allison stared at her. "Jesus, Deena. You're in love with this guy. I'd like to think you'd kick some ass. His, hers, somebody's!"

Deena lowered her gaze. "I've never hit anyone before."

"Well, then, let me tell you, sister, it's one of those wrong things that feel absolutely great. You know what I mean?"

Deena thought about her grandfather, calling interracial couples an abomination, and then remembered Tak making love to her.

"Uh, yeah. I do."

"Alright then. So, you'd probably sock him."

"I could never hit Tak."

Allison watched John out the corner of her eye. "I bet you could if he stumbled home drunk one night with lipstick on his collar."

John leaned over the railing, watching as the two women stood just out of earshot, Allison's hands on Deena's shoulders.

"You'd better get her," John warned. "Allison's probably sullying the Tanaka name right now."

"Why? What do you think she's saying?"

John shrugged. "I don't know. Probably that you're a gigolo and she shouldn't waste her feelings on you."

Tak drew up to full height.

"And why the hell would she say that?"

John grinned. "Cause you look like me."

"Bullshit," Tak said. He relaxed a tad. "You look like that balding father of yours."

John laughed. His father Yoshi's hairline had gone from receding to retreating these last few years.

"Well, you know, Tak, people have always thought we looked more like brothers than cousins."

"They were trying to make you feel better."

Tak watched Allison as her arms flailed and thought back to John's comment. "Jesus, John, what did you do?"

John shrugged. "I don't know. That's the problem."

"I don't follow."

"Well, here's the gist. Buddy of mine had a bachelor party. I got wasted and came home in a taxi I don't remember flagging down. But I sobered up real quick. Allison found lipstick on my collar and gave me a black eye."

"Shit, John. But you're still . . . together . . . right?"

"Due to no small amount of begging on my part."

"Well, shit, what'd you expect? What were you thinking?"

"I'm pretty sure *thought* wasn't part of the equation. More like scotch, tits, testosterone, and a bit of encouragement from the guys."

Tak stared at him. "So you don't love her?"

A flash of irritation crossed John's face. "It's always so damned black and white with you, isn't it? Of course I love her."

Tak turned back to the water. "Just scotch and tits get in the way sometime, huh?"

"Listen!" John spat. "Here you are in your first serious relationship for all of, what? Twenty minutes? And you want to judge me? I can remember when you were fucking girls from here to San Diego. No dinner. No relationship. Just you, her, and a bed."

"Yeah, OK, can you keep your voice down though?" Tak glanced around surreptitiously. "Anyway, that's not me anymore. Before the other day I hadn't had sex in over a year."

"You expect me to believe that?"

"I don't expect you to do anything."

"You're telling me during that whole 'friendship' stage you weren't somewhere getting laid every once in a while?"

"Didn't want to."

John blinked. "Wow. What the hell did she do to you?"

Tak stared at the dark waters and beyond it, to New Jersey.

"I just love her. She's everything I'm not. Brilliant, driven, and resilient as hell. And she's solid, you know? You know what you're going to get from her every time."

"And beautiful. That doesn't hurt," John said.

Tak grinned. "Hell, no, it doesn't hurt."

"And those tits are like, what? Good solid D cups?"

"Alright. Settle down."

John grinned. "I forgot. You're in love with this one. So, before we were skating around those Playboy Bunny tits you were talking about how reliable she is. Proceed."

Traffic blared loud behind them, New York loud, and the temperature continued to soar.

"Back to you," Tak said. "You never answered me."

"Yes. I love her. Of course," John sighed as if expecting the question.

"So, it's just the problem of forgetting when you're drunk then?"

John shot him a look of impatience. "Listen, this is *my* neck of the woods, samurai. I'll dump you in the Hudson, and it'll be like an episode of *Law & Order* around here."

"Right," Tak said. "They'll be drawing a chalk line around your ass right about here."

"It's just space and opportunity, *itoko*. Space and opportunity," John's palms touched, bowing with the challenge. The gesture was a relic from their childhood, deference to the karate films they imitated as children.

Allison sighed, watching as two overgrown men tussled on the sidewalk.

Deena glanced at her. "Should we do something?"

She shook her head. "If we're lucky they'll fall in the river."

She took in Deena's shocked expression and snorted. "I'm kidding. If we're lucky, John'll fall in the river."

"You don't mean that either," Deena said.

Before them, John yelped, struggling to wiggle free of Tak's headlock.

"I can look at you and tell how much you love him."

Allison shrugged. "My burden."

"Love isn't a burden. It's a gift."

"You say that now. I'll check back with you in a year or so, when your love is no longer a fresh novelty."

Deena remembered Tak's words in Chicago. "Relationships take work, Allison. Anything worth having takes work."

She sighed. "I know, I know. And deep down I know John's a good guy. But the lipstick hurts nonetheless. But I guess I was to blame for that as much as he."

"How's that?"

"Haven't you been listening? I didn't make my needs clear. Our relationship was never spelled out in so many words. So when he got backed into a corner, that's what he relied on—the fact that we never specifically agreed to a monogamous relationship—despite spending every day together. And as angry as I was, I knew that technically he was right. While I'd been committed to him, I'd never required the same of him. I just . . . assumed."

Allison watched as Tak helped John to his feet. "I know you trust him and that's good. You should. All I'm saying is, don't make the same mistake I did."

Tak watched Deena fold her arms, face pinched with agitation. No sooner had they returned to the hotel room than did she pull him aside and begin ranting.

"I swear to God, Deena, I don't know what you're talking about," he said after attempting to follow her for several moments.

"I'm talking about you, Tak. And me. About . . ." She took a deep breath. "All I'm saying is, I don't want some big-breasted woman kissing on you!"

Wide-eyed, Tak glanced past Deena to John, who was busy pretending not to smile as he flipped channels on the flat screen.

"Outside. Now."

Tak grabbed Deena's wrist and pulled her into the hallway.

"What the hell was that? What are you talking about?"

"I don't know. I just—Allison said—"

"Allison?"

"Yes. Allison thinks," she took a breath, "I think that I need a commit from you."

Deena took a deep breath and tried again. "I need a commitment from you."

Tak stared at her. "OK."

"OK what?"

"OK, you've got a commitment from me."

She blinked.

"That all?" he asked.

She lowered her gaze, suddenly embarrassed. "Yeah. I guess so."

"Allison, I'm telling you, you need to learn to mind your own business!"

"And you need to learn to keep your dick in your pants!" Allison squared off before John, fists balled.

John threw hands over his face in exasperation. "Good Lord! How many times do we have to do this? I didn't have sex with anyone, and you know it!"

"*I know it? You* don't even know it! How the hell am I supposed to know it?"

"I'd know if I'd fucked someone!"

"How?"

"I don't know. I'd just *know*."

"How? 'Cause your cock wasn't shiny when you got home?"

"Listen," John held out hands before him as if attempting to calm him and her, "could we not do this right now? My cousin's only here a few days. You said you wanted to see him, and that's the only reason you're here. But if you're just going to fuck up his perfectly good relationship so you can tear me down, then you should just leave."

Allison's mouth fell open.

"Tear down? Tear you down? How dare you! I have done *every-thing* for you! Everything! When my father was going to flunk your ass—"

"Oh! Here we go again! How many times do I have to hear *that* shit? How many nights have I stayed up trying to help your ass figure out some fine point of law?"

Allison glared at John Tanaka, the six foot tall, broad-shoul-dered, too often arrogant son of a used car salesman who'd earned everything he had through a combination of brains and brawn. She hated and loved him all at the same time, and hated herself for both.

"What did you end up ordering?" John asked, peering into Tak's brown paper bag as they rode up the hotel elevator.

"Chicken parm. And you?"

John shrugged. "Whatever you got. That's what I told the guy. I said, 'Give me what he's having.'"

Tak glanced at him. "No, you didn't."

"Yes, I did. I'm trying to be more adventurous. Allison says I need to be more adventurous. 'Like your cousin,' she said. 'He took his girlfriend on a cross-country trip on the *spur of the moment*,'" John mocked.

Tak laughed. "And what did you say? 'Fuck you'?"

John shook his head. "I should've. But I said, 'She wasn't even his girlfriend when they started.' To which she answered, *'Well, that's worse!'*"

Tak grinned. "Yeah, I'm not really sure where you were going with that one."

John shrugged. "Who knows these days."

He paused. "So, you say she's never been to a nightclub before? This'll be her first time?"

"Not exactly. She went once while we were in Atlanta."

As the elevator rose, Tak dug in his pocket for his room key.

"Hundred bucks says I can get Deena to dance before you."

"She'll dance, John. She just needs a little prodding. Your variation of it probably won't work though."

"Two hundred."

Tak sighed. "John, I don't think you want to—"

"Two fifty."

"Alright. Your funeral."

They stepped off the elevator. "Now remember," Tak said as they arrived at the door, "I don't take sob stories and I don't take checks."

Allison stared at the white pants suit with its conservative cut and frowned. "You're not going to wear that, are you?"

Deena froze. "What's wrong with my suit?"

"Nothing. I mean, what is it? Gucci?"

Deena nodded.

"Well, yeah, it's a beautiful suit, if you're looking to sell some real estate or something. But you're going out to shake your ass."

Allison disappeared in search of the black duffle bag she brought.

"You know, I haven't figured you out yet, Deena. You try your damnedest to hide shit the rest of us are in line to buy. What gives?"

Deena frowned at Allison's backside as she dug through the bag. Before she could respond, the blonde stood, a dash of black fabric in her arms.

"Here. Wear this."

"I don't even know what that is."

"It's a dress, Deena. Now stop being my grandmother and put it on." Allison held it out.

Deena shook her head. "That's what you were going to wear."

"I brought three outfits with me, because I never can make up my mind. I'll wear one of the other two and you this. You've got the body for it, trust me."

Deena frowned. "I don't think I should."

Allison held the dress. "I know you should. It hugs and flows in all the right places, and Tak's jaw will drop when he sees it."

Deena hesitated. "You really think he'll like it?"

"I *know* he will."

Tak froze at the sight of Deena. Dark curly hair, soft tendrils falling onto creamy bare shoulders, lips painted crimson, and pale brown eyes sharpened with smoke-gray eye shadow. The black fabric sculpted her body, clinging to a shelf of soft, supple cleavage with the tease of an ultralow neckline. Tight from top to hem the dress split midthigh for a dramatic flash of leg. Her tanned and toned calves were accentuated with sleek black pumps.

Tak's mouth opened . . . then closed. He looked from Deena to Allison, who stood behind her beaming.

"She looks incredible, doesn't she?"

Tak's lips parted and still, he failed to speak.

Deena's face fell. "You don't like it?"

Tak shook his head, sputtering. "No, no, I love it. I'm just—just taken aback is all."

"I look stupid. I'm taking this off." She turned away.

"No!" Tak cried. "Don't—don't change a thing. You look incredible. Please . . . don't change anything."

Deena turned, brought a hand to her cleavage. "It's not too much?"

John shook his head with a laugh. When Allison cleared her throat, he snapped to attention.

"And you look beautiful, baby," John blurted.

Her gaze narrowed, arms folded. "This is what I had on when you left."

Tak turned to his cousin with amusement.

"Right. I meant every day though. You look beautiful every day."

"Sure you did. Now give me my dinner before I belt you."

Club Echo was a posh multilevel club in Midtown Manhattan. When Tak led her inside, Deena gave a gasp.

An HDTV covered by a thick layer of glass served as the floor. According to Tak, both it and the walls reflected the club's ever-changing theme. On this night the floor was a vast pool of crystal blue and the walls a perpetual waterfall. Masked beneath the loud and pulsating pop was the sound of crashing water. It, combined with vaulted ceilings, gave the feel of standing in a fast-filling cup of water.

Deena turned to Tak in astonishment. He gave her waist a little squeeze. "I knew you'd like it."

"Like it? It's awe-inspiring! I mean, take away the hip hop and you'd be in a museum exhibit about the importance of water!"

Tak grinned. "The last time I was here the place was set up like a jungle. Every so often, a monkey would swing by or an elephant would trumpet. Now *that* was awesome."

Deena turned from him and scanned the crowd. Packed tight, each clubgoer gyrated to the blast of the beat, encased in sweat despite the unrelenting air-conditioning. They were over twenty-one but under thirty—blond and brunette, deep chocolate and soft tan, each with brightly colored drinks in their grips as they moved. To Deena, everyone looked in his or her element . . . everyone else that is.

Tak glanced at Deena's predictably apprehensive face and smiled. "How about we start with a drink, huh?"

The bartender was a dirty blonde with a big smile and a tight white tee. Tak waved her over and ordered a beer for himself and a Screaming Orgasm for Deena.

"Lucky you," the blonde winked before disappearing.

"Tak!" Deena blushed. "What the hell was that?"

"A drink. But if you'd prefer to think of it as a promise, that's always an option." He didn't have to look at her to know she was embarrassed.

When the drinks arrived, they swallowed them quick. Tak ordered another round, and they too, went down.

"So," Tak placed a hand on Deena's arm as she swallowed her third Screaming Orgasm, "how are you feeling about all this?"

Deena snorted. "Are you kidding? I can hardly believe I'm here. In a club, in Manhattan, in this dress, and I'm drinking a Screaming Orgasm." She looked down at herself as if verifying she were not someone else. "My grandfather must be clawing through his grave right now." She brought the drink to her lips with a giggle.

"Any regrets?"

"About what? You?"

He nodded.

Deena shook her head. "Not one."

John and Allison danced to a few familiar songs, a random selection from the top twenty pop and hip-hop charts, and in between, downed a few drinks. Three beers for him, two Daiquiris for her. He was loathed to admit it, but his cousin's presence had done them some good. Before Tak and Deena's arrival, their relationship had been teetering on the brink of certain extinction. Fights about washing laundry and drinking the last swallow of milk seemed to drive as much of a wedge between them as his lipstick on the collar. But there was something about Tak and Deena, something invigorating, encouraging. Something about the way he leaned into her when she spoke, as if fascinated by her. Or the way he placed a hand at the small of her back or on her arm, as if a never-ending need to make a connection with her fueled him. And the way she looked at him, looking as if absorbed, as if the object of her infatuation was not only adored but admired.

John wanted that for himself. And could see that Allison wanted it, too. When had they lost their ability to laugh, to play, to love so easily? Long before the lipstick on the collar, before the months of laundry-induced screaming—too long perhaps to remember. But as Allison pulled John into her arms, and the soft curves of her body melded into the contours of his, he knew that it was his to have back, should he want it.

Tak watched from the bar stool as John and Allison approached. Four Screaming Orgasms and twelve hit songs later and Deena was fast becoming an immobile part of the furniture. John grinned, leaning in for his cousin to hear.

"It doesn't count if you drag her onto the dance floor unconscious, Tak."

Tak laughed. "She's not the victim here. She's the one ordering all the drinks. I'm just paying."

"Sure you are."

John waved for the bartender. "Send a pitcher of beer to the table over there. We're going to run a tab, courtesy of this guy." He clapped a hand on his cousin's back, who thanked him rather dryly.

Minutes later, the four sat in a corner, music blaring, as they downed a round of Heinekens.

"I've been meaning to ask you, Deena. Like, what are you? What's your ethnicity?" Allison shouted.

Deena tensed instinctively. "Black. Black and white."

Allison's eyes lit up. "Really? Like what specifically? Irish? Italian?"

Deena shook her head. "I—I don't know."

Allison frowned. "Well, maybe we can figure it out."

"Allison . . .," John warned.

"No, John," she waved a hand. "It's cool. Deena's cool. And I'm really good at this. Now what's the surname? That's a good place to start."

"Knight," Deena said.

"Knight? Yeah, that's not very helpful. Is it your mother's side or your father's? Because maybe you could ask—"

"There's no one to ask," Deena snapped.

"Hey!" Tak leapt to his feet. "Feel like dancing? Allison?"

"Dancing?" She blinked in surprise. "Yeah, I guess. Just a minute. Let me just . . ." she turned back to Deena.

Tak touched Deena's shoulder. "You mind if we hit the floor?"

"No, it's fine. Whatever."

"Good. One song. We'll be back." Tak grabbed Allison's hand, feigning ignorance of her hesitation and near-dragging her away.

John stared at Deena over the pitcher of beer. After a brief pause and an indulgent sip from his mug, he spoke. "She means well. She doesn't know any better, but she means well."

He was met with a flicker of irritation. When she neglected to speak, John pushed on.

"They both have good intentions. But you can't expect other people to know what it's like to be half of something and all of nothing."

Deena looked up.

"Take me, for example. My mother's white. There's this whole side of my family that's blue-eyed and lily-colored. Now, they've never mistreated me, never said an unkind word to me, but still, I don't feel white."

"I don't feel white, either," Deena said.

John grinned. "Problem is, I don't feel quite Japanese, either. I feel more Japanese, but not all Japanese." He shrugged. "Maybe that's because I'm always treated like an outsider." He looked up at her, waited. She seemed to weighing something in her mind, hesitant still.

"For a long time," John said, "I tried to prove I was one of them. My *Nihongo* is pretty damned good, and my history is stellar. But if they take one look at these eyes, then all that's worthless."

Deena lowered her gaze. "We're a lot alike, Mr. Tanaka."

John shrugged. "Only if you're lucky." He refilled her glass with beer, his smile teasing. "So," he said, "which side do you identify with? Black or the white?"

Deena shrugged. "It's hard to say. I mean, I don't even know the white side. After my mother ki—"

John froze, midpour. "After *what?*"

She lowered her gaze. When she looked up again, it was past him to where Tak and Allison danced. From there, it was an arbitrary point on the wall. Finally, she faced him again, noting with disdain that she still had his attention.

"After my mother killed my father."

John stared at her, the beer now overflowing. "Are you kidding me? 'Cause if you are, that's the worst joke I've ever heard."

Deena burst out laughing. Only a Tanaka could make her laugh about something so terrible. "I'm not, John. My mother killed my father. She shot him. And I can't believe you made me laugh about it."

He looked down, noted the mess he made with his still-pouring beer, and reached for a fistful of napkins. "It's a certain charm I have," he explained.

Together the two mopped the spilled brew. When he looked up, he did so as if remembering something. "Tak says you don't dance."

"Oh, I do. A little. Just not well," she smiled sheepishly.

John shrugged. "No, no. I understand. I'm the same way. But I like to do it just the same." He paused, stole a glance at her. "I thought everyone did."

"I suppose so."

John leaned forward. "Allison's like Tak, you know, a real good dancer. She won't even dance with me. She says I make her look bad."

He was betting that she'd been too busy at the bar to see him dancing in the corner.

"That's horrible!" she blurted.

John tried not to smile.

"It's OK. I mean, I wouldn't want to dance with someone who was really good at it anyway. It'd be nice to dance with someone who was a little uncomfortable or wouldn't mind if I lost the beat."

"Someone like me?" Deena whispered.

John's eyes widened. "You'd do that for me?"

Deena nodded.

"Well, then," John stood. "What are we waiting for?"

Tak stood in astonishment as John and Deena moved on the dance floor. He would've laughed at the absurd way his cousin insisted on thrusting his pelvis had Deena not looked so damned sexy. Her hair was loose and damp, and a thin sheen of sweat covered her, causing her to glisten. Hands in her hair, Deena's hips swayed. When John whispered something in her ear, she threw her head back and laughed.

Tak pushed his way through the crowd and tapped John on the shoulder roughly. He turned to face him midthrust.

"You mind?" Tak said. "You've earned your money already."

"I can see why you like her so much, Tak," John grinned.

"Get your ass out of here," Tak said, and yanked John by the collar.

Tak fell in step with Deena thereafter. "Hope you left some of that for me," he said appreciatively.

Deena grinned. "It's all for you."

With a bite of his lower lip, Tak pulled her in close and dropped his hands to her waist. Deena's arms found his neck.

"I missed you," she admitted.

"Somehow that doesn't make me sad."

He turned her so her back was to him, wrapped arms around her midsection, and pulled her in close.

Dancing came natural to him; it was about feeling the moment, as all art was. As they moved, his hands worked her body, their hips one with the pulse of the music fueled by lyrically laced promises of sex and wild fulfillment coupled with alcohol and skin on skin for an ethereal intoxication. His hands slipped from waist to hips, hips to stomach. He could touch her all day.

"You feel incredible," Tak whispered.

"So do you," Deena replied.

His breathing came loud and labored. Finally, Tak dragged wet lips across her throat as the strobe lights bathed them. He cupped her breast, grazing, and fell away, too tempted. His erection pierced her back.

"You're killing me, Dee. I can't—"

She turned and kissed him, swallowing his words. Emboldened, he met her head-on, his mouth opening with hunger. He gripped the back of her head and tilted, wanting more than her kiss could give. With a grunt of frustration, he inevitably pulled away.

Tak sliced the crowd in his rush to the bathroom, hand clasped tightly with Deena's. The two disappeared into the men's restroom, and as John watched, a slight smile crossed his lips. He turned back to the bartender and nodded toward his now-absent cousin. "Give me your best, on his tab. Clearly, I'm gonna be here awhile."

Chapter Twenty-three

When Tak and Deena woke the next morning it was not because of the time—nearly noon by then—or the bright rays of sun baking the window, but rather, because of the blare of Deena's cell phone. Groggily, she reached for it, frowning at the disturbance of her sleep and the pulsating of her skull.

"Hello?"

"Deena! What an unequivocal pleasure. To hear your voice on this, the twenty-third day of a thirty-day vacation."

Deena bolted upright. "Daichi?"

Next to her, Tak sat up, startled.

"Indeed. Are you enjoying your holiday?"

"Sir, I—"

"It's a simple question, Deena. Have you found this leisure time pleasurable? Fulfilling? Satisfactory at the very least?"

"Sir—" Deena swallowed. "It's been satisfactory, yes."

"Twenty-three days away and 'satisfactory' is your assessment? A disappointing conclusion for those of us who continue to toil."

"Well, no, sir. I'm enjoying my immensely. I—"

"Perhaps my abrasive tone continues to escape you. Could it

be that your idle time has led to atrophy of the mind, leaving you unable to assess an individual's given demeanor?"

"No, sir, I can tell that you're upset."

Deena glanced at Tak.

"Good. Provided you're still interested in work as an architect at the Tanaka Firm, I would recommend you report to my office on Monday morning, 9 A.M."

Deena swallowed. "Yes, sir. Thank you, sir. I'll be there, sir."

Daichi hung up.

Chapter Twenty-four

Deena hustled into the Tanaka Firm Monday morning and rode the elevator to the thirteenth floor, hands trembling. Sliding glass doors parted for her as she stepped off the elevator and onto the gleaming marble logo. Angela, Daichi's secretary, greeted her with a tight-lipped smile.

"He's waiting for you, sweetheart." Her eyes were sympathetic.

Deena swallowed and gave a nod, unwilling to speak and thereby give voice to the extent of her fear.

She'd only been to the thirteenth floor a few times. It was vast. Once past the soundproof sliding glass doors, the receptionist lobby where Angela was housed, a twenty-foot high ceiling, lacquered maple wall paneling, and chocolate Spanish marble flooring greeted those entering. An acoustic sound system mimicked a babbling brook, while a seating area comprised of sleek Italian furnishings graced the waiting area. She'd seen the same set in an interior magazine with a list price of nearly thirty grand.

The entrance to Daichi's office was nearly as daunting as the man. Massive round-top double doors of thick African mahogany were made even more prominent by the polished Tanaka logo inset in stained Tiffany glass. The doors, she suspected, were worth more than her salary for the year.

Deena raised a fist to knock, took a deep breath, and shot Angela a single look of poorly suppressed distress. But the older woman was distracted, her face in files, so Deena turned, fist wavering, only to find the door open.

Daichi stared at her, his square face hardened by a perpetual frown. He stepped aside and let her enter, lids heavy with his watchful gaze. When Deena entered, he slammed the door behind her and took a seat behind a dark, broad desk.

"Close to a month of vacation, Ms. Hammond, and you've earned my undivided attention. Do share what one does with such an abundance of time."

Deena froze. She'd spent close to an hour with his son, trying to anticipate his questions. But they had not anticipated this, the first.

Daichi's fingertips formed a steeple over which he shot a critical frown. "Are you . . . unable to recall?"

"Yes, sir. I remember."

"Well, I've not the time to linger, in case you were wondering."

She lowered her gaze. "I went on a road trip."

"Oh? Where?"

"A few places. Atlanta. Memphis. St. Louis." She wanted to stop, but his silence seemed to demand more. "Chicago. Cleveland. New York."

"Ah. And did you see the Gateway Arch? The Willis Tower? The Empire State Building, perhaps?"

"Yes, sir."

"How charming." Daichi's smile was ice. "And do you feel that you've earned such a celebrated vacation by way of the caliber of your work here?"

She lowered her gaze. "I don't know, sir."

"Well, I do." Daichi stood. He rounded the desk, hands clasped behind his back.

"You are an undisciplined talent, Deena. Neither hot nor cold. Idealistic yet ambivalent, presumptuous and timid. You are as inconsistent as you are capable, a greater sin than ignorance. And with your tepidness, you've proven yourself dispensable."

Daichi ventured to the broad floor-to-ceiling windows and frowned down at the cobalt waters of Biscayne Bay.

Deena's vision blurred. Even as a pigtailed girl she'd wanted to be an architect. It was her father's dream that she become one. The two of them would spend hours holed up in a single room, drawing and planning, measuring and building a small-scale community they called Hammondville. The name still made her smile; it was so stupid. Back then, they'd maneuver the streets of Brickell, admiring the brilliant towers of Miami. "That one there," her father would say, "nothing compared to what you'll make." And Deena would look at him and feel pride and purpose.

But he'd been wrong. She'd make nothing important. At twenty-five, she was done.

Daichi whirled, startling her from pain-filled nostalgia. His approach was quick, confrontational, as he closed the space between them.

"I ask you, Deena, what good is talent without gall? Brilliance without conviction?" His dark eyes narrowed in disgust. "It's but spilt milk before the mouth of a hungry babe. You have nothing because nothing is what you desire. You lack the audacity for greatness. You've not the stomach for it."

When Deena opened her mouth, she found her voice small, weak against the weight of accusations.

"That—that's not true," she said.

Daichi stared down at her, as if disgusted with her presence. "No?" He raised a brow. "How many designing competitions have you entered? Prizes have you vied for?"

Deena shook her head. "I—I've been busy with other projects. I've had a full load—"

He stared at her until she lowered her gaze, too ashamed to continue.

"What good is it, Deena? What good is any of it? Encyclopedia-like knowledge? Limitless talent? What purpose does it serve when you sit on your laurels, content to design wheelchair ramps and take monthlong vacations?"

He was shouting at her, and she was crying. She could think of nothing to stop it; she knew it disgusted him, yet she continued and murmured heartfelt apologies for disappointing him all the while.

"I'm sorry. I don't know. I'm just sorry."

He turned away. "You'll be handling the predesign phase of Skylife. On my desk in one week, I expect to see the following . . ."

Stunned, Deena glanced around wildly before common sense instructed her to grab her briefcase. She fumbled with it for pen and pad, cursing herself for not considering the possibility she might still have a job.

He paused, his first showing of mercy. "I expect to have the agenda for this project. Concrete goals. Anticipated obstacles. Your design team."

"My design team?"

"Yes." Daichi turned to her. "The individuals you anticipate will best be suited to carry out your vision. You should have covered this in an undergraduate course."

"Yes, sir, I did. But where do I get them? From here? The firm?"

Daichi rolled his eyes. "From Bangkok if need be."

He began a slow pace. "Your work will serve as the blueprint for the entire project." Daichi paused to glance at his watch. "You have one week. Seven days, to the minute, to deliver what I've asked for."

Deena nodded and tucked away horribly scribbled notes into a battered briefcase.

"Failure to provide this will be indicative of your desire to no longer be in my employ. Do I make myself clear?"

"Crystal, sir."

Deena stood and hesitated, briefcase in hand. "Daichi, I—I want to apologize for—"

He held up a hand. "You are young. And it is to this that I attribute your inability to ascertain the best time to exit. So I will tell you." He gestured to the door. "Now. And no more vacations."

Chapter Twenty-five

Deena sat staring at her desk as she contemplated how to lay the groundwork for a structure worthy of the Tanaka name. In a week's time she was to turn nothing into something and something damned good. Failure meant the loss of her livelihood.

She thought back to her initial conversations with Daichi about the project. In them, they'd agreed that originality, consciousness, sustainability, and function were most important. And the more he talked, the more Deena came to know how he'd earned his rightful place as a brilliant mind in the annals of architecture.

"You err when you think of sustainability as a set of practices to reduce our carbon footprint," Daichi told her. "You must look at it as survival. Whose survival? you might say. Ours is the obvious answer. Or the planet's, perhaps. But as an architect, you must look at it as the survival of the building. What is the building's unique contribution to the community? To our craft? To the world? When you can answer that, you've created a design that is truly sustainable."

Deena stared at her desk. Her task was clear. She was to create a building whose contribution to the world was unequaled. She had one week to lay the groundwork for it.

An hour later, she abandoned her staring contest with the desk in the hopes that fresh air would bring fresher ideas. When Deena stepped out of the posh marble lobby, heat and humidity accosted her like a wall to the face. She squinted at the sunlight, paused, and took a deep breath of the stifling heat.

She rounded the firm, eyes on the structure in admiration of its discretely layered symbolism. The glass sheath of the building invoked fluidity, the running water, renewal. Its triangular shape was a primitive symbol for fire, the only naturally occurring element man could create. Thus, fire as an element bridged the gap between mortals and gods. At least that was the way she'd learned it.

The Tanaka Firm stared back at Deena, a towering prism of prestige. It taunted her, warning her that she could never emulate all that it encompassed—that she could never emulate Daichi Tanaka. Somehow, she knew it was right.

Deena turned to the pristine blue bay at the building's backside and lost herself in the lull of the waves. It was there that the answer revealed itself eventually. She could not be Daichi. That much was simple. And as she remembered his words, she understood. Understood that this was a dare. A dare to challenge his ideals, not as a scrubby college kid asserting herself in a snow-covered parking lot, or as a green-nosed intern in the heat of debate, but where it counted—out there, in the world. And in doing so, she would fly in the face of those who claimed he was the last word in contemporary architecture—unapproachable, unequivocal, and irrefutable.

She could do this. She lived through her father's murder, her grandfather's abuse, and put herself through the toughest college on earth. She could do this. She would have to.

"You lack the audacity for greatness," he'd told her. *"You've not the stomach for it."*

It was a dare. An attack. A lie. And she had one week to prove it.

Chapter Twenty-six

Not long ago, there'd been a boy that Lizzie liked, an eighth grader who played basketball and made good grades. He was from a better part of town, had two parents, and wore the best clothes.

She made up her mind one day that she'd talk to him. That day, Lizzie dressed for school in the sexiest getup she could muster without getting expelled. It consisted of a short-sleeved cinched corset that lifted and cupped the best tits around and shimmering, painted tights of the same cerulean blue. When she got to school that day she found him. He was in the company of a teammate, a power forward named Walt who rarely spoke. Together, they stood in the school's hall.

"Lucas, right?" Lizzie said, knowing full well she knew her crush's name.

He lowered her gaze to her body, not with the appreciation she'd expected, but with a critical, assessing eye.

He could see through her, through the clothes she'd earned on her knees to the tainted blood that coursed through her veins. She wanted to walk away, not willing to stand the humiliation. But then, Lucas smiled.

"Yeah, I'm Lucas." He frowned thoughtfully. "You're Lizzie, right? Or something like that?"

Lizzie nodded. Her heart thundered. He knew who she was. And didn't mind.

"Well, what can I do for you, Lizzie?"

"Do?"

"Yeah. You wanted something, didn't you?"

Lizzie swallowed. "Yeah. I, uh, thought that we could go out sometime."

"Go out?"

Lucas glanced at Walt, who raised a brow.

"You know, catch a movie," Lizzie explained.

Lucas paused. "You're Lizzie, right? Lizzie Hammond?"

She nodded.

Lucas and Walt exchanged another look.

"OK. I'm game. How's this? There's a party tonight at my place. My parents are gone all night so it'll be great. Come and uh . . . be my date."

"Wow. Okay, sure. I'd love to," Lizzie gushed.

"She'd love to," Lucas said to Walt, who grinned. He turned back to Lizzie. "Excellent. I can't wait."

Lucas Strong's house was by far the nicest Lizzie had ever seen. It had two stories, a white picket fence, and a pool in the backyard. All of that was on top of the lake it faced. Sabal Lake was what it was called, and Lizzie had never heard of it before that night. Even before she saw the house, she knew Lucas was well off. His mother was an elected representative who made him go to public school for PR purposes, he told everyone. One look at his house let Lizzie know he had no business at such a shitty public school.

Lucas, tall and nearly filling the frame, greeted Lizzie at his front door and instinctively, Lizzie warmed. He grinned at her, a clutter of boys at his back, before waving her in.

"Where is everyone?" Lizzie said, glancing at the dozen guys present.

Lucas shrugged. "I invited people. Hopefully they'll come. Someone else may be having something though."

Lizzie frowned. She couldn't imagine any other party she'd rather be at.

"You drink?" Lucas asked. Briefly, his gaze lingered on Lizzie's dress, a backless and thigh high electric dress she was suddenly grateful she wore.

"Yeah, of course," she called. She'd never actually had a drink, but didn't want him to know that.

"Good," Lucas said, turning to shoot her a smile. "Let's set you up then."

Lizzie followed him, thrilled when he took her hand, smiling at the stares she was earning. They wanted to be with her, all of them. But they couldn't have her. She was with Lucas.

The kitchen surprised her. She'd never seen one like it, in person, at least. Shiny marble floors, wallpaper, and a high ceiling. She even saw one of those rigs where pots and pans could hang from overhead, like in a restaurant.

Lucas grinned at her wide-eyed stare as he mixed a quick drink. When he handed it to her, she took a sip and winced.

"I thought you said you were a drinker."

Lizzie nodded. "I am."

"Good." He brought fingers to the bottom of her glass and eased it upward. "Drink up. Then we'll dance."

With the bitter alcohol down, Lucas laced fingers through hers and guided her to the center of the living room. No one was dancing to the music, as there were no girls to dance with. Lizzie felt sorry for all of them. They watched, some with beers, others with soda, as she gave Lucas her undivided attention. Lizzie smiled. She would show them how lucky Lucas was to have her, how much of a prize Lizzie Hammond could be.

Lucas pulled Lizzie close and immediately they began to grind. The music was loud and insistent, a frenzied thump of bass, cymbals, and nasty lyrics, shredding for a high-octane booty mix. She placed her arms at his neck as he gripped her waist, their bodies moving in tight, concentric circles. Her tits swayed with the beat, loose in her strapless, braless outfit. She was sexy, so sexy, and could feel it.

When his hands found her butt, she let them, cause he was cute and she liked him. Lucas grinned and squeezed ass with both hands, dick pressed at her abdomen. He began to kiss her, hard, open-mouthed and sloppy. Ironically, Lizzie didn't have much experience kissing on the mouth and worked to keep up with him as he smothered her. Lucas kneaded her ass, pressing her flat, grinding less like a dance as he pulled her dress. Behind Lizzie a cheer erupted as a blast of air-conditioning hit her thong-clad ass.

Lucas backed her to the wall, never slowing as she stumbled, pinned her there, and fumbled at the crotch of her panties. With one hand, he unzipped and thrust into Lizzie.

He fucked her there, on the wall, at his party. With a leg around his waist, she stared at her audience, blank-faced and numb as harsh, hurried stabs pounded her. When he pulled down the front of her dress, she didn't stop him. When he lifted her other leg, on the instructions of another boy, she didn't stop him. And when he grunted in her ear that she was "one slutty bitch," she didn't tell him he was wrong. Lucas sweat and moaned as he clamped down on her ass, leaving Lizzie to stare at the onlookers who were enjoying the show. Somehow, Lizzie had believed she could keep the truth from Lucas and her audience. But looking at them told her they knew. They knew who, or rather what, she was and wasn't. And in the end, she'd only kept the truth from herself.

He came in her that night before stepping aside for Walt. Tall and strong, Walt dropped his pants and carried her to the couch, where he shared her mouth with another short and sweaty guy that Lizzie didn't know.

There were five in total. Five boys that did whatever came to mind for however long they could stand it. They came in her, all five, and never once did she protest. But afterward, Lizzie made a decision, her best one yet. Never, would she be fucked for nothing again. Ever.

Chapter Twenty-seven

Back at her desk, Deena withdrew pen and paper. She printed "Skylife" at the top of a legal pad in large, neat letters and stared at it.

What did she know about the project? She numbered the lines of the page and began to list facts as they came to her. A multiuse facility—residential and commercial. Marked for wealthy residents. Advantageous ocean access. Impressive views of the bay.

Deena sighed. She was young, twenty-five, and had graduated just four years ago. How could she create a design so impressive that people would fork over millions of dollars for a sliver of *her* vision? How could she create a standard of luxury that made a unique contribution to the world, when she had spent most of her life in poverty?

She groaned. This line of thought was counterproductive.

She turned to the function of the building. It was a multiuse structure with commercial and residential units under the same roof. It was a community. Deena began to scribble everything that came to mind about communities. A group interacting in a shared environment. Shared resources, preferences, needs, risks.

What else could her building do for this community, aside from the obvious task of providing shelter? Many architects tried to impose a sense of community cohesion through common space. It was a good notion, but she wanted to take it further. Could she, through her designs, create this same sense of cohesion not just with the residents of her building, but with those in the surrounding area, too? Could Skylife, in essence, draw the outward in?

Deena chewed on her pen in thought. She envisioned outdoor common spaces, a gym and sauna open to the community, and an outdoor café for the business tycoons who worked steps away. Skylife would not be a world unto itself, but rather, a seamless part of a larger existence.

Deena frowned. The idea was good, but it was just a start. People would not pay millions to inhabit squares, no matter how many coffee shops were nearby.

Spacious lofts came to mind, with 180-degree views of water and floor-to-ceiling windows like the ones in Daichi's office. Still, she needed more.

She wanted people to rush home, breathless in anticipation, to fawn over their million-dollar lofts, dashing from one corner to the other as they proclaimed their love not just for the panoramic views but for every square inch. Each apartment should be alluring, enchanting, intoxicating. Each apartment should be loved.

Deena tore off a fresh sheet of paper.

Love.

It was the very thing that had eluded her for so long. And yet, even she'd uncovered it. Love. How could she look at it pragmatically?

She thought of Tak, jotting down words as they came to her. Beauty. Pleasure. Bonding. Familiarity. Intimacy. Reciprocity. Could she re-create these same attributes in her design, and by proxy, manufacture love?

It sounded outrageous. But outrageous, so far as she knew, was not the same as impossible.

Chapter Twenty-eight

Kenji Tanaka lay on his back, the door before him closed. He was in his weekend bedroom at his older brother Tak's house and on his nightstand was a stack of graphic novels. On the television, *The Sopranos*, turned low. Briefly, he considered a romp with one of the half-dozen adrenaline-rushing video games he owned, but a glance at the clock on his nightstand made him decide against it. He had a baseball game the next day and it was nearly ten all ready. Late nights playing pseudo NFL games wouldn't get him a starting position at UCLA. So he flipped off the TV and the lamp, pulled the Marlins comforter up, and snuggled in.

Even before Kenji heard the faint squeaking of bedrails and the occasional lusty moan from his brother's room, not long back from his vacation, he knew things had changed for Tak and Deena. It was no one thing that had convinced him, but instead, a bunch of little ones. They suddenly had this endless need to touch for starters, subtle but ever present. A question with a hand on the arm, a suggestion with a hand on the back, it never seemed to stop. And what was with the double talk? Everything Tak said made her blush, as if it all had a second, more seductive meaning.

Kenji sat up. His headboard and Tak's faced each other, and the pounding coming through the walls was not conducive to sleep. With a frown, he flipped on his lamp and snatched one of the graphic novels off his nightstand.

They were not comic books, as the ill-informed tried to call them. There were distinct differences between the two. Important differences. For starters, they were novels not serials that required you to return to them again and again for short fixes. Second, and more importantly, they were gritty, mature, and more reflective of the real world.

Take the one in his hand, for example. It was from Guy Robin's Groove Town series. In it were pimps, prostitutes, drug dealers, mobsters, and a corrupt police force, all realistically conveyed in the film noir style. What could be better than moral ambiguity and sex? He grinned each time he imagined the timid Peter Parker tangling with Guy Robin's 5th Street Girls, a clan of prostitutes steeped deep in vigilante justice. Those Spidey webs would do no good in Groove Town.

He was guessing, of course, about whether Guy Robin's take on criminal life was realistic. Despite being raised in Miami, a city with a murder rate higher than New York and Los Angeles combined, Kenji had never so much as seen a purse snatched, let alone anything reasonably dangerous. He lived in a house so posh it had been on the cover of designing magazines, and even then was called an "estate." It was surrounded on three sides by the bay and had two pools, a tennis court, fitness center, movie theater, and a private dock for the two boats his father kept. There wasn't even a semblance of normalcy at the public school he attended. Shuffled there by zip code, it was home only to the extremely well off, and to Kenji, had all the trappings for an episode of nauseating teen drama.

There was a knock at his door and Kenji set aside Guy Robin.

When Tak stepped into the room, he wore only a pair of white cotton pajama pants and an awkward expression. He cleared his throat before speaking. "Hey, little bro. Got a minute?"

Kenji nodded, and reached for the Rawlins baseball he kept near his stack of graphic novels. "Yeah, sure, come on. I'm not going anywhere."

Tak took a seat on the edge of the bed as Kenji stretched out and began a one-man game of catch.

"We should talk. There's something I need to tell you."

Kenji glanced at him, never slowing in his game of catch. "No need. Already know."

Tak hesitated. "And . . . you're okay? I mean, I know you like Deena, and I know she hangs out with us a lot already, but I don't want you to feel like this thing is going to come between us or anything."

"Nope. It's cool."

"She'll be over here some weekends though," Tak said hesitantly.

"Yeah, I figured," Kenji countered dryly.

Tak took a deep breath. "Well, I know this is probably a surprise but—"

"It's not."

Tak grinned. "OK, then. It's not a surprise, and you are OK with it?" Kenji nodded. "Alright then," Tak continued, "enough with the awkwardness. Tell me what I missed while I was gone."

Kenji shrugged midtoss. "A lot. I mean, it was twenty-four days."

Tak lowered his gaze. "Yeah. About that, I won't do that to you again, okay?"

Kenji looked away, features twisted with masked annoyance. "You're a grown man. You want to leave for a month, who am I to say something?"

"Yeah, just the same. I won't do it again. Not for that long at least." He paused. "So, how was it?"

Kenji shot him a look. "You know how it was. Dad was in Asia or Africa or some other continent we're not in, and Mom was in a bottle."

"And you? What were you doing?"

"Reading, practicing music, baseball. Made the six o'clock news one night."

"You what?" Tak sat up straighter.

"I made the six o'clock news last. Triple play, bottom of the ninth."

"And you didn't call me?" Tak demanded incredulously.

Kenji grinned. "Figured you were busy."

Tak laughed. "Then you had more faith in me than I did."

"Come on, Tak. You've never met a girl you couldn't have."

Tak reached over and messed his hair. "Spoken like a true little brother."

He stood to exit and looked down at the younger version of himself. Tak smiled with quiet admiration. "Bases loaded and you're sending 'em home, huh? Well, I'll be damned."

After an afternoon at the game rooting Kenji on to victory, Tak stood over Deena in the place where he'd left her four hours earlier. She was in his living room, frowning over a legal pad that had become her constant companion. She scribbled, scratched, and scribbled again, before lifting one of the half dozen or so thick books from the coffee table. Next to them were stacks of loose-leaf paper, newspaper clippings, magazine clippings, and Post-it Notes, many stapled together in thick, helter-skelter wads. Tak picked up one such stack and examined it. He lifted the glossy magazine clipping of a fuzzy-faced man to read the Deena-created fact sheet beneath.

Aamir Mahmoud
Electrical Engineer
Age 52
Native of Beirut, Lebanon
Current Residency, Los Angeles, CA
Ph.D. Harvard University
M.S. & B.S. from MIT
Major Projects:
Waldorf Astoria, United Arab Emirates
Bank of Tokyo, Tokyo, Japan
Capitol Building, Sacramento, CA

Leaguer Fields Stadium, Nashville, Tennessee
Pluses: Renowned for meticulousness. Recently published a book on risks in architectural design
Minuses: No major residential projects to date

Tak set aside Mahmoud's profile and picked up another. This one had a passport-size photo of a fat-faced Asian woman alongside a stack of notes. He turned to the fact sheet.

Margaret Lee
Electrical Engineer
Age 63
Native of New York, NY
Current Residency, West Palm Beach, FL
Ph.D. Northwestern University
M.S., Columbia University. B.S., NYU
Major Projects:
Miami School of Design, Miami, FL
West Palm Beach School of Arts, W. Palm Beach, FL
Bennett Regional Hospital, Children's Wing, Fort Lauderdale, FL

Tak frowned at Maggie Lee's fact sheet and he thought back to Mahmoud. He had a state capitol and an NFL football field while Ms. Lee here had a wing in a hospital, admirable, but certainly not equal.

"What's up with the drastic departure, Dee?"

She looked up. "What?"

"The drastic departure between Mahmoud and Maggie Lee. What's up with that?"

In the kitchen, Kenji nuked a fresh round of popcorn, snack food before he returned to his job of clipping and sorting for Deena. He'd taken to his job of assisting Deena in the organization of her prospects. To Tak, it was almost as if helping her succeed would be the equivalent of thumbing his nose at their dad.

"Mahmoud's a huge deal," she explained. "And I have to be realistic." She turned to her legal pad. "Besides, I probably won't even contact him."

Tak sat down. "Of course you will."

He picked up Mahmoud's sheet again. "Where's this picture from?"

"*Architectural Digest*," Kenji said, returning with his popcorn. "Found it myself. There was a feature in there talking about his new book on fault tolerance."

Tak blinked. "On what?"

"Fault tolerance," Kenji said. He shoved a fistful of popcorn into his mouth. "It's a fail-safe for when part of an electrical system hits the skids. Keeps it operating."

Tak stared at his brother another moment, shrugged in surprise, then turned to Deena. "Maggie Lee seems OK. Better than okay, even. But you shouldn't let Mahmoud's credentials intimidate you. Let *him* tell you no."

Deena shook her head, not bothering to look up. "You don't get it. I'm a kid to these people. A nobody."

"So?" Tak sighed. "Listen to me. You're brilliant. Anyone who saw your design," he reached for a roll of paper on the table, "who saw *this*, would want to work with you."

Deena blinked.

"Call Mahmoud. Please. And don't take no for an answer. Not, at least, without letting him see this."

Chapter Twenty-nine

Two hundred pages bound and color-coded. Six graphs with corresponding appendices. Three flow charts, a budget, and one sleep-deprived architect. Deena's moment of reckoning was less than ninety minutes away.

In those moments of near-neurotic fear, she flipped through her proposal in an effort to calm herself. Her work was good. But good wasn't necessarily good enough.

It was an ode to organic architecture, and as such, a contradiction. Who'd ever heard of a skyscraper that mimicked nature? A jutting bolt of man-molded steel claiming to be a complement to God's natural order?

But life was contradiction.

Deena turned to the profiles in the rear of her proposal. Mahmoud was still there, alongside other prominent names like Michael Hudson, professor of landscape architecture at Yale and a consultant for the '96 Olympics. Steve Marshall, a civil engineer and professor at the University of Southern California, whose books on coastal engineering were architectural gospel. And Claudia Oppenheimer, a designer whose name was outside the sphere of their world, but akin to that of Armani and Vuitton.

Of the three heavyweights she'd invited, Oppenheimer had been added to the team in a stroke of madness, brought on by Tak's contagiously naïve encouragement. Now, as Deena stared at the potential design team, a veritable rock group in her world, her naïvety and presumptuousness, her recklessness even, stared back at her, brewing and spreading a potent sort of horror.

She could hear Daichi as he flipped through the proposal—*Mahmoud, Hudson, Oppenheimer. Impressive. While we're at it, we'll have the Beatles in the lounge and Julia Child in the kitchen. Next on the agenda: digging up Walt Disney so he can sprinkle the fairy dust necessary for all this to come true.*

Deena closed her proposal and rose from her desk. Her design was a good one. And she was a good architect. She would succeed. She repeated the mantra silently as she made the trek from her office to the conference room. And when she entered, she found Daichi already seated at the head of the table with four junior partners in tow, two on each side. Daichi glanced at his watch and nodded. The clock was ticking.

With shaky hands, Deena set up the PowerPoint presentation she'd spent a night's sleep fussing over, her pulse reiterating the importance of the moment. She slid a copy of her proposal to each of the men present and waited. Deena stared at Daichi, and Daichi stared back.

"Well?" he said rudely.

She closed her eyes and heaved a prayer at the heavens. When she opened them, her heart raced. It was win or go home.

Chapter Thirty

Lizzie stood at her locker, moments after the shrill of a five-minute warning bell and tried to remember her combination. The last time she'd opened it had been more than a month ago. With a grunt, she punched the aluminum slab and turned away. She didn't even know why she was there, at that stupid school with those stupid teachers and their stupid students. She scowled at them as they milled by, girls in trendy tanks or swanky skirts, boys in baggy shirts and fitted hats with the tags stilled attached, all of them in the newest and the latest. She glanced down at her own clothes, a white and cotton candy pink shirt that said *Sweet and Sour*, a pair of glittering and faded jeans, and the perfect high-top Converse. Lizzie watched the girls as they passed, laughing and gossiping, and wondered just briefly, if the things they wore were as hard to come by as the things she wore.

"Lizzie?"

She was startled by the sound of her name. She turned to the unfamiliar face, a short and dark boy with big black glasses, shiny, spit-filled braces, and an odor two stoplights past wrong.

"Go away," Lizzie said and turned back to her locker. She fumbled in frustration, aware of the boy still relentless at her back.

"I'm Harold," he said as if she'd been wondering. "You're in my sixth-period English class."

Lizzie shot him an exasperated look. "How the hell would you know that? *I* don't even remember what I have for sixth period."

Harold shifted his weight, dark skin glistening with sweat despite the cool corridor.

"I saw you in it, at the beginning of the school year. Back, you know, when you used to come."

Lizzie tried to concentrate on remembering her combination. The numbers ran from 0 to forty, and there were five numbers in the sequence—or was it six? She frowned. If there were five, and five times forty was two hundred (was that right?), then that meant that she would have to try two hundred different combinations before she found the right one. Lizzie sighed. She wished she had her sister's brain. She was always so good in math and science and English . . . and everything.

"I—I heard about Lucas's party."

Lizzie froze.

"What the hell did you just say?"

"I—I just said that I heard about the party. Everyone has, really."

Lizzie turned and took a single menacing step toward him. "Do I look like I give a fuck what everyone has heard?"

She did, of course; had skipped school for two weeks just to avoid the stares and whispers of boys who'd had her. But damned if she'd admit that now.

"I—I only said that because, well—"

"Well, what?"

"Because I got a hundred dollars for my birthday and—and I thought that I could give it to you. If you—you know."

Lizzie stopped. "A hundred dollars? Cash?" She eyed Harold with interest now.

He nodded.

"Is it with you now?"

Again, he nodded.

She thought of what she could do with a hundred dollars. She could get a cell phone or an iPod, maybe even some makeup—the expensive kind that they let you try on at the cosmetics counter in the mall.

"You want to do it now?" Lizzie asked.

"No." Harold recoiled. "I—I've got class and—and anyway you can suspended for that."

"So your house, then? After school?" She didn't want to miss out on that hundred bucks.

Harold shook his head. "My parents won't just let me bring a girl over and . . ."

Lizzie sighed. "Fine. Whatever. Just meet me at my locker after school. I know a place."

When Lizzie met Harold at just after three, the sun hung dull in the sky, rays blunted by an overcast sky. They walked for fifteen minutes—across a six-lane intersection, through an open field littered with trash, and past an old railroad track. Near a series of blackened warehouses was an old hatchback, its make, model, and color singed beyond recognition. Rumors abounded as to why it'd been burned.

"In here," Lizzie said, prying open the door. "This is OK if we hurry up."

Harold stared as she tossed an old tire iron from the back and pushed aside yellowed newspapers bums covered themselves with when they slept.

Lizzie turned to him, took in his sickly expression. "What? Are you scared?"

"A little," Harold admitted.

Her eyes became slits. "Well, either way you pay me, since you're the one who's reneging."

She folded her arms and waited, thoughts of the Mac counter at Aventura Mall coming easier with the passage of time.

"No, no. I'll do it." Harold nodded. "Just . . . get in."

When Lizzie climbed in, Harold slid in next to her. The interior was pungent. It was hot and smelled of bum funk, Harold, and piss. Still, she wanted that makeup. She peeled off her shirt and scooted out of her jeans. And when she sat before Harold in not a whisper of clothes, he stared back at her in lip-trembling astonishment.

Chapter Thirty-one

Deena shoved open heavy double doors and spilled into the sanctuary. She tugged on the hem of her ivory jacket, tucked her black leather Bible under her arm, and squeezed onto the front pew between her grandmother and sister.

"You late," Grandma Emma said, scowling as Deena tuck wayward brown tendrils into her bun. After a night of Tak's fingers in her hair the coils were willful, unruly.

Deena wondered if she looked different. She certainly felt different. So much of her life had changed in the last two weeks. A single reckless presentation and a night in New York had changed everything for her.

"You needs to be on time. Ain't nowhere you needs to be more important than the Lord's house."

Deena met her grandmother's stare, aware of her ever-present blush. She just couldn't suppress it.

"Yes, ma'am," she muttered with what she hoped was deference.

Still, her thoughts were with the presentation. Had that been a twinkle of pride in Daichi's eyes, or a sliver of wishful thinking? And he'd actually said, "well done"? Certainly, not!

Grandma Emma continued to glare, and ordinarily, it would've been enough to upset her. But these days, little could deflate Deena Hammond. With her name attached to the most prestigious construction project in Florida, and with a human aphrodisiac, an insatiable, irresistible, positively indulgent Takumi Tanaka waiting for her at home, no amount of staring from Grandma Emma could dampen that. With the realization that she was smiling at her grandmother's hardened expression, Deena turned her attention to the pulpit.

"It ain't like you missed something," Lizzie mumbled, rolling her eyes.

Deena frowned, then scowled at her sister's spaghetti straps. Her blouse sculpted her boobs with the aid of a diving neckline which allowed them constant movement.

"Pull your shirt up before you lose those things."

Lizzie rolled her eyes, but obliged.

Deena faced forward, shifting in the tight seat. Her mind wandered already. *Preliminary estimates for the Skylife project. Tak's hands. Follow-up phone calls. Tak's lips. The construction time line. Tak inside her.* Deena sighed.

She turned to the choir as they filed onstage. Two dozen men and women in bright white robes and not a single one with a distinguishable feature. Her vision blurred and melded together as she scolded herself for sinful thoughts in the house of the Lord.

They sprung to action, the pianist belting out a quick flurry of notes, the percussionist jumping in with a snare, and the choir with a hand-clapping sway that was instantly contagious. Next to Deena, Grandma Emma rocked with the music, her wide-brimmed hat bobbing with the beat. The sound from the choir chimed full and rich, and instinctively, a foot-tapping number about leaning on the Lord in times of adversity came together. It was rousing but humble, exciting the way only Black gospel can be. Deena clapped in time with them, her distractions forgotten. But when Cicely Williams stepped out for her solo, Deena knew what would follow.

"That should be *you* singing," Emma shouted over the congregation's enthusiasm.

Thirteen years ago, when Deena was twelve, she'd brought the church to frenzy with the voice of a timeworn woman and the aid of the very same song. She'd been a child though, and not so much moved by the power of Christ, but rather, the necessity to show an equally young Cicely Williams who the better singer was. She'd peppered her song with a few well-placed "hallelujahs," and after that, there'd been no disputing it. Even back then, she was competitive as hell.

Deena wondered what Tak was doing. She'd left him in her bed with the promise that she'd be gone for a few hours only. She glanced at her watch, unable to keep from wishing she hadn't left him at all.

After tapering off to silence four or five times, Cicely dove back into song with foot-stomping, hand-clapping fury. When it ended, Deena half-expected the girl to roll on the floor, white robe and all, but, of course, she didn't. Next to Deena, Grandma Emma brought a lace handkerchief to her face and dabbed sweat. Holy Ghost Fever was what Anthony used to call it, an ailment he was certain was three parts bullshit and one part hoopla.

Deacon Moore wanted them to pray, so Deena closed her eyes. He said something about tenderness and temptation and her thoughts turned to Tak. She bit her lip with the memory of his words after the first time they made love—husky, breathless, provocative whispers of how he dreamed of her, craved her, and loved her. She remembered the way he teased her to fruition, touching her, filling her, his hardness forcing its way into an opening that seemed not to exist. She'd clung to him as he bore into her, shooting pain and pleasure with his penetration.

Eyes shut, Deena's breath ran shallow with the memory, her very core pulsing and heating in the sanctuary.

"Girl, what in the world are you doing?"

Deena's eyes flew open at the sound of Lizzie's voice.

"What?" Deena blinked.

"What's wrong with you? What are you doing?"

She looked around. Prayer was over, and if the sight of Deacon Moore resting in his seat was any indication, it had been for some time. Deena looked down at her hands, clutching the pew in a white-knuckled grip and blushed.

"I—I don't know. I had something on my mind."

"Well, whatever it was it looked pretty damned good."

Deena looked away. "Shut up. And stop swearing."

Reverend Lincoln was a short and slight figure with a black beak of a nose and a voice that bellowed in the rafters. He'd been a friend of Grandpa Eddie's and shared a platoon with him in Vietnam.

When the reverend found the pulpit, he cleared his throat, adjusted his reading glasses, and instructed the congregation to turn to First Corinthians, Chapter 6, Verses 9–11. With a hand to her mouth, Deena stifled a giggle at the horrible irony of him choosing one of Grandpa Eddie's favorite passages.

"Do ye not know that the unrighteous will not inherit the kingdom of God?" Reverend Lincoln gave them a hard look. "Do not be deceived. Neither fornicators, nor idolaters, nor adulterers, nor homosexuals, nor sodomites, nor thieves, nor covetous, nor drunkards, nor revilers, nor extortioners will inherit the kingdom of God."

He looked up, his gaze falling on the front pew. The Hammond pew.

"And such were some of you."

At the end of the service, the congregation spilled out onto the sidewalk. With their exit Grandma Emma turned a glare on Deena.

"Your mind was not on the Lord's Word today."

Deena shrunk back. "I—I have a lot going on right now. With work."

"Mmm. Jus' so longs as you keeping the Lord's work on your mind, too, namely this here fellowship hall. You wasn't at the last two meetings we had to discuss it. Reckon cause you was in New York."

Deena hesitated. "About that, Grandma. You guys are—are going to have to find someone else."

"What you mean 'someone else'? You the only one in the church that knows—"

"I understand that. But I just started this new project at work, and I have to devote all my effort to it. I can't be distracted with this."

She was drawing the reverend's attention and a few others, including Cicely Williams and her mother Mabel. Already, her family, including Aunt Caroline and Aunt Rhonda, were by her side.

"Chile, what you mean 'distraction'? I know—"

Deena held up a hand to stop her. "I'd be more than happy to give the church a referral, but I can't do this. I won't do this."

Her grandmother stared, and her Aunt Caroline asked her who the hell she thought she was. Meanwhile, Deena dug out her phone and sent Tak a message.

DON'T WANT 2 WAIT 2 SEE U.

After service, she was supposed to help with dinner at Grandma Emma's house.

But his response came quick.

BE THERE IN HALF.

She looked up again, a smile broadening her face. "Oh, and, uh, I made other plans for dinner."

Lizzie grinned. "Me too. I've got other plans too."

Deena shot her a look of warning before waving good-bye to the family, though she doubted they noticed. She then started off for the two-block hike in pumps to the Starbucks where Tak would meet her.

Chapter Thirty-two

She could hear them at the water cooler, talking as if she wasn't there, Whispering and giggling as if she didn't matter. There were two of them this time, but there'd been others at other times. The ones who didn't participate weren't exactly casual spectators either, as they sat around their tables in the break room, laughing and beaming with pleasure.

Jennifer Swallows stood, arms folded over her massive bosom. She had a round and scowling face, pitted and lean-lipped; her nose a quick beak. She wore drab grays and dull darks over an otherwise dumpy frame. If her bullet-point breasts were any indication, Deena guessed the bra she wore was as old as her career.

"I'm telling you, it's some huge housing development venture. It's going to be a private subdivision in Brickell. And that's after she disappeared for a month." Jennifer shot Deena a contemptuous look, and Deena froze, tuna rye halfway to her lips.

"It's on Fisher Island, Jen. Only one of the wealthiest Zip codes in the nation," Walter Smith said. A bright-eyed and petit architect, he prided himself on an unscrupulous sense of fashion.

"It's not Fisher Island, it's Brickell. And at twenty-four years old," another look from Jennifer, more sinister than the last.

Walter fished in the pocket of his charcoal slacks and came away with loose change. Jennifer followed him to the vending machine as he made his selection.

"Makes you wonder, doesn't it?" he said. "The sort of talents a girl has to have to land a gig like that. Architecture aside, *of course.*"

"*Of course.*"

Deena colored.

A smattering of laughter echoed through the break room, and Walter flashed an innocent, yet pleased smile. But when Daichi entered, the room silenced.

He made a beeline for Deena.

"Stop eating."

Deena froze, sandwich in hand. They had the attention of the room. The whole room.

"What's wrong, Daichi?"

"I had no idea you took lunch so early." He frowned at his watch. "In any case, I've made reservations at Del Mar. We can start—"

"Del Mar!" Walter cried.

A forbidding sort of silence penetrated the room. Daichi turned on Walter and closed the distance between them.

"You've an objection, Mr. Smith?"

Automatically, Walter took a step back. "No, sir. It's just—well, with all due respect—"

"Please. Such preambles are contrived and insincere. Do not impose on my time by subjecting me to one."

"Well, OK. I just wanted to say—well, everyone wants to say, really—"

"Everyone?" Daichi scanned the break room. With better than twenty architects present, he found that only Deena would look at him.

"Has there been an election, Walter? Are you now an elected representative?"

"No, sir. I just—"

"My patience wears thin."

"Sir, does seniority not play a part in your decisions? I've been with this company for seven years and—"

"Please, I've not the aptitude for company politics. If you've a direct statement please make it at this time."

"Alright, fine." Walter's slight chest swelled with the deep breath he took.

"I would like to say that I think you could've picked someone more qualified to assist you on the Skylife project. Someone who knows more than her. Someone who doesn't take unauthorized vacations for weeks at a stretch."

Deena swallowed.

"I see." Daichi scanned the room. "Who feels that they would've been better suited for this project?"

Slowly all hands went up.

"I see," he repeated. Briefly, Daichi scanned the mutineers with interest. He then turned to their elected representative. "Walter! Tell me this. What are the three principles of *firmitatis, utilitatis, venustatis* that all good buildings must satisfy?"

"I beg your pardon, sir?"

"Deena?"

She leapt to her feet. "Yes, Daichi?"

"The three principles. Name them."

"Durability, utility, and beauty, sir."

Daichi brushed past Walter, his eyes falling on a lean and gray-haired peer.

"You. Give us a common interpretation of Islamic architecture."

The gray-haired man blinked. "Islamic, you say?"

"Deena!"

"The repeating themes in Islamic architecture commonly evoke Allah's infinite power and suggest infinity."

Daichi moved quickly to a long and raw-boned man with blond hair and small eyes. "Daniels. Criticisms of sustainable architecture. Now."

"Sir, I wasn't aware that—"

"Deena."

She fired off automatically. "Sustainable architecture isn't a discipline within our field exclusively, but a concern for the construction industry as a whole."

Daichi turned on Jennifer Swallows, eyes daring her to so much as move. "Shall I question you as well, or was the humiliation of your ignorant peers sufficient enough?"

"More than sufficient, thank you."

Daichi nodded and turned on his audience, smiling broadly. "There now, pupils, not so grim. You've earned more fodder for your rumor mill. Now, you and your peers can speculate as to how long you'll be gainfully employed."

With a nod toward Deena, Daichi exited a deathly silent break room. She tossed her sandwich and scurried after him, careful not to look back.

Chapter Thirty-three

They met at the close of each day to discuss her progress on Skylife. In the early stages, these meetings ran only until dinner, with Daichi questioning or making suggestions and Deena sitting, pen in hand, eager to lap up his thoughts. But as the year progressed, and her dream team assembled—Hudson, Marshall, and even Mahmoud—their meetings grew longer and took on an altogether different tone.

"Your design has been garnering quite a bit of excitement," Daichi said, his eyes on Deena as she scooped Pad Thai from the take-out container they shared.

"So I've heard."

"People are saying it's where eco-friendly will finally meet opulence."

Deena rolled her eyes. "Eco-friendly is a vague and commercialized term with no real value. And even if it weren't," she paused to brush bits of crushed peanuts aside with her chopsticks, "it would be an inherent contradiction."

"The best architecture in the world is contradictory, Deena." He paused long enough to place food in his mouth, chew, and swallow. "Have you prepared the briefs on site selection yet?"

Deena nodded. "I have a clear favorite, but of course, the choice is yours." She pushed aside a stack of papers on his desk, reached into her briefcase, and handed him the briefing.

"And your favorite is?"

"Key Biscayne. South Pointe is second."

"Fine. I'll keep it in mind."

Daichi watched Deena, his scowl deepening each time she picked through her food. "Why don't you just have them omit the peanuts?" he demanded impatiently. "Why do you always go to such trouble?"

He swiveled out to the fridge behind his desk, grabbed two bottles of Perrier, and handed one to Deena. Behind him, open blinds revealed the city skyline and the ocean just beyond, enveloped in darkness.

"Because you like peanuts. Whenever we have Thai you get extra."

He softened. "Peanuts are an excellent source of protein. You shouldn't omit them from your diet without careful consideration."

Deena rolled her eyes. "I like peanuts fine. Just not with my chicken."

Daichi took a sip of imported water before returning to his carton for more Pad Thai.

"Have you seen the latest copy of *Issues in Design*? There's an excellent article on the benefits of beach nourishment," he said after several moments. Beach nourishment was the replacement of sand lost through erosion.

"I read it," Deena said.

"And your thoughts?"

"You know my thoughts." She looked up. "It's a risky enterprise. When improperly done it has a drastic impact on the ecosystem. Even when properly done the rate of erosion is obscene. The article skirted that. It read like propaganda."

Daichi grinned. "But you must realize the advantages. You live on a stretch of beach that has benefited from just such a practice.

There's ample research to indicate that the breadth of a beach has a direct impact on storm surges and—"

Deena waved a dismissive hand. "I know the research. And as always, you speak in absolutes."

"Absolutes?"

"Yes. As if there are no alternatives," she said dryly.

His smile widened. "Like revetments."

"Exactly."

Deena maneuvered more Pad Thai into her mouth with chopsticks. "Beach nourishment is a commercial enterprise fueled by the tourism industry, and it needs to be presented as such. Don't tell me about the benefits during a hurricane when the real issue is the benefit during tourist season." She chased her food with a gulp of water. "By the way, I can't stay late tonight."

"No?" A flash of disappointment crossed his face.

"I'm going to a baseball game tomorrow. It's a long drive. Five hours. And though it sounds trivial, it's really important that I be there." After all, she thought, it wasn't every day that Kenji made it to the state championships.

Daichi eyed her carefully. "There's work to be done."

"There's always work to be done. And I always do it," Deena said.

Daichi shrugged as if conceding the point. "You must be quite the fan," he said finally. "I never would've envisioned it. You, among the drunkards, perhaps in a smart pair of slacks, reveling in America's favorite pastime."

Deena smiled. "Not so much. I'm a fan of one player, in particular." As an afterthought she nearly added, *your son.*

These were the cracks in the dam, when her reverence for Daichi battled the reality of him being a shitty father. Before her disappointment could leak through, however, her phone rang. She fished it out of her briefcase and answered.

"Hey there, sweet cheeks. Dad still holding you hostage?"

It was just past 7 P.M., and a Friday night.

Deena smiled. "Yeah. Sort of. I don't know how much longer I'll be. We're just now eating."

"Tell him I said not to make you wait so long. You know you get those headaches when he overworks you."

"I'll do no such thing," Deena laughed. She glanced at Daichi, who scanned her briefings with a frown.

"Listen, I'll catch a cab to your place and let myself in."

"At which point you'll tie me to the bed and overpower me with rough hot sex, right?"

Deena laughed. "Riiiight."

"So say it."

"I will not!"

"Repeat after me. Say, 'I'm sorry, Daichi, but I have to go fuck your son now."

A shriek of laughter escaped Deena, and she quickly clamped a hand over her mouth. Out the corner of her eye she caught Daichi staring. "I'm hanging up. You're making me look like a fool."

"Fine. I'll see you when you get off. Try not to make it midnight again. We leave early tomorrow."

"Yes, Ta—," she froze with the slip and was met by Tak's laughter. "Don't be so thrilled," she said instead. "I'll see you soon."

She turned off the phone and looked up.

"Boyfriend?" Daichi guessed.

"Yes, sir."

"Not surprising. You're attractive enough." He returned to his food. "Has he been with you since the start of the project?"

Deena nodded. He frowned as if thinking this over.

"It's a difficult endeavor, you know, balancing professional ambitions and personal entanglements. Some of us are less successful than others."

Deena shifted, her eyes on Daichi's cluttered desk. He had no idea just how well she'd been versed on his personal shortcomings.

"You know, you don't strike me as the sort of woman satisfied with the trappings of mediocrity," Daichi suddenly said.

"I beg your pardon, sir?"

"The trappings of mediocrity. Commonness, if you will. I strain to envision a Deena Hammond satisfied with a subservient role as wife and mother."

She raised a brow. "When I become a wife and mother my role will be as equal, not subordinate."

Daichi shrugged. "Perhaps. But do you suppose you might find happiness in a life weighted with the roles of mother, wife, and career woman? These are not complementary responsibilities. Often, you'll find that your success as an architect will be at the expense of your duties as wife and mother. Perhaps even now you can see it in your shortcomings as a romantic interest."

Deena paused, thinking of Tak's warning not to arrive at midnight once again.

"My boyfriend's very understanding. His father is . . . a successful businessman. He knows the demands."

Daichi watched her. He cleared his throat and leaned back in his seat. "Make your choices wisely, Deena." He toyed with a weighty gold pen emblazoned with his signature, eyes trained on it and not her.

"Too often, it appears beneficial to sacrifice leisure for career, family for success. I, more than anyone, am guilty of this transgression." He looked up. "One cannot succeed in one regard without failing in another. *Time* and *People* call me the face and future of architecture, but my wife and sons call me a stranger."

Chapter Thirty-four

Before New York, Tak and Deena spent each evening together, and after, each night. Sometimes, Deena would watch Tak's work unravel on canvas, other times it was her who brought the office home—frowning over drafts or fussing over notes. Most evenings they were content to walk along the shore, brooding over nothing, over everything. They would whittle away their time, cooking elaborate and sometimes disastrous meals, musings really of what they thought they had at a Mexican or Thai, Italian or French restaurant, just days prior. And the week-ends, why, Deena's weekends were chock-full now, Saturday nights at a club, Sunday afternoons sailing, and Kenji's baseball games, whenever they happened. Nowhere in the mix was her family, and for that, Deena was grateful.

When Deena let herself into Tak's place, it just before nine. In one hand was leftover Pad Thai, which was promptly taken from her with a kiss on the cheek by Kenji; and in the other, her purse and briefcase, lifted and tossed aside by Tak. He greeted her with a warm and lingering kiss before following Kenji into the kitchen to help dispose of their father's take-out.

As Deena stretched out on the couch, pumps discarded, the Tanaka brothers joined her, two heaping plates of Pad Thai in tow.

"So, what did you guys go over?" Kenji asked as he took a seat.

Deena shrugged. "Oh, the usual. The vision for Skylife—my vision, his vision, the investors' vision. How we can all be happy and stay within budget." She gave a tired laugh before turning to Tak.

"Did you get much done today?"

"Some. Not much. Mostly just bullshitted with Kenji."

His kid brother grinned. "By that he means practiced the drums."

Tak shot him an impatient look. "If you could call that practice. Seemed more like a tutorial to me. Apparently *all* of us were on a monthlong vacation."

Kenji blushed. "So, um, Deena? The project's going good then?"

"Very," Deena tried not to smile.

"And working with my dad? Being around him? That's okay, too?"

"Surprisingly."

Kenji frowned. "What's it like?"

"What's what like?" Deena asked, stifling a yawn.

"Being around him. I mean, what's he like?"

Deena froze with the realization of what he was asking her.

Tak got up, set down his plate, went into his bedroom, and slammed the door. Kenji watched him before turning back to her.

"Did I do something?"

Deena shook her head. "No, of course not." She glanced at Tak's closed door, then back at Kenji, deciding Tak would have to wait.

"You—you wanted to know about your father?"

He nodded. "Is he, like, angry all the time with you, the way he is with me?"

Deena blinked. "What makes you think he's angry with you?"

Kenji shrugged. "I can tell. I don't see him much, and even when I do see him, he doesn't look glad to see me. Sometimes he calls me names."

"Names? Like what?"

"One time he called me a mute, because I never talk around him. But I just don't know what to say." Kenji paused. "Did you know that he didn't want me?" He glanced at Tak's door cautiously.

"Kenji! Why would you say something so horrible?"

"'Cause it's true."

"And how could you possibly know that?"

"I overheard him once. He said that it was irresponsible for them to have a second child since he's gone all the time and Mom's a drunk. He said that they took the proper precautions, and he didn't see how it could happen."

Deena cringed. "He still loves you, Kenji."

"Love me?" Kenji snorted. "He doesn't even *like* me. I've said more to you in this conversation than I have to my dad in the last twelve months."

"I know it's hard, but—"

"Hard? I never see my dad. How much worse does it get?"

Deena smiled ruefully. "Have I—have I ever told you about my father?"

He shook his head. "Is he like my dad? Always busy?"

Deena smiled. "No, sweetheart. He's dead. And my mother killed him."

Kenji frowned. "Well, what did he do?"

"Do?" Deena echoed, the word tasting foul in her mouth.

"Yeah," Kenji said. "People don't just . . . kill people, right? So, what did he do?"

Deena swallowed. It was an obvious question, but one never posed to her, never asked as far as she'd known.

She sat back, eyes blurring momentarily.

"I'm going to bed, Kenji. Good night."

Chapter Thirty-five

Florida in June kicked rocks. The air was too thick, the sun too bright, and the temperature like hell on repeat. Still, it was the only place Tak had ever called home, and he suspected it would always be.

Their seats were good ones—middle of the pack and down center. Deena was wearing his favorite UCLA cap, threadbare and pulled low, as well as a pair of jeans and a baby tee. She tugged on the shirt constantly, as if still getting acclimated to the new and relaxed wardrobe and the outfit that revealed a tad of her midriff.

Tak brought a hand to the cap he wore and tried to bend the brim. New and ill fitting, he'd ordered it online with the realization that his trusty standby was gone for good. Both caps were white with gold letters trimmed in purple, but his—or rather Deena's now, was broken in just right, while the other saluted like a soldier.

Eyes on the field in search of his kid brother, Tak thought back to a conversation with Deena a few nights ago. In it, she told him that after her father had been killed, she and her siblings spent ten days in foster care. Ten days. He just couldn't fathom why. True, her family was poor, but lots of people were poor.

The Tanakas, none of which who'd fared as well as his father, would've mobbed the place in an instant. They would've fought like hell—Uncle Yoshi, the used car salesman, would've argued that as second oldest he was entitled to the kids, while Aunt Asami would've pointed out that she had more money. In the end though, his grandmother would've won.

Tak wondered about Deena's mother and her family. Her mother had been born and raised in Miami; it stood to reason that someone from the family was near. Didn't Deena want to know them?

He glanced at her cautiously.

"What do you know about your mother's family?" Tak asked.

Deena turned from the warm-up on the field and frowned. "My mother's family? Why?"

He shrugged. "Just curious, I guess."

"Not much. A few names. And that I have no need for them." She turned back to the field.

"No need? Why?"

"Well," Deena said. "I've never met them, not one of them, not even when my mother was around."

"But there could be a million reasons for that. Maybe they don't even know about you. Or maybe—"

"It's a great day for a game, isn't it?"

She tugged on the brim of his cap and shouted "Go, Kenji!" The young man scanned the stands, spotted them, and waved vehemently. Though silenced, Tak's mind continued to race. He just couldn't shake it.

"Day Two in foster care, Miss Measley, our caseworker, comes in and tells me that Jeff and Laura Wright, my mother's parents, would be there to pick us up that afternoon," Deena finally said, eyes still on the field.

"And?" Tak said quietly, almost afraid to go on.

Deena glanced at him. "And, I'm still waiting."

Chapter Thirty-six

On her way home from school, Lizzie rounded the corner just as the first raindrops fell. She used a hand to shield her face. The rain in Miami was unpredictably violent, and she knew that she'd never make the three blocks home before it caught her full force. Thunder clapped and lightning flashed. Lizzie jumped, then double-timed her efforts. Another clap, and all at once, rain fell in gusty, torrential bursts. Everything around Lizzie turned gray and cold.

Next to her, a white Monte Carlo pulled over, barely visible in the storm.

"Hurry up. Get in."

It was Snowman. He threw open the door, and Lizzie jumped in, dripping onto his seat.

He stared at her.

"You look good wet. Sexy as hell."

"You think so?" She looked down at herself.

Snow laughed. "You fucking kidding me? I get a hard-on every time I see you, anyway. You and that sister of yours."

Grinning, he placed a hand on Lizzie's leg. "But you the only one know how to use what you got."

Slowly, he began to knead her thigh, working inward in tight circular motion. She said nothing, used to the way men touched her. They couldn't help themselves. She knew that. Lizzie glanced at the windows, now fogged as rain blasted the car.

"Let's get in the backseat for a second. My defroster isn't working, so we'll have to wait this out."

Lizzie hesitated. He'd fucked her before, ever since she'd lost her virginity. He had this way of nudging himself in regardless. Slipping over to Lizzie's place when his kids were there to visit, only to corner her in the bathroom and pin her to a wall; offering to run to the store when Grandma Emma needed milk or juice and asking Lizzie to ride, only to pull over halfway and pull himself out. And now spying her in the rain and offering a ride.

Lizzie climbed into the backseat. Snow was too tall to scale over as she'd done, so he threw open his door and dove into the back. Drenched by the rain, he turned to Lizzie and kissed her, no questions asked. Rough, calloused hands squeezed and groped, tugging on her clothes until she had none.

"Come on," he said, pulling on his pants. "Suck my dick." Before she could answer, he'd placed a hand behind her head.

An hour passed. An hour she spent swallowing him, underneath him, on her knees for him.

Finally, when he'd spent himself in her, he reached for his jeans and pulled his wallet out of his pocket. "What I owe you?"

Lizzie hesitated. She hadn't been sure if she'd get paid since she hadn't made it clear. She would charge him the usual price. No friends and family discount here.

"Let's see, twenty for the blow and a hundred for the fuck."

Snowman peeked in his wallet dramatically. "I've only got ten on me."

Lizzie flared. Next time she'd collect up front. "Give it to me," she spat.

He handed her the crumpled bill and watched her slide it into her jeans. "How much you made today?" he asked.

Lizzie eyed him suspiciously. "Why?"

"'Cause I want to know."

She shrugged. "A hundred fifty."

"And how many dudes you fucked for that?"

She shrugged. It was none of his business.

"What if I told you that you could make a lot more money doing the exact same shit?"

Lizzie frowned. "I'm not standing on no fucking street corner, Snow."

He sat up straighter. "Naw, listen. I know dudes with real money. Dudes that pay two hundred, two-fifty for what you just did."

"Two hundred dollars? For one guy?"

"With a body like yours? Hell, yeah. You better do while you young." He nodded to himself approvingly. "Now what I'm thinking is that you and me can clean up. I send 'em your way, I get my referral fee, and you get the rest."

"Referral fee? How much is that?"

"Does it fucking matter?" Snow hissed. "You're not paying it, they are. What I'm saying is I can send one guy your way that'll pay you for what you're getting for a shitload of guys. So, you with it or what?"

Lizzie laughed. She could hardly believe her luck.

"Hell, yeah, we're in business. Hell, yeah."

The drugs came fast. Alcohol and weed first, X, coke and heroin later. They were what she needed, and they made getting through the jobs easier. Snow was the one who gave her the stuff and when his supply ran dry, Lizzie began to look elsewhere for a high. She began to look anywhere.

Chapter Thirty-seven

When Grandma Emma and Deena were ushered into Principal Williams's office, the man brightened at the sight of his former pupil. He'd aged in the years since she'd last seen him, sprouting a belly where a tight stomach once sat, and white speckle in his crop of thick black hair. But his smile was the same; big and congenial, eyes nearly shutting with the joy of seeing Deena.

He gushed over her momentarily, eager to know about her life and career, before ushering them to the hard-back plastic seats in front of his desk. Lizzie sat in a corner donning a fitted white T-shirt that failed to reach her waist and had "Hot and Bothered" printed on the front. Not even in hell would this shirt and skirt be within the dress code.

"What are you wearing?" Deena hissed.

Principal Williams shot her a sympathetic look. "Ordinarily, we send students home when they dress like this, but quite frankly, we'd be sending Elizabeth home every day if we did."

With everyone seated, Principal Williams folded his hands and gave a tired smile. "I wish we were here under better circumstances. I am so proud of you, after all."

"Thanks," Deena said quietly.

She shot Lizzie another reproachful look. There wasn't a lot of time to dawdle, considering she'd taken Tak's car and left him back at the firm. Despite what he'd said, she didn't want him to have to catch the bus on her account.

"Mr. Williams, I know you told my grandmother over the phone that you wanted Lizzie out of your school, but isn't there any other alternative?"

The principal frowned. "I know it was quite some time ago that you were a student here, but do you remember the zero tolerance policy I had?"

"You mean about illegal activity?" Alarmed, Deena looked at her sister. She wouldn't meet her gaze.

"Illegal activity is *exactly* what I mean," Principal Williams said.

He reached into his desk and pulled out a sheet of folded paper before sliding it over to Deena.

The first set of handwriting was in pencil, scrawled in haste, but clear nonetheless.

WHAT CAN I GET FOR $25?

The answer was small, careful, tightly written. Lizzie's handwriting.

A BJ.

Deena dropped the paper.

"She also offered her services to me," Principal Williams said too loudly. "When I told her that I would have to withdraw her from school."

"She's troubled, Mr. Williams," Deena blurted, pushing back the hot and sour feel of her stomach. "Don't kick her out. You— you know my family. You've had them all here! My aunts and cousins! You know better than anyone how troubled we are!"

"Yes, but—"

"So give her another chance! I'm begging you!" Deena glanced at her sister, gum popping and indifferent, then back to the stern face of her former principal, singularly aware of the momentousness of the fight she now faced alone. "You know my family. We have babies in high school and go to jail before we're twenty-one. I'm trying to teach her what's right, but all around her are bad examples! She needs you around. She needs to see people who are educated and self-respecting, who look like us." Her eyes filled with tears. Nearby, both Grandma and Lizzie were stone silent.

"Deena, I have to treat this with an even hand. If I found a male student pimping out girls, everyone would expect me to deal with him harshly. I can't appear light in this matter." He sighed. "I can't have her prostituting herself."

"It's not the same. Exploiting others is not the same as exploiting yourself." Deena turned to her sister. "And she won't do it again. Right?"

Lizzie nodded as if bored. "Yeah, sure thing."

Principal Williams gathered Kleenex from the box on his desk and handed them to Deena.

"Stop crying. I can't have you in here crying." His gaze skated reluctantly to Lizzie. "If she promises . . ." he hesitated. "I guess I'll let her stay."

"Oh, thank you!" Deena cried.

"But not today. Take her home and get some sensible clothes on her. Tomorrow we start again, and I expect to see a new attitude."

"Yes, sir," Deena was already standing. "Thank you so much. God, thank you."

Williams nodded. "Alright, alright. Go on now. And no more crying."

Outside, Grandma Emma strode right past Tak's Ferrari and kept moving. She clutched an oversized black pocketbook in both hands and her feet moved faster than Deena had ever seen.

"Grandma, where are you going? It's this car, remember?"

She whirled on her, like thunder and fury. "What? You think I'm so ignorant I can't remember the fancy car you drove up here in?"

Her mouth creased to a single trembling groove, dark eyes now slits. Around them, high schoolers poured out the double doors to mill in the street.

"No, I—"

"The next time you want to go somewhere to bad-mouth my family, you leave me at home. You hear me?"

Deena paused. "Bad-mouth?"

"Yeah!" Grandma Emma took a step closer. "Or do you talk like that so often you don't even know when you doing? Talking 'bout how we uneducated and what-not!"

"I didn't mean it as a slight. I just—"

"If we shames you so, why don't you go back to that *other* family you got? The white one that likes to kill people? Or don't they want you?"

Deena's lip trembled. "I never said I was ashamed—"

"You didn't have to!"

"Grandma—"

"I takes you in. I clothes you. I feeds you. And you bad-mouths me and my family."

She started off again, an angry gait ailed by arthritis. But Deena didn't follow.

"Me and my family," she'd said.

Her family.

Hers.

Chapter Thirty-eight

Tak turned to Deena, smiling at the sight of wild brown locks framing her heart-shaped face as she lay on the pillow. She was frowning. It was the end of the summer, August, and he knew what occupied her thoughts at this time of year.

"You don't have to do this. They can't make you." Tak propped up on an elbow, his tanned skin contrasting with the stark white of the bedsheets.

Deena sighed. "They'd die if I didn't. I'd never hear the end of it."

"You'd hear the end of it if you stopped listening."

"Anyway, I'm the reason they do it every year. I came up with the idea."

He couldn't fathom why she would want to not only attend a banquet honoring the life of her grandfather, but plan one. Yet, she'd done so year after year, celebrating a man who'd spent years grinding her into the dirt. She owed him nothing. In fact, she owed him more than nothing. She owed him hatred.

Deena stared at him until a smile cracked her sullen expression. "Maybe it won't be as bad as last year."

Last year, he thought, *God help us if it were.*

She'd planned her menu with care, calling it a "veritable smorgasbord of the safe and daring." It included cracked crab and caviar, shrimp cocktail and pâtés, canapés and imported cheeses; and all that was before the rosemary lamb chops and herb-crusted salmon she'd serve as the main course.

Tak and Deena had argued in the caterer's office and in the car afterward, and she started to cry. He couldn't understand this, he'd shouted; wouldn't understand this. And she dashed tears, trying to explain.

"You think I don't know how my grandfather felt about me? Do you think I need you to constantly remind me?" She shook her head.

"It isn't for him," she said finally. "It's for my grandmother. The only person in the world that wanted us. Eight days we sat in that foster home before Grandma Emma and Grandpa Eddie came. They took one look at me and disappeared for another two. Later on I found out that my grandma used that time to convince him to take us in."

He was treading in deep and treacherous waters, he knew; where a banquet was no longer a lavish dinner but gushing gratitude for crumbs kicked her way. So he backed off and let her be. And the result had been a sobbing and heartbroken Deena, returned from the banquet with a stain on her dress and stories of how they made fun of her, of her food, her clothes, her everything.

This year she stayed firm in not planning the event. Tak suspected part of that was due to the fight she'd had with her grandmother following the visit to Principal Williams's office. At the last minute, when the Hammonds realized that Deena wasn't going to be footing this year's bill, they threw something together, and it was this something that she considered attending.

Tak sat up with a thought.

"Tell you what," he said. "Let's stay busy today. Then you won't have time to think about it."

Deena shook her head. "I have to at least go, Tak. My grandmother'll be disappointed."

He shrugged. Last he'd heard, she still wasn't speaking to Deena.

"Disappointed in *what* is the question, Deena. And maybe the answer is in not having you to bully."

He swung legs out from the bed and stood. "Not sure how sad you need to be about that one."

Deena closed her eyes.

He knew what she was thinking. They could be a cruel bunch, those Hammonds, and not going could be worse than enduring. She'd go, he thought, because in the end, that was easier.

She opened her eyes.

"What'll we do instead?"

Tak grinned in surprise. "Whatever you want. Large or small. Name it and it's yours."

Somehow, that didn't seem enough. Then an idea occurred to him.

"Hey, let's redecorate your place. Looks like the inside of a mausoleum, anyway."

Deena pouted. "That's a bit strong."

"No, not really," He reached for the pajama pants he'd discarded by the bed the night before and pulled them over his naked torso. "Listen, I'm an artist. You can't possibly expect me to spend so much time in such drab surroundings."

Deena stood. "Humph. I wouldn't have thought you'd notice. Your eyes are closed so often."

Tak stared at her. "What was that? A sex joke?" He snatched a pillow and heaved it at her. "That was terrible. Now get dressed so we can get to work."

Like everything else about her, he found her penchant for bad jokes adorable.

They spent the morning shopping and the afternoon redecorating. Sunshine yellow curtains, goldenrod paint, a cream throw rug, several pieces of his artwork and a crystal floor lamp were all in tow when they finally returned to her apartment. Deena never knew a man could be so fussy about shades of color.

At the furniture store she'd balked at the idea of a living-room set, crying poverty and the like, only to have him spring for the one she showed the most interest in. When she complained about the amount of money he was spending, he threw in an entertainment center as well.

They changed clothes, moved the old futon to the center of the room, and went to work layering the floor with newspaper and cracking open cans of paint. They worked in silence for a while, with nothing but the slick sounds of wet paint being slathered onto walls to entertain them.

"You're making a mess, Dee," Tak scolded, scowling at her poor painting skills. She looked at him baffled, then down at herself. In an effort to paint higher than her wingspan allowed, she'd leaned against the wall, lathering paint all over the torso of her T-shirt. She stuck her tongue out at him.

"Sorry," she mocked.

He frowned at her, knowing he was only being particular because they were painting. Even this was art to him. He turned back to the wall, then rounded on her suddenly.

"Hey! Isn't that my shirt?"

Knowing that it was, Deena began to whistle innocently as she returned to painting with renewed vigor.

"That *is* my shirt!"

She whistled even louder and made bold, dramatic sweeps of the brush to demonstrate how busy she was.

"Can't talk right now, Tak. Got a lot of work to get done over here."

"What! You're gonna give me back my damned shirt!"

He rushed Deena and hoisted her over his shoulder. Laughing, she squirmed to get free of his powerful grip. Paint smeared his shoulder and back as he carried her through the living room, past the bedroom, and toward the bathroom.

"Sticking your tongue out at me! Ruining my shirt! I'll show you!"

Deena laughed fitfully as he carried her away.

"And didn't I tell you that you were making a mess?"

He dumped her into the bathtub. Doubled over with laughter, she attempted to escape before he turned the shower on full blast. Yellow paint seeped from her now transparent shirt and lounge shorts, draining into the tub beneath her.

With a determined expression and a single hand, Deena snatched him in, and in seconds they were saturated and giggling, her body beneath his. She kissed him as cold water rained down.

"Uh-uh. Don't try to distract me. You still haven't taken off my shirt." The water plastered razored black hair to his forehead and neck as he murmured between kisses.

"That's because I'm not going to." Deena traced the bridge of his nose with a single finger, then kissed him again. He raised an eyebrow.

"Oh yeah?"

"Oh yeah," she replied. Suddenly they were struggling again as he yanked at the shirt and she fought to keep it. But her fight was brief, and her laughter long.

"Deena, you made that way too easy."

Tak kissed her again, tossing his sopping wet T-shirt of a prize from the tub. He returned to Deena, heart pounding the way it always did when she was within his grasp.

Chapter Thirty-nine

Deena ran the flats of her palms across the broad dark table and tried to ignore the glares of those around her. Jennifer Swallows, sixty-nine, with the firm twelve years, in the industry forty. Sam Michaels and Donald Mason, each in their fifties, had been with the firm over twenty years. Herb West, at sixty-seven, had been with the firm ten, but in the industry forty. There were others, twenty-five in all, and each had something Deena did not. Decades of experience. And yet she was there, among this elite group, with seventy-five other architects on the other side of the door, snubbed from this all-important meeting.

Daichi entered the room with a scowl and closed the door behind him. He held no briefcase, no notes, nothing to indicate the meeting's purpose. He allowed his gaze to rake over each of the architects present, twenty-three men, Jennifer and Deena, and spared no one the invasive appraisals that bordered on molestation. Still, Daichi's entrance conjured up stirring images of Tak, flickering like an 8 mm film—Deena's office door, a bare leg, his mouth at her neck . . . then lower. She cleared her throat and shifted in her seat. This would be a long meeting.

Deena's cell phone vibrated from its resting place in her purse. She glanced down at her lap and willed herself not to peek. Turning to Daichi, she willed herself to concentrate on the cut of his Armani suit, the polish of his Prada shoes, the glare on his face. The phone vibrated again. She peeked.

THOUGHT OF U. THINKING OF ME? CALL WHEN U CAN.

Deena ran a finger along the screen, as if in touching the words she might touch Tak. Of course she was thinking of him. She was becoming incapable of not thinking of him.

Hurriedly, she punched in a response. *IN MEETING. CALL AFTER. DAD LOOKS MAD.*

Deena raised her gaze to Daichi as he paced.

"Whenever there is an economic downturn you will find that the building industry will suffer exponentially. A look out the window will show you that construction has all but halted in this city. Our economic crisis is a global one, with far-reaching ramifications," Daichi said.

Deena's phone vibrated. She glanced down. From his seat next to her, Herb West scowled, his distaste with her inattention clear.

TELL HIM YOU'D MUCH RATHER HEAR WHAT HIS SEXY-ASS SON HAS TO SAY.

Deena stifled a giggle and rushed to reply. *I'LL NEED HIS SEXY-ASS SON TO SUPPORT ME AFTER THIS CONVERSATION IS DONE.*

Deena stared into her purse, waiting impatiently for her phone to vibrate. The answer was quick.

U GOT IT.

"Deena? Deena, I'd like to hear your thoughts."

She snapped to attention. "Sir?"

"Your thoughts. I find you often have an opinion. I'd like to hear it now."

Oh shit.

Every eye turned on her.

"Well, Daichi, I agree with you."

"You do?"

"Yes, sir. Absolutely."

She had to stick firm. Wavering now would invite more questions.

Daichi stared, everyone stared until beads of sweat wet Deena's forehead. She thumbed the phone in her lap, unwilling to move and draw attention to it. She rushed to remember a snippet of speech. Something about construction demand waning.

Deena cleared her throat. "It's . . . inevitable that our industry would suffer. A recession prompts people to panic, to save, not spend. Without demand, there's no need for supply. That's basic economics."

They gasped. Deena looked around, wondering what she'd said, only to see Daichi's scowl melt into quiet admiration.

"I find your candor in this matter a mark of maturity and confidence. A bold, yet necessary statement, Deena, considering the numbers I've illustrated."

He turned back to the board, using a wooden pointer for emphasis as he spoke.

"The Miami location, our largest as headquarters, will see the biggest layoffs at 20 percent. Our offices in Tokyo, London, Mumbai, and Mexico City will experience major cutbacks as well, not only in architects employed, but in support staff as well. As I've already indicated, I expect a 15 percent decrease in overall personnel, effective immediately."

Daichi turned to Deena with a smile, oblivious to the horror dawning on her face.

"Again, Ms. Hammond, thank you for reiterating the need for this in plain speak. As always, your candor and astuteness is appreciated."

Lunch would have to be brief. Daichi's meeting had been an unexpected part of her day, and as such, had eaten into time she would've spent on the project. With a site selected and the design plans finalized, they were scheduled to break ground at the start of the new year. That meant that Deena was in project management mode.

She glanced at her watch. She had forty minutes to eat and make to the meeting with the Skylife investors. As Deena stepped out of the conference room, however, Daichi stopped her.

"A moment of your time, please."

Deena moved out of the steady stream of exiting architects and joined Daichi near his dry erase board.

"You'll be meeting with the investors alone today."

Deena's eyes widened. "What? Why?"

"Because I have a scheduling conflict. And because you're capable of doing so."

Deena's breathing shallowed. "Yes, sir."

"You'll be fine, Deena."

"Yes, sir."

"You may go now. Unless there's something you'd like to say."

She wanted to tell him that she hadn't been listening, that she never would've stated in such cavalier terms the need to lay off so many people. Better than two hundred of them gone because she'd been text messaging his son.

"Deena?" Daichi said when she failed to respond.

"Yes, sir?"

"Something on your mind?"

"No, sir. I'm leaving,"

Deena scurried from the conference room, head cowed.

"It must be nice to know you've got job security at what . . . nineteen?" Sam Michaels said from his spot behind Deena in line at the lunch truck.

"Ah, but what it must cost," Donald Mason sighed. "Still, some women find it easier than others, I suppose."

Deena swallowed hard in an effort to keep her eyes trained on the selection before her. Tuna on rye. Ham, turkey, bologna, all with American cheese. A Caesar salad with wilted lettuce.

"He's got great taste though. She's young, firm, got everything in all the right places. He could do worse," Herb said as the line moved.

Donald laughed. "At this firm? Easily!"

She would get the turkey. She would get the turkey and an apple. With twenty-five minutes to spare, she would take her lunch under a tree somewhere far from Sam, Donald, and Herb and gross speculation. The line moved again. Two more until Deena's turn.

"Still, if she's gonna be a whore, he shouldn't be the only one to benefit. Senior staff should be able to petition for perks. Blouses with lower cuts . . ."

"And hand jobs on the side," Sam added.

Donald hooted in approval.

Hand jobs on the side.

And so it was that Deena was a whore again. With her grandfather, Eddie Hammond, in the ground nearly a decade and a single lover in her life, she'd been reduced to that emblazoned word once more. Whore. She brushed away hot tears as she ordered turkey. Underneath her tree, she would find the bread stale and the lettuce wilted. In this world as Daichi's prized protégé, nothing was what it promised to be.

Chapter Forty

You know," said William Lewis Henderson, "I have a real problem with the way the bottom line on this project keeps inflating. We've seen an additional $50 million increase since the initial estimate—"

"Well, sir, we've made some changes, changes that you were among the first to approve. Remember?" Deena said.

"Of course I remember!"

Henderson was a pale and portly man, red-faced in his anger, with sunken silver eyes and never-ending beads of sweat. His suit was Versace, his shoes Armani, and his gold pinkie ring inlaid with diamonds. He rolled gray eyes in impatience. "What time is Daichi arriving?"

Deena sighed. "I've already told you that Daichi won't be joining us."

"We're paying top dollar to work with Daichi Tanaka, not, not some intern," said Maurice Wilcox, the son of James Martin Wilcox of The Wilcox Group.

The Skylife project was the brainchild of William Lewis Henderson and his wife Maria Garcia, a Miami socialite whose family made their riches during the Cocaine Cowboy era. In the late '70s and early '80s, when the majority of cocaine entered the U.S. through Miami, it was by way of families like Maria Garcia's. Years later, the Garcias reestablished themselves as a respectable family with a history of philanthropy and very deep pockets.

After marrying Maria Garcia, William, a Miami attorney with a brief and spotty political career, established Henderson Properties, the principal investor for the Skylife project. He brought on two other development firms, The Wilcox Group and Allen Young Investors, who provided additional capital for the project.

"I am not an intern," Deena said quietly. "I'm an architect, same as Daichi."

"Oh? Were you in *Time* magazine as well? How about *People?* Were you in *anything?*" That was Maurice.

Deena rubbed her face tiredly. Today was not the day for Maurice's snide remarks. She stared at him as he continued to bark, ruddy face seemingly scorched free of facial hair, jowls jiggling as he spoke.

"Daichi is the principle architect on this project, as you were promised. I work under and answer to him. I can answer whatever questions you might have."

Maurice stared at her, unconvinced. As he opened his mouth, William interrupted him.

"I'd like for you to answer my previous question, which you've made every attempt to ignore. Why has the cost of this project soared from $300 to $350 million?"

"Sir, I've already told you—"

"No. I want you to go over to that dry erase board and line itemize every expenditure for us to see. Then I want you to justify every single expense until we're satisfied. Now," William pointed a single long thick finger at the board behind her.

Deena closed her eyes, tears threatening her. She'd never seen them this way, impatient, belligerent, condescending. She glanced at the door with a simple prayer that she knew would not be answered. Daichi was in his Mercedes en route to Orlando for talks of another major project. She'd heard whispers that it was with one of the major theme parks. He would not be walking through the door for a project he'd already secured, when the enticement of immortality lay at the precipice.

Deena stood and made her way over to the dry erase board. And with her back to the investors and tears pooling in her eyes, she began to write line-by-line the expenditures of a $350-million project. And when Steve Young, the project manager, arrived twenty minutes later, she would be forced to start the presentation from scratch.

Three hours after a meeting that should have taken one, Deena sat at her desk staring at the caller ID. It was her grandmother.

She greeted her as she dabbed her eyes with Kleenex.

"Don't you 'hi, Grandma me.' Where you been? You was supposed to be at your granddaddy service the other day!"

Deena sighed. "Can we talk about this another time? I'm at work and swamped and very stressed."

"No, we can talks about it now. You always at work, always swamped, always stressed. And since we talking about work, when you gone get back on that fellowship hall?"

"I already told you; I don't have time for the fellowship hall."

"And I already told you that you ain't gone shame me. Now where you been? I called your house the other night and ain't gets no answer. Now where you spending your nights?"

"I'm at home every night. I—I was probably just asleep."

"Mmm. Sleep *where* is the question. When you was supposed to be at your grandpa service you was sleep den, too, I reckon."

"I just . . . forgot, Grandma."

"Forgot! After all that man done did for you? Supporting you all them years? I reckon you gone do me da same way when I'm dead and gone."

Deena traced a finger along a shiny paper clip. She marveled at how small and slight, how tightly wound, that piece of wire was. Like her. "I have to go, Grandma."

"Go? Your grandfather was just likes a father to you. Better than a father cause he wasn't your father yet he treats you like he was. He was a good man, and he done right by you. And you, well, you just a ungrateful little—"

Deena slammed the phone into its cradle. She wouldn't take another word of how her grandfather had been the father she never had. Not another goddamned word.

Chapter Forty-one

Dee, baby, I've got awesome news. Guess whose upcoming gallery showing is being featured in *The Herald?*"

Tak switched the sleek black phone from the left to the right ear, a piece of charcoal for sketching in his hand. He frowned slightly at the canvas before him.

His excited declaration was met with sniffles.

"Baby? Baby, what's wrong?"

"Nothing," Deena said. "*The Herald* is—is wonderful news. And you work so hard. You deserve the recognition."

"Yeah, but why are you crying?"

"I'm fine, Tak. Just . . . having a rotten day. A really rotten day."

Tak stepped back from the rough sketch of Miami's skyline and frowned. There was a discrepancy between the buildings and their reflection in the bay. It needed a do-over.

"I'm listening," he said

"I just—I just fired like two hundred people, and the investors are angry at me and—and Sam and Donald called me a whore, and—"

He dropped his charcoal. "What?"

"I said that I fired—"

He shook his head. He didn't know how Deena could fire anyone or who in the hell Sam and Donald were, but he'd be damned if he wouldn't know shortly.

"Hey, hold on. You're at work, right? I'm coming to you."

He hung up before she could protest, grabbed the keys to his Ferrari, and made tracks for The Tanaka Firm.

Tak popped the top on a Bud Light and handed it to Deena before returning to the cooler to get another for himself. She took it with a grateful sigh. They sat in silence with the hot sand beneath them and the cool, glistening waves before them. On the horizon, the sea and sky were a seamless and perfect blue, indistinguishable in the distance.

Tak waited for her to finish her beer and then spoke. "So, how are you feeling?"

Deena shrugged and eventually gave a deep inhale. "A little better. The view is nice. The company nicer."

"That's good. So who was it again that called you a whore?" he said impatiently.

"What?"

"You said on the phone that someone called you a whore. Who was it?"

"Oh. That. Just these guys at the firm. Sam and Donald."

"Well, do Sam and Donald have last names?"

"Tak, there's no reason—"

"Last names, Dee."

She shot him a pained expression. "Sam Michaels and Donald Mason."

"Michaels. Mason. Got it."

"Tak, what are going to do? Are you going to get them fired?"

He would've preferred feeding them his fists, but yes, fired would have to do.

"Nothing. I'm not going to do anything," he lied. "Here's an idea. How about we just enjoy the breeze and try to forget about this day?" He stretched out on his back, hands behind his head, his face being warmed by the heavens.

"Oh. Let me say this first. Then we forget. A couple things. I talk; you listen." When she nodded, he proceeded. Tak held up a finger. "One, you're not responsible for all those layoffs."

"But—"

"Let's review the rules. I talk; you listen."

Deena sighed.

"Second," another finger joined the first. "You're not an intern, but an architect. A brilliant one, with more talent than my father even."

"Tak, your father—"

"What amazes me is that despite your brilliance, you're having trouble with these simple rules. I talk. You listen." He shot her a look of impatience. She met it with stony silence.

"Three. You don't owe anyone anything, not even your grand-parents. And four, you're not a whore."

He sat up. "Look at me."

"I am looking at you."

"No. *Really* look at me." He beckoned her with a single finger. When she leaned in, he cradled her face with both hands. "You're not a whore. You're not a whore. And you're not a whore." He smiled at the glisten in her eyes. "Now, you tell me."

Deena took a deep breath. "I'm not a whore."

"And you're everything a man would want."

She blushed.

"Say it."

"And—and I'm everything a man would want."

He lay back down and returned his gaze to the sky.

"What is it that you want, Dee?"

"Want?"

"Yeah. 'Want.' Is it your family's acceptance or their love that you want?"

She hesitated. "Their love, I guess."

"And if you never get it? Could you be happy?"

"Could anyone?" she asked in disbelief.

Tak sat up. "Did it ever occur to you that might find the very thing you want somewhere else?"

"I don't know what you mean."

"I mean with me, Dee. With my family. This thing that you think is beyond your reach—well, maybe it isn't. Maybe you're just looking at it wrong."

She blinked profusely, cheeks tinged with red. "If this is a marriage proposal, Tak, it's a pretty shitty one," she said finally, smiling.

Tak grinned. "Duly noted. Work on presentation skills before proposal."

Deena rolled her eyes.

"Tak, please, this is all talk. Your father doesn't even know about us."

"We could tell him."

"I can't tell him. You said he would hate it. And I can't have him hating me when, for the first time in my life . . ." Deena trailed off, head shaking, bursting with words she couldn't bring herself to say.

"For the first time in your life, what?" Tak said carefully.

"It's just that everything in my life is a fight. Work, family. Being with you is the only time I get to just be. Don't take that from me. Not yet."

Tak exhaled in defeat.

"OK," he said. "Alright."

Chapter Forty-two

For Deena's first gallery showing, she was nervous, even more so than Tak. A write-up in *The Herald* meant the possibility of a huge turnout. Any sort of buzz for an artist was good, but she knew Tak's art had undergone a drastic departure and worried that attendees might resent the lack of nefarious underpinnings he'd come to be known for. His art these days was decidedly more self-indulgent.

Tak and Deena arrived at Frankfurt P's Art Gallery at 6:30, some thirty minutes before the opening reception for the private exhibition. The single double doors on an assuming stretch of sidewalk gave no hint of the gallery's enormity. Maple hardwood floors, ecru walls, and cream-paneled cathedral ceilings combined to give the room an understated elegance. Each of Tak's paintings were mounted on a stretch of wall or a fit of easel and made prominent with an unassuming spotlight.

Once introduced to Deena, the gallery's owner, Tate Hutchinson, chatted idly with Tak about the buzz his opening night had generated. Hutchinson was a fifty-something-year-old with the purchased body of a man half his age and the annoying habit of wearing shades indoors.

"Jana and I are expecting an awesome turn out," Tate said to Deena, a glass of red wine in hand. Jana was his wife.

"This guy's a rising star. Soon he'll be bailing on Frankfurt P's for the grandeur of Paris." Hutchinson rolled his eyes in exaggerated fashion. "As it is, I've already got to share him with those bozos in Manhattan."

With a grin, Tate slapped Tak's back good-naturedly.

Boredom plain on his face, Tak turned from Tate to Deena. His gaze traveled the length of her discreetly. She wore a simple cream dress, the neck of which plunged to reveal just a hint of cleavage. A thin strand of shimmering pearls and sleek cream pumps completed the ensemble. Deena smiled at the furtive attention.

"Let me get you some wine." Tak took her hand and led her to a broad banquet table covered with cream cloth.

"You look delicious," he murmured.

Deena blushed. "Delicious?"

Tak paused to open a bottle of merlot and pour her a glass. He handed it to her with a smile. "Delicious," he reiterated. "Appetizing. Mouthwatering. Succulent."

The doors opened and a cluster of five entered.

"Game time," he said. He gave her a hurried kiss, threw back the merlot he knew she wouldn't drink, and disappeared toward the crowd.

As the gallery erupted with life, quickly Deena lost Tak to the crowd. He moved from group to group, working the room like a silver-spooned socialite, clearly in his element among the people. He had the talent of his father and the social graces of a debutante. People were drawn to him, wanted to hear what he thought, what influenced him, what made him. He took their compliments with a gracious smile and a humble word, made them laugh with effortless quips and always, always thanked them for their interest.

For Deena, the whole picture that was Takumi Tanaka always amazed her. His art always amazed her. There were times when he created things that gave her emotions she couldn't articulate. She would want to reach out and touch his work, was compelled to do so, but knew she couldn't. It was the same with these people. They stared at his creations, lifted hands to touch them, hands that waivered with both want and knowledge that they could go no further. His art moved people, inspired joy or sorrow, hope or hopelessness, with an ease that had no equivalent. Deena knew that one day his fame would come from this very thing.

She moved from painting to painting scrutinizing each with a laymen's eye. A seaside village in blinding shades of amber and sage. A glistening pool of turquoise in an otherwise barren desert. A man and woman locked in naked embrace and near-blotted from view. There were names for each, like *Serenity, Respite, Rhapsody*. They were in keeping with the emotions they invoked.

Deena continued in this fashion, giving each painting careful attention before stopping at a crush of attendees gathered around a single large canvas. Off to the side Tak and Hutchinson busied themselves in muffled disagreement.

A slender white-haired woman peered at the single large canvas as she lifted a glass of red wine to painted and wrinkled lips. "It's a transitive piece. Like the caterpillar midmetamorphosis, if you will. Provocative, yet emotionally layered. A unique insight into women, I'd say."

"And brilliant no less," added another, behind her. Still the crowd, so thick, prevented Deena from seeing what they meant.

A portly and balding man draped in black spoke next. "He's managed to retain many of the markings of Expressionism—the reliance on emotion as a mainstay, for example. Yet there are unmistakable elements of Impressionism—the visible brush strokes, the emphasis on light, the ordinary subject."

"Ordinary?" balked the white-haired woman. "She's clearly beautiful."

The fat man sighed. "Ethel, 'ordinary' is hardly an insult. The term is connotative of her accessibility as a woman. The curvature of her frame, for example, is indicative of womanhood as a whole and not the oftentimes unattainable societal standard of beauty. She is, as my wife would say, 'a real woman.'"

Deena pushed her way through the crowd, now impatient, and found a space between the bickering pair. She froze at the spread of canvas and could feel the eyes of the crowd on her as she inspected it.

Skin like toffee. Wide gold-flecked eyes. Hair, a thick potpourri of browns. She was naked, save for a crimson scarf snaking up the woman's ankle, sheathing flesh and curves in its ascent of her body. She clutched the vibrant red fabric in her fists as it unraveled, airborne like a kite. The scarf spread and grew, fanning out before her as it faded from crimson to pink to white.

She was beautiful.

She was free.

She was Deena.

Underneath the painting was a simple gold label.

Unfolded

Takumi Tanaka

PART Three

Chapter Forty

Tak scanned the bedroom to ensure everything was packed. He folded his oversized UCLA sweatshirt, because he knew Deena would want it for the plane, and tossed both it and his iPod into the carry-on bag. Deena rushed past him, mumbling to herself, list in hand, as she checked off items.

"Dee, we've got to go. We'll miss the flight." He watched her scurry by and smiled despite himself. She was adorable in her little pink dress and wide brim hat as she muttered about toiletries and charge cards.

"I'm afraid I'll forget something, Tak. What if I forget something?"

"Then we'll get it in Mexico," Tak smiled slyly. "And hurry up. I'm trying to join the Mile High Club."

Deena snorted. She darted past him again when her cell phone rang.

"Don't you dare answer that," he warned even as she dug the phone out of her clutch. Tak groaned. They'd never make the 4 o'clock to Puerto Vallarta. When they went to Montego Bay for their one-year anniversary, she did the same thing—scampering through the room in search of something, anything to bring. They arrived at the airport so late they weren't allowed to check in their luggage. This time it seemed they'd miss their flight altogether.

Deena shouted into her phone. "Lizzie what? For how long?"

Tak shook his head. The mention of her sister was never a good thing. He took a deep breath and collapsed onto the bed. He was certain that there would be no trip to Mexico.

Deena's sister Lizzie was missing—again. The night they were to fly to Puerto Vallarta for their second anniversary, Tak and Deena spent it scouring the streets of Liberty City. It was not the first time they'd done so either. Tak was becoming adept at tapping on the shoulders of bums, pimps, prostitutes, and drug dealers, forcing them to look at a picture of a troubled teen he'd never met. He cringed as women with missing teeth promised him the blowjob of his life and as dealers offered him X, snow, smack, rock, and half a dozen other things he hadn't heard of. Tak was laughed at, harassed, and threatened, but he continued nonetheless. For him, it was easier to face the perils of Liberty City then to return home to a weeping Deena, certain she'd lost yet another sibling. She was unable to eat or sleep, and unable to stop crying. And each day he felt certain that her heart, his heart, or both, would break from her grief.

Lizzie reappeared three days later. She offered her family no explanation and no apology, and Tak felt certain he could kill her. He remembered the morning the police found a woman's body in a dumpster in Allapatah. He'd felt prostrated as Deena sobbed, certain it was her sister. He remembered Deena's shriek of relief when she failed to recognize the bloated teen on the table at the ME's office. But even as they stared at that strange girl, Tak wondered how many times they'd be forced to return, hoping yet again that it was not her sister.

The day after Lizzie returned, Tak and Deena left for Mexico. They vacationed at his father's summer estate, Villa Paraísa, in a tiny coastal village just north of Puerto Vallarta called Sayulita. Daichi's sweeping six-bedroom home on the coast of the Riviera

Nayarit boasted a rooftop terrace, mangrove estuary, and a mile of private ocean access—all surrounded by mountainous terrain. But it could've been a box washed along the shore for all the attention Tak and Deena paid it, as they were consumed by each other, and little else.

They made love leisurely each day they were in Sayulita, savoring the feel of their passion under the sweltering spring sun. Each movement was deliberate and measured; as if convinced they had a lifetime together. This growing sense of permanency was evident in everything they did while there. It was in the way they made plans to visit Tokyo next year, and Italy the year after that, in their jesting about Daichi and Grandma Emma eventually meeting, and in their imaginings of Japanese children with wild brown hair.

"We should say something soon," Tak said as he and Deena lay side by side in poolside lounge chairs.

She lifted her head. "What?"

"We should say something. About us. To my dad. To your family."

Deena shook her head. "What's your hurry?"

Tak scowled. "It's been two years."

"So what?" Deena shrugged. "Two years, ten, what's the difference?"

Tak searched her face for some indication that she was joking. There was none.

"Dee, keeping this thing quiet was supposed to be temporary."

"I know," Deena snapped.

"So, tell me then," he said in controlled fashion, "how much time do you need? Three years? Five? Ten?"

Deena sat up in a huff. "What's your deal, Tak? Aren't things good? No problems, no complications, nothing families would bring." She shook her head. "Why in the world would you want to change that?"

Tak stared at her incredulously. "Our families are part of who we are, Dee. You can't escape that."

"Not my family," Deena hissed, lying back down.

"*Yes*, your family. *Especially* your family," Tak said.

Deena chewed her bottom lip. "Give it a rest, Tak. You're working my nerves."

He rolled his eyes. "Yeah, well, we can't have that now, can we?"

Deena's gaze shrunk to aggravated pinpoints.

"Yeah, Dee, your family has shaped who you are," Tak's hands clasped behind his head as he lay on his back, staring at the sky. "Your wants, your hopes, your fears—everything. Just look at you. You won't even think for yourself; you're so afraid you'll be voted off the island."

Deena stood. "This is my goddamned life. Not some game."

He smiled ruefully. "You're the one who wants to play games. Skulking around, whispering. Pretending you don't know me when it suits you. Acting like you've never heard of me when you've just finished fucking me. What's it like, Dee? To fuck me one minute and not know me the next? Hmm?" He turned to her, raring for a fight, only to find her crying. He reached for her, feeling like an utter jackass, cursing himself involuntarily, but she bitterly recoiled from him and rushed for the house.

"Dee!" He leapt to his feet, eyes on her backside as she rushed away. "Dee!"

The door slammed soundly behind her.

After spending half a day on opposite sides of a locked door, Tak convinced Deena to come out and eat. They decided on Don Pedro's, an oceanfront gourmet restaurant, and walked in silence to the town square. Once there, they took their seats on an outside deck so close to the shore that the occasional ocean mist wet their feet.

"Dee, I owe you an apology." Tak reached across the table and covered her hand with his own. "I love you too much to talk to you the way I did earlier."

Deena stared at his hand cupped over hers.

"Dee, come on," Tak said. "I can't know how you feel, or what motivates you to do some things. But I do know this. Before you, there was something missing from my life. I'd go around trying to fill a void with art, friends, anything, really—never knowing that it was someone and not something I needed. But that all stopped when I met you."

Deena looked up, offering him the slightest smile. He'd take it. Tak drew her hand to his lips and kissed her fingertips.

"I think you know how much I love you," he said. "But if there ever comes a day when I'm being an ass or I otherwise put that in doubt, forgive me. There are few things in this world I'm certain of. But I'm certain about this. God made you for me and me for you. Remember that."

Chapter Forty-four

Sunday dinner always began with a blessing of the food by Grandma Emma after which the family dug into an impressive spread of her best fare. The menu would include deep fried chicken, catfish, neck bones, chitterlings, collard greens, butter beans, stewed okra, and corn bread.

Deena could remember when she'd arrive early enough to help her grandmother with preparation, but since Tak two years ago, she found herself arriving later and later, and occasionally missing dinner altogether.

"So, Deena, where've you been? We haven't seen you for a while," Aunt Rhonda said as the family settled into their meal.

"I've been a little busy," Deena said quietly. "I, uh—have a big project at work that's taking a lot of my time." She would not tell them that her "big project" was tanking—that key investors were threatening to pull out, that construction was delayed, and that the budget was hemorrhaging.

"Oh yeah?" Grandma Emma asked as she piled fried chicken on her plate. "What they got you building?"

"A beachfront condominium," Deena said. "A skyscraper."

The truth was *she* wasn't building anything. She'd signed on to the project believing she would be Daichi's proxy, only to become his puppet. Though his workload demanded his presence in Rome and Tokyo, Dubai and Moscow with endless regularity, Daichi continued to micromanage Skylife. Every e-mail, every phone call, and every fax had to be routed halfway around the world so that he could do everything from responding to routine questions from material suppliers to ensuring that building contractors were remaining true to his designs. This resulted in delay after delay as the cost of the project soared.

"Damn, a skyscraper, Deena?" Aunt Caroline said with flecks of collard greens wedged between her gold teeth. "You ought to see if you can get them to put your name on it."

Deena's cell phone rang. She turned away from the table and answered.

"Hey, there. Still alive, I see. How's dinner?" Tak asked.

Deena smiled. "Fine. Everyone's staring."

"Good. Say something sexy."

"No!" Deena blushed.

"Say what you said last night."

"Oh my God, shut up. I'm *so* going to kill you tonight!" Deena gushed.

"It's what I'm hoping," he murmured seductively. "But I won't keep you. I just need to know what time to pick you up." He couldn't stand the thought of her catching the bus in the rankest part of town, standing next to a bench that doubled as the bed for a foul-smelling homeless person. He'd begun picking her up about three months after her brother died when a bum grabbed the hem of her dress as she stood waiting for the bus.

"Six o'clock. Starbucks, like usual," Deena whispered, feeling the collective heat of everyone's stares.

"Good. Till then, love." He hung up.

"I suspect that the reason you ain't got no time to help come Sunday." Grandma Emma scowled as Deena put her phone away.

"I don't know what you mean," Deena murmured.

"She's talking about your soon-to-be baby daddy over there," Deena's cousin Keisha, piped up.

Deena balked. "I have never, nor will I ever, have a 'baby daddy.'"

Keisha raised a brow. "Why you gotta say it like that, Deena?" she demanded, thinking of her four children and their four fathers.

Keisha never liked Deena. Right from the start, she thought Deena acted like she was better than everyone else, with her light eyes and white folks' skin. When they were kids, she would go on and on about her good grades like someone gave a damn. And when they were in high school, she flaunted her virginity like it was fucking priceless. And the guys, well, they'd act as if it were some precious prize, too. Keisha could still remember the way they'd stand by their lockers rambling on about Deena's pussy like it was the Holy Grail.

When they were in the 9th grade, Keisha had sex with Snow in the school's broom closet. She'd never forget what the eventual father of her child would say as he pulled up his pants. "Man, if only your cousin was so easy, I'd be in heaven." If ever there were a moment when Keisha became certain of her hatred for Deena, that was it.

And as the family continued with their meal, Keisha stared at Deena, with her matching manicure and pedicure, her light eyes and her light skin, and wished her all the harm in the world.

"You know, Deena," Keisha's mother Caroline piped up, "nobody'll get mad if you wind up pregnant. I mean, your mother was pretty much a ho and well, you know what they say." She stood and reached over Lizzie for the bowl of collard greens, her tank top and jeans squeezing her belly so that it looked like a split peach.

"Shut up, Caroline," Grandma Emma snapped. "The only one been having kids is your children. Look at that son of yours, Shakeith. Seventeen with a baby on the way." She shook her head. "And anyway, Deena ain't interested in affronting the Lord no more than her presence already do. Ain't that right, child?" Emma turned to her granddaughter.

Deena sighed. "Yes, ma'am." She avoided Lizzie's piercing gaze.

An awkward silence followed before Rhonda reached over and touched Deena's hand. "Tell us about your friend."

Deena trusted Rhonda, and if there were anyone she'd want to tell about Tak, she would be it. When Deena moved in with her grandparents seventeen years ago, Aunt Rhonda had been the only member of her new family that she knew from her old life. Even after Grandma Emma and Grandpa Eddie disowned Deena's father for marrying her white mother, Rhonda visited her older brother each week. Deena loved her aunt at first because her father loved her, but after his death, that love grew when Rhonda became her only ally.

Still, Deena hesitated. "Well, he paints for a living."

"Paints!" Grandma Emma bellowed. "Who done heard of scraping a living like that?"

"Lots of people, Mom. They're called painters," Rhonda rolled her eyes. "Go ahead, Deena."

"Well, he's really talented. His work is featured in two galleries—one in Coconut Grove and another in Manhattan. He sings, plays three instruments, and writes music in his spare time." Deena ticked off each item proudly. "Oh! And he's fluent in three languages: English, Spanish, and—" Deena faltered, horrified by what she almost revealed.

"And?" Rhonda prompted.

Deena looked down at her plate. "And Japanese."

Keisha snickered. "I can't see no Black dude speaking Japanese."

"I know, right? All that ching ching chong!" Aunt Caroline hooted.

Deena sighed. They were impossible. If she were another woman, a braver woman, she'd stand up and demand an end to this foolishness. She'd declare her love for Tak and do so unflinchingly. She would seize this opportunity, and in doing so, tell them everything. But she couldn't. She thought of the way Aunt

Caroline would look at her after finding out she was sleeping with an Asian man—as if she were somehow less Black, and less of a woman for desiring him. And she thought of Grandma Emma and the way she'd turn her back on her when she found out that Deena was sinning against the Lord.

Rhonda glared at Caroline. "Must you always be offensive?"

Caroline rolled eyes at her younger sister. "Boy, I swear! Let a nigga go to college and they come back siddity every time," neck rolling with each word.

"Maybe a li'l bit o' college would of did you some good, Caroline," Emma surmised with a point of her fork. Her eldest daughter was fifty-two and a shift manager at a fast-food restaurant.

Rhonda turned back to her niece. "What's your friend look like, Deena? Handsome?"

Deena's cheeks flushed scarlet. "Well—"

Grandma Emma's fork clattered to her plate. "Child, what is this foolishness? You think somebody here thinks this just your friend?"

Deena turned to her food, adamant about avoiding her grandmother's glare.

Emma sighed in exasperation. "Well, is he a good man at least?"

Deena looked up, surprised, smiling. "Very."

"Not liable to run off and leaves you with no kids, I 'spect?"

Grandma Emma glanced out the corner of her eye at Caroline and Keisha. Caroline stared back at her mother, saucily.

Deena thought of Tak's playful declaration while in Sayulita that he would accept no less than a dozen children from her.

"No," Deena assured her grandmother. "No chance of that."

"Well, then, child," she nodded to herself thoughtfully, prodding at black-eyed peas with a fork, "when you finds a man you loves, you make sure you keep 'em. Any fool can tell you that."

Chapter Forty-five

Deena concentrated on her clock in an attempt to ignore the pulsating pain at her temples and the insufferable waves of nausea. Were it not the day they broke ground on Skylife she would've stayed home. But this was her opportunity to pose alongside Daichi, the city's mayor, and powerful businessmen who had the potential to be her next clients. So, she would spend the morning grinning for pictures with pangs of nausea and too high pumps, smiling a smile that never reached her eyes.

At the groundbreaking, William Henderson, the project's primary investor, spoke of the Skylife project as though he were the one to design it. It was a "reenvisioning of the Miami skyline," he said, and a challenge to investors everywhere to start rethinking their place in history. Would they rise to the challenge, as he had done, and create models for the future of environmentally conscious yet posh accommodations? Or would they fall short, as so many do, in making excellence meet conscientiousness?

As she listened to his jabber, Deena's head throbbed with the heat of the morning and the memory of their battle over expenditures. She couldn't recall him possessing such lofty principles on that day.

"As I conclude," Henderson said with a flourish of the hand, "I ask each of you not what architecture can do for you, but what you can do for it."

Deena groaned.

"And here I thought I was the only one unable to stomach Henderson's grandstanding," Daichi said as he stood next to Deena. He turned with a secret smile. "Perhaps we should let him lay hammer to nail, as he seems so inclined to do."

Deena giggled.

Deena spent her morning hobnobbing with bigwigs. She was most excited not by that, but by the opportunity to meet Mahmoud, Hudson, and Marshall, her dream team-turned-reality. The four of them, along with Daichi, took pictures and answered questions, and when *Miami Design* asked Deena if they could have a word with her, she nearly hemorrhaged on the spot.

When Deena finished shaking the hand of the stocky blonde who'd interviewed her, she found her way over to Daichi, centered in a cluster of fellow architects. He ignored the refreshments as he usually did at events and opted only for a bit of soda water.

"So, I tell this intern, 'Listen, if you want to be "imaginative," then head down to Brickell and see if Tanaka's accepting new recruits. He's got interns over there working million-dollar projects,'" Michael Cook guffawed.

Cook, the former professor who saw fit to confront Daichi so many years ago during his MIT appearance, was met with a roar of laughter as he brought a glass of ice water to his lips. Deena wasn't surprised that he didn't remember her as a former student; he could never be bothered with learning the names of undergraduates.

Daichi wasn't smiling. "Interestingly enough, I've found that genius discriminates not in terms of age or race. Perhaps if my peers were better able to grasp that concept, then our field might better reflect the populace."

The laughter died.

"Incidentally, Ms. Hammond's not an intern. She's a registered architect and the genius behind the innovative design you've spent all morning fawning over."

He gestured to the small-scale model on display. A stately stem, once completed, Skylife would be the narrowest, tallest, most graceful creation to dawn Miami's skyline to date. With a walkway like an undulating ribbon, the building curved in its ascent as if to mimic ocean waves. Its lean appearance gave residents a startling three-sided view of the water while its 125 floors served to shatter the skyline.

"She designed this?" Cook said incredulously, no doubt considering the engineering ingenuity such a slim structure demanded. "You're being far too generous."

Daichi stared at the man with impatience. "I'm not." He glanced at Deena. "Are you ill?"

Deena blinked in surprise. He'd only spoken to her once that morning and she could think of no other time where he'd so much as looked her way.

"I'm—I'm feeling a little under the weather."

"Then why are you still here? Are the hors d' oeuvres so delightful?"

"No."

"Then leave."

"Yes, sir." Deena turned away, then paused. "Would you like me to meet you back at the office?"

"Is that where the ill go? To the office?"

"No."

"Then no, Deena." He turned back to Cook.

Still, she hesitated. In her four years at the firm, she'd never taken a sick day. Better still, her days of the monthlong vacation weren't far enough in her rearview mirror for her to feel comfortable.

"So, Daichi," Cook said, "I hear you've been short-listed for the Pritzker."

The Pritzker Prize was the architectural equivalent of a Nobel. Daichi rolled his eyes.

"I've no information indicating such and considering what I know about you, I suspect you know even less. Now, if you'll excuse me. I have business elsewhere."

Chapter Forty-six

Deena had no idea that something could be both really good and really bad at the same time. But she'd discovered just that when Daichi invited her to his California mansion for the holiday season. He wanted the opportunity to comb through their plans and ensure perfection for what was fast becoming a daunting project. His extended family would be in attendance because of the New Year, as it, and not Christmas, was the apex of the holiday season for the Tanakas.

It should've been cause for excitement. Meeting her boyfriend's grandmother, aunts, uncles, and cousins. And it was, except for the fact that they couldn't know that Tak was, in fact, her boyfriend. Or that she even knew him.

Two weeks at Daichi's estate, under the same roof as Tak, forced to feign indifference. The thought made her sweat.

Daichi's sweeping estate was in Encinitas, a cliff-side retreat just north of San Diego. It boasted twelve bedrooms, three floors, five bathrooms, two dining rooms, a private stretch of ocean, and a tennis court. Its views of the Pacific were breathtaking, made possible through generous floor-to-ceiling windows and sliding glass doors.

Daichi hired a driver to pick up Deena at the airport. He was a dapper fellow, with white gloves and the lot, and it was all Deena could do not to giggle as he took her luggage and helped her into the back of the Town Car.

When she arrived at the estate, she was met by Tak. Her face lit up when he answered the door. At this point, he'd been in Encinitas for four days, and therefore, away from her.

He squeezed her quickly before releasing her and glancing over his shoulder. He took her hand and led her inside.

"Where's your family?" she whispered.

He shot her a sneaky smile and brought a finger to his lips. They left the luggage in the foyer and made their way down the hall. Past the reading room, past the den, and past the dining room before he pushed her in a closet and closed the door behind them.

"Tak! Your father—"

"Quiet, Dee, I'm busy."

He smothered her words with a kiss. She pulled him closer, instantly emboldened by the notion of a tryst in the closet, enveloped in darkness.

He returned to her mouth, pulling away clothes in his haste.

"You should've come sooner," he said, mouth at her throat and a teasing hand on her breast.

Deena uttered something that even she couldn't understand.

"Uh-huh," Tak mumbled distractedly. He snatched her skirt upward, fumbled, and slipped into her with practiced ease.

Deena bit down on his shoulder and let loose a stifled moan. Somewhere in between were thoughts of him and his father. Was he on his way? Pulling into the drive? Or already there?

Tak slowed as if reading her mind. She thumped him on the back.

"God, no, Tak. Don't stop, just—just *hurry*."

When Tak and Deena parted a half hour later, they veered in different directions, making it only a few steps before hearing Daichi's voice.

"Deena!"

With a hand on the stair's railing, she froze, sweat from his son coupling with a now fresh sheen of her own.

She turned to face him.

"I contemplated forming a search party for you. No one seemed to have seen you arrive."

Daichi folded his arms as he stood at the foot of the staircase. "Now how did you ever manage that?"

Tak stood back, near enough to intervene, yet seemingly struggling with the decision.

"I, uh—wasn't feeling well. The flight. Air sickness," Deena said.

"And are you better now?"

"I think so."

"Good." With a clap of the hands Daichi turned to Tak. "Then I'd like you to meet my son, Takumi. Takumi, this is Deena Hammond, a colleague from the firm."

Tak watched Deena descend the staircase. Would she really stand there, moments after having him inside of her, after whimpering her love for him—after all that, could she really stomach pretending they were strangers?

She could.

As Deena extended a hand to him, nausea washed over Tak. He thought about ending the charade, blurting what they were, what they'd done, and would have, were he not certain she'd leave him looking the fool.

"Takumi," she said softly, the smile on her lips not bothering to reach her eyes. She sensed it too, the insanity of it all, of two adults pretending to be nothing to each other.

"Deena," he said coolly.

Tak clasped her hand, fingers stroking the palm and brushing her fingertips as she withdrew from him. He met her gaze, challenging, daring her to do something about the intimacy of his touch. She did nothing.

Chapter Forty-seven

Daichi grabbed Deena's luggage from the foyer and showed her to her bedroom. Once inside, he cleared his throat as if uncomfortable with the intimate quarters of his own guestroom. His gaze swept the confines in subdued appraisal before returning to Deena.

"And how do you find your accommodations, Ms. Hammond?"

Her first reaction to the room had been awe. "It's beautiful, Daichi. Everything you make is just so beautiful." She thought of his son and blushed. "I mean—architecture, of course."

"Of course."

"There are so many little touches." She scanned the room indulgently. "The stretched ceilings, for example, are amazing."

They were polished white and cast a gleaming reflection of the room. The four walls alternated between ecru and a rectangular maple wood grain. A four-paneled eggshell room divider mirrored the queen-sized platform bed and its pristine white linen. All of it was accented by bamboo stalks on either side of the bed that reached to the ceiling.

"And the wood grain paneling is wonderful. The geometric patterns give dramatic play to the lights and shadows."

Daichi stared at her. "Dinner's being served in a moment. I'm not sure how familiar you are with Japanese fare, but you'll find that the Japanese American family is the originator of so-called fusion food." He flashed a smile.

"There'll be some sushi," he continued, "which I know you enjoy, probably some teriyaki and tempura, and always a great deal of seafood. As an aside, you'll find that our vernacular vacillates between English and Japanese. We make every attempt not to do this with guests, but occasionally we err. I feel obliged to apologize in advance." Daichi paused. "Perhaps I should brief you on etiquette."

"I'll be fine, Daichi. You're not the first Japanese American I've encountered."

Daichi's lips curled into a smile. He offered a curt nod, and then opened the door. As they descended the stairs, Deena spotted Kenji at the bottom. Back to her, he faced a diminutive man with broad frames and an even broader grin. Deena placed him at thirty.

Kenji turned at the creak of the stairs, face aglow at the sight of Deena.

"Hey, Deena!"

Two steps ahead of Daichi in her descent, she froze. Cringing, Kenji looked from Deena to his father, realizing his error.

"You've met?" Daichi asked.

Kenji's mouth opened and closed, furious with the labor, but still, no sound emerged.

Deena turned to Daichi, her smile desperate. "We met earlier. Briefly. Probably when you were wondering how I managed to be so stealthy."

Daichi frowned. "And have you met my nephew Michael, as well?"

He gestured to the slight and awkward creature beside Kenji. She shook her head.

"Then Michael, this is Deena Hammond, an employee at my firm. Deena, Michael. He's a systems analyst with IBM. Attended your alma mater, in fact."

Michael's eyes lit up. "A fellow Beaver? What class?"

"'03. And you?" Deena extended a hand.

"2000. The brass rat says it all."

With their hands clasped, Michael turned his hand clockwise, giving Deena a view of a gold class ring. The bezel held the MIT mascot, a beaver, the school's shield, and the year of graduation. "Never leave home without it."

Deena smiled politely. She was not so fond of her days at MIT. She found the winters harsh and the people impersonal. She took away no mentors and no friends, though she suspected that much of it was due to a protective shell made long before collegiate days.

"Do you have your class ring? I'd like to compare the designs."

She hadn't been able to afford a class ring, but she wouldn't tell him that, even if he did look like a shrunken and unsightly version of Tak.

"Those rings are far too bulky for me, I'm afraid."

Michael grinned a grin with too much gums. "You know, William Wang once said that there are three recognizable rings in the world: The Brass Rat, West Point's, and the Super Bowl ring."

Daichi scowled. "I don't bring guests here for you to berate them down with worthless trivia, Michael. Now, we are weary and famished. Has your *obachan* finished dinner?"

Michael nodded and jabbed the bridge of his glasses with an index finger. "She's been waiting for you."

"And yet you detain us?"

Daichi pushed past his nephew and led Deena through the foyer and into the dining room.

Like the rest of the villa, the dining room was decorated in simple, subdued earth tones. Warm cream and soft browns came together in a streamlined, sophisticated homage to the Orient. The dining-room table took a sleek and minimalist design, made of dark birch wood. Long and narrow, it held seating enough for fourteen. Beneath the table lay a splash of bright, in the form a cream tatami mat that offset the dark table and ebony wood paneled walls splendidly. Rice screen doors with dark wood trim folded back to reveal broad glass doors, and beyond that, a panoramic view of the Pacific.

"I can see that this room meets your approval," Daichi said with a teasing smile.

Deena returned it. "If I didn't know you so well I'd ask who you hired to decorate."

Daichi rolled his eyes. "Now you simply flatter."

The Tanaka brood watched them. Tak sat on one side, sandwiched between John and Kenji. There were two middle-aged men—one that would've been striking if not for his widow's peak, and another, with a pudgy face, comb-over, and too-thick eyebrows. Deena knew which was Daichi's brother, John's father.

"Deena, might you do a fellow Beaver the honor of breaking bread together?"

Michael appeared at her side, slender arm already extended. He donned a Dodger blue T-shirt, bare save for the stylized arrowhead just over his heart. A master's degree and five years among the geeks at MIT told her it was a Star Trek tee. On this evening, he'd paired it with some snug jeans.

Deena glanced at Tak, who made a point of looking away.

"Well? What do you say?"

She turned back to Mike. "I—I guess so."

"Great!" Mike led her to a seat across from John and took one across from Tak.

Deena lowered herself into her chair and gave John a sheepish smile. He responded with a short wave that was more fingers than hand. John turned to Tak and whispered something. Tak whispered back. When John turned back to Deena, he was all smiles.

He stood abruptly and offered a hand across the table. "John. John Tanaka. Pleased to meet you." His gaze was steady, as challenging as Tak's handshake.

Deena stood, aware of the attention of the entire Tanaka family. "Deena Hammond," she said quietly.

"If Michael can reign in his unadulterated eagerness, I will, in fact, offer formal introductions to all," Daichi said, taking a seat at Deena's left hand, his variation of an apology to John for supposed rudeness.

A blush colored Deena's cheeks as Michael mumbled "Sorry." With Tak, John, and Kenji across from her, she felt as though under a firing squad

Daichi glared at Mike a moment longer as if to ensure his silence, and then turned his attention to the elderly woman at the head of the table.

"Deena, this is my mother Yukiko Tanaka. *Okasan*, this is Deena Hammond, a colleague of mine."

She was a regal figure, short and wraithlike, with bone-straight, glossy black hair running the length of her back, bronzed skin, and wide, expectant eyes. When she spoke, her voice was no surprise—silken and aged, soothing.

Yukiko rose, her diminutive stature leaning over the table, and offered Deena a tiny hand. Deena stood and took it. Here was Daichi's mother, Tak's grandmother. It seemed to Deena that everything she now was, was somehow because of this stranger.

"It's a great honor, Mrs. Tanaka."

She lowered her gaze. "Likewise, I am sure."

The old woman found her seat again, careful not to sit on her silken locks. Daichi turned to the fat man with the comb-over at the left hand of his mother. "And this is my brother, Yoshiaki."

Deena stood, attempting to stifle astonishment. It was this man, with the beer belly and the greasy comb-over, that was John's father, Daichi's brother—not the man at the other end in peak physical condition.

Yoshiaki offered a hand. His mouth was stuffed with what appeared to be rice, though no one else was eating. He glanced at his palm, spotted grease, and wiped it on his pants. When he offered it again, Deena took it reluctantly.

Across from him, Daichi glared.

Deena met Yoshiaki's wife next, John's mother June. A wide-eyed and angular woman with stringy brown hair and a smidgeon of freckles, she had a wide mouth with pink lips and a catty laugh that she reacted to everything with. She was white.

They had another daughter, a teenage girl named Lauren, as slim as she was solemn. Dark makeup circled her eyes and painted her lips, a gross contrast to her pale pallor. When she greeted Deena, she used no words, only a hand, the fingernails of which were painted black.

The man Deena had been certain would be Daichi's brother was actually his brother-in-law. Ken Wantanabe, a microbiologist for the Centers for Disease Control. He and Daichi's sister, Asami, had a five-year-old daughter named Erin, who seemed to simmer more than sit. Deena thought her adorable.

And she met Tak's mother, Hatsumi Tanaka. A slender beauty, she had alabaster skin, creamy and polished, ebony salon-styled curls, and mournful gray eyes. She wore a silk white blouse and creased gray slacks. Her makeup was daring yet well done, shimmering silver above the eyes, a hint of blush for the cheeks, and lips the color of cherries. She looked flawless.

It was only when she stood and clasped Deena's hand that her awe-binding spell was broken. Her touch felt cold, too cold, and with it came the memories of stories Deena had heard. Of neglect and alcohol, of indifference to everything.

Still, she was beautiful.

The spread before them was impressive. She'd never seen such an assortment of fresh seafood in one home. Boiled Maine lobster, raw oysters, and steamed mussels shared space with an assortment of sushi and sashimi, gyoza or steamed dumplings, miso soup and soup of another kind, clear with large prawns in it. There was soba with sliced duck breasts, shrimp and chicken tempura, steamed white rice, fried rice, and a few steaming one-pot dishes that Deena couldn't identify.

"Everything looks so delicious," Deena said to no one in particular.

"My mother is quite the chef," Daichi said. "She's the one to thank for such a lavish meal."

He lifted the miso soup, ladled out a bit into the porcelain bowl before him, then passed it to Deena. She took some and felt the incredulous eyes of Tak and Kenji on her, both of whom knew that she didn't care for miso soup.

"I find it fascinating that you're an architect," Michael said suddenly. "It isn't a field with a lot of women, let alone beautiful women."

Daichi's spoon clattered to the table.

"Will you force her to listen to your nonsense endlessly? Even sweatshops allow lunch breaks."

John snickered into his hand.

"But I was just making conversation, *oji!*"

Daichi returned to his soup. "Well, do a better job."

They ate in silence, and after the soup, passed around trays of seafood and sushi. People plucked at random. Deena took some of everything so she wouldn't seem impolite. She also took only a little, as taking the last of anything she knew would be rude.

Michael slid a one-pot dish toward her. "This is especially good, if you like beef."

Deena peered into the dish. She spotted soba noodles, firm tofu, slices of beef, cabbage, and mushrooms.

"It's sukiyaki," Michael said. "You know, there's a great fable about sukiyaki and a medieval nobleman. It goes like this. One day—"

"Michael, maybe you should just let her get some before it gets cold," his mother suggested hastily.

Again, John snickered.

"Could you not have quite so much fun?" Tak whispered.

His cousin turned serious with the scolding.

Deena grabbed bits of the sukiyaki with the back of her chopsticks and shot John a warning look. He returned it with wide-eyed innocence.

Tak's grandmother, Yukiko, cleared her throat. "And how is your art these days, Takumi?"

Tak's glare melted. "It's good, *baachan*. Just a few weeks ago I had a gallery showing in Manhattan, the most profitable to date."

His grandmother beamed. "Your art inspires people. Even your grandfather said so."

Tak shrugged. "There's always room for improvement."

"And your music? Do you keep up with that, still?" John's father, Yoshi asked.

Daichi scowled. When Tak was a boy he had music lessons three days a week—piano and violin. One summer with Yoshi and the boy returned with a knack for the drums and a need for a guitar. When Daichi refused to buy him either, his uncle did, and Tak taught himself.

"You know I practice." Tak simulated a guitar riff, and Yoshi grinned, his mouth was brimming with rice.

"So, you studied architecture at MIT, huh? A difficult program to get into," Michael said. "But then again, aren't they all?" he chortled obnoxiously.

Deena shrugged. "I suppose so."

She brought white rice to her mouth with chopsticks.

But Michael mistook her indifference. "You suppose so? You must be a sharp one. But I knew that already since you work for my *oji*."

Deena massaged her temple tiredly.

"So, were you an active participant in the social scene?"

"No. Not really," Deena whispered. She openly searched for a rescuer, but found no takers.

"Funny. I would've pegged you for a folk dancer, easily."

Tak dropped his utensils. Michael glanced at him and turned back to Deena, unfazed.

"I was very active with the Science Fiction Society and the Model Railroad Club. You probably had friends in one or both."

Deena sighed. How was it that Tak and John and Kenji could all be so warm and funny, and this guy—this guy could be so . . . *awful?*

"You know, there are times when I find myself missing MIT," Michael said, dunking his gyoza in soy sauce before dropping it into his mouth. "Are you the same way?"

"No." Instantly, her curtness embarrassed her. "It was . . . too cold for my tastes."

Michael grinned and nodded as though he were privy to some great inside joke. "Indeed, indeed. Still, there are times when I wish for that old school spirit, you know?"

Deena scooped a sliver of beef out of her dish and ate it. She had no idea what he wanted her to say.

"We should've crossed paths on campus at least once. And I know we didn't, because I would remember a face as pretty as yours."

Both Daichi and Tak glared openly at him.

"What?" he finally said.

Deena met Tak's gaze. He was pissed. At Michael, at Deena, and at himself. She could see it. She shot him a look of pity, hoping to convey that she was suffering as much as he, but he met it with a hard, indifferent glare.

"Perhaps you would allow Ms. Hammond to enjoy her meal instead of feeling obliged to humor your fruitless advances," Daichi said.

"Hey, come on, Daichi. Don't start that."

That was Yoshi.

Daichi turned to his brother. "You've something you'd like to say, Yoshiaki?"

"No. He does not. And neither do you," their mother answered. Everyone fell silent.

"Maybe after dinner I can show you some of the sights here," Michael offered.

Deena could feel Tak's eyes on her.

"Um, no. Tak—Takumi has volunteered to do that."

"Oh?" Michael looked from Deena to Tak, paused at the thinly veiled annoyance on his cousin's face, and then turned back to her. "Okay. Maybe some other time."

When dinner ended, John made eye contact with Deena and nodded toward the back door. He stepped out onto the terrace, and she followed.

"Quite the show you've got going." He closed the sliding glass behind them.

Deena sighed. "So is Tak ready to commit domestic violence or what?"

John grinned. "You'd have to cop to a relationship for it to be domestic violence."

"Is that your legal opinion?"

John snorted. "Hey, toots, you're pretty and all, but if this goes down, I'm Tak's lawyer not yours." He paused, slipped a hand in his pocket.

"Tell me something, Deena. I'm just curious here. You guys have been at this thing awhile now. I mean, formally, for close to three years, and informally, even longer. How long do you keep things up like this?"

Deena frowned. "Now you sound like Tak."

"No. I sound like a guy who's about to get caught between his brother and his cousin—a cousin of which happens to be his best friend."

She ran a hand over her face and through wayward curls before exhaling in fatigue. "I don't know, John. I don't know what I'm doing. I'm just hanging on by a thread—trying to keep everything and lose nothing, when I'm not even sure if that's possible. I just wish that I could—"

She fell silent when the doors opened and Mike stepped outside.

"So, uh, post-Renaissance, you say, huh?"

Deena blinked at John, slow to catch the tactic. "Oh, yeah. Post-Renaissance."

Desperately, she searched for an application to the phrase. "Well, there was more unity in construction back then. And, uh— and more consciousness of the surroundings, at least as far as designing was concerned."

"At least," John said distractedly, his eyes on his brother.

"Now this is a new interest," Michael said. "John and architecture."

John scowled. "Mom and Dad thought the same thing when they saw you talking to a girl."

Michael's smile faded. "Pretty enough to tear brothers asunder, huh?"

John sighed. "I'm bailing. Talk later, Deena."

She watched him go with reluctance.

"Maybe I should go, too."

Michael nodded. "Alright, then. I'm sure we'll talk again."

Chapter Forty-eight

Deena sat in the window seat of her bedroom and admired her view of the Pacific. The waters were dark and shimmering as the light of the full moon illuminated her face. She'd been certain Tak would come to her when the house was still and everything seemed safe. But as the hours dragged on and night crept toward morning, there was still no Tak. When Deena did fall asleep, it was with a heavy heart.

Deena woke in the night and jumped from the arm draped about her. If that weirdo went so far as to—

She turned and exhaled in relief, her heart thumping wildly. It was Tak. Deena snuggled in close, now facing him.

"When did you get here?"

He shrugged. "One, maybe two minutes ago."

"I thought you were mad at me."

"I am. I was going to slip in here and steal a little undetected sex."

Deena snorted.

"Okay. Maybe you would've detected after a second or two.

Point is, I've decided not to be mad since I agreed to do this crap, and since it's your dream to work for my dad and what-not."

Deena smiled in unfettered gratefulness. "That is why I'm so crazy about you!"

"Yeah, and I know someone who's crazy about you."

She pulled a face. "I don't like him, Tak. Not at all."

Tak grinned. "Mike has that effect on women. Now if only we were a couple, I could just tell him to go away." He brought a finger to his chin as if contemplating a solution.

"Not mad, remember? Not even passive aggressive."

His gaze narrowed. "Not sure I agreed to that one."

"I see. You know, John warned me you might resort to domestic violence. He said that if you do, he'd be willing to defend you."

"John's a tax attorney. I'd probably wind up with the death penalty after slapping you."

Deena giggled. "Good. Keep that in mind when you're busy being mad."

They stared at each other, smiling, noses near touching in the dark. It still amazed her that she could be so comfortable with someone, so close without self-consciousness. She hadn't even thought it possible.

"Your grandmother's beautiful," she said. "And your mother, too."

"Uh-huh."

"And I get the joke now, about John looking like his father."

"Oh you do, now?" Tak sat up. "What are you trying to say?"

Deena sat up as well. "Nothing. I just—"

"What? That he's fat? Ugly?"

"No, Tak. I would never. I just—"

He seized her, tickling as she squirmed, as she giggled her apology. He clamped a hand over her mouth and leaned over to whisper in her ear. "I can't believe you're going to sit here and laugh in my face," he said.

"I'm not. All I said was—" her words muffled and distorted.

"And John, that poor bastard, do you see what he has to look forward to? What he'll look like in a few short years?"

Deena giggled.

"Again, with the laughing in my face." Tak sighed, finally freeing her mouth. "And Mike, Jesus, he's on the fast track there, isn't he?"

When Deena laughed this time, she clamped a hand over her mouth to stifle it. Tak frowned at her.

"You're doing it again."

He paused, as if with a thought. "And poor Lauren. Can you picture her in a few years? With that comb-over and that gut?"

This time when Deena laughed, he tickled her till she thrashed. "I'm gonna teach you some manners, little lady. Right now. Gonna give you some punishment."

He grabbed her by the wrists, pinned them overhead, and kissed her neck. His body felt lean and hard, and hers, instantly turned on.

Chapter Forty-nine

When Deena ventured into the kitchen the next morning, beckoned by the smell of coffee, she was greeted by the Tanaka women—Yukiko, Daichi's mother, June, his sister-in-law, Hatsumi, his wife, and Asami, his sister. Erin, Asami's daughter, sat at the breakfast nook swinging her feet.

"Can I get you some coffee?" Yukiko asked in that soothing voice of hers.

Deena nodded and pulled out a chair from the table. Despite the kitchen's broadness, it still pulled off a cozy feel.

She took a seat across from Asami, who sipped tea as she watched her. June took a seat next to Asami and also began to stare. Deena smiled nervously.

"So, we hear that you work for Daichi," Asami said.

Petite and pretty, she had wide dark eyes and black hair that fell to her shoulders, streaked with chestnut. Her clothes were expensive and reserved—dark tailored slacks and a sleeveless blouse; Deena recognized them from the new Dolce & Gabbana lineup.

"It's going well. We're in the middle of a major project that we're very excited about."

"Yes, yes, we know that," Asami said dismissively. "But how is it to work *for* him?"

"Oh, it must be horrible," June blurted. The women looked at each other and giggled as if they thought themselves naughty.

Deena went to work preparing her coffee. A touch of milk, two spoons of sugar. "Every architect considers it a great honor to work with him. Myself included."

June rolled her eyes. "Yes, we've been told. By him."

Again with the giggles.

Deena shifted in her seat.

"You know," Asami said, bringing a fist to her chin, "you're not what we were expecting. Not at all."

"No?" Deena said.

Asami shook her head. "When my brother said he was bringing a colleague home, well, we thought . . ."

"A man?" Deena suggested.

"Well, yes. One that was older . . ."

"And whiter," June blurted, as if oblivious to her own whiteness.

Deena grinned. "Then I must really disappoint."

"On the contrary," Yukiko said, joining them at the table. "You're a breath of fresh air."

Deena smiled at her. She couldn't help it.

"So, tell us about yourself," Asami said as she stirred her tea. "Where are you from? Where are your parents from? How many brothers and sisters do you have?"

"Well," Deena began, "I'm from Miami, and so are my parents. And as for my siblings, I have two. A brother, who's dead, and a sister. Both younger."

"Your brother is deceased? My goodness, I'm sorry. That must've been terrible for you," Asami said.

"Was it a long time ago?" June asked.

"It doesn't matter how long ago it was, June. You never get over that sort of thing," Yukiko scolded.

Deena offered a sad smile. "I cope. It's been a few years now, so, I've learned ways of dealing."

"You must be so strong," June said. "I wilt at the slightest bad news."

"And she means it," Asami said. "She was inconsolable when they cancelled *Sex in the City*."

They all laughed, June included. And Deena wondered when had she last sat with women and did something as simple and pure as laugh. Maybe never.

Asami stood and began clearing dishes. June rose to help her.

"You're so young," Yukiko said. "Your family must be awfully proud."

Deena lowered her gaze and said nothing. But when she looked up, she had their undivided attention.

"Anyone would be," Yukiko continued softly, as if sensing something just beneath the surface.

Deena sighed. *Would you?* she wanted to ask.

Wanted to, but didn't dare.

Chapter Fifty

They didn't work that first day, on Christmas Eve, or on the second, Christmas Day. Though there were no lights and mistletoe or none of the traditional trappings of a Christmas, there was still a decidedly festive atmosphere.

Deena spent the morning on the terrace chatting with the Tanaka women about nonsense matters like clothes and makeup, movies and celebrity gossip. Afterward, June took her into the bathroom and demonstrated a few techniques for concealing her freckles.

The women marveled at how well Deena coped with being away from her family on Christmas Day. It was all she could do not to smile. Somehow, she didn't miss the shouting and fighting, or the crass and belligerent way the Hammonds celebrated the holidays.

That afternoon Daichi and Yoshi stood before the stainless steel gas grill with its six individual burners and watched the meat cook. Behind them, their children splashed in the pool and sunned on the deck. Deena stretched out on a lounge chair, her face in a book as Michael sat next to her with a smear of sunblock on his nose.

"You know, Daichi, you should've gotten a charcoal grill. The food would taste better," Yoshi said.

Daichi prodded a skewer of chicken, onions, and green peppers. "Charcoal masks the tastes of food. Propane provides a purer experience."

Yoshi scowled at him. "Dad used a charcoal grill for thirty years, and you never complained."

"If you wanted your food from a charcoal grill, Yoshi, you should've brought one," Daichi said idly.

Yukiko arrived with a tray of seasoned chicken and Daichi added them to the grill. He basted half with barbecue sauce and the other half with sweet teriyaki.

"Where's the yakitori?" Yoshi demanded.

"There is no yakitori," Daichi snapped. "There are chicken breasts and wings, legs and thighs, beef and pork ribs, lamb chops and steak, hamburgers and hot dogs. Certainly even a man with an appetite as robust as yours can be sated with this selection."

Yukiko's eyes narrowed. "Daichi . . ."

"Humph. Well, when did you start adding lamb chops to the menu?" Yoshi demanded. "Was that after you made the first or second million?"

Daichi sighed. "There are some of us with more discerning palates," he said carefully. "I am one, and Ms. Hammond is another. But for you there are hot dogs."

"When we were kids hot dogs suited you just fine," Yoshi countered.

"Yes, and you enjoyed flying kites and playing baseball." Daichi lowered his gaze to his brother's stomach. "But clearly you've given that up."

"Daichi! You know that your brother struggles with his weight! You should support his efforts, not ridicule them."

Daichi closed the lid on the grill. "I'll be sure to do that, as soon as I witness them."

Yukiko sighed. "Daichi—"

"No, *okasan*, it's okay." Yoshi drew up to his full weight, turned to Daichi, his stomach round and solid looking beneath the tuck of his Polo shirt. "Maybe I'm not some hotshot architect that people look up to. And maybe I'm not rich and fit and important. But I'd rather have people like me than fear me."

Daichi eyed him with amusement. "Then you're a fool."

Yoshi squared off, fists clenched. "This fool might not have your money, but he could teach you a thing or two about being a father."

Daichi nodded. "Foremost among fatherly duties is the ability to provide shelter for your brood. Take you, for example, Yoshi. You still find it necessary to rely on your mother for monetary assistance from time to time in this regard."

Yoshi turned to Yukiko, his face beet red. "You told him? You told him about the house?"

Yukiko looked from one son to the other with helplessness. "I had no choice. There was no one else that had that much money."

She'd called Daichi only when Yoshi faced imminent foreclosure.

"But you let me think it was from you."

"You wouldn't have taken it otherwise, Yoshi!"

Yoshi stormed past his mother, pride tarnished. There was now something else his brother could lord over him, a debt of $13,000 that could never be repaid.

With a sigh, Deena closed both her paperback and eyes. Clearly, Michael Tanaka would allow for no reading today.

"We should go dancing sometimes," Michael said. "I know you wouldn't think it, but I'm a great dancer. Not as good as my brother, mind you, but not many people are."

Deena lowered her shades. "John's a good dancer?"

She thought back to the nightclub in Manhattan and his spastic thrusts.

"Are you kidding me? When we were growing up, John used to run with this group called . . . Explosion, I think it was." He shook his head. "They did all kinds of stuff. Like crazy, break dancing, break-your-neck kind of stuff. I mean, the guy was amazing. You show him anything and he can repeat it right back to you, just like that. It's insane."

Deena sat up. "John? John Tanaka?"

Michael scowled. "You know, you should really hang out with more Asians. You'll find that we're a lot more than the stereotypes people attach to us."

Deena nearly laughed. "I spend plenty of time with Asian people, thank-you-very-much."

Michael sat up. "So, you're not adverse to . . . dating one?"

Deena sighed. "Of course not."

"And do you think you could find an Asian guy attractive? Sexy, even?"

"The right one, yes."

He smiled. "That's good to hear."

It didn't seem to occur to him that he might not be the right one.

Mike followed Deena's gaze to the pool where Tak and John were midway through a game of water volleyball.

"I know you wouldn't think it," Michael said, "but I'm quite the athlete. As children, that was a sport I managed to dominate."

Deena had heard enough stories of Michael's childhood— sprains during tee-ball, nosebleeds in flag football, and fractures during Frisbee, to recognize a lie when she saw one.

"Really, now?" she said dully.

"Oh, absolutely. Athleticism comes natural to me—a rarity when combined with my academic prowess," he said earnestly.

"Well, then, you shouldn't let me keep you from doing what comes naturally to you," Deena said, giving a nod toward the game.

Michael blinked. "Are you kidding me? Even the excitement of competition pales in comparison to you."

His flattery nauseated her. Deena shifted and sighed in relief when she spied John climbing from the pool. He reached a towel, dried himself, and approached.

"Deena, let's walk."

"Walk where?" she said.

John raised a brow. "Does it matter?"

Already she was getting up.

~*~

"Daichi, your brother looks up to you. And your words effect him," Yukiko said, closing the patio door. "And too often, you're careless with them and his feelings."

"*Okasan*, if my words were important to him, he would not be a used car salesman with a wife and three children he can barely support," Daichi said with forced evenness. He glimpsed Yoshi just on the other side of the glass door, peering at the grilling meat. Daichi scowled.

"You're not being fair, Daichi. Yoshi did what he thought was best, given the circumstances. Both your father and I were proud of him for the tough decisions he's made."

Daichi stared at his mother. "I see."

"*Musuko*, don't say it like that."

"Like what?"

"Like nothing. Just try to treat your brother better."

Daichi nodded. "Fine. Are we done here?"

Yukiko sighed. "I suppose so."

"Good. Now please excuse me, Mother. I have . . . culinary duties to attend to."

Forced indoors by the rain, Deena and the Tanakas took their meal and settled in at the dining-room table. They drew her into their conversations effortlessly, interspersing talk of sports and food and travel destinations with questions about her. When Daichi presented her with a Christmas gift afterward, she was grateful for Tak's warning that he might do just that. He gave Christmas presents to Christian colleagues, he said, as a matter of good business practice. It wasn't a far cry from Tak, who'd given her diamond studs that morning and insisted he wanted nothing in return. Still, Deena was glad that she'd taken the time to find a gift for Daichi.

Daichi unwrapped the paper carefully, folded it, and set it aside before opening the box. Deena watched cautiously, nerves taut, as he lifted the first book.

"*Structure and Nature,*" he read. "*Finding Harmony in Discordance.*" He chuckled.

He dug for the next treat.

"*Organic Architecture: Molding Earth and Form.*" And finally, "*Nature and the Artificial: Man's Arrogance in Architecture.*"

"The lady doth protest too much," Daichi teased.

She smiled. "Until I have my way."

"Your way," Daichi laughed, "would be an onslaught of low-income housing, all with beachfront access, fitness centers, and the latest in architectural innovation."

"Affordability and innovation aren't necessarily divorced."

Daichi grinned. He found her youth and compassion refreshing.

"No," he agreed. "But affordability and the wealthy architect are." Daichi tipped his glass to her and took a drink.

"Well done! Bravo!" Yoshi clapped. "The sooner you abandon your principles the sooner you can be rich. My brother here can offer you all the guidance you need on that."

"Yoshi," June said. "It's a holiday. And we're all having such a good time."

"Yoshi is welcome to air his grievances holiday or otherwise. He's certainly entitled to a few, considering the substandard life he's forced to endure." Daichi sipped his tea.

"Daichi. Yoshiaki. That's quite enough," Yukiko warned.

"Yes, yes, remind us again of how important you are. My brother on the cover of *Time* and *People* and *Newsweek.* Daichi Tanaka, the most important Tanaka. Everyone take note!"

"The most important Tanaka?" Daichi laughed. "And what does that distinction require? A university degree?"

Tak sighed. John rubbed his face tiredly.

"Daichi!" Yukiko cried. "You've gone far enough!"

Daichi shrugged indifferently. "Perhaps."

Deena looked from Daichi, in his white button-up and navy slacks, legs crossed, and sipping iced tea as though he were bored, to Yoshi, his face bloated and red, mouth working without speaking, food forgotten.

~*~

Michael sat on Kenji's bed, surveying the spread of comic books. Each one seemed to impress more than the last, and he lifted them with the respect and admiration of a long-time fan.

"You've got a few vintage here, Kenji. *DC Marvel vintage.* How'd you ever get this stuff?"

Kenji shrugged. The DC Marvel stuff was for bragging rights only. He still preferred his graphic novels. "Got it on eBay. How else?"

"Having a rich dad must be awesome." Mike picked up yet another book.

Kenji thought about his uncle's job as a used car salesman. "At least your dad was home a lot."

Michael laughed. "Too much if you ask me." He paused. "Can I ask you something, Kenji?"

Kenji glanced at him. "Yeah, sure. What is it?" He began stacking his comics in order of release, making neat piles on his nightstand.

"Deena's beautiful, isn't she?"

Kenji froze. "What?"

"That girl, Deena. The one that works for your dad."

Beads of sweat peppered Kenji's forehead. "Yeah. What about her?" He was having trouble breathing.

"I saw you with her today. On the beach. You must've spent hours with her. And you guys went for ice cream afterward, didn't you?"

Kenji swallowed. "Yeah."

"Well, tell me about her. What's she like?"

Kenji stared at him. "I—I don't know." He lowered his gaze. "I don't really know her."

"Kenji, come on. You're with her all the time. Today you were with her forever. What did you talk about? What did you learn? What did she laugh at?"

Kenji shook his head. "I don't know what to tell you. I don't know what she likes. And we just talked about stuff. Baseball. Comic books."

He was lying, of course. They'd talked about him screwing up and greeting her like an old friend on the staircase. They'd talked about the way he dusted the opposition in last year's state championship. And they'd laughed about Michael not being able to take a hint.

"So she likes comic books? I knew it!" he leapt to his feet, thrilled. "I knew I'd have so much in common with her. I just felt it. This meant-to-be thing." He began to pace. "I'm putting everything I've got into winning her over. And I want you to help me."

Kenji wiped his forehead. It was damp. Really damp. *"But why?"* he whined inadvertently.

"Why what? Why do I want to win her over?"

"Yea—yeah. I mean, why do you have to want her so bad?"

Michael shook his head. "Because she's beautiful, Kenji! That hair. And those eyes. And she's smart. I'm willing to bet she's brilliant. And that's the sort of woman I was meant to be with."

He stopped pacing. "You know what, Kenji? I think I'm in love with her."

"What? No! You can't be." Disbelief marred his face.

Michael stopped and gave him a once-over, as if seeing him for the first time. "Ohhh. I get it. You like her too, huh? A little boyhood crush?"

"No! God, no. She's like a sis—" Kenji bit down. "Listen, I don't like her. Not the way you think."

Hurriedly, he lowered his gaze to the stack of comics. God, where was Tak when he needed him? Or a flight to Miami? "Besides," Kenji muttered disagreeably, "you barely even know her."

Michael shrugged at the minor inconvenience. "That's why I need your help. Help me get to know her. Everything I try seems wrong. I can't make any progress. Find out what she likes for me. You're a kid. She'll trust you. She'll think you're adorable."

Kenji shook his head. "I can't help you, Michael. I can't talk to her, I can't—"

"What do you mean you can't talk to her? You just spent the whole afternoon with her! Make her laugh again, then slip in a good word about me."

Kenji closed his eyes. What could he say? Denying Michael this would cause him to wonder. Yet, helping him would be betraying his brother. He needed a compromise. Or at least, the appearance of a compromise.

He sighed. "Alright, Michael, alright. I'll help you."

Chapter Fifty-one

After a robust breakfast of steak and eggs, Daichi and Deena retreated not to the study as she'd expected, but to the terrace to work. Donning a floppy straw hat, sundress, and sandals, she followed Daichi out, amused once again by his casual attire. On this day, it was a crisp oxford, sleeves rolled up, tan chinos, and a pair of Italian leather loafers. Daichi minus a jacket still looked strange.

He led her to what was undoubtedly the most impressive patio furniture she'd ever seen. Curved wicker benches of a deep espresso, padded with thick couture cushions, surrounded a round glass table adorned with bone china settings for four. An oversized umbrella in a soft cream shaded them. They had prime viewing of the private stretch of beach and the volleyball game Tak and John, Kenji and Mike were about to start.

Tak was shirtless, his bronzed chest sweat-glistened under the morning sun. He ran a hand through his hair, saturated and falling into his eyes. Deena exhaled.

"Are you fan?"

Deena blinked. "A what?"

"A fan. Are you a fan of volleyball?" He opened his briefcase, never taking his eyes off her.

"No. Well, not really."

"Yet they seem to have your attention."

"No, I was just . . . thinking that . . . someone should tell them not to . . . play so soon after eating," she finished lamely.

"I see. Would you like to take a moment to do so?"

Deena blushed. "Of course not. We have work to do. And in any case, they should know better."

Daichi nodded. "Agreed. Now let us get to work."

They labored through lunch, triple-checking their work as they snacked on finger sandwiches and sipped iced tea. Deena ignored her cell phone as it vibrated, certain it was her grandmother yet again. She had this well developed habit now of making frantic calls when Deena was out of town.

Deena turned her phone off and pushed through the sludge that was their work. And when Daichi set aside their stacks of paper and eyed Deena with interest, she stared back warily.

"Something on your mind, Daichi?"

"A curiosity. Unrelated to work."

Now she really was nervous.

"Okay," she said with forced evenness.

He cleared his throat. "I find you to be a capable architect, Deena—more than capable even. Talented, astute, driven. So, my question to you is this. What has consumed you so singularly?"

"Sir?"

Daichi nodded as if her hesitation were due to something reasonable and other than confusion.

"I should hardly expect your candor without offering you such accessibility." He leaned back in his seat.

"My success as an architect was at the expense of my wife and children. There are times when the reality of that consumes me. It prompts me to toil, to accomplish more, as if said accomplishments can assuage the bitterness of sacrifice. So, I'll ask you again. What has consumed you? What sacrifice have you made in the name of architecture that now requires such relentless commitment?"

She lowered her gaze. "Maybe I'm just ambitious."

"You are," he conceded. "But burdened, as well."

She swallowed. When she spoke next, her eyes were on the crumb-laden dish before her and not on her boss.

"When I went away to college my brother Anthony was eleven and my sister Lizzie, eight. They did all the things kids at that age do. Anthony would draw and do puzzles, and Lizzie, well . . . Lizzie was content with finger painting and dolls."

Deena shifted, paused.

"When I returned from MIT my brother was a drug dealer with two years left to live and my sister, well, my sister was already quite adept at giving out sexual favors."

The words didn't shock him the way she thought. He nodded as if he'd expected something so sordid. "And your parents? What of them?"

"My father's dead, and my mother's in prison."

"Am I to presume they're related?"

Deena nodded, suddenly feeling tired.

"And . . . you blame her? For the fate of your brother and sister?"

Deena sighed. "I blame her. I blame me. I don't know."

Daichi fingered the doily at his table setting. "It is—the burden of an oldest child to accept responsibility for all things. I too am guilty of this."

He looked up. "Have you ever—inquired as to her motivations for murder?"

"No." Deena lowered her gaze. "No."

"I see." And to Deena, it seemed as though he did see.

She looked up suddenly. "Plenty of people have made a success of their lives without having a mother. I'll do the same."

"I suspect that you will."

Their eyes met, and he looked sincere. Deena smiled.

Daichi swallowed the last of his tea and began to stack papers. He placed them in his briefcase.

"Are we done so soon?"

"Yes. Perhaps a stroll might do us some good."

Deena looked up and spotted Kenji, the lone straggler from that morning's volleyball game, sitting on the beach, watching waves.

"Maybe Kenji could use some company," she said softly.

Daichi glanced at the boy, and for a second, a look of uncertainty crossed his face.

"Actually, I believe there's some unfinished business that requires my attention."

"I see," Deena said.

He picked up his briefcase and turned to leave.

"You know, Daichi . . ." she said.

"Yes?" He looked up.

She had no idea what to say. She glanced over at Kenji and couldn't help but feel that in her silence, she was betraying him.

"You have to confront it," she said. Instantly, she wanted the words back.

"What?"

She looked at Kenji again. "The thing that consumes you. I think you—I think we have to confront it."

He stared at her, for an eternity it seemed, though truly he didn't seem to see her. Finally, he offered a short nod.

"Perhaps," he said softly. "Perhaps."

Daichi headed for the door again, stopped, and faced her. "You should know that I haven't been completely honest about my requiring your presence here, at this time."

Deena froze.

"Claudia Oppenheimer has a home about an hour north of here in Beverly Hills. She's considering your proposal to come on board as the interior decorator for Skylife. But she would like to meet you first. On Thursday."

He disappeared.

Chapter Fifty-two

John wondered how his brother could ever miss the signals between Tak and Deena. The gazes and lingering smiles, the innuendos and "accidental" touching. Just the day before Tak inadvertently called her "muffin" or "cinnamon" or some other kind of digestible nonsense. It was enough to nauseate a man.

John and Tak stood on the terrace, their eyes on Deena as they spoke. She lay poolside, a book in her hand, a red two-piece on her body. It fit like wet latex on curves.

"So, why didn't you bring Allison?" Tak asked casually.

John glanced at him. "You kidding me? Allison and Daichi? I want no part of that."

"It's inevitable though."

"Yeah. This from the guy who was just 'introduced' to his girlfriend of the last three years."

Tak rolled his eyes. "Don't remind me."

"Of course, I will. I'll remind you every time I'm feeling self-righteous."

Chapter Fifty-three

You wouldn't help me 'cause your brother wants her!"
Michael stormed into Kenji's room.

"What?" Kenji sat up. He was getting so confused. He just
wanted to go back to Miami, where keeping this farce up was easy.

"Your brother tells me that he's interested in Deena, too. And
that's fine! I just know where your allegiances are now."

Michael paused. "Just promise me you won't help him. He
doesn't need help."

"Help with what?" Kenji cried.

"With her! Help pursuing her. A guy like Tak doesn't need
help!"

Kenji frowned. "I think you should sit down and talk to Tak
about all this. He can help you understand. And keep me out of
it. This is between you guys, anyway."

Mike paused. "Is he in his room?"

Kenji breathed a sigh of relief. "Yeah. He should be."

Michael padded down the dark hall toward Tak's room. As he
walked, he thought about what he would say. He would reason

with him. Make him see that there were plenty of girls that he could have, plenty that he had had. Why not leave this one to Mike? For Tak, it was all the same anyway.

Mike raised a hand to knock on the door and froze midmotion.

The sounds were muted, but distinct. He'd know them anywhere. He had a monstrous pay-per-view bill that could attest to his intimate knowledge of those sounds. He cracked the door slightly, praying that it didn't squeak. It didn't, and he peeked in. It took a few moments for his eyes to adjust to the darkness, but when they did, the heavens blessed him. The faint spring of coils, the moaning, and then two bodies coming into focus. He could see them, and it was incredible.

She was beautiful, even from that side view—*especially* from that side view. Her hair curled like a waterfall, and her breasts swayed as though they were heavy. Mike was certain they were heavy. Tak's hands were at her waist, and he was guiding her, balancing her, heaving the full weight of her atop him. And she was begging for him. God, she was begging for him.

Tak and Deena. Tak and Deena. Mike bit on his fist, struggling to understand what this meant. But he could hardly think clear. Not with her before him and naked.

But what did it all mean? They'd met days ago, and yet Tak, ever the ladies' man, was here making love to her.

Maybe she was one of those new age girls, free and in tune with her body, who sought sexual gratification constantly and made a practice of exploring their sexuality. He wondered if she'd been with a woman, or if she'd had multiple partners at once.

Mike looked down at his erection, then back and forth between the bedroom and down the hall. Much as he wanted to, he dared not nurse it. There were about half a dozen things wrong with this situation, and him doing something about his arousal would add a dozen more. He turned his attention back to the pair.

He had to rethink his approach. Anyway, he should've known better. She was an intelligent woman and beautiful, painfully beautiful. What made him think that she would want what every other woman wanted, when she was clearly like no other woman? A woman as brilliant as this must have boundless desires and an open and progressive attitude. The thought excited him. He'd approached her time and again, appealing to her intellect, her interests. But his cousin had shown him the way.

Mike would appeal to her appetite.

Chapter Fifty-four

Claudia Oppenheimer was a tall and svelte German woman with platinum blond hair and a body like an exclamation point. The fur about her neck sat brushed to a gloss, worn in spite of the warmth. Oppenheimer positioned herself across from Daichi, who wore an oxford with the sleeves rolled up, and Deena, whose short-sleeved blouse was the most appropriate for the weather.

Oppenheimer, who sat taller than both Daichi and Deena, looked down a beak of a nose as she spoke. The conversation she insisted upon was completely irrelevant and consisted of what Deena thought of men who played polo or women who gouged on strawberries. When she confessed that she had no idea such women existed, Oppenheimer laughed as though Deena had a knack for comedy. Daichi sat through it all, pain-faced and quietly obliging, leaving Deena to do most of the talking.

In the end, Oppenheimer agreed to come on board. Deena's aura was pleasing, and her palate sensible, and with that, they could form a formidable team, Oppenheimer said. Deena and

Daichi exchanged a look of curiosity, a look of "what-the-fuck" as Tak was fond of saying, before smothering a laugh they would later enjoy.

That afternoon, Tak, John, and Kenji tossed a Frisbee on the stretch of beach behind the house as Deena thumbed through a book on the art and architecture of ancient Egypt on the terrace. Intermittently, she looked up to watch Tak, shirtless and hard-bodied, wet with sweat and ocean water as he moved. At least once, she shivered.

"Deena," Michael said, appearing at the back door. "Just the person I was looking for. Mind if I join you?" He took a seat on the swing without need of her answer.

Mike reached over and lifted her book for a peek. "Ancient Egypt, huh? That mind of yours doesn't rest. Not even on vacation."

Deena met his gaze. "I'm not on vacation. You are."

He nodded. "Sorry, I forgot." He took a deep and dramatic breath. "Deena, I've something to tell you. I—I think you're breathtaking."

She lowered her book with a sigh. "Michael, I'm not in the market for a boyfriend."

He nodded. "No, no. I understand."

He leaned forward and whispered in her ear. "I know what it is that you want. And I want to give it to you."

"Give it to me?" Deena echoed. She leaned back to place a buffer between the two of them.

"Yes. I know what you need, and I'm man enough, mature enough, to give it to you. You want to be free. You want sexual freedom. I can give that to you. I'm telling you, I'd give you anything."

"I want *what?*" Deena echoed, confused.

"Exploration. And I don't mind. I have to be honest with you. The moment I saw you, I was breathless. I'd do anything to be with you. I'd—"

"Mike, wait. There's something you're not understanding."

"No, I understand. And I'm okay with it. You might not think it, but I can please you. Just give me a chance. Try me out."

Deena stood, her book clattering to the floor. "I don't know what you're talking about, but I want you to stop talking about it."

"Just think about it," Michael said, kneeling to scoop up the book. He paused to dust it off. "I know your type, and I know that in certain circles, your lifestyle isn't acceptable."

"My *lifestyle?*"

"Yeah. I mean, I don't use words like 'slut' or 'whore.' They're judgmental and sexist. But we're missing the point. I don't want to be cumbersome. We could start with a one-night stand if you want, no commitment, of course, and—"

"A *what?* Oh my God! Get away from me!"

Deena pinwheeled back into the terrace railing, upturning a glass of lemonade in her descent.

Michael's gaze narrowed in confusion.

A few yards away, the Frisbee glided to the ground as Tak stood watching Deena fall. He took in her cowering posture, backed into the porch railing, and tore across the hot sand to reach them.

"What the hell's going on?" he demanded on arrival.

Deena's eyes watered. "He called me a slut!"

"He *what?*"

Tak turned on Mike.

Mike sighed. "That's not what I said. All I said was that girls like her tend to prefer sexual freedom."

Tak took a step closer. "Run that by me one more time."

"I said that girls like her prefer sex—"

Spittle flew with the insertion of fist to face. With a yelp, Mike toppled, blood spewing from his mouth. He staggered to the ground in stages, a hand to his face as he shrieked.

"Fuck!" Tak said. With a grimace, he shook his hand, a hand streaked with blood.

"Fuck!"

Tak's head dropped as he gripped his wrist; eyes squeezed shut, he bent forward.

Behind Tak, John and Kenji tore across the beach. When they got to the terrace, John placed a hand at Tak's chest to hold him in check.

"Feel better?" John said quietly.

"You better fucking believe it."

John grinned. "Thought so."

From his cowering position on the floor, Mike began to yell. "You hit me! Why the hell did you hit me?"

Tak took a step, only to have John push him back.

"'Cause you don't listen, Mike! She's my girl. *Mine.* And I warned you."

Mike sat up with a whimper, a hand at his nose. Blood coursed between his fingers.

"Shit," John said. He turned on his brother. "Why the hell couldn't you just back off?" He went and offered a hand. Mike slapped it away.

"You're taking his side? I'm your brother! Your goddamned brother!"

"You're an idiot is what you are." John turned to Deena. "Do you see what happened? Didn't I tell you that this would happen?"

Deena's eyes widened. "You're blaming me?"

"Shit, yeah, I'm blaming you. The only reason it didn't happen sooner is because me and Kenji have been running interference all over the goddamned place!"

"I was supposed to know Tak would break his hand on Mike's face?"

"Yeah! I did!"

John turned to Tak with a look of disgust. "Now what? You probably broke his fucking nose—and, and by the looks of you, your hand, too."

Tak winced. "I think you might be right."

John brought his palms together before his lips. "Okay. Just— give me a minute to think."

"Think? Goddammit, *do* something. He just—just punched me in the face!"

"Well, it's not like you didn't deserve it!" John cried. He shook his head and turned to his cousin.

"You see, Tak?" This is why I told you to just tell him. You know how he is. He never quits."

"I'm sitting right here," Mike said, his hand slick from the still-gushing blood.

"Well, what are we going to do? We can't just take them in the house like this," Kenji said.

"I know, I know." John looked at Tak, who clutched his wrist in an effort to steady the afflicted hand. "Are you alright?"

Tak shook his head. "The pain's killing me. And my hand's swelling up."

"Never mind me, who's bleeding to death on the floor," Mike said.

John sighed. "You should've left her alone. Daichi said so, Tak said so, and she turned you down every chance she got. I don't know, Mike, maybe this is what you needed."

John pulled his brother up and wrapped his arm around his shoulder.

"There something wrong with your legs?" he asked, wondering why it was so difficult to steady his older brother.

"I'm dizzy. I need to lie down."

John sighed. "Shit. You guys need a doctor."

Tak shook his head. "I can't go to a doctor. If my dad finds out—"

"We'll just have to make up something then."

Mike balked. "And if I don't want to go along with your lies?"

Tak took a step forward. "Then maybe I can give you a little encouragement with the hand that still works."

Mike looked from his cousin Kenji, to his brother, each with gazes devoid of sympathy. He sighed.

"Fine. What's the story?"

Chapter Fifty-five

Yukiko was no longer listening to Takumi's cumbersome explanation. She simply couldn't, lest her migraine grow worse.

They were playing football.

Michael *was playing football?*

Well, he was nearby.

Close enough for an elbow to hit him yet not in the game?

Yeah.

And your hand?

What about it? There's nothing wrong with my hand.

It looks disfigured.

Oh that. Slammed it in a door earlier.

And you played football afterward?

Uh, yeah.

Yukiko made her way to Daichi's study with thoughts of Michael's face and Takumi's hand plaguing her. Clearly the two had found one another, and she was certain she knew why.

Michael's advances toward Deena seemed to border on manhan-
dling. Anyone with more than a passing interest could see the way
Takumi squirmed when Michael made advances. Her son Daichi
failed to have more than a passing interest.

Daichi met Yukiko's tap on the door with a gruff "What?" She
bristled, despite the knowledge that he would soften once realizing his mother stood on the other side. Yukiko stepped inside as
Daichi set aside a legal pad riddled with careful print. He turned
in his custom-made swivel chair, retail price $3,000, and gave his
mother a cursory nod.

"Afternoon, *okasan*. What can I do for you?"

Daichi didn't smile at his mother, but then again, he didn't
frown either.

"It's about Takumi," she said.

Daichi's face darkened.

"What is it now? I've a great deal of work. I can't be bothered
with trivialities." Daichi turned back to his desk.

"Takumi is not a triviality. He's your son."

She shifted her weight, heavy-lidded eyes on the broad of his back.

"Are you here to lecture me, *okasan*?" Daichi's fingers formed
a steeple as he stared at his cherry wood desk. "If so, I've much
work to do."

Yukiko sighed. "What you do here is not work, Daichi. What
you do here is chase ghosts." She took a seat on the mauve leather
couch behind him as Daichi lowered his head.

"I don't know what you mean."

"You are a brilliant man. I've no doubt you do."

Yukiko nibbled on a wrinkled, painted lip as she thought about
the lavish estate that was her home, designed and built by Daichi.
She thought about the five vacation villas he owned and the jug-
gernaut that was his architectural firm.

"Time does not rewind, my child, no matter how hard and fast
you wish it so," she said.

Daichi studied his fingernails. They were manicured and shined
with the clear polish of a pampered man.

"Your sons love you. Your wife loves you. But you must repair the bridge that divides you. No one can do this for you. I think you know that."

Daichi stared through his desk, eyes glistening. He was the greatest architect the world had ever seen. *Time* said so. *People* said so. Two dozen honorary degrees said so. And yet, it was these words that pierced his heart.

"Time is escaping you, Daichi. Your stubbornness, your intolerance, your willfulness is the source of your unhappiness. And the stakes now are higher than ever."

"*Okasan*, if you have something specific to tell me, please do so."

"Alright."

Yukiko stood. "I just left the hallway, where I found Michael with a broken nose and Takumi with a broken hand. They claim that football is the culprit, but I suspect the lie is for your benefit."

Daichi sighed. He had no idea what she expected from him.

"Too often, when our children lie we lash out without looking inward. Sometimes they lie because we've closed the door to the truth. They lie because we've made telling the truth impossible. They lie because we require it."

Yukiko stood at the door, a hand on the knob.

"Whether you like it or not, Daichi, you are the eldest and head of this family. And your opinions affect everyone. In your quest for perfection, you've begun to see the world in black and white. You've made shades of gray impossible. But they will exist whether you acknowledge them or not. With your intolerance, you drive a wedge through this family. With your intolerance, you demand the lie."

Chapter Fifty-six

A **boxer's break was** what Tak had, a fracture of the knuckles that was the perfect complement to his cousin's shattered nose and concussion. Tak's injury took a cast and six weeks to heal, during which time he was unable to paint or play his guitar. His father hadn't required much of an explanation; Tak told him that Mike had simply gotten on his nerves. Interestingly enough, he took that without question.

Deena sipped iced green tea as she sat at her desk. The tea was a gift from Asami. She was at work on a Sunday, brainstorming ideas for a designing competition a few thousand years out of her league. The competition was for a so-called "City-Within-A-City," a megaresort in the Dominican Republic that would be the equivalent of an everything-and-the-kitchen-sink dive into the tourism industry. It was an architect's dream, with eighty acres of space and very few guidelines. A $7 billion enterprise, the commission alone guaranteed $560 million. Every architect in the world salivated at the venture, letting Deena know she had an ice-cream sundae's chance in hell of getting the gig. Still, it was about the process, and as she worked, she remembered Daichi's words of advice. Study the culture. Remember the culture. Reflect the culture. She wasn't sure how much it would help her though, since he was entering the competition as well.

She should've been at home, curled up with Tak and his newly freed hand. Despite the desire to earn a name for herself, she kept turning to silly and trivial thoughts. Something Tak said, something John did, something Kenji wanted. She needed discipline. In the past, she'd had it in droves. What had the Tanaka men done to her? She could only imagine the answer they'd give.

They had this way with her, Tak, and John even, of making her laugh when logic defied joy. She'd been standing in the mirror that morning, staring at her reflection, when she turned to Tak and said, "You know, one time, my grandfather told me I looked like a baboon."

He'd looked up at her with a frown as serious as it was contemplative. "You want to go kick over his tombstone?"

She'd laughed, of course, knowing he would've done it had she agreed.

Deena chastised her wandering mind. The "City-Within-A-City" was her ticket to freedom. Win that, and her days of a stingy five-figure salary with Daichi were over. She smiled.

Fantasizing was fun. And now back to work. After all, she had a full day ahead of her. A few hours at the office, a trip to Babies 'R' Us and a baby shower for an expectant fourteen-year-old. Somehow, her itinerary failed to excite her.

Deena stood in line at the Aventura Babies 'R' Us, a baby mobile in one arm, a nursing pillow in the other. She tried not to think of the gift's recipients, the fourteen-year-old girlfriend of her seventeen-year-old cousin, Shakeith, but her thoughts had a will of their own. As she stood, she pondered how such a family could exist—a helter-skelter mix of welfare receiving, low-achieving, blissfully satisfied souls content with self-destruction.

It wasn't that she believed healthy families existed apart from problems. But she knew the difference between that sort of family and one without hope. The day after Tak broke his hand on Mike's face, he pulled his cousin aside and offered an apology. It was important to him that he had his cousin's forgiveness, and for Mike, once he realized what Deena was to Tak, he was horribly embarrassed and wanted Tak's forgiveness, too. So when the cousins parted at the end of the week it was on good terms. Once, Aunt Caroline and Rhonda had argued over the price of postage stamps. The argument escalated, Caroline hit Rhonda, and the two didn't speak for a year.

Shakeith was Caroline's son. A seventeen-year-old smoker, drinker, and soon-to-be father, he idolized Deena's deceased brother, Anthony. Whenever Shakeith wanted to emphasize one thing or another, he would do so by invoking the name of his cousin. "Man, I put that on my dead cousin Tony," he'd say with a shout. Tony, who was third-in-command in the tyrannical R.I.P. gang, Tony, who moved more cocaine in and out of Liberty City than any two dealers combined, and Tony, who'd become so powerful someone believed he had to die.

Tony. It was how Deena sifted trash from treasure. Tony versus Anthony. One was a murderous gang member, the other her brother. And all it took to separate them was the dropping of three small, yet powerful letters.

Shakeith wanted to be Tony. It was in everything he said and did. In the way he'd invoke Tony's name when challenged, as though his cousin had written an evocative and compelling manual on the art of gangsta living. It was in the way he dressed and walked, that funky gait that dared onlookers to test him. And it was in his life's philosophy, that of doing as Tony Hammond would've done.

Deena gave him a year to live. Maybe a little more, but not much. A single year and the Hammonds would bury another.

Their story would be compelling were it not so commonplace. Prisons were brimming with brothers and cousins, fathers and sons, all harbored within the same maximum facility. What was impressive to Deena was the stories of those who didn't fill those walls. The Deenas and Rhondas who kept their footsteps high as they trudged through the sludge. To Deena, the honest way was the hard one, and the other, easy.

She couldn't understand the lure for Shakeith. Her brother was dead. Despite all those who had feared him, maybe even because of it, Anthony Hammond had been hunted, captured, and slaughtered.

Chapter Fifty-seven

Morning arrived without fanfare. The simple shimmer of sunlight through the windowpane woke first Deena, then Tak.

"Mmm. You feel sublime," he mumbled, running a hand down the length of her body. Immediately, he felt a familiar stirring. "I want to be inside you," he whispered, planting kisses along her neck. His body pressed against her backside as remnants of Cartier aftershave and tequila wafted in the air. She eased away from him, rubbing her eyes in an effort to become oriented. Her phone beeped, insisting there were several missed phone calls. Just as she rose to retrieve it, Tak tugged at her camisole.

"Not now, Dee. No Lizzie, no Skylife, no problems," he insisted.

She smiled at him and settled back into his arms. No problems. The idea was as seductive as the kisses he planted along her neck. The phone beeped again, and she plucked it from its resting place on her nightstand before he could stop her.

No problems.

The idea was laughable.

Deena looked at the phone's screen and groaned. "Your dad," she said, noting the missed calls. "I'd better call him," she rubbed the side of her face wearily.

"Come on, Dee, forget that." Tak pulled her into his arms impatiently, relishing the soft flesh of her backside against his chest.

He continued planting kissing along her throat, slowing long enough to appreciate the slope of her breasts and the flat of her stomach before moving on to the curve of her backside. His manhood stirred its approval, and Deena laughed sleepily.

"Is that all you do?" she asked. "Think about sex?"

Tak chuckled. "Oh, baby, I can do more than think about it."

In an instant, he was atop her, parting her legs as she laughed, pushing her back as she struggled to sit up.

"Tak!" she squealed. "Would you go back to sleep? I have to call your father!"

"Sleep?" he scoffed. "What, are you kidding me? I'm not going back to sleep and neither are you." He pushed her again. "Now stop playing hard to get! I've got a seed to plant, woman."

Deena shrieked as he began to kiss her body relentlessly, pushing aside the straps of her camisole, tugging at her panties. "Tak! Your father—"

He groaned and lifted his head momentarily. "Dee, I gotta tell you. You're killing my ego here with all this talk of my dad."

Before she could respond, he returned to her body with vigor, licking, biting, and sucking. When she cried out in delight, he lifted his head with a smile of triumph.

Tak was poised to enter her when the doorbell rang. Once, twice, three times, all in quick succession. Startled, Deena sat up, causing him to dismount her. Not easily thwarted, he attempted to reclaim his position, only to be deterred again.

She pulled on Tak's UCLA sweatshirt and an old pair of shorts before rushing to the door. As she approached, the bell rang twice more.

"Make it quick, Dee!"

Deena threw open the door, prepared to slam it provided it were a Jehovah's Witness, salesman, or some other equally unwanted rascal.

It was Daichi.

"Daichi?" Deena croaked.

He adjusted his crimson tie.

"Deena, I expect my associates to answer when I call them, and consider it highly problematic when they do not."

"Sir—"

"We need to discuss this project. *Now.*"

He pushed his way past Deena and into her apartment.

Deena's horrified gaze followed him. "This is a really bad time right now, Daichi. If you want, I can throw on something and meet you at the office."

She cast a single, sickly glance toward the bedroom.

"A bad time?" Daichi echoed in disbelief. "A bad time? Construction is stalled, Deena, and has been since yesterday afternoon. Every day it continues we burn a quarter of a million dollars. *A quarter of a million dollars!*"

Deena's mouth opened, but no words came out. She was aware of the budget, of the opposition they took for the slightest expenditure, but her mind was fodder. Tequila, fatigue, and fear muddled her thoughts. She glanced at the bedroom door again.

"You know, Deena, this is incomprehensible, and frankly, I'm stunned. Rarely have I misjudged a person's character. But you," Daichi wagged a finger inches from her nose. "You are forcing me to question your professionalism, your aptitude, and your judgment. I would recommend you salvage this ordeal, immediately."

Sickened, Deena looked from Daichi to the bedroom door yet again. She needed a moment, a moment for thinking, clarity, a plan.

Behind him something crashed.

And the bedroom door opened.

"Dee? Who was it?"

Tak stuck his head out and glimpsed only a partial view of Deena. Grinning, he pressed on. "Quit playing hard to get and climb your ass back in this bed."

When she failed to respond, he padded into the living room with a brazen smirk, intent on finishing what he'd started and froze at the sight of his father.

"Oh my God," Tak whispered. In nothing but a pair of form-fitting boxer briefs, his libido died, instantly.

Daichi looked from Deena to Tak and back again, his face a myriad of astonishment.

"Now, Dad, before you go crazy—" Tak reached for his father in an effort to calm him.

Daichi turned to his employee, his gaze narrowing. "I see your aspiration knows no bounds, Ms. Hammond."

Deena gasped.

"Dad, when we met we had no idea that you were the common denominator."

"When you met . . ."

"OK, I know what you're thinking. And you're absolutely right. We should've been more forthright. We should've been upfront. And we shouldn't have pretended that we were meeting in California for the first time. But you have to understand—"

"When you met . . ."

"*Otosan*, just—just hear me out. Please."

"How long this been going on?"

Tak cringed. "*Otosan*—"

"Don't '*otosan*' me! How long has this been going on?"

Tak swallowed, suddenly speechless, motionless. Daichi pointed an emphatic finger at the couch, and without a word, Tak sat.

"Takumi, I will not ask you again." Daichi stared at his son until he looked away with a sigh.

"Three years."

"Three—"

At this revelation it was not his son he looked at, but Deena. Deena who'd listened to his confessions of parental ineptitude, of resentment and regret, all while feigning ignorance.

"Daichi, I didn't—I never—" she shook her head. "I never told him anything you said."

This time it was Tak's turn to look up.

"What? What are you talking about, Deena?"

She looked from the elder Tanaka to the younger, desperate.

"He confided in me, about—things." She turned back to Daichi. "But I never betrayed you. Not once."

Tak's eyes narrowed, and in them, Deena saw the seeds of something new.

Distrust.

Daichi turned to his son.

"Takumi, you know I can't accept this."

Tak sighed.

"You know how I feel about this matter."

"*Otosan*, please. Just listen. I love her, and I have for years. She makes me happy. Doesn't that count for something with you?"

Daichi sighed. Here was his son, sniveling about happiness. It was always that way with Takumi, so engrossed with himself. But Daichi knew he needed look no further than a mirror for someone to blame. He'd always given his son whatever he wanted, believing it the best way to express his affections. When he turned sixteen, he bought the boy his first car, a Ford Mustang convertible, because it was what he wanted. When he graduated from UCLA, it was a three-bedroom condo in South Beach, and for his twenty-fifth birthday, a luxury yacht for cruising the Caribbean.

Daichi was most comfortable when his love could be expressed with gifts, as opposed to the emotional outpours everyone else seemed to prefer. But in showering his son with gifts, Daichi had created a man whose values did not match his own, who had no sense of the group's greater identity, who constantly sought pleasures of the self and of the flesh. Takumi, he found, knew nothing of modesty, restraint, or sacrifice and was at least to Daichi, the very antithesis of Japanese.

"This is your problem, Takumi. Everything is about you. What Takumi wants, what Takumi likes. No reason, or values, or anything. And what has Takumi decided he wants this time? A little flesh."

"And what about you, Dad? Don't you go to any lengths to get what you want? Isn't that what my whole life has been about?"

Daichi's gaze narrowed. "This is neither the time nor the place."

"No? Well, can you have Angela pencil me in and get back to me?"

Daichi's eyes narrowed to nothing. "Listen to me and listen closely. I am your father. You know better than anyone that I will not tolerate insolence. We will not revisit this. I forbid this. I forbid *this*," he pointed a finger at Deena, and like that, he'd reduced her to an object, a thing, a *this*.

"Dad." Tak's voice broke with frustration. "Don't be this way. If you just—if you knew how important she was to me," Tak sighed. "I've always done as you asked, regardless of whether we saw eye to eye. So you must know that I—I don't do this lightly."

"Takumi. What would your *ojiichan* say? What would he think?"

Tak sighed, thinking of the proud historian that was his grandfather. What *would* his *ojiichan* say?

"*Otosan*, I can't help how I feel."

Daichi closed his eyes. When would the boy learn? Learn that what mattered was not issues of the self, but of the group, the greater good.

"You're my oldest son, Takumi. You're supposed to be my pride and joy."

Daichi's head was lowered. He was no longer shouting. "When I am gone you're supposed to head this family. To preserve our history, our traditions, our way of life. You know how important this was to your *ojiichan*, how important it is to me." Daichi ran a tired hand through his hair. "I know I have not been the ideal father. Absent when I shouldn't be, whether through mind or through body, but such a thing doesn't negate your responsibilities. It doesn't negate who or what you are."

He raised his head. "You cannot be so color-blind as to erase the color from your own skin. You are not as others are. You are of Japanese blood and your history is rich and important and worthy of preservation. Know this before you know anything."

Daichi paused with the memory of him and Yoshi learning Japanese on Saturdays, going to Dharma school on Sundays, and a host of ethnic and cultural events—Hana Matsuri, Sakura Matsuri, Tango no Sekku, and the Obon street festivals. His father had been adamant about Daichi and Yoshi knowing and taking pride in their culture.

"There are things greater than you, *musuko*." Daichi looked at his son pointedly. "You must ask yourself, this woman that you love— will she follow our traditions? Will she honor your ancestors at the Obon festival? Build a *butsudan* for you, for me, when we are no longer here? Because Christians are not in the habit of fashioning altars to the deceased, no matter how much they've loved them."

Tak thought of how willing Deena had been to let things unravel because his ethnicity proved an obstacle. He thought of the lengths she went to hide who and what he was—lying, skulking, hiding indefinitely. He couldn't be certain she'd ever embrace their traditions. They hardly ever fought, but when they did, it was because he'd grown tired of deceiving his father or keeping quiet when Grandma Emma called. She'd never able to give him a straight answer as to when they could pull the shroud back from their relationship. Perhaps, she'd never intended to. Perhaps, after three years together he already had the answers to his father's questions and simply refused to accept them.

Tak stared at the floor. "I don't know what she'd do, *otosan*. I can't be sure."

Daichi stared at his son, boldly. "I'm leaving."

He turned to Deena. "And you are off the Skylife project."

"What?" she exploded. "You can't do that to me! You have no right!" It was her project, her vision, *hers*.

Daichi chuckled. "*I* have no right? *I* have no right?"

He took a single menacing step toward her. "*I* have *every* right. I am Daichi Tanaka. *That* is *my* firm. And I began it with little more than the sweat of my palm. That is *my* son, born of *my* flesh and blood. *You*, Deena Hammond, are the one with no rights."

Deena shook her head, flustered and near tears. "But this is personal. You can't kick me off for—for dating your son."

"No? How about because your project is overbudget? Or because your inaccessibility this weekend has caused an estimated loss of $2.3 million as we searched for documents that only you seem to know the whereabouts of? So, tell me, Ms. Hammond, would you find any of those reasons more to your liking?"

Deena closed her eyes, felt a tear spill. "Daichi, please. I'm begging you."

He turned away, unimpressed. "And as for you, Takumi, I will pretend that this never happened. And you will do the same."

Tak and Deena watched as Daichi smoothed his charcoal jacket, straightened his posture, and sauntered out the door. Silence followed.

"Tak?" Deena said weakly as he disappeared into the bedroom. When he emerged, he was fully dressed.

"Tak? Tak, talk to me." His silence frightened her.

He shot her a single, impatient look, brushed past her, and slammed the front door behind him.

Chapter Fifty-eight

Deena tore out the door after Tak, oblivious of the wild jutting of her two-tone curls, and barreled down the creaking staircase. She shouted his name in desperation, certain he intended to exit not only her building but her life. She found him partway down, frozen at the sound of her voice, as he waited for her to catch up with him.

"What, Deena? What do you want?" He sounded tired, anguished.

"What do I want?" Tears obscured her vision. "I want you to come back. Why did you leave like that?"

Tak took a deep breath. "Why do you want me to come back, Deena?" Still, he wouldn't look at her.

Deena searched the expanse of his back. "What do you mean? I love you. Why would you—"

He turned to face her. "Alright then. You love me? Then let's make this thing solid. When do I meet *your* family?"

"Tak," Deena shook her head in exasperation, "you can't—you know I can't let you." Deena sighed. "We keep *talking* about this!"

"Right! We keep talking about it. And it's going to keep coming up." Tak shook his head in disbelief. He took a step upward, toward her.

"Just what is your plan here, Dee? To keep me hidden forever? And just how the hell am I supposed to feel about that?" It was exactly as his father said; she wanted more from him than he should ever have to sacrifice.

"Tak, please. I love you. But you've got to understand how things are for me."

"How things are for *you*? This whole relationship has been about 'how things are for you'!"

"I know, Tak, and I love you for it. I know this is a strain on you. But this is hard for me, too. There are consequences to this relationship for me."

Tak stared at her. "And what? You haven't decided whether you're willing to accept these consequences yet?"

"That's not the point, Tak."

"No, Deena. That *is* the point. You love me? Then, dammit, you need to act like it. I mean, what kind of watered-down love is this, anyway? You love Lizzie, and you fight like hell for her. You prowl up and down the streets at God knows what hour, without a fucking thought for yourself. You love your grandmother, and you fight like hell so she'll show you an iota of affection."

Deena's nostrils flared. "Is that it, Tak? I don't show you enough love?" she sneered.

Tak shook his head. "This is such bullshit. I'm out of here."

He turned and barreled down the stairs. Deena followed.

"Don't you dare walk away from me in the middle of an argument!" she called.

"We weren't arguing. I made a statement, and I departed shortly thereafter."

"What are you now, Daichi? Smug and self-righteous?" Deena shouted as they rounded the last set of stairs.

"My father's a wise man," he said as he reached the bottom of the staircase, "and he knows exactly what he's talking about—when it comes to you, at least."

He cast her a single hard glare before taking off again. She gaped after him.

"What the hell's that supposed to mean?" She quick-stepped to meet his long stride across the lobby.

"It means just what I said."

"When it comes to me?" Deena echoed. "No way. You don't get to make some sweeping statement like that and just walk off."

Tak shot her a look before shoving open the heavy double doors that led to Collins Avenue.

"Fine, Dee. You know what it means?" Tak said as their argument spilled into the bustling sidewalk. "It means that he's a hell of a lot smarter than me. He's smart enough not to let love derail his values." He shot her a look of disdain. "But I guess you two are alike in that way."

Deena shook her head in desperation. "Tak, come on! You know I love you. God knows I do. I don't know how to be any plainer than that! If we were in a perfect world, I'd already be married to you." Deena's eyes filled with tears.

"Well, we don't live in a perfect world! So you need to decide whether you'd be married to me in this one."

He jumped into his silver Ferrari, staving off her plea with a slam of the door. Tak started the car, backed out of his space, and whipped a furious turn into the street. In their anger, both were oblivious to the wild SUV barreling toward him until too late. With the screeching of tires and the folding of metal, Deena screamed as the convertible, and the man she loved within it, were crushed.

Ruby red lights pulsed as frantic sirens signaled the severity of Tak's condition. Within the tight confines of the racing ambulance, Deena bit back the threat of hysteria as she took in his motionless body, blood-soaked clothes, and swollen blue lips.

A burly paramedic strapped a pressure cuff about Tak's arm. He paused, then frowned at the gauge.

"I've got BP at 100 and dropping!"

Deena looked in desperation from the thin redhead with the messy ponytail to the thick man with the wire frames and wondered which, if either, could save Tak's life.

"90 . . . 80 . . . 75!"

The redhead clamped an oxygen mask over his face and paused. "Shit," she said. "This guy's going into cardiac arrest!"

Deena could see nothing but Tak's dying body and the pale hands as the paramedics worked to revive him. An anguished sob tore from her lips.

They arrived at Ryder Trauma Center under a hail of red lights. Men and women in white jackets and scrubs dashed to meet them. A flurry of hands assisted in the transfer as Tak was hoisted from ambulance to hospital. Deena rushed after them blindly, padding through the smatterings of blood leaking from Tak, trailing crimson footprints in her wake.

The trauma team burst through the doors of the resuscitation room and swarmed on Tak in a blaze of needles, tubes, sponges, knives, scissors, and white jackets. Nurses worked to cut away his clothes as Deena watched in horror—the fitted tee from Old Navy, a gift from her, faded Levis with a perfect fit, and white boxer briefs, Calvin Klein—the only kind he'd wear. Two IVs went into his arms as a tiny blonde slipped a needle into the back of his hand and retrieved multiple vials of blood. A pressure cuff was strapped to him and tape patched to his chest.

The EKG screeched to life, indicating that Tak had flatlined.

"Call a code!" screamed a white jacket.

The hospital's paging system blared to life.

"Code Blue, Shock Trauma Unit. Code Blue, Shock Trauma Unit."

"No," Deena whispered. "No."

"Code Blue, Shock Trauma Unit. Code Blue, Shock Trauma Unit."

They slipped a chest tube into Tak. Crimson flooded from his torso, rushing to fill a plastic hose.

"God, please."

He couldn't do this to her, wouldn't do this to her.

"Code Blue, Shock Trauma Unit. Code Blue, Shock Trauma Unit."

Her father, her brother, and now, the man she loved. The Grim Reaper followed her, haunting her with the promise of everlasting sorrow.

Hot tears streaked Deena's cheeks. She closed her eyes and whispered a prayer wrought with grief and desperation. Never would she take him for granted again. Never, if given another chance.

"Though He causes grief,
Yet He will show compassion
According to the multitude of His mercies."

Grandpa Eddie would whisper that verse from Lamentations as he sat on the edge of his bed clutching a yellowed portrait of his son, her father, Dean Hammond—dead at twenty-eight. And as she stood there facing the frantic shriek of the EKG monitor, she whispered the verse over and over, the words pouring from her lips in a mangled mesh of despair. Tears filled her eyes as an endless stream of blood pumped from Tak's body into a container on the floor.

A white jacket turned to Deena as if seeing her for the first time. "You need to go, ma'am. There's a social worker in the hall that needs information from you. And she'll want to contact his family."

Deena thought about the life she could've had. Her life if she'd tried to stop her mother from killing her father, if she'd stayed with Anthony instead of going home the night he was murdered, and if she'd only agreed to let Tak meet her family. Her stubbornness and their argument had sent him barreling into the street. Her words had sent him to his death.

Deena paced, as if to tread a groove in the floor. Her brain went numb, her mouth dry, her eyes a flood of endless tears. In her mind, tires screeched, bones crunched, and there was yelling—so much yelling. Was it her? Was it him? God, was he really pinned by all that metal? Her stomach lurched.

They'd lived as though they had forever. And there was no excuse. Fate had given her ample warning that time and love were precious. She'd always taken him for granted, up until the last moment. She strung him along, coddling him, humoring him, ignoring his desire to have more than a cloak-and-dagger affair. In doing so, she assumed that his friendship, his companionship, his love, were all unconditional, irreversible, and timeless. A life without Tak was what she deserved—deserved for never having the guts to love without condition or to purge the demons that haunted her. And so she stood, with an hourglass in hand, and the sand all emptied out. Their time together was done.

Daichi burst into the hospital like a torpedo. His jacket unfastened, his hair tousled, his face a deep crimson.

"You!" he shouted. "What's going on with my son?" He grabbed the arm of an orderly near the entrance, who instantly appeared terrified.

"Takumi Tanaka! I demand to know his status!"

Three steps behind him a woman entered with her head lowered. Mounds of freshly styled curls cascaded about her shoulders as alabaster skin sheathed a long, graceful body. It was Hatsumi.

"Deena!"

Daichi spotted her and shoved aside the orderly, who stumbled. He closed the space to Deena and pummeled her with questions.

"Give me a status report. What's going on? Where is he? What's his condition?"

Deena shook her head, slowly. "I-I don't know."

"What? Well, is he conscious? Dead?"

"I don't know!"

Daichi stared at her, his breathing shallow; his stomach nauseated. His thoughts were muddled, incoherent, as he struggled to concentrate. He was losing control. A white-hot panic brimmed beneath the surface, threatening to overwhelm him. Sweat beaded his temples as Daichi clenched his fists, his nails piercing the palms until they bled. The pain was a distraction, and with it, he was able to refocus. He needed information. With information, he could make decisions, give orders, right this wrong. With information, Takumi would be alright.

Daichi turned his wrath to the woman at the reception desk.

"Takumi Tanaka. Right now," he slammed a fist on the desk. "Tell me what's happening."

The gray-haired woman fumbled with a folder. She was slight and mousy, cowering under the fury of Daichi Tanaka.

"Right goddamned now!" Daichi screamed. "Takumi Tanaka!"

The woman behind the counter disappeared in search of information. With his head bowed and palms flat on the counter, Daichi took a deep breath, allowing only the slightest tremble to escape. His tears were sudden and silent, and brushed away in impatience. Eyes closed, he spoke to his long-dead father.

"*Otosan*, please," he trembled involuntarily, "I've done so many things wrong. I've been prideful, arrogant, and abusive. I've taken my son for granted. Please help me." He broke off. Swallowed. "I'm begging you."

Daichi inhaled deeply before lifting his head. He smoothed out his suit. No further grief, no more indulgences. He turned to Deena who sat gasping and trembling, sobbing into her hands. He watched and he marveled. Daichi had seen this expression only once before, such stark bleakness, such wretchedness—on the face of his mother when his father had died.

He extended a hand to Deena and gestured for her to come forward. She looked at him with distrustful, bloodshot eyes. She searched his face for some sign of his intentions. The embrace was a surprise.

Chapter Fifty-nine

When Yoshi joined Daichi in the waiting room, he took a seat next to his brother and stared at the floor. A one A.M. flight out of Denver, just four hours after he'd received word of Tak's condition, placed him in Miami at just after nine A.M. It took a single bag of luggage, a six-hour flight, and a rental car going ninety miles an hour, to get him there at eleven. But even in his haste, he'd not beaten his son John, whose flight from LaGuardia brought him in just before midnight, the night of the accident.

Yoshi searched for words. His heart wanted to say one thing, his mind another. Grief crippled his thoughts. They were fractured, incomplete, like a heartfelt letter with pages missing. This was his nephew, teetering on the edge of death. The boy he'd taught to play drums and the guitar against his brother's wishes. The boy he'd spent summers wrestling with and took to Disneyland when his brother hadn't the time. He loved him as if he were Michael or John, loved him more in some ways. He was equal parts Yoshi and Daichi, the better of the two without any of the worst. He couldn't lose him. He simply couldn't.

"When you prayed," Yoshi said as tears began to blind him, "when you prayed to *otosan*—did he answer?"

Daichi fell silent for a long time. "No," he said simply.

Yoshi sniffed. "He didn't answer me either."

He paused momentarily. "When we were kids," Yoshi began, "I used to think you were invincible. I used to think you could do anything, be anything, and have anything. Till yesterday, I think some part of me still thought that."

Yoshi brushed away tears, half-laughing at a fifty-year-old man who still believed his older brother omnipotent. "I'd give anything to still believe that right now."

Daichi stared at the floor, his eyes shadowed with worry.

"I hope you can forgive me one day, Yoshi. I've been a terrible brother. Always have been."

Yoshi shrugged. "That's not exactly true. A little rough sometimes, but not terrible." He nudged Daichi. "You taught me a lot of things. How to tie my shoes, how to ride a bike and eat a taco at the same time, and how to get a girl to let me kiss her on the first date." Yoshi grinned. "All very important."

Daichi shook his head. "I don't know how to forgive, Yoshi. I've been unable to forgive you for doing as you pleased with your life. And I've been unable to forgive my wife for having an affair."

"She had an affair? When?"

"Eighteen years ago."

"Oh."

"But even that seems to be my fault. You of all people know how intolerable I can be."

"Yeah," Yoshi said slowly. "For fifty years I've been trying to get through the door of Daichi's approval. And in that time I've figured out that not only is it narrow, but sometimes it doesn't exist at all."

Daichi rubbed his face as if to wipe away the self-loathing.

"I've made so many mistakes," he said pitifully. "Left so many things unspoken. Every cross and thoughtless word, every moment of neglect and forgetfulness, it plagues me and convicts me, Yoshi." Daichi dashed tears away. "I need a second chance. Desperately."

Yoshi sighed. "We all do, Daichi. We all do."

Chapter Sixty

A **balding white physician** with the face of a cherry pie stood before Deena and the Tanakas in the waiting room a full fifteen hours after the accident. He introduced himself as Dr. Frank Moore and offered a hand as ruddy as his face. He looked from Hatsumi, who continued to dab the corners of her eyes, to Daichi, red-faced and stiff, before turning to Deena, who held her breath altogether, hands clasped in anticipation. He recognized her as the woman he'd thrown out of the resuscitation room hours ago.

"Mr. Tanaka," Dr. Moore began, "arrived with cardiac arrest after enduring blunt force trauma to the chest. This resulted in a massive hemothorax, or in laymen's terms, blood in the chest cavity. After we performed resuscitation and an emergency thoracotomy, we located and stopped the bleeding. In addition, he suffered a break of the right fibula and tibia and several contusions and lacerations."

"So he's alive?" Daichi breathed.

Dr. Moore grinned. "And awake, no less."

Deena shrieked with delight and hugged first Kenji, then John. Hatsumi clasped a hand over her mouth and stifled a sob. Daichi stared at Dr. Moore distrustfully. It was his brother, Yoshi, who swept him in a bear hug, the first they'd shared since adolescence.

"My God! Can we see him?" Deena asked.

The doctor frowned, shaking his head. "He's in ICU. Right now what Mr. Tanaka needs is lots of rest. We'll monitor him tonight. We expect he'll be able to see you tomorrow."

~*~

The ICU allowed two visitors every two hours, for a total of fifteen minutes. Visiting hours began at 10 A.M. and ended promptly at 8:15 P.M., allowing each patient a maximum of ninety minutes' company a day, should visitors leave and return each hour.

At 10 A.M., Daichi and Hatsumi rushed in, eager to see their son, and thereby relegating Deena to a spot in the waiting room. It was then that the influx of Tanakas arrived—Grandma Yukiko, in on the red-eye from Phoenix, Asami and Ken, who drove all night when they could find no flight from Atlanta, and Mike, who made three connections to get from Seattle to Miami in eight hours of travel time. That was in addition to Kenji, John, Allison, Yoshi, and June, all of whom had arrived within hours of the accident. By the time visiting hours ended at 8:15, Deena found herself still sitting in the cramped quarters of the waiting room, but this time considering the possibility that Tak wouldn't see her.

She returned the following day only to watch it unfold as the one before. She arrived early, resumed her spot in the hard-backed chair near the lone water fountain, and watched as Daichi and Hatsumi led the usual procession of Tanakas. Tak was angry with her. He had to be. He had to know she was there. Why wouldn't he ask for her?

"Deena?"

A nurse approached her, piercing her thoughts.

~*~

Deena followed the nurse down a brightly lit hall and into a spacious private suite. Bright lights, stark white walls, and polished linoleum illuminated the room. In one corner was a leather recliner, in the other, a matching couch. A small table with magazines sat at the arm of the sofa. A 27-inch flat screen was mounted on the wall. He was there, in the center of the room, as an IV and chest tube protruded from his body and a medical monitor recorded his vitals. His face and arms were covered in bruises, his leg in a cast, but he was alive.

She was eager to hear him, to feel him. But as Deena rushed to his side, he held up a single bruised hand which stopped her. She drew back, confused.

Tak cleared his throat, attempted to shift his body for comfort and thought better of it. The words he'd speak would be hoarse and wreak havoc on his chest, but he'd say them nonetheless. They would be the first words he spoke to her, in this, his new life.

"I love you, Dee." He cleared his throat again and pushed on despite the pain. "I've never doubted that you were the woman for me." He paused.

"I want to share my love and my life with you, and if you'll have me, I want you to be my wife."

With effort, he opened a hand to reveal the Tanaka family engagement ring. His father purchased the band of white gold when he sought his mother's hand in marriage. It now belonged to Tak as he sought Deena's hand. Perched upon it was a polished natural pearl more than seven generations old. The lone valuable of a once-wealthy family, that pearl had seen the docks of America at the turn of the twentieth century, been buried in haste with the forced internment of Japanese Americans, and would adorn the finger of one more Tanaka woman, so long as he got the answer he desired.

She answered in a whisper, soft yet clear nonetheless. It was the word which had been in her heart all along.

Yes.

Chapter Sixty-one

When John slipped into Tak's room, a day or so after his transfer from intensive care to the general ward, he found Deena snoozing in an armchair and Kenji by his brother's side, flipping through an old and battered copy of *Sports Illustrated.*

"I hear congrats are in order," John said, closing the door behind him.

Tak smiled. "Word travels fast."

"Man, you should hear Allison. You've got her ready to elope right now. She's all 'they didn't even know each other when we started dating!'" John shook his head. "You try to make me look bad."

"Don't have to try hard."

John leaned against the door and gave Tak a once-over. He had more beeping machines around him than the *Starship Enterprise* and looked like someone had hurled a can of whoop ass at him, but hell, he was alive, and for that, nobody was more thankful than John.

"Enjoying your vacation?" John asked.

"It's great." Tak attempted to shift and winced. "Just the break I needed from the monotony of life."

"You got a break alright. One for the leg, another for the rib cage." He shook his head. "How many bones you plan on breaking this year?"

Tak's laugh was like wisps of smoke, thin and barely there. "The plan was all, but I think I'll tap out now."

John looked up and spotted Kenji's scowl. He knew the kid didn't have the self-deprecating sense of humor that he and Tak shared, so he took Kenji's red-eyed glare as a sign to back off the jokes. He'd never known Kenji to hit anyone, but he wanted no part of that just the same. Something about being the test subject for a kid *The Herald* claimed didn't hit balls so much as snipe them didn't exactly whet John's appetite.

He glanced at Deena. "She's been here as long as I think?"

"Longer probably."

"Well, they're all excited out there. You should hear them cackling about spring colors and summer weddings and caterers from L.A. or some shit."

Deena stirred in her chair. "Are they really?" she said.

John laughed. "Go out there and talk to them. See for yourself. They're ready to make you a Tanaka tonight if you'll let them."

She sat up. "Are you . . . sure?" She lowered her gaze. "Maybe they're just being polite. I'll bet they're being polite."

John raised a brow. "Maybe you weren't paying attention in California, but the Tanakas tend to be a blunt bunch."

He tilted a head toward the door. "Check it out. And take your new brother with you. I'd like to shoot the shit with Tak."

Deena rose, her smile shy. When Kenji stood, he balled up the old issue of *Sports Illustrated* and tossed it in the garbage. John raised a brow.

"Babe Ruth, all-time greatest player." Kenji rolled his eyes. "Gimme a break."

John grinned as they disappeared into the hall, and Kenji continued to mouth off about Ruth's impressive stats in a league that was all-white.

With the door closed behind them, John turned back to Tak. He eyed his cousin with interest.

"Now, how are you?"

Tak sighed. "Tired. Sore as hell."

"The other guy, the one that hit you, he showed up with flowers back when you were still in ICU. It took security and every orderly in the building to get our dads off him."

Tak rolled his eyes. "Your dad, maybe. My dad was probably just trying to find an exit. I'm sure he had a flight somewhere."

Silence filled the room. In it, John ventured over to the floral arrangements stacked on the nightstand with overflow on the floor. He lifted one and admired it. They were lilies or lilacs or something like that.

"He offered me a job," John said.

"When?"

"When we were in California. In-house tax attorney for the firm."

"You gonna take it?"

John shrugged. "I'm thinking about it. It's more money than I've ever seen. Good even for an Ivy League grad at the top of his class. And I wasn't at the top of my class."

Tak sighed. "He talks with money."

"You know, you're right. Problem is, he can't get you to listen." John gave his cousin a wink, snatched the remote from his hand, and tossed it to far side of the room. With a grin, he closed the door to the sound of Tak's pained laughter.

Chapter Sixty-two

Daichi sat in his home office pouring over drafts and notes for a single project he'd become obsessed with over the last few weeks. It should've been a simple enough task—a public library, but something about the designs bothered him. There was simply—something left to be desired.

Lately, concentration was something else left to be desired. Daichi's mind insisted on wandering to the moments after his son's accident. The feelings of helplessness, of inadequacy, of despair. Never had he felt so impotent, so desperate. But when his son regained consciousness, Daichi failed to do as most fathers would. He didn't rush to his son's side, embrace him, and whisper words of fondness. Instead, their encounter was brief and awkward, and when they parted, he was left feeling empty and feeble. To this day, the feeling remained.

~*~

After a series of strengthening exercises in the full-service weight room in his parents' home, Tak thanked his therapist for the visit, showered and dressed, and went in search of his mother. In the hospital, he'd spoken candidly with her about her drinking and the need to quit. With the doctor's promise that Tak would live came his mother's commitment to detoxification. A somber bit of reality coupled with Alcoholics Anonymous meetings had given her two months of sobriety.

The family maid told Tak that his mother was out walking in the garden. Their "garden" was closer to an arboretum than the patch of field most people toddled around in planting herbs and lilacs. His body revolted against the idea of searching for her. He headed for the door.

Tak didn't know what made him stop to speak with his father. Maybe it was the way his office door was cracked instead of welded shut. Maybe it was the glimpse of him doing nothing, save staring at the wall that caused Tak to pause and tap on the door.

He was told to enter.

His father's home office was pretty big. The desk he sat at was broad and made of cherry wood, the chair behind it leather and ergonomically correct. He'd pushed back his PC's flat-screen monitor as if it annoyed him, and piles of paper were stacked neatly in its stead. On the far end, against the wall, were a series of double-wide cherry wood bookshelves, polished to gleam. In one corner was a drafting table and the various supplies his father used when he went old-school—pencils, a T-square, and a compass. At the back of the office was a leather couch, black and soft.

"Got a sec?" Tak said.

Daichi nodded. He pushed away from his desk and turned to face his son. Tak hesitated. His father didn't usually stop working just because someone wanted to have a word with him.

"Mind if I sit?"

Daichi shook his head.

"Are you alright? You don't look well," Tak said after a brief but awkward silence.

"I'm fine. How is your rehabilitation going?"

"Good."

More silence. The two glanced at each other, then looked away.

"She liked the ring," Tak said suddenly.

Daichi nodded. "She should. It's three hundred years old."

Tak conceded the point.

"And the therapy? You said that it's going well?" his father asked again.

"What? Oh, yeah, yeah. Pain management. Breathing techniques, strength and endurance. That's the gist of it."

"And is there much . . . pain?"

Tak shrugged. "Sometimes. The incision site bugs me. You know, where they had to stick in the chest tube. And it hurts to cough. That kind of thing."

"I see. Well . . . let me know if there is anything I can do to help."

"Yeah. Okay."

Tak cleared his throat.

"You know Mom—Mom's stopped drinking."

Daichi turned back to his desk. "Is that right? Is that what she's taken to saying these days?"

Tak's gaze narrowed. "She hasn't had a drink since the day of the accident."

His father unraveled a draft. "Perhaps."

Tak stood, scowling. "There is no 'perhaps.' She's not drinking. She says she's not drinking, and I believe her."

"The woman is a drunkard, Takumi. She revels in the feel of intoxication."

"She's trying. Why can't you even give her that? Why can't you give anyone anything?"

Daichi sighed. "I don't know what that means, Takumi."

"It means that I'm sick of you. I'm sick of you being so damned crass and indifferent. I'm sick of you not giving a damn."

"And what would you like me to give a damn about?" he said quietly.

"Your wife! Your kids! Me! I mean, come on, Dad. I nearly died, and for you it's just an inconvenience in your schedule!"

Daichi swiveled to face him. "Is that what you believe? That I care for no one? For nothing?"

"I know you don't!"

Daichi leapt to his feet. "How dare you! How dare you come into my home and speak with authority about what matters to me." He began to pace with the heat of his fury.

"When you lay dying in that hospital, it was me who was so overcome with grief that I could neither eat, nor sleep, nor function. It was me who tortured himself with every decision, every unspoken word, every measure of affection I ever withheld from you. Me, who spent the night weeping, even after hearing you were alive, as I lay there convicted by every cross word I ever spoke to you. It was me, Takumi, your father, and no one else. And you have the audacity to tell me that I don't care for you? That I don't love you?"

"And Mom? Does she have to die for you to love her, too? Is that what it takes?"

Daichi turned on Tak, enraged. "Who the hell do you think you are? You've crossed the goddamned line."

"Well, I'm so sorry! I didn't know we recognized lines! Not since you habitually encroach on mine!"

"You think I didn't love your mother? You think I didn't ever love your mother? You wouldn't even be here if I didn't love your mother. Why don't you sit down and shut up about things that you know nothing about?"

Tak crossed his arms defiantly.

"Goddamn it, Takumi, I said sit down!"

Reluctantly, Tak lowered himself onto the couch, partially surprised by his outburst of emotion.

Daichi faced him.

"I loved your mother. I loved your mother more than anything. She was beautiful, smart, compassionate—she was everything I wanted in a woman. I worshipped her."

Tak's eyes narrowed. "So what the hell happened?"

Daichi sighed. "When I met your mother she was a freshman at Harvard while I was in the last year of my graduate studies. She was curled under a tree, reading Emily Dickenson. Back then, Emily Dickenson consumed her. I walked up to her, took the book from her, and recited Lord Byron's 'She Walks in Beauty.'"

Tak blinked, trying his best to conjure an image of his father, underneath a maple, wooing his mother with poetry. The image never came.

"We dated for six months, and then married. At our ceremony, she was already six weeks pregnant with you."

Daichi slipped his hands in his pockets, leaned against the edge of his desk, and sighed. "She left school to marry me and to have you. She was so full of potential and so brilliant, the guilt from that plagued me. I wanted so badly to give you both a better life that I lost sight of what constituted 'better.' I thought that 'things' meant better. So, I pushed for bigger contracts and worked longer hours. And by the time I accomplished what I set out to do, well, your mother and I were strangers. The distance brought the alcohol, and the alcohol, animosity."

Tak lowered his gaze. "And what about Kenji? Most days it seems you can hardly stand to look at him."

"I don't know. When I look at you, there is so much of me, and of my father. But when I look at Kenji, I just see—your mother—timid conformist, crestfallen wife, adulterer."

"She had an affair?"

Daichi waved a tired hand. "It was a long time ago. Nothing for you to be concerned about."

"You don't—you don't doubt that Kenji's yours, do you?"

Daichi smiled. "No. Of course not. We had not decimated just yet."

He rubbed his forehead. "Kenji was conceived in a time when our marriage was difficult, whereas with you, it was a time when I was full of optimism and hope, joy and love. By the time your brother was born, your mother and I were divorced in all but the most literal sense. Through no fault of his own, Kenji symbolizes everything that has gone wrong with my life, and you, all that has gone right."

Tak chewed on his bottom lip. "Do you—still love Mom?"

It was a question Daichi had been asking himself for two decades. He and Hatsumi had shared so many years, more unhappy than happy, but he'd remained with her nonetheless. In fact, he'd never considered leaving her. Not on the countless occasions he'd found her too inebriated to care for their children and not when he found her in the arms of one of his interns eighteen years ago. But he wasn't sure that his reluctance to abandon her was tantamount to love. Perhaps it was the guilt and self-loathing he felt whenever he saw her presented in exquisitely perfect fashion, with her makeup and hair in place, as though nothing were more important. He'd look at her and think of that beautiful freshman, hair slightly disheveled as she read Emily Dickinson. He'd think of the bright future she must've had before Daichi Tanaka derailed her. Perhaps the guilt kept him there.

"I don't know if I love your mother. But I do know that I love you, and I'm willing to say it until you believe it."

~*~

When Tak returned home that evening, he exhibited signs of forgetfulness, confusion, and disorientation. He put things down and forgot where they were, faltered midway through sentences, and stumbled over words.

Since Tak's accident, Deena had delved into medical journals and self-help books in an effort to monitor and assist in his recovery. His behavior was symptomatic of head trauma, something that could exhibit symptoms immediately or over a period of time.

So she followed him around, asking probing questions about sensitivity to light and headaches until he turned to her quite suddenly, as if noticing her for the first time.

"Did you know that my mother was already pregnant when my parents got married?"

Deena froze, a copy of *Treating Trauma* in her hands. "No."

"Oh. Okay."

With a shrug, he took a seat on the couch and began untying his sneakers.

"He told me he loved me today."

Deena's eyebrows shot up.

"Who did?"

Tak grinned. "My dad."

Chapter Sixty-three

Daichi entered the master bedroom and cast off his plush robe and slippers. He changed into a pair of silk black pajamas and slid underneath the covers next to his wife. She lay on her side with her back to him. Daichi, taking in the slow rise and fall of her body and the otherwise lacking motion, determined she was asleep.

He put on his wire-framed reading glasses and delved into the latest issue of *Architectural Digest*. He fully expected to enjoy it, the last of the season, as it featured a retrospective look at the year's innovations. But his mind was on Takumi and the conversation they'd had. Never had he spoken to someone with such candor, with such vulnerability. Never had his son seen him cry.

Sighing, he set the magazine back on the nightstand. There would be no *Architectural Digest* tonight.

"Hatsumi?"

She turned to face him. How many nights had they shared like this one? With her back to him, never speaking, never interacting, just him reading until he fell asleep and her simply listening?

"Yes, Daichi?"

He'd always thought her voice beautiful. As a foolish young man, he'd imagined that if something as sweet and pure as fruit could speak, it would have the voice of Hatsumi. How was that young man defeated? And better yet, why hadn't he put up a fight?

"May I speak with you for a moment?"

Hatsumi drew herself up on one arm, and Daichi frowned at her attire. He was certain what she wore constituted negligee—black satin and lace cupped her breasts and hugged her midsection, held up by only the slimmest of straps.

"Why are you wearing that?" he demanded. "It's much too cold for that."

He kept their home as cool as possible to ward off bacteria.

Hatsumi lowered her gaze. "You wanted to speak with me about something?"

Daichi looked away.

"Yes. I, uh, wanted to ask you something. Ask your opinion, rather, on something." He took a deep breath.

"Do I love you, Hatsumi?"

She frowned. "I'm not sure I understand what you're asking." She shifted in her chemise, the cool air upon her breasts. Daichi's gaze faltered momentarily.

"I want to know whether or not I love you," he said simply.

Hatsumi hesitated. "I don't think so."

He blinked a few times and nodded to himself. When he turned to her once more, she shifted again, her nipples pressing through the lace of her chemise.

"You're cold," he observed. "Allow me to get you something." He was out of bed and searching for a robe before she could object.

The last time he'd volunteered to do something for her was two weeks before Tak's accident, when he offered to pour a bottle of alcohol directly down her throat, thereby dispensing with the constant refilling of her glass.

The robe Daichi handed her was his own. Standing to take it, she revealed the full cut of her nightie—the sheerness of material, the slight curve of her slender body and long bare legs. He was rendered breathless where he stood, recalling a time when his lips would trace the length of those legs, delighting in the sweet fragrance he found there.

"Thank you," Hatsumi said, tying the belt of the oversized cotton robe about her waist.

"You're welcome," he said quietly. When he looked away, it was in frustration.

"I, uh, spoke at great length with Takumi today," he said.

Hatsumi blinked.

"We talked about many things, Takumi and I. This is why I asked if I loved you, as it was the question posed to me by him."

"And what did you say?"

"The truth. That I didn't know."

Hatsumi walked to the large window facing the foot of their bed and gazed out at the bay, and beyond it, the Atlantic Ocean.

"When we were younger you looked at me and you saw a beautiful woman, an intelligent woman, a woman you were honored to have by your side. But as time went by, that vision deteriorated. I became a woman who sacrificed a promising life, foolishly according to you, to have your child and be your wife. Quite simply, I became a fool."

She turned to face him. "But where is it written that I can't be all those things—beautiful and intelligent, wife and mother? When you look at me, you do so with regret. You think of what I could've become. You measure greatness by outward appearances and superficialities."

She swallowed. "No, there are no monuments erected to pay homage to my ego, and no, I don't grace the covers of magazines, but I have two beautiful sons and a family that I love. So, I do not meet your standards of greatness, but I am no one's failure."

Hatsumi turned away from her husband.

"Why do you stay, Hatsumi? Why do you stay in this empty, hopeless marriage?"

She sighed. "Because . . . we can find each other again."

Daichi stared at her back, pained by the temptation her words afforded him. Suddenly, he knew why he'd never leave. Daichi, like his wife, had held out hope that love would find them again. Each in their own way longed for something, anything to rejuvenate the passion they'd once shared.

Hatsumi took a step toward him and allowed her robe to cascade to the floor. She revealed deliciously subtle curves under dark and yielding fabric. Daichi stared, his thoughts imbued with images of long pale legs and the delectable enticements he'd once savored.

Aroused to the point of madness, his hands, his mouth, his body found hers before his mind could convince him otherwise.

Chapter Sixty-four

The library still plagued Daichi. True, once completed it would be the largest in the state, shared by four colleges clustered in Broward, but it was just a library. He'd designed facilities for some of the largest companies in the world. His work donned the covers of magazines and the glossy pages of books in cities all over the earth. Could a library really be such a challenge?

At four o'clock, exactly six hours after entering his study, there was a knock at the door. Absentmindedly he told whomever it was to come in.

Kenji stood with a hand in the pocket of his relaxed jeans, head down, voice soft. "Mom wants to know if you're hungry."

"Perhaps."

Daichi frowned at the computer-generated renderings of his flawed vision. He grunted. "I just can't . . ."

Kenji took a step closer and frowned at the screen. "You can fix it if you make your promenade wider. And put reflecting pools on both sides."

Daichi looked up. "What?"

Kenji faltered. "I said you should make your—n—never mind."

Daichi stood. "You understand what you're looking at?"

Kenji's gaze returned to the floor. "I guess so."

Daichi frowned. Suddenly seized by an idea, he snatched a pencil and sheet of paper from his desk and drew frantically. When finished, he held the sheet up before Kenji.

"What's this?"

He looked from the paper to his father's expectant face.

"A column."

Daichi pursed his lips in impatience. *"What kind?"*

Kenji looked again. "Tuscan."

Daichi allowed the paper to fall as he snatched another. He sketched frantically, then wielded his work once again.

"And this?"

"A trefoil."

Daichi whirled as if seized by madness, searching, rummaging wildly. "And this? What's this, Kenji?" He brandished a copy of *Architectural Record.*

"A magazine."

"The building, son, the building."

"Oh." Kenji gave it a second look. He bit his lower lip and looked up uncertainly.

"You can do it, Kenji. You're my son. It's in you."

Kenji frowned before returning to the picture.

"It's a church."

Daichi sighed, already turning away.

"Gothic Revival."

"What?"

Kenji hesitated.

"Look again."

Daichi held up the magazine, and Kenji studied the cover carefully.

"Now what is it?"

He frowned. He was trembling ever so slightly, never taking his eyes off the cathedral on the cover.

"What is it, Kenji?"

He looked up. "Gothic Revival?"

"Say it like you mean it."

"Gothic Revival."

"Louder."

"Gothic Revival!"

Daichi tossed the magazine aside and took his seat again. "Tell your mother we'll take our lunch in here."

Kenji raised an eyebrow. "We?"

Daichi looked up. "Yes, 'we.' Unless you're unwilling to share a meal with your *otosan*."

Kenji grinned and disappeared from the room.

PART FOUR

Chapter Sixty-five

Deena's khaki Louis Vuitton clutch was perfectly suited for the iridescent capris and form-fitting three-quarter length white button-up she chose to wear to meet her grandmother for coffee. Grandma Emma, on the other hand, donned a barnyard red potato sack dress complete with looming white buttons and off-white orthopedic slippers. As they exchanged icy greetings, Deena was perfectly aware of the violent contrast they made.

They'd not spoken since Deena brought Tak over for Sunday dinner two months prior. The meal had been a fiasco from the onset. When they arrived, Grandma Emma peered behind the two as if she were expecting a second, more acceptable man, as Caroline, Keisha, and Lizzie gaped in wide-eyed astonishment. And the questions! Deena's cheeks still burned with the shame.

"So, Tic," Aunt Caroline said as she leaned forward, "what part of China you from again?"

"His name is Tak not Tic. And he's not Chinese," Deena said.

"I'm—I'm actually from here," Tak replied.

"What do you mean 'here'?" Caroline demanded.

"I mean here, here. Miami. I was born here." Tak shifted in his seat and cast Deena a single, amused glance.

"Oh," Aunt Caroline said.

"Well, where your daddy from?" Grandma Emma asked, mashing collard greens and corn bread together with her fingertips. "What parts a China he from?"

Tak sighed. "My father's from Phoenix."

"But he wasn't born there though, right? He was born in China, right?"

Tak shot Grandma Emma a pointed look. "My father was born in Phoenix, and his father in San Jose." He took a sip of water. "But I do know what you're asking me. I'm Japanese."

Deena recalled the poise with which Tak handled everything from being offered pig entrails to fielding questions as to whether he was "some kin" to the Chinaman who ran Chan Wok's on 69th. And just when she'd been certain that she could tolerate no more, Deena discovered she was right.

"So, you been down to the prison to tell your momma you getting married?" Caroline asked sweetly.

Deena closed her eyes and buried her face in her hands. She would not cry. She refused to cry. Next to her, Tak squeezed her shoulder.

"Humph. You know she ain't told him that. No man in they right mind going to fools with a woman got that kinda evil in her blood. You carries that stuff in your blood, you know. Evil ways," Grandma Emma advised with a wave of her fork.

"Actually, I know all about her mother," Tak said. "We talked about it a long time ago."

"Well, you know, Emma, not everybody even believes in good and evil, God and the devil. The boy probably don't even know Jesus Christ died for his sins." Deacon Moore, an increasing regular at the Hammond table, turned his attention to Tak. "Do you know that, boy? Do you know that Jesus died for your sins?"

"Oh my God! If you don't shut the hell up!" Deena cried. "Will you all just shut the hell up?"

"This girl has lost her damned mind," Keisha whispered.

"I knew she lost her mind when she brought that Chinese boy 'round here like somebody ordered wonton soup," Caroline said.

Deena stood. "One more word. One more word about him and as God is my witness I will come across this table and—"

"Deena," Tak grabbed her arm.

"You'll what? What are you gonna do to my momma?" Keisha stood to meet her.

"Bring it, Keisha," Deena said through gritted teeth. "You bring it, and I'll shove it down your goddamned throat."

Grandma Emma stood. "Sit your ass down before I come cross this table! Anybody gone be putting hands on somebody it's gone be me laying holy hands on your ass for bringing this Chinese boy 'round like dis."

Deena and Grandma Emma stood staring at each other as Keisha lowered herself into her chair. Around them, each Hammond gaped as Deena, still on her feet, defied the will of their family's matriarch. Never had it been done so brazenly.

"I don't answer to you," Deena said. "Not anymore." She turned to Tak. "We're done here."

When Deena and Tak left, it was with the belief that she'd been ejected from the fold. After all, had not her grandparents turned their backs on their only son when he married her mother, a white woman? Had they not remained steadfast in their contempt up until his death ten years later? So it was with shock that Deena answered the phone when Grandma Emma called weeks later and suggested they meet.

"Can I get you something, Grandma Emma?" Deena asked with a touch to the old woman's shoulder. Emma looked up from her work-worn and wrinkled hands.

"They got Sanka?" Grandma Emma asked from her seat in the center of the Starbucks. Deena sighed. Shaking her head, she made her way over to the counter, to stand in the weaving line.

After ordering two cups of venti decaf, Deena carried the sweltering brew to a corner table in the eclectic coffee shop, where she gestured for her grandmother to join her. While she told her-self that she'd chosen the corner table in regard for Grandma Emma's hip and back concerns, she was aware that it offered a semblance of privacy from the boisterous regulars that crowded the café. The spot seemed detached from the rest of the room.

"Deena, you know I love you. I love you more than anything. I raised you and your brother and sister like you was my own. So when I tell you things it's with your best interest in mind." Grandma Emma tapped her temple.

"I know you think so," Deena said carefully.

"No. No. No. I do. I don't tell you things for my own benefits. Like this here I got to tell you. For your own good."

"For my own good," Deena echoed distrustfully, her eyes trained on the wisps of steam escaping the lid.

Grandma Emma looked up at her, nodded, then leaned for-ward conspiratorially, her synthetic wig shifting in the process.

"You can't marry that Chinese boy."

"Japanese," Deena said.

"Chinese. Japanese. Really, when you gets downs to it, it's the same thing," Grandma Emma stated.

Deena stared at her. "Alright. I'll humor you. Why can't I marry him?"

Grandma shook her head. "Your whole family against it. Ain't that mean nothing to you?"

"Not anymore," Deena murmured.

Grandma Emma stared back in shock. "Look here, gal. Ain't they got no black men whereabout you could find?"

Deena's patience evaporated. "I don't want a black man. I want him, Grandma. I love him. Weren't you the one who told me that if I found a man that I loved, that treated me right, that I should hold on to him no matter what?"

"Chile, you takes my words and you twists 'em. You twists 'em to suits you."

Deena sighed. "You're impossible."

Grandma Emma shifted in her seat. "Look. It ain't jus' that he's a Chinese. Listen. This what I know. You two go hot tailing up out of here and get married, both your families gonna be upside down." She waited for Deena to deny this. When she didn't, her lips curled into a satisfactory smile.

"I'm pretty sure his peoples want him to stay with his peoples like we wants you to stay with yours. That's the first thing. Second is this. I mean, let's just be real here. Y'all two get together and you bound to have a funny-looking child!"

Grandma Emma whooped with laughter, clapping her hands all the while. Deena knew she couldn't wait to tell the ladies of the church how she just came right out and told her what was what, right to her face.

"See, people like you don't ever think about who you effecting, just yourself," she said, eyes suddenly narrowed with seriousness.

"Well," Deena said carefully, "I could say the same thing about you."

The women stared, a dark silence passing between them. Then Grandma Emma's face darkened. "Listen, I'm here 'cause I am a woman of God."

"And I'm not?" Deena blurted.

"No, now it ain't that," Emma held up her hands, gesturing for Deena to calm down. Was she the aggressor now? Deena wondered.

"You was raised in the church now and even though you got some ways about you like you wasn't, you still was."

Deena began to massage her temples. "I don't follow you."

"Those people don't believe in Jesus Christ!" Emma shouted.

Deena nodded wearily, conceding her point.

"Uh-huh. Deacon Moore says they *Buddin*. And that they pray to a fat Chinese man. Now who in they right mine ever heard of a fat Chinese man being the son of God?"

Deena closed her eyes, counted backward from ten, and spoke. "Yes, lots of Japanese people are Buddhist, Tak included. But I don't see your point. In fact, I think you need to learn to tolerate other people's differences." She regretted the words in an instant.

"What! Girl, Jesus Christ died for your sins! He laid down and died for you! For you, Deena!" Grandma banged her fist on the table for emphasis. "They nailed him to a cross and—"

"Grandma, calm down," Deena hissed, eyes darting in humiliation. "Calm down right now!"

"You think Jesus laid down and died so you could marry a Buddin?" Emma cried. "No! I don't think so!"

They'd drawn the attention of the go-getters, the early-morning suits who consumed both caffeine and the morning's headlines as if they needed both to survive. Among them she spotted William Henderson, the wide-eyed, pudding-faced investor in the Skylife project with whom she'd traded barbs with on more than one occasion. He, like the other onlookers, gawked at the unfolding debacle.

"Grandma, would you please keep it down? People know me here, for Christ's sake."

"No! Jesus Christ—" Grandma Emma screamed.

Deena stood. The lively café had fallen sinfully silent, despite the multitudes present. Aside from her grandmother, all Deena could hear was whirring from the refrigerated display case.

"Grandma, if you don't shut up right this second, then I will consider this conversation over," Deena hissed.

Grandma Emma struggled to her feet. With a single, hard glare she reeled back and smacked her.

Deena's lips parted in disbelief. Tears filled her eyes as she brought a hand to her stinging cheek. Despite the threats, despite the harsh words, it had never been Grandma Emma who hit her. Never.

"I won't . . ." Deena's voice broke. With the eyes of the café on her, she decided to salvage her dignity by bringing their meeting to an end.

"I won't stand here and be hit, Grandma. I don't care how much I disappoint you. I will not tolerate being hit."

With a trembling hand, Deena dug into her purse and retrieved a sheet of gold embossed parchment. She held it out to her grandmother, who stared at it. Deena cleared her throat and set it on the table.

"My wedding is in six weeks. The details are on the invitation. Come if you like. But as of now, the matter is closed to discussion."

Chapter Sixty-six

The day was hot even by Miami standards. Nowhere was this more evident than in Daichi's attire, the most relaxed she'd ever seen him. He wore his standard oxford, sleeves rolled up, first button undone, and paired it with crisp Armani slacks, cuffed to avoid the ocean current. Beads of sweat plastered hair to his forehead while next to him, Deena walked in silence. At their backs, on the coastline, was Deena's architectural rendition of love—Skylife, completed and reaching for the heavens. She had no idea where her next project would take her; already she'd received the letter thanking her for her entry in the City-Within-A-City competition. Unlike Daichi, she was not a finalist.

"You were right," Daichi said suddenly. "This view is quite enjoyable."

Deena's cell phone rang. She pulled it from her pocket and gave it a peek. It was her grandmother. Ever since she'd delivered the news of her engagement, Emma had been ransacking her phone line.

"And how are the Hammonds taking this news?" Daichi asked, as if reading her thoughts.

Deena shrugged. "About as bad as expected."

He laughed. "Worse even than my initial reception of this love affair?"

"Much worse."

They continued in silence.

"It turns out that Cook was right," Daichi said suddenly.

Deena blinked. "Michael Cook? About what?"

"About my being short-listed for the Pritzker. Turns out he knows something after all."

Deena's eyes widened. "My God, Daichi, that's such an honor. When will you know if you've won?"

He shrugged. "Yesterday. I got the call yesterday. The ceremony will be in May."

"What!" Deena shrieked and embraced him before realizing she'd done so. She pulled back with a blush and got to see something as rare as a Nobel Prize winner in the flesh. Daichi embarrassed.

"I'd like for you to accompany me. The ceremony's in Melbourne, Australia."

"Me? You want me?"

"Is that so impossible to conceive?"

Deena shook her head. "I-I don't know. I thought you'd want someone—important."

Daichi shrugged. "I'd say a daughter's pretty important."

He flashed a grin at her, the most generous she'd seen, one she couldn't help but return. But he had no idea the effect his words had on her. She'd never entertained the notion of having a father again, and what it would mean, what it could mean. She never thought that she could be a daughter again. And yet she would be.

Soon.

Chapter Sixty-seven

Emma stood at the narrow stove and waited for the hot-cakes' edges to brown. In a nearby saucepan grits boiled and bacon sizzled in a frying pan. She glanced at the coffee pot and watched it gurgle. In another moment, her biscuits would need to come out of the oven.

Emma slipped the 5x7 from the pocket of her housecoat and peered at it. With a single crooked finger, she traced the outline of the man in the portrait. He was a fine-looking young man with the gleam of youth in his eyes, bright like diamonds, and just a trace of stubbornness. Emma held that gaze, lost to her forever, before reluctantly tucking it away again.

She'd come across that old picture in Eddie's keepsake box. Facedown. It was hidden just beneath a pair of cuff links given to him by his father, a Cuban cigar from the day their son Dean was born, and a Purple Heart he'd received from his tour of duty in Vietnam. Emma stood motionless, with that picture in hand, her mind weighted with buried memories. And when sleep failed to come for her that night, she stared at that picture and tried to remember the day when she'd become so old and hardhearted.

As Emma removed the hotcakes from the griddle, she thought about the invitation Deena gave her two weeks ago. She'd never laid hands on such fine paper. It was sturdy, sophisticated, beautiful. And those letters! Why, they were raised up on it as proud as anything she'd seen. And while she couldn't do much more than guess as to what that invitation said, she couldn't help but notice the similarities between it and her granddaughter.

Emma surveyed the spread she was preparing and glanced at her watch. Deena would be there at any moment. She was on her way over to pick up a copy of her birth certificate so that she could apply for her marriage license. Her wedding day was just weeks away.

When Deena arrived, she refused the breakfast Emma had gone to the trouble of preparing. Juice from fresh squeezed oranges, flapjacks, bacon, eggs, biscuits, grits—she would let them all go to waste. She wanted the birth certificate, and she wanted to leave.

"Grandma, you'd said that you would have it out for me by the time I got here," Deena complained, surveying the spread of food in disapproval. "I don't have time to waste this morning."

Emma shook her head. "Chile, a good breakfast ain't time wasted. Now come on in here and make yourself a plate. And afterwards, you can help me fine that paper you need."

Deena watched as her grandmother turned from her, retrieved a plate from an overhead cabinet, and began to fill it with food. When it seemed that the dish could hold no more Emma turned to her granddaughter and watched her reluctantly pull out a chair to sit.

The two ate in silence, with only the occasional scrape of fork and knife against plate and Emma's smacking to interrupt them. And when their plates were empty, Emma reached into her pocket and dug out her old picture. She kept her eyes on Deena as she placed it on the table.

With a trembling hand, Deena reached for the picture. A long and lean man with rich chocolate skin, wide almond eyes, and a good-natured grin stared back at her. Wrapped in his tight embrace was a smiling woman with a wide and pouty mouth, cornflower blue eyes, and hair like stalks of wheat. They were Deena's parents.

Deena gripped the picture until it shook, tears blinding the nearly forgotten faces. Her father, Dean Hammond, and her mother, Gloria, eligible for parole in the year 2032.

Emma watched as Deena's mouth became a hard line. Her jaw clenched, and her eyes grew cold. Deena set the picture back on the table.

Emma stared at the portrait thoughtfully. "You think you ever could forgive her?"

"What?" Deena said. It was not the question she'd been expecting.

"Your mother," Emma tapped a finger on the picture. "I asked you if you ever gone forgive her for what she done."

Deena shook her head "I don't know, Grandma. I've never thought about it."

Emma nodded. Twenty-five years had passed since she'd last heard her son's voice, fifteen since she'd placed him in that pine box. Time, she discovered, marched on in cruel, unforgiving bursts.

"Maybe," Emma said as she lifted the picture from the table, "you should thank about forgiving her. It's a hard, hard thing to want your child's forgiveness and find it beyond your reach."

Deena met the old woman's wet eyes. "What?" she whispered.

Emma lowered her gaze. "For a long time I looks at you and your brother and your sister and I sees my boy. I sees what I loss, and I hates you for it. I hates you for making me see that every single day."

Emma swallowed hard, her voice harsh and broken. "I takes that hate out on you and I treats you wrong. But it's not cause I don't love you, it's cause I can't—I can't stands to see him no more. I can't stands to see my son looking back at me and asking why I threw him away."

She rubbed her face tiredly. "Listen, Deena. Gone and marry that boy. I ain't gone stand in your way no more."

Emma nodded toward the picture of her son. "I reckon this the closest I'm gone get to a second chance, anyway. I suspect I better take it." She stood, brushed away a tear, and collected the dishes.

Epilogue

The little girl lifted her menu, peered at the upside down script, and lowered it again. "*Ojiichan*, do you think they have french fries here?"

Her grandfather's lips curled into an indulgent smile. "If they don't we'll go somewhere where they do."

Deena lowered her menu with a sigh. "Don't tell her that." When she turned to Tak, it was with an accusatory glare. "I thought you said you were going to talk to him about this. About spoiling her."

"I did. You see the good it did."

Deena turned back to Daichi. "Well, I'll tell you myself. Stop spoiling her or she'll be unbearable in a few years." She shook her head. "And anyway, there are other people here besides her. I, for one, have been waiting for weeks to come here."

She looked up to see the waiter place a sushi and sashimi spread before them.

"Lord Jesus," Grandma Emma murmured.

Daichi smiled at the old woman before turning to the tray,

examining the spread with a critical eye. "Looks good," he said cheerfully.

Emma snorted. Tak and Deena exchanged knowing, smothered smiles.

"Now listen here, Emma. You'll honor our agreement. I held up my end of the bargain, and now you'll do the same," Daichi warned.

Mia squealed. "When *ojiichan* ate chitlins his face was red!"

Daichi laughed. "You see? You owe me."

Emma sighed. "But this hardly seem equal."

"You're right. I was forced to eat pig entrails, whereas you have a fresh selection of the highest quality in seafood."

"But you ain't cooked none of it!" Emma cried.

Daichi clapped his hands in delight. "You're a real treat, Emma, a real treat. But a deal is a deal." He leaned forward and with chopsticks began plucking the various pieces he wanted her to eat, setting them on the empty plate before her. "Let's see . . . We'll do a bit of sashimi here, salmon, *and* tuna. Also some eel and cucumber—"

"Come on, Dad, give her a break," Tak laughed.

"What?" Deena cried. "When we were dating you gave me eel *and* salmon roe!"

"Good point, Deena," Daichi grinned. "Let's add a bit of gukanmaki to this plate and you're ready to go. That, of course, is sushi with three types of roe in it."

"Now what the devil is roe?" Emma asked, jabbing at one of the hand-rolled pieces of sushi.

"Oh my God, don't tell her. It's better if you don't her," Deena warned.

Daichi offered wasabi and soy sauce to Emma under the rapt attention of the table.

"Lord, I guess it's now or never," she murmured, raising the eel and cucumber to her mouth.

"Place it all in at once," Daichi advised, his eyes dancing. "It's better that way."

With two fingers, Emma jammed the sushi into her mouth. Mia shrieked.

"Lord have mercy!" Emma cried.

"My God, I never thought she'd do it," Deena whispered, turning to Tak.

"What, are you kidding? My dad would've rode her forever," Tak murmured.

As Emma chewed, her eyes watered.

"Swallow it! You'll only prolong it this way," Daichi laughed.

Emma spat in a napkin and burst into a coughing laughing fit.

"You don't expect that one to count, do you? I swallowed a record nine portions of your chitterlings! You'll never get anywhere spewing pieces from your mouth like that," Daichi said.

"I don't know why he's doing this," Tak said. "When he gets back from Japan, she told me that she's gonna make him eat possum."

"What?" Deena laughed. "Where in the hell is she gonna find possum?"

Tak shrugged. "She says she knows a guy that goes back and forth to Mississippi all the time, and that he's going to bring her some. She claims she hasn't had any in forty years, but she's making some especially for Dad."

Deena laughed. "This'll go on forever, you know, them trying to one-up each other."

Tak touched her hand. "I can think of worse ways this could've turned out." A tiny smile played across his lips. Deena matched it before dropping her gaze to his hand. Instinctively, it fell to the faint and jagged scar running crosswise from his index finger to wrist. It was an ever-present reminder of traits she tried to forget. Cowardice. Selfishness. Deceit.

"*Chee-chee pah-pah chee—*"

Deena looked up, roused from a memory. "Baby, don't sing at the table."

Mia hesitated, mouth open mid "*chee.*" Wide, silver-plated saucers stared back at her mother.

Deena could see every part of herself in her daughter Mia, sifted through and made better. From the wild and silky jet-black curls pinned diva-style in two oversized pigtails to the dollop of cinnamon on oatmeal skin and eyes like wide and polished sterling silver, heavy with the weight of her value. She had the look of a girl who could do or be anything, even at five.

She admired her already.

Mia Tanaka, who ate soul food and spoke *Nihongo*, who frequented festivals with her *ojiichan* and Sunday worship with her great-grandmother, had learned in five years of life something it took Deena twenty-five to figure out. That even with all of these seemingly contrary traits, she was just what she was intended to be.

Tucked away in Deena's wallet was a family portrait from the year before. In it, she and Tak sat side by side, her in a simple cream sweater and slacks for Christmastime, him in a white button-up and blue jeans. His hair, of course, tousled just right. Before and between them was Mia, black hair braided in zigzags before flowing free into two bountiful pigtails. Her *ojiichan* kept her in runway best, so on this day she wore her favorite Burberry romper accented by a Tahitian pearl long since lost to a sandbox.

Deena wasn't sure why she'd sent the picture to her mother, or why she'd gone to the trouble of restoring the one of her parents and including it, as well. Two portraits, palm-sized, in a single white mailer to Gloria Hammond, care of Broward Corrections. No letter inside, no explanation.

When she received a letter back, with that telltale prison stamp, less than a week had passed. Deena took it, and placed it with the others, unopened.

Not yet, she thought.

Not yet.

Book Club Questions

1. What were your overall impressions of Crimson Footprints?
2. What was unique about the setting? Did you feel the setting enhanced or diminished the novel?
3. What were the themes? What message, if any, did you feel the author had for the reader?
4. Did the characters seem realistic? Why or why not?
5. Which characters could you relate to, if any? Did you have favorites?
6. What conflicts were present through the course of the novel? Which were most challenging?
7. How did the death of Deena's father figure into her romance with Tak?
8. Was Tak right to stay the course with Deena? Would you have done the same?
9. Was Deena right to stay the course with Tak? Would you have done the same?
10. In what ways did Deena change? What events triggered this change?
11. Do you believe that Tak changed? Why or why not?
12. What other characters evolved during the course of the story? Did this enhance the novel?
13. What parts of Crimson Footprints made you uncomfortable? Why? Did you think these portions were necessary?
14. Were there characters you loved and wanted to meet? Ones that you despised?
15. How would Crimson Footprints be different if it took place in another part of the United States? Or a different period in time?
16. What does the title mean to you, if anything?

CPSIA information can be obtained at www.ICGtesting.com
Printed in the USA
LVOW061024231212

312972LV00002B/135/P

Book Club Questions

1. What were your overall impressions of Crimson Footprints?

2. What was unique about the setting? Did you feel the setting enhanced or diminished the novel?

3. What were the themes? What message, if any, did you feel the author had for the reader?

4. Did the characters seem realistic? Why or why not?

5. Which characters could you relate to, if any? Did you have favorites?

6. What conflicts were present through the course of the novel? Which were most challenging?

7. How did the death of Deena's father figure into her romance with Tak?

8. Was Tak right to stay the course with Deena? Would you have done the same?

9. Was Deena right to stay the course with Tak? Would you have done the same?

10. In what ways did Deena change? What events triggered this change?

11. Do you believe that Tak changed? Why or why not?

12. What other characters evolved during the course of the story? Did this enhance the novel?

13. What parts of Crimson Footprints made you uncomfortable? Why? Did you think these portions were necessary?

14. Were there characters you loved and wanted to meet? Ones that you despised?

15. How would Crimson Footprints be different if it took place in another part of the United States? Or a different period in time?

16. What does the title mean to you, if anything?

17. Did the story end the way you expected it?

18. Was the book what you expected? Did it leave you hopeful or disappointed?

19. Would you recommend Crimson Footprints to other readers?

20. It's easy to vilify those who are opposed to interracial marriage. However, in the scene where Daichi discovers Tak and Deena together, Daichi presents a practical argument against it. Did you find his argument persuasive? Why or why not?

CRIMSON FOOTPRINTS 2
New Beginnings

COMING FEBRUARY 2013

*If you enjoyed this book as I enjoyed writing please leave
a review and tell a friend.*

About

S **hewanda Pugh** is a native of Boston's inner city. She has a bachelor's degree in Political Science from Alabama A&M University and a Master's in Writing from Nova Southeastern University. Fueled from a young age, her passion for crossing societal boundaries like race, class and culture, is the inspiration for both her cluttered bookshelf and her writing. When she's not busy obsessing over fiction, she can be found traveling, nursing her social networking addiction or enjoying the company of loved ones.

Facebook her at: https://www.facebook.com/shewanda.pugh
Follow on Twitter: @ShewandaP